ALLIANDRE RISING

ALLIANDRE RISING

Book One of The Knights' Trials

DANIEL E MYERS

Wyvern's Aerie

Copyright

Foreword

I want to take some space to thank a number of people who made this book possible. First off, everyone reading this now, for taking the time out of your busy life to read it. I hope you enjoy the story.

None of this would be possible without the support of my wife, Kelly, who is my Marion. Anyone who has ever met her knows her wonderful qualities I expressed through Marion. I love you baby. And I hope for many more happy years together.

All of my children helped in some way as well, telling me in no uncertain terms when the plot was weak or the storylines sucked. So, thank you Lauren, Haley, Caitlin and Jake. Your personalities are expressed throughout the book, whether you see them or not.

One of my oldest friends, Roger Stockman for cutting the book apart and making it focus on the story. Part developmental editing, part line editing, part proofing, and all helpful, I should give him co-writing credits.

Another of my oldest friends, Erik Olsrud, for creating the Forest Spirit world, which I unabashedly stole and then changed. I hope you don't mind the changes I made!

Roger and Erik, along with Greg Mueller, Jerry Prindle, and Rick Trieweiler. Forty-year friends who created many of the characters and inspired the story. Without you, none of this would have happened.

Tom Kratman, for writing a series that held my interest long enough for me to get back into the habit of reading.

My editors. Besides Roger, Deborah Murrell, Claire Ashgrove and Beth the Writer! All of you made my story readable.

Thanks to the following CONvergence guests who stopped by the Wyvern's Aerie and said nice things about the book! You have no idea how much that encouragement means to me.

Libo Hanto, Bailey Lake, Jen Ruth Wyrk, Laura Thursten, and Ashley Deleon

DEDICATION

This book is dedicated to Dennis Zonn, who gave me a Tom Kratman book and inspired me to start reading again. OK, he nagged me incessantly until I finally read the book, but I loved it and started reading books again. Thank you, my friend!

Contents

I

⸙

The Trail to Foresight

25th of Frendalo, Year 1124 AGW (After the Great War)

Burned and frostbitten, Victor was having a terrible day. How easy it had been for the stranger wearing the black cloak with the red hood to talk him and his friend Mortimer into waylaying travelers to the Jubilee. When Beauregard, Victor thought the stranger had called himself, first proposed it to him and Mortimer, it sounded like a splendid idea. They could attack individuals traveling to the city. This close to the Great Chasm, few who survived the barrage of long-range spells would give chase. Easy money both Victor and Mortimer needed.

Both hoped to pay for more training, Mortimer to become a great mage. *Too bad Beauregard is leaving so soon, he could have trained him.* But there were plenty of mages in Foresight. Rumors were there was even a mage trying to reincorporate the Red Crest Magistry. If so, they would be looking for mages to bulk up their membership; they might even waive the dues. If not, they should have enough, depending on the cost of keeping Mortimer alive.

The first three travelers they encountered went down easily, then Beauregard left. They were thinking about packing up when a lone rider appeared. They readied their spells and then, bad luck hit. The traveler survived Victor's fire blast and Mortimer's spirit missiles, then retaliated with an even stronger fire blast of their own. Victor saw the blast coming. He stopped casting his next spell and ducked behind the stone in front of him, hoping it would protect him.

The misaimed blast turned the already dry morning air into a furnace. Victor saw Mortimer's singed hair as the smell of flash-burned flesh filled his nostrils. Victor noticed the clothing Mortimer wore insulated his skin from the charring; however, his friend's exposed face would have blisters forming soon.

Despite his obvious pain, Mortimer followed up with a shot from his longbow, but even the poisoned arrow failed to drop the traveler. Nor did the horse go down, the rider spurring it to a gallop. Victor considered casting a ray of lightning, but the fleeing rider galloped out of range.

***

Puffs of dust from the hard-packed ground rose with every step of Leaf Dancer's steady trot. Even at this pace, the precise movements looked more akin to a circus performance than a horse carrying a rider and packs. She often received stares, as a Silver Aelf riding a warhorse. She had sold the lavish saddle, pads, and cloth barding she had received with Leaf Dancer years ago. A sturdy blanket and saddle were all the horse carried now, along with Ariandel and her packs. Still, her small stature did not match the stature of the horse. Even without the armor and tabard, she looked a little out of place.

The blanket was made of dyed wool, softened by years of wear. Ariandel had learned the magical trick of cleaning and mending minor items. She performed it as needed on the blanket. Otherwise, it would have worn out in the many years since she had bought it at a small bazaar in Candeltin on the plains near her home. She favored blue, and she wore a dark blue cloak over a pale blue blouse with brown wool riding pants tucked into rugged black leather boots. She carried a dress of the same color blue in her pack to wear in town. A lovely, if plain, dress, the narrow hips and the hem made it impractical to wear when mounted.

She could stop at a village along the way, but Ariandel hoped to find a sorcerer, or maybe even a bard, to provide her training. She had much to learn before the Comórtas le Haghaidh Banríona. Shivering a bit with excitement, she imagined herself as a powerful mage, queen of all the aelf. She had worked so hard up to this point, and she couldn't wait to continue her training. She would have to earn some money first, but if she could find a quiet room, she could write some scrolls and sell them. She had one written already, written on silver bark linen, but the linen alone was worth more than she expected the training to cost.

She reflected on the spell she worked on with her teacher in the Black Woods, a portal which would carry her and her horse to anywhere, instantaneously, but she did not have the knowledge or experience in manipulating the spirit energies to perfect it yet.

Near midday, and almost past the Great Chasm, Ariandel still had many miles to travel to get to the Central Kingdom's capital city of Foresight. The small hills to the south went on for several miles before ending at the border of the human kingdom. Scattered trees and bushes and even patches of grass appeared as she neared the plains west of the Great Chasm. Small rodents scurried out of her path, and an occasional snake sunned itself on a rock or a patch of the hard-packed dirt. The fall weather arrived, and the smell of prairie grass floated on the light breeze. Thankfully, this region received precious little rainfall, even during the wet season. Muddy trails would have delayed her enough she would have had little chance to make it to Foresight before nightfall.

A blast of fire exploding in front of her interrupted her thoughts. The heat beat through her cloak and singed the hairs on Leaf Dancer. He reared, almost unseating her. She regained her balance and looked around for the source. As she did, several flashes of light came at her from an outcropping of rocks to her left. They struck her squarely; her necklace glowing before shrinking noticeably. But the necklace absorbed the magical impact, saving her a good deal of pain. She ran through the stamins she had memorized and summoned her energy, sending her own flaming ball to explode where the lights had come from. Spurring Leaf Dancer, she galloped away as fast as she could.

An arrow flew at her, piercing her shoulder with a splash of poisoned gel. It burned deep inside, but she rode on. As she rode, the poison continued to burn. She could feel her strength ebbing as the poison and burns took their toll. She faded in and out of consciousness while Leaf Dancer continued on, following the trail even after she could no longer summon the strength to prod him on. She knew the stalwart horse had borne an injured rider out of an ambush more than once. Her eyes closed, then went wide open as she landed hard on the ground. Lying still, her eyes fluttered as Leaf Dancer prodded her with his hoof, standing guard over her, challenging any to disrupt her body while he still lived. Then her eyes closed again.

***

Great clumps of dirt and rock flew into the air as each step of Aeris' great hooves drove the beast across the uneven ground. Red scale mail armor glistened and flashed, reflecting the midday sun as Alliandre galloped across the plains just north of the foothills surrounding the Great Chasm. A great lance rode in its straps, pointing straight up at the sun, blue-black legs carrying the massive steed at a seemingly unsustainable pace. In fact, not even moving half-speed, Aeris could maintain this pace for hours if need be. Even with the armor and armored rider he carried on his back.

Alliandre Del Nileppez Drol Hulloc rode with purpose to Foresight. Being the vanguard of the Party of the Seven, he needed to set up rooms and stables for everyone before they arrived and before the inns filled with other travelers. As almost all towns in the Three Kingdoms were set a day's wagon ride from each other, travelers would arrive late in the afternoon. This offered plenty of space for farms and growth. It also ensured travelers would not have to camp in the wilderness at night, unless they wanted to do so.

But with less than a week until the Jubilee in Foresight, travelers would arrive in great numbers, taking up any available spaces at the inns. Those arriving after the inns were full would be forced to stay in the inevitable tent city outside the gates. Even now, Alliandre suspected a good-sized tent city grew already as the knightly orders and adventuring parties showed up for the games. The Party of the Seven would not be among them if he could help it.

Alliandre was not opposed to sleeping in a tent, or even on the ground if need be. Raised in the court of the Southern Kingdom, he had been forced to flee. After, he had been a squire to the knights in the Freehold of Dragonsbane and trained as a warrior. Those experiences accustomed him to being "in the field" for weeks or months at a time. At fifteen, he spent the better part of nine months in survival training in the Northern Kingdom's tundra with just a cloak and knife.

But not Fairwind Duine Fionn, Princess of the High Aelf. She loathed lying on the ground. Her idea of camping outside involved casting spells which created a small wooden palisade and bedding for a score of people. Real cots, not just bedrolls on the ground. She wrote scrolls to carry with her in case they couldn't make it to a town with a decent inn. They had all stayed in one such keep the prior night.

Alliandre thought fondly of the aelf princess, despite their history with the Del Nileppez line. She always smelled of flowers, reminding Alliandre of his great love, Marion the Virtuous. Despite her tendency to demand creature comforts, she had proven herself to be a tenacious ally during their many campaigns together. She traveled the world to experience life. For an aelf princess, her attraction to danger and excitement matched some humans. She lived for it, Alliandre thought. While she gravitated to the other nobles, she always treated Alliandre kindly. And she almost always smiled when she called him Drullock, his nickname from childhood everyone seemed to have learned.

He chuckled to himself at the thought, then stopped and turned as a flash came from the hills to the south. The flash turned into a bolt of electricity. The hairs rose on his body as the lightning nearly missed him. Nearly missed wasn't the same as missed. He jerked uncontrollably for a second as the shock went through him. Aeris also trembled, but

Alliandre knew through experience how his mount resisted electricity quite well. Fire and cold also, Alliandre had learned over the years.

Alliandre spurred Aeris to a full gallop and drew the sword from his left bottom scabbard. "Fuair Seifean Ghaoithe." He yelled the command words as he pointed the sword toward the outcropping of rock where the lightning had originated. It caused little visible effect, just a cyclonic gust of air springing from his weapon. Crystals of ice formed on the ground in the direction he pointed the sword. The outcropping of rocks sprouted their own ice crystals, as Alliandre bent over his charging mount.

He did not have time now to delay hunting highwaymen, confident these brigands were no threat to his companions behind. In fact, Braxlo the Brave, Hero of Formount Pass, would enjoy the exercise entailed in riding them down. He had to get to Foresight and notify the guards, as well as get everyone cleared for entry to the city. With no more attacks coming from the rocks, he spurred Aeris on.

***

Ariandel awoke with a pounding in her head, and pain all over her body. Her mind blurred with her eyesight. She could not see as consciousness fled and reappeared. Her left shoulder burned with a deep pain, the rest of her arm numb. Her exposed skin was burned, as the blisters on her hands attested. Her first experience being ambushed popped into her head. She tried to focus on it to stay awake. Instead, the memory stayed with her as she drifted off into a dreamlike torpor.

A hand lifting her head broke her pain-induced mini-coma while someone poured water across her lips. She sputtered and choked on the first drops, but then drank as best she could. The smell of oiled leather and metal assaulted her nostrils. She opened her eyes and saw a stub-nosed dragon head staring back at her. Her entire body jerked in terror, and she twisted and turned to escape its grasp.

It took a few seconds for the shock to wear off. When her brain regained its function, she realized the helm had been forged to look like a dragon. She stopped struggling and sat up, motioning for more water. She drank several small sips, stalling for time to think. The stranger had not bound her, but she doubted she could do anything against such a hulking, frightening man. She glanced around for Leaf Dancer, and saw the horse several yards away, secured to an even larger, blue/black course-haired beast much resembling a horse.

Looking closer at the man as he stood up, he looked to be as tall Leaf Dancer. No, she guessed, even taller. Not near as wide, but he had the lean musculature of someone who spent his life fighting in armor. And he wore magnificent scale armor, designed to look like dragon scales. Bright red, with plate reinforcements which were lacquered the same color. She noticed he carried swords. Not just one or two, but several. Two on his body, and it looked like there were more on his horse? "That cannot be right," she muttered to herself, squinting as she tried to focus her eyes.

"Can you ride?" asked the man. He sounded angry. *Why should he be angry with me?*

"I said, can you ride?" The man had squatted down in front of her and spoke slowly, as though he was speaking to a child.

Alert now, she asked him, "Do you have any healing?"

"Of course, I have healing." He stood again. "What kind of fool travels near the Great Chasm and doesn't have healing?" By his withering glare, she had a good idea he thought he was looking at that exact kind of fool.

It may have been the headache, or the painful burns, but his attitude put her off. "Listen here, you honorless brute. I appreciate you stopping, but if you didn't want to help, why did you bother at all? If you have some healing, I will pay you for it, and you can be on your way. Or if you do not wish to help, just be away so I can continue my journey."

"Fine with me. Glad you only bruised your ego." He turned smartly, walking over to mount. He rode right up to her before reaching into one of his packs. He pulled out a small jar and tossed it to her.

"Here, this stuff smells bad. However, it will make your body heal your wounds quickly for a few hours, then you are going to be exhausted and have to rest. Make sure to eat something." Turning, he galloped off again.

"Thanks," she yelled after him angrily, then in a much quieter voice, "grendlaar spawn!"

* * *

Victor woke up later to find Mortimer near death. He retrieved their horses, hoisting Mortimer across the back of one. The cost of keeping Mortimer alive and tending his wounds would not take all they had gotten, depending on the sword they recovered. They had been friends since Victor came to Foresight. He would do anything he could to keep his friend alive.

Victor rode the horses hard as they traveled back to the city. Within view of the city gates, he noticed the blue/black horse. He didn't think the rider had gotten a good look at him, but he also didn't want to take any chances. So instead of approaching the gate, he went around the northern wall. He passed the gate and rode around to a sally port covered by a small rise. He rode through the ditch surrounding the walls, then went up the uneven stairs, guiding the horses with their loot and Mortimer. He and the horses disappeared into the dark tunnel.

"We should have enough to get you back into the Mages Guild after this," Victor told his unconscious friend. "I may rejoin the guard. The guild is too expensive. I could make captain in a few years." The tunnel, although short, turned frequently, and leading two horses slowed him considerably. He continued talking just to break up the tomb-like atmosphere. "My father may take me back if I can show him I am more than just a pickpocket."

He reappeared inside the walls, on the western side of the city, hurrying to a back alley behind some stables. A wiry stableboy sitting on a barrel pretended not to notice in order to avoid trouble. Victor led the horses around the corral and farrier's shack, and through narrow, muddy streets to a small cottage. The thatched roof looked like it kept most of the water out when it rained. The single window had great shutters which were open, but when closed, would stop anyone from entering through the window. He went up to the door and went inside, carrying Mortimer and some of the loot they had gained. After seeing to the comfort of his friend, he left for one of his favorite shops.

Outside, sturdy stones made up the wall of the shop and it had actual planks for a roof, rare in this part of the city. No windows, and an imposing steel reinforced door. Inside, the shop looked just the same as many shops around town. Clothes on racks, and shelves along the walls with bracelets and necklaces and other jewelry. A section by the door held capes and cloaks, and a small case sat at the counter. Behind the counter, several swords of varying length and even a halberd hung on the wall or in display cases. Victor tried on a coat and thought about palming a ring as the owner helped the only other customer, then decided against it. He doubted it would fool Jeremy, and it would not be helpful in the negotiations if Jeremy caught him stealing. Jeremy finished making the sale and the other customer left.

Balding, with a small beard and bulging belly, the man greeted Victor as he walked to the counter. They displayed more expensive items on shelves in large cases behind the counter where the smallish Jeremy stood.

"Hello Victor, how have things been going for you?"

"Pretty good." Victor lied. "I have some loot Mortimer and I picked up near the Great Chasm a few days ago. We thought you may have some need of it." Victor laid the sword and dagger on the counter. Pointing at the runes on the sword, he said, "The sword is enchanted and has this nice ruby for a pommel. What do you think, Jeremy?" He held up the sword, turning it so the man could see the light reflecting off the iridescent red gemstone.

"Where did you say you got them?" the shopkeeper asked.

"Mortimer and I were exploring over by the Great Chasm. There were brigands hiding in a cave there. They attacked us, but we drove them off. There were a few who were unconscious, so we stabilized their wounds and looted what looked like it might be of value. Mortimer received a serious wound, so we returned home. He is still laid up. I am just trying to see if there is enough here to buy some healing." Victor always thought it best to add as many truthful statements as possible to his lies. If anyone reported highwaymen near a cave, his story would seem to be supported.

"I hope you reported them to the Guard. With Jubilee, they will not be happy about highwaymen so close to the city."

"We got in late, but we told the guards who let us in the gate. Perhaps I will go back today and tell the Sargent of the Guard directly." Then, grabbing the sword hilt firmly, Victor gave a command. "Chama Encesa."

The ruby on the hilt turned from a dull red to a glowing bright red, the blade bursting into flame. Jeremy jumped back. "Chama." Victor spoke again, and the blade returned to normal.

"Well Victor, you hit pay dirt, my friend. I can give you a hundred turots for the sword."

Victor had heard enchanted blades could run several hundred turots. Still, he had little experience with buying and selling enchanted weapons. He could not enchant them himself and did not know what a flaming sword would be worth. But he thought a lot more than a hundred turots.

"Five hundred turots for the sword," he declared. "You know it is worth much more than that."

Jeremy put on a shocked face. "Five hundred, are you crazy? It is just a simple enchantment, and I still need to repair and polish it and clean it up. The scabbard too. But Jubilee is here. If I can get it ready in time, I should get a premium, so I will give you a hundred and fifty for it."

"If I had the time, I could sell it myself at Jubilee and get the five hundred easily. But I want you to make some money. We are friends after all, so how about four hundred?"

This went on for several more minutes, Victor walking out with two hundred and ten turots.

***

Sivle and the group of riders rode up to the lone knight sitting on a jet-black stallion. The knight seemed to study the ground and underbrush. "Trouble, Sir Braxlo?" asked one rider, an aelf female in an exquisitely detailed riding cloak. Cornflower blue, with white and red lace, and gold and silver embroidery in the shape of a majestic tree. The great branches held golden birds which matched her long, golden hair perfectly. In the branches were also silver nests, one of which allowed the cloak to be clasped with a bird from the other side, cleverly designed to sit inside it. The scent of wildflowers and honeyed soap radiated from her, and the knight inhaled deeply. Looking her straight in the eyes, the same color as her coat, he disciplined himself not to get caught up in her beauty. Fairwind, looking like a human woman barely out of her teens, had that effect on many men. He himself never grew tired of being in her company and smiled at her before continuing.

"Fire and lightning, Your Highness," said the knight matter-of-factly. "An hour ago is my guess, judging by those tracks." He turned and pointed at great clods of ground torn up in a path leading along their route. "Drullock came this way. I found evidence of two men, maybe three, over in the outcropping due south. They were hit by some fire as well, and blasts of cold, possibly. My guess is from that damned sword of his." Turning to another companion, he added an aside. "I will never understand why you made it for him, Sivle. Like he wasn't insufferable enough."

Sivle smiled at the old complaint between them. For all his up-bringing in the court of the Southern Kingdom and the best teachers the kingdom could afford, Alliandre seemed to reject the manners and etiquette they had worked so long to instill in him. Once the Southern Kingdom fell and the Knights of Dragonsbane rejected him, he decided the direct approach favored him. And Sivle, being his friend since they were infants, enchanted swords and armor and anything else which would keep his friend alive.

"First, you know Alliandre does not like to be called Drullock, even when he is not around," Sivle replied, then smiled at Braxlo. "Second, I enchant his weapons and armor so he can stay alive long enough for the rest of you to join the fight."

Ignoring the taunt, Braxlo continued, "There is also a cave where it looks like they kept their horses. Four bodies in it, all of them still alive, but unconscious. Someone put some poultice on their wounds. Grendlaar were all over it too at some point. Looks like they didn't bother the unconscious ones, maybe thought they were dead. It looks like they had another tied up there but escaped. Must have been a mage, because the tracks went to the front of the cave and then they were just gone."

"Excellent, Braxlo. Nice work," said Sivle. Wearing scale armor fashioned to look like a dragon, an exact match to Alliandre's, only in blue, a nasty-looking mace hung from his saddle, with a silver tree hanging from a cord around his neck. "We will need to notify Foresight when we arrive if Alliandre has not."

"About the grendlaar?" the black-clad knight asked.

Sivle thought for a moment. "No. The grendlaar didn't seem to cause any harm. No sense sending out troops to antagonize them."

"You still think they can be reasoned with?" Braxlo laughed. "They lack the intelligence to even use the spirits, what makes you think they can negotiate? And would they even keep their word?"

"Remember the trip to the Great Chasm when we found the Roxora? The grendlaar there didn't seem hostile. They even offered us water."

"Brackish, poisoned water. Yeah, I remember."

"It wasn't poisoned, just stagnant. They were drinking it too. But they didn't attack us. So for now, let's just report on the brigands."

"Do you want me to track them?" asked Braxlo. Tallish, with a battle-hardened face, he wore armor in the style from his knighthood days. An older design, with a blackened exterior, even blacker than his skin. Both Fairwind and Sivle had enchanted it several times. His sword, also blackened, all but crackled with magical energy, even in the scabbard. He carried himself with the sure confidence of someone who had great skill with it. So much skill he had no need to advertise it.

Like Alliandre, he had trained at the Freehold of Dragonsbane. However, he had taken the oaths of the Order of Dragonsbane, had been a knight there for twenty-five years, and retired before Alliandre arrived. With his duty to the Freehold completed, he became a simple farmer, raising cattle and wheat with his wife. Several years later, after his wife had died and his children had grown, he explored the Great Chasm.

During this time, the story was, he met Her Royal Highness, Princess Fairwind Duine Fionn. Her golden hair resembled sunlight radiating from her head. Her face had the ever-youthful glow all aelf seemed to hold for several centuries. With no idea who she was, or what her goals were, he pledged his sword to her right there, traveling with her ever since. Almost ten years together. Even during the last five, when they had all gone their separate ways, he stayed with her. Every year they all met at the Freehold, twice finding interesting quests to fill their time.

"No," replied Sivle. "If Alliandre thought they were a threat, he would have taken care of them. I think we are safe to continue."

The last member of the group, a tall, wiry man dressed in black robes, spoke up, "Or maybe his eagerness to see Marion took over." That drew chuckles all around.

Continuing the familiar joke, Braxlo added, "Let's get moving then, or we will miss their wedding. I will go back on point."

They rode on for several more hours and were nearing the end of the morning when they came up a rise and saw Braxlo stopped with his fist in the air. They rode up carefully, Sivle whispering as he got next to him, "What are we looking at?"

"Someone seems to have fallen here." Pointing at some matted vegetation and scuffs on the ground, he continued. "It looks like Drullock rode by here and found someone down. You can see where he dismounted Aeris over there," pointing several yards away, then at the matted ground, "then came over next to this indentation. Then he appeared to ride off." Scratching his stubbled beard, he continued, "There is another set of tracks which follows his tracks. We can assume they are from the fallen rider. Pretty well-trained horse too. I would have guessed a warhorse of some sort, but it does not have the heavy armor

I would expect. With its prancing, it could be a circus horse of some type, I suppose."

Braxlo removed his helm, pausing to take a long draught from his water bag. Sweat dripped off his graying hair and down his face. "Nothing to worry about in the immediate area, but we should be on alert. I would suggest we ride in a starburst formation about thirty feet apart. I will ride ahead. Makes for a boring ride, but we don't want to be massed if spellcasters are about."

They rode on four more hours. The sun passed its zenith, traveling down when they came up a rise and saw Braxlo stopped with his fist in the air again. They rode up and Sivle whispered quietly, "What are we looking at?"

"Down behind the rock formation. Single rider, female aelf, horse looked to be down, but she got it up and moved it behind the rocks when she saw me. I am sure I saw her pull out what looked like a scroll case. I rode around looking for ambushers, but I did not see any."

"So, it may be just what it looks like, a single rider with an injured horse?"

"Could be. Could also be a trap. No telling if there are any others hidden in those rocks."

Sivle paused for a moment as he looked over the scene. They had traveled miles from the Great Chasm, and there were no longer the rocky hills to the south. Instead, rolling hills covered with prairie grass and wildflowers went as far as the eye could see. Foresight sat visible in the distance, still several hours' ride away. Here and there, small boulders or outcroppings of rocks and earth dotted the landscape. It would have been a beautiful scene if they had been able to enjoy it. With the evidence of the earlier ambush, he thought it would be best to be careful. "Any sign of Alliandre?"

"Pretty sure he rode past here several hours ago. Doesn't look like they bothered him."

Sivle decided on a course of action. "Erich, go down and see if you can determine if she is friendly or not."

Erich swung his black cloak around his crouched body. Whispering some commands, he seemed to disappear as the cloak swirled and changed color to match the surrounding grass. Sivle and Braxlo could see his path for half a minute as he left for the outcropping, but Sivle lost him before he had gone a quarter of the distance. Braxlo watched and pointed him out until Erich reached the halfway point, then Braxlo lost him as well. Looking at each other, Sivle and Braxlo just grinned.

Sivle's longtime friend, Erich the Black, ostensibly a priest of the Forest Spirits, advanced high in the ranks before leaving the priesthood to travel and see the world. He intervened in a fight outside of Tristheim, saving a noblewoman from some brigands. It turned out the brigands were members of a Thieves Guild from Kai, and the noblewoman turned out to be the wife of a high-ranking member of Tristheim's Thieves Guild. The nobleman, Jonas Del Banks, convinced Erich to join the guild.

Erich spent a dozen years in Tristheim. Through the guild, he had learned how to be stealthy and get into places people were trying to keep him out of. Unlike many members, Erich rarely used these skills to rob people, but they had come in handy while adventuring. It was when he first left Tristheim that he and Sivle met and became friends. Erich claimed to want to obtain the riches of the Great Chasm, and said he saw Sivle as his greatest chance. While Sivle suspected some of Erich's story to be exaggerated, he had been a strong ally in their years together.

Ten minutes later, Erich stood above the outcropping, yelling up, "Just an aelf girl and a knight's warhorse, by the looks of it. They both look injured. They will survive, but they look exhausted."

***

Terrified, Ariandel trembled as she hid in the tall grasses. Leaf Dancer lay several yards away beside a large bolder. She hoped the black rider had not seen him. Although just eighty years old, she still recognized the symbol of the Snow Dragon which adorned the black knight's shield. She could feel adrenaline affecting her. Tunnel vision narrowed her sight, restricting her view to the area where the knight's companions had joined him. Her hearing increased until she could hear a bee ten paces away, even over the grass rustling in the wind. She dropped her head to avoid being seen and tried to slow her breathing.

She jumped at the sound of someone shouting right behind her. She looked up and saw a tall, thin man dressed all in black. His cloak shimmered, seeming to blink in and out, making him difficult to see when he turned a certain way. His jet-black hair, long for a man, fell below his shoulders, and he had some sort of symbol around his neck, a family crest or a religious symbol of some sort. His gray eyes and sharp, hooked nose made him seem almost birdlike. Nonetheless, she found him quite attractive. He looked away, so Ariandel opened her small scroll case in case she needed to cast the spell inside.

A few minutes later, four imposing strangers surrounded her. Well, not all of them so imposing. She recognized one as a High Aelf noblewoman, which she took as a good sign. But the man in the black cloak, and the other in black armor, with skin almost as dark, looked like they could kill her and take all of her belongings, not losing a moment's peace about it. And the third man wore blue armor which matched the rider she had encountered earlier. This set her on edge. *They must be together.* If they were friends of his, they were probably NOT nice people. Eventually, the man in the blue dragon armor dismounted, giving her a formal bow.

"I am Sivle Si Evila Drol Revo. With me, Erich the Black, high priest of the Black Woods Shrine. Sir Braxlo the Brave, Hero of Formount Pass, Knight Errant of the Freehold of Dragonsbane. Last, Her Royal Highness, Fairwind Duine Fionn, youngest daughter of Their Majesties, King Aedengus Duine Fionn and Queen Rionach Finn Duine Fionn. We offer you any aid we can provide. Please be at ease and tell us what brought you to this lamentable condition."

Ariandel looked at the four standing over her and thought about how she should respond. The speaker introduced himself as Sivle Si Evila Drol Revo. Si Evila indicated a bastard of someone unknown, and not a noble. But Drol Revo indicated a noble mother. *He must be in good standing then.* The tall man in black, a priest it seemed, scared her the most. The armored brute wore the markings of a knight of Dragonsbane. Definitely not good. *They hate aelf.* But he traveled with an aelf princess so...

Did he say aelf princess?

She decided either she would be safe, or it didn't matter anyway if she wasn't, so she told the story of the obstacles she had faced that day. It got interesting once she got to the meeting with, "... that pig-headed, ill-mannered, ill-bred, thundering oaf." Her heart pounded as she remembered the encounter. "To think I lay there wounded and un-conscious, and he didn't give me so much as his name or even offer to give me a ride on his huge porcupine horse."

She sighed, then continued, "Then, just when I thought he would be helpful, he gave me this!" She held out the empty jar and continued, "Now I am so tired I can barely walk. My horse is the same, the sun is going down, and I am stuck out here waiting to get accosted by ban-dits. I won't even be able to relearn my spells since I cannot get some-where quieter!" Her story finished, she flung out her arms, throwing the empty jar out into the grass and sat down, exhausted by the effort of her long tale.

Perhaps because of the exhaustion, she sobbed. Then she looked up, angry again, as the two men, Erich and Braxlo, the blue-armored man had said, were laughing. She thought they were laughing at her until she noticed the annoyed look on the man in the blue armor.

"That sounds like Drullock alright!" bellowed Braxlo.

"Hahahaha, he HATES that stuff. Why do you bother giving it to him, Sivle?" roared Erich.

This went on for far longer than Ariandel would have thought possible. By the time they wound down, she smiled, liking this group despite their familiarity with the oaf. Drullock, they said his name was. *Hmmm. That name seems strange.* The same name as a rodent in the far west, which emitted a foul-smelling odor as a mating ritual or when startled. It would be odd for someone to name their child after it, even stranger among the civilized humans not to have the surname of at least one of their parents, Del for the father, Drol for the mother. Only the knights took other titles. *Perhaps he is some sort of barbarian or lived across the White Hills to the west. Or maybe it is a nickname. Drullock.* She knew she would remember the name.

Sivle broke up the verbal belittlement, motioning to Erich. "Could you take care of the horse please, Erich, while I see to this young maiden?" He then laid his hands on her head, saying a few words. She could feel energy coursing through her, restoring her strength. A moment of euphoria came over her. When it passed, she opened her eyes and saw Leaf Dancer stand up and prance around like a young colt. Erich pulled an adamon out of his pocket to feed to the horse.

Then, the princess addressed her. "My dear, why don't you accompany us to Foresight. We will make sure you get there safely." Then, with a grin at Sivle and mock admonition in her voice, "It is the least we can do after the abhorrent treatment you received at the hands of our companion."

"Yes, Your Highness! That would be delightful," she said as she rose to her feet so she could give a proper curtsey.

"No bowing out here, my dear. In court, you can bow. Outside the city, you need only be our friend."

***

Alliandre stopped with less than a mile to go before he reached the city. He dismounted before rummaging through one of Aeris' packs. From it he pulled a banner, a silk embroidered tabard for himself, and a large velvet caparison for Aeris. It took several minutes to fasten the caparison on the massive beast and don his own. Then, mounting Aeris and attaching the banner to his lance, he raised it high as Aeris walked slowly to Foresight.

This was, perhaps, the only courtesy of court he observed. Whenever someone of import, or any armed group, arrived at a city or castle, they would raise a banner and move slowly to the gates. This gave the guards time to summon the Captain of the Guard, and for them to send an escort. It also gave them time, depending on the person or persons in the party, to arrange for a high-ranking person to greet them once admitted through the gates. Customarily, the guards would confiscate and hold any weapons or potentially harmful magics the visitors carried and charge a small fee for their storage. Even small villages kept this tradition. Frequently, armed travelers who did not show this courtesy met with a sizeable portion of the town guard when they arrived.

Alliandre noted the guard dispatched a detail out from the gates to meet him. A short while later, the banner of riders hailed him. "Who goes there?"

"I am Alliandre Del Nileppez Drol Hulloc, vanguard of the Party of the Seven, friend of the Central Kingdom and subject of the lost king, Tristan the Bold." Bowing in the saddle to the leader of the banner, he continued, "I have arrived to announce the Party of the Seven, renowned adventurers and heroes of the Great Vreen War. We have come for the Jubilee, and to pay our respects to their Majesties King Henry the Great and Queen Persimone the Fair. All hail the king!"

"All hail the king!" the guards replied in unison.

Handing a scroll case to the captain, Alliandre continued, "I also have this certificate, from the king, allowing us privileges against confiscation."

"Hail and well met!" replied the captain as he looked over the letter Alliandre handed him. Pausing several moments while he scanned the letter, he spoke. "We shall escort you to the gates. There you will declare all weapons and magics you intend to bring to our fair city. With Great King Henry suspending confiscation for you, we ask you to abide by, and assist the guard in enforcing, the laws of the city as stipulated in the letter. We ask you to pay a small fee as well."

Technically, the letter had waived all fees, but the captain thought he would at least ask. If nothing else, to see just how friendly to the Central Kingdom this man was, he added, "To pay for the increased security."

"Of course," Alliandre assured him, tossing a small bag over to the captain.

Feeling both the weight of the bag, and the crystalline items inside, the captain said, "I only requested a small fee. This is quite generous."

"I hope you remember that," laughed Alliandre.

"Then follow us, and we will get you processed as quickly as possible."

"It will not be quick, but fear not, we have time before the Party of the Seven arrives."

The accompanying soldiers first looked crestfallen at losing the opportunity to pocket a few stray coins and lighten the bottles of liquor from this illustrious traveler's baggage. Now they stared in wonder at the pouch of valuables in their captain's hand and probably wondered if any of the contents would fall their way.

They rode the remaining way together, with Alliandre surrounded by the banner for protection. Smiling to himself, Alliandre couldn't help thinking if someone did attack, he would likely do most of the protecting. The captain sent two men ahead. To set up a pavilion they said, but Alliandre knew they would first summon the guard commander and more guards just in case his intentions differed from those stated. The ride continued uneventfully. Within fifteen minutes they sat under the shade of the pavilion drinking chilled wine while discussing the items Alliandre carried. The mayor had shown up as well, welcoming Alliandre with a deep bow.

***

Earl Alberto Del Comaste Drol Seville, Mayor of Foresight, had heard of the Party of the Seven. Nearly everyone in court had. He had even met one of them, Sir Lolark the Luckless, frequently. Alliandre was not a holy paladin like Sir Lolark. Not even a knight, though Alberto knew he had trained at Dragonsbane. Not even a nobleman, if the reports were true. But he came from the line of Drake Del Nileppez, and he had saved the life of the king's son during the Great Vreen War. The chancellor's instructions had been clear. Alliandre Del Nileppez Drol Hulloc had the same standing as any visiting nobility. So Alberto had put on his finest clothes, his golden stole identifying his position and title, then rushed down to the gate to meet the rider. Hopefully, before he reached the guard tent. He wasn't sure if Alliandre would take offense to being handled by the Captain of the Guard.

"It is with great delight we welcome you back to our fair city, Master Nileppez. It has been too long since your last visit. I have spoken to the Royal Chancellor, and you are to be shown every courtesy. Their Majesties would enjoy seeing you again, and you are welcome to petition an audience while you are here. To save you time, you require no declaration of arms. Although if you can spare the time, we would be grateful to you if you would indulge the guards. For appearances, if nothing else." He gave Alliandre another deep bow.

Bowing in return, Alliandre replied, "Well met, Earl Del Comaste. We are just as delighted to be visiting the great Central Kingdom, and the wondrous city of Foresight." The captain looked a bit astonished this stranger knew the mayor's name and title. Alliandre continued, "We are at Their Majesties' command while here and will be honored to be granted an audience. In one week's time, we will request an audience. As far as declaring our possessions, I would not think of entering this fine city without doing so, as the king has been so gracious as to allow us to provide our own security over them. Let us begin."

Alliandre drew a sword and laid it on the table, "The sword Equite." Drawing and laying another sword onto the table, "The sword Liberte..."

***

Over an hour later, Alliandre finished the list. A pile of swords, daggers, two shields, a belt, his lance, several robes, rings, amulets, jars, and bottles covered the table. A chest filled with small bradnut-sized gems, and another filled with platinum and silver coins, sat on the ground next to it. He had also set his own coin purse on the table, filled with a mix of the coins of the realm. Alliandre handed the captain and the mayor a small stack of parchment which contained the lists of items carried by Fairwind, Braxlo, Erich, and Sivle. With a grand flourish, Alliandre bowed again and said with a big grin, "That is all we brought with us on this trip!"

The mayor attached his seal to the parchments and returned them to Alliandre. He did the same with a list made by the captain as Alliandre had gone through the items. Bowing back with a grin of his own, "I am sure you will want to get a meal and a room, so I will delay you no further. Do you need a guide to one of our fine inns or taverns?"

"No, thank you. I am going to arrange rooms at the Wyvern's Aerie, and I know the way. Please direct the rest of the party there when they arrive."

With the formalities completed, and another small bow, Alliandre began repacking and equipping the weapons and items with which he had arrived.

It only took him fifteen minutes.

***

The rest of the ride to Foresight passed uneventfully. Ariandel watched as a banner of the Knights of Gold Keep rode by. Their conical helmets and angled armor were all burnished in hammered gold, and their shields had the image of a great keep, also in hammered gold. They looked like they would crowd the small group, but Braxlo returned, moving to the front. The rest of the group fell in behind him and rode in a line, making it clear they would not move. At the last moment, Braxlo pulled out his shield, displaying the Freehold of Dragonsbane heraldry. The knight's commander gave a small nod, then barked a command. The knights made a precise movement into a single file line of their own, and they passed uneventfully.

"I thought the Freehold of Dragonsbane would have gone away when the war ended since there is no reason to kill aelf anymore," Ariandel said out loud, to no one in particular.

Fairwind responded first. "The Great Aelf King of Kings gave up the aelf claims on the Freehold. In return, the Freehold members agreed to repair the damage they had done to the Black Woods, the Great Woods, and the Great Tree. They also promised to construct a magnificent temple to the Forest Spirits within the Freehold. They have been allies of the aelf ever since. They even stationed a full spear of aelf paladins there, and the knights and the paladins train together."

"Yep!" added Braxlo, "Now we only get to kill aelf on special holidays," he teased, with a growl to his voice and a fierce look which made Ariandel wonder. Fairwind's quick smile and gentle head shake dispelled her fears.

"Not to change the subject," the half-aelf in the blue armor interrupted, "but what is a, aelf from the Silver Woods doing this far east, riding a knight's horse, but wearing beggars' clothing? No offense intended."

Ariandel winced. Her clothes were not beggar's clothes. Well-made and sturdy, she had to admit they were somewhat plain, at least compared to the finery in which these people traveled.

"First, my clothing is quite well made and practical, thank you very much. Second, the horse, well," she thought of how to best explain Leaf Dancer. "A kind knight who saved my life bequeathed Leaf Dancer to me. I am doing what many of our people do, traveling and learning about the world. I may not have traveled as long as you have, but I have been selected from my village to compete in the Comórtas le Haghaidh Banríona. Whether or not I am chosen, I will make a name for myself in the world and they will know me as Ariandel an Láidre."

"You are a bit young, are you not?" Fairwind asked politely.

"I am only fifty years younger than the current queen when she was chosen. The prince is young, even younger than I am. I have decades before he is of age. Can you imagine it? Being the first queen with a full aelf king in over a thousand years."

"We all wait for the day when an aelf once again rules over us. But the prince is not the deciding person, my dear." Fairwind smiled gently. "The king is nearing sixty, and there has not been a king who lived past seventy. You have at most ten years to train."

Ariandel had not considered the king's age. She could learn much in ten years, but not enough to impress the current queen. Considering her options, she straightened stoically. "I will make a name for myself because I must. I trust the spirits will guide me."

That drew snickers from the men in the back, but Sivle rode up next to her and continued. "I am curious. How do you intend to make this name for yourself?"

"I intend to become the greatest mage of the Silver Bark Woods. One of my reasons for coming to the Jubilee is to find a mage under whom to continue my training. I am already one of the strongest mages in my clan, and my mother says magic runs strong in our family. My great-great-great-grandmother was Elandra Gruag Fionn. She stood among the mages who helped stop the knights of Dragonsbane in the last battle, forcing their surrender."

"It wasn't the spirit-damned aelf which forced our surrender," Braxlo growled as he turned his horse around. "Drake Del Nileppez had a vision of some sort and called the truce. If he hadn't, he could have burned the entire woods, including the big oak you all worship." Ariandel pulled back a bit, terrified as Braxlo rode toward her. He had no weapon drawn, but his grimace seemed menacing enough.

"I'm sure both sides have their histories of the war," Fairwind said, trying to calm the situation, giving Braxlo a stern look.

"Of course, Your Highness," Braxlo replied meekly. "I meant no offense." Turning his horse back around, he spoke not quite under his breath, "At any rate, it happened a millennium ago, and none of us were there to know the truth."

"Actually, my great-great-grandmother is still alive, and she grew up hearing all the stories of Drake the Defiler and passed them down to us." This brought her a look from Fairwind as well, and Braxlo began turning his horse once again.

Sivle attempted to regain control of the conversation, querying her further. "Never mind the ancient history, who was your aethorn?" he asked, using the aelf word for teacher. With a wave of his hand at Braxlo, he turned his horse in between the two of them.

"Toron Drol Versa," she replied proudly. "I met him while he traveled through the Silver Bark Woods and he agreed to teach me the basics. I studied under him for over a year."

"A human? Teaching a Silver Aelf. Hmmmm, interesting. I met Toron several times in my youth and trained with him as well. A fine man. Didn't have a great love of aelf, though." Then, shaking his head, he continued the interrogation, "What was the first lesson you learned from him?"

Ariandel began her recitation of the lesson every spirit user learned. "The Forest Spirit energies traveling in the aether are what we use to create our spells. Once we understand a certain form of energy, such as fire or air or earth or water, we can manipulate it to do our bidding. Organizing the energies and combining them in certain ways is how we create our magics. Therefore, we study the great mages and the spells they were capable of, to learn what is possible."

"Why can't everyone use the spirits?"

You must reach into the aether with your innate energies. While everyone has some innate energy, not everyone is strong enough to manipulate the spirits.

"Why do we write our spells?"

"We write the stamins of the spells once we have figured them out so we can memorize them and recast them without trying to figure it all out again. This is why the spell books of the ancient wizards are so valuable and so well protected."

"Very good," continued Sivle. "Although, I have come to disagree with the last part. We would advance our knowledge faster if we shared more. But that is another discussion. So here is a thought for you to ponder. What if there are not many unique spirits, but only one?"

Surprised, Ariandel blurted out, "That is ridiculous."

"You are so sure? Explain, please."

"If there were only one spirit, we would have no need of stamins to weave the different energies together. We know the different disciplines use different energies for their spells. For example, bards use air and aether spirits, which is why a bard has never created a blast of fire. Instead, their spells focus on inspiring and drawing magnificent feats from themselves and their companions. And why they can project their voices over great distances, or in noisy rooms. If there were only one spirit, anyone could weave blasts of fire, for example."

"You have learned your lessons well, it would seem." Sivle's expression said he did not believe it. But he continued, "Speaking of bards, the bard Mirandel Amhrán órga told me when I studied under her years ago, in order to be a great mage, I would have to unlearn everything I knew. I have grown to believe her and would return the favor by giving the same advice to you. However, unlearning is difficult."

"You trained under Mirandel?" Ariandel stopped Leaf Dancer, looking agog at Sivle. "Now I know you are lying. It is said Mirandel has taken no students for over a century. She believes her power to be too dangerous. But you claim she trained YOU?"

"Sivle never lies, my dear." Fairwind spoke matter-of-factly, as if she had said the sky is blue. "I can vouch for him. Mirandel did indeed train him."

"Then who ARE you, REALLY?! Is there no one you have not met? I cannot tell if you are well traveled nobles or just convincing liars, no offense intended. You seem genuine," looking at Fairwind, "but you claim to be a High Aelf princess." Turning to Sivle, "And you knew and trained under two of the greatest mages in the last five hundred years. Next you will tell me Sir Braxlo is a descendent of Sir Robert Bloodaxe."

"Nay, milady," Braxlo chimed in. "My great-grandfather killed Sir Robert Bloodaxe."

Ariandel looked at Braxlo in shock.

"He's joking," Fairwind said disgustedly. "Braxlo, what did I tell you about being nice to this young bhean. She has been through enough. Her opinion of us did not get off on a good foot with Drullock. We do not want her thinking we are all uncouth barbarians."

"Yes, Your Highness. Sorry, milady." Braxlo bowed from his horse and waited for Ariandel to acknowledge his apology.

Looking sternly, she told him, "You have an evil streak in you, Sir Braxlo, to torment young helpless maidens like you do, but I forgive you." Adding a devilish smile, "I am sure you will be just as forgiving when it comes time to repay all your kindness."

Braxlo groaned, turning his horse back onto the path, trotting ahead next to Erich.

As he rode off, she continued, "I mean no offense, as you may be all you say you are, but this is quite overwhelming." Sighing, she finished, "At least you have confirmed one thing for me. I had thought at the time this 'Drullock' must have been a barbarian, and now I know I was right. It explains a lot."

Fresh laughter burst from Braxlo and Erich. They turned and rode together for a bit, passing jokes back and forth. She couldn't hear everything, although Ariandel no longer believed they were at her expense. By the time Braxlo galloped forward to run point, she was liking these travelers even more.

***

A short way from the city gates, they rode up on Braxlo setting up a small tent. Sivle and Erich dismounted to assist him. In no time at all, they erected the tent. On the top flapped a small leaf-shaped pennant of cornflower blue, with golden trim. Ariandel recognized the crest of the High Elves and the laurel ringlet signifying the royal family. She had been curious whether her new traveling companions were telling the truth, but no one would be foolish enough to display that unless they were brave or stupid.

The tent itself was a brilliant white, with the Great Tree of the High Aelf on each side, blue crenellation adorning the top. She wondered how they kept it so clean. Braxlo held one flap open and gave a deep bow. "Ladies."

Fairwind dismounted and grabbed a pack from her horse, motioning for Ariandel to do the same. "Let's change and freshen up. Drullock should have cleared us at the Northern Gate by now."

Ariandel dismounted Leaf Dancer and grabbed her dress, although unsure how she would be able to ride in it. She supposed she could ride sidesaddle, but it would be an uncomfortable trip. Fortunately, the city gates were only a five-minute ride, so she strode into the tent, smiling sweetly at Braxlo as he held the flap for her as well. "Thank you, Sir Braxlo. So nice to be in the company of such a noble knight." She said it sarcastically, but she could have sworn the gruff man's lips twisted upward.

Once inside, she took out her dress and began changing.

"Excuse me my dear," the aelf princess began, "I do not mean to be rude, but perhaps you would care to wear one of my dresses into town. I have plenty, and you can return it anytime. I am afraid if we go with you dressed like that, people will assume you are a servant, or worse."

Ariandel looked at the dress Fairwind held out to her and scoffed. "My apologies, Your Highness, but if you do not mind my saying so, I would look like your servant in THAT dress, magnificent though it is. I also would not feel comfortable putting on airs and wearing something other than the clothes I am used to. Besides, I would feel horrible if I damaged it."

On cue, Ariandel caught her foot in the skirt of her dress, grimacing as she heard the telltale ripping of fabric. Inspecting her dress, she found the rear half of the skirt hanging like the flap on a pair of men's winter under-breeches. She looked up, ready to cry, then decided against it. Instead, she cast the ruined dress to the ground. Standing as tall as she could, head held high, she said in her most courtly voice, "On the other hand, I might enjoy being your servant for the day, Your Highness."

Fairwind looked at her, standing so proud in nothing but her stockings. With a giggle, she ran over and gave her a giant bear hug. "Today, I name you Ariandel Cara Ríoga, my royal friend! Come with us. We shall make sure you find a mage to train you. If you do not, I will teach you myself." She became a whirlwind of activity, pulling out shoes, stockings, petticoats, and crinolines, along with a beautiful gown of robin's egg blue with silver threaded lace on the skirt and a high collar of red with gold stitching. Next came a red and gold trimmed corset with the great silver tree of the High Aelf embroidered on the front of the blue panels. The blue stockings ended above her knee, secured there by straps hanging from the petticoats. Then sapphire-colored shoes which seemed to be a size too small, but they matched the dress perfectly. It took some time for the two of them to get dressed, and by the time she finished, Ariandel would have happily gone back and put on her plain dress, torn skirt or not.

They walked out of the tent to find the men looking scarcely different. Erich was dressed all in black, although now all velvet and silk, with his cloak gathered over one shoulder. High black leather boots covered the bottom of his black velvet trousers, with an ethereal black silk shirt peeking out from under his velvet jacket. Ariandel thought there might have been a vest under the jacket as well, but the lack of contrast made it hard to tell. Only the keenest eye could detect hints of more than a few blades tucked behind the jacket flaps or under lace trim.

Sivle still had on his armor, having polished it to a bright luster, and adding a tabard, the garish-colored fabric made him look quite foppish. He covered his horse's barding with a great velvet caparison containing the same garish pattern. If he had a lance, someone might have mistaken him for a knight from Wyndgryph Castle. The yellow, red, and blue colors reminded her of seven brightly colored shields, all joined at their tips. Looking closer, she noted one of the "shields" matched the design on her corset.

Braxlo had a similar tabard on, with a similar caparison on his horse as well. A pennant attached to his lance also bore the strange device. Ariandel decided it must be their crest, although she wondered why Erich and Fairwind did not display it as well. She pondered their crest as she looked for Leaf Dancer and saw someone had removed his saddle and put on a new caparison which looked like autumn leaves falling. Looking closer, she noticed, under the silken covering, straps holding a harness for her to ride in, sidesaddle. They had outfitted Fairwind's horse with a caparison of robin's egg blue. A great trunk spread up the back, with branches reaching out, covering the entire surface. Along the bottom hung red tassels, almost touching the ground. No doubt her caparison hid the same harness.

Braxlo assisted the ladies onto their horses, bringing two folding tables which acted as stairs, holding their hands while they got situated. Braxlo led the horses at a slow walk. Even Leaf Dancer's precise gait did little more than rock Ariandel. With her feet firmly in the stirrups attached to the straps, and at this pace, she rode quite comfortably.

"Drullock will have gotten us cleared, but you will need to declare any magic items or weapons," Braxlo called back from the front.

"I have only this dagger, and a few potions and a scroll," she called back.

"No need to announce it to the world. Just prepare to declare it at the gate. You have money for the confiscation tax, yes?"

"Surely, they would not confiscate these insignificant items. I can see why they would take your swords and magic items, but this tiny dagger?" She pulled the dagger out to show him, but Fairwind motioned for her to stop.

"It will not matter," she stated confidently. "We have sent a list of our belongings with Drullock, so just be quiet and sit tight. Hopefully, they will not ask about you."

She began replying, when Braxlo called out, "Riders coming!"

Sure enough, a dozen riders were charging their way. Ariandel recognized the crest on the banner as from the Black Aelf, and she knew immediately they were aelf paladins. The lean horses had long legs built for speed. They had long manes which were braided down and around the necks, dangling across the steeds' chests. Barded with chainmail and scales, they seemed to flow across the field. Braxlo rode forward to meet them. After a brief conversation, he moved to the side, as did Erich and Sivle, when the riders closed. Within minutes, they surrounded Fairwind and Ariandel, all facing outward, lances lowered. They rode their horses in formation. Walking backward, sidewards, or at an oblique, the riders maintained their formation all the way to the gates.

***

Braxlo rode ahead, waved over by an official-looking man under a pavilion. When he arrived, the gentleman bowed deeply. "Sir Braxlo the Brave, I presume. Allow me to give you an official welcome to the city of Foresight. I am your humble servant, Mayor Alberto Del Comaste Drol Seville. Please be welcome." Handing Braxlo a glass of chilled wine, he continued, "Your companion Alliandre is arranging rooms at the Wyvern's Aerie, but first, if it would please you, we have a prince of the Black Aelf here who has requested an audience with the princess. I'm sure you noticed his guards." The mayor looked at Braxlo with a patient expression.

Braxlo took a sip of the wine, then another while he pondered the request. The aelf of the Black Woods were not normally outgoing. Their kingdom had borne much of the initial fighting in the Great War, the Knights of Dragonsbane annihilating most of their male population, driving what remained out of the Black Woods. They then harvested more than half the trees to build siege weapons and to fuel their camps. For this and other atrocities, Drake Del Nileppez received the name, "The Defiler". He so devastated the Black Aelf they were forced to practice polygamy for five centuries after.

Braxlo decided it best to grant the request. No sense in creating resentment if unneeded. "Are we free to enter the city, then?" he asked the mayor.

"As your papers are in order, of course," the mayor answered with a slightly apprehensive look. As he spoke, Braxlo cut him short.

"The invitation honors Her Highness. She shall collect her things and join the prince shortly. Please inform him immediately. And thank you my lord, for wasting no time delivering the invitation." Braxlo bowed his head a bit. Here stood Alberto Del Comaste Drol Seville, mayor of one of the great human cities, an earl no less, playing messenger boy for two of the aelf visitors to his city. "Oh well," he muttered under his breath as the mayor turned to leave, "I guess it comes with the job."

Turning to the party, he called out. "Sivle, Erich, they have cleared us to enter the city. Drullock has set us up at the Wyvern's Aerie. Big surprise. Leave without us, please, as it seems Her Highness has a prince who would like to meet her." As he offered his hand to help Fairwind dismount, he looked over at Ariandel and gave her a deep bow. "Little waif girl, it looks like you are on your own. Safe travels to you, my lady."

Ariandel began to reply, but Fairwind had dismounted and she and Braxlo had already begun walking toward a dark-colored tent. Sivle and Erich spurred their horses across the road toward the massive gates. She sat there somewhat stupefied for a moment, then followed the two heading into the city. In her confusion, she neglected to notice she still wore the gown of a High Aelf princess.

***

Fairwind entered the large pavilion after Braxlo, through the door flap Braxlo held for her. She scanned the interior of the tent. A large desk sat directly across from her, with a small table a quarter of the way around to her right. She could smell the cinnamon and clove indicating some spiced wine and noticed the pitcher sweating in the center of the table. Three chairs sat around it, and three golden glasses for the wine. In the middle of the tent, head down on one knee in a reverential bow, a well-dressed aelf knelt beside a young human girl.

Although common for aelf nobles to have servants, rarely were they human servants. When the aelf of the Black Woods took humans, they usually took them as slaves. They kept the appearances up of them being only servants, but Fairwind knew well their hatred of the humans. Even after a thousand years had passed. In fact, only the Golden Aelf hated the humans more. She understood the animosity, as the Black Woods had been almost destroyed. The knights of Dragonsbane had been true to their word, planting trees and protecting the lands around the Black Woods, but even after all this time, the woods were still just a shadow of their former glory.

She whispered back, "He seems to have expected you as chaperone, dear Braxlo."

"Welcome, Your Highness!" The aelf prince rose and stepped forward to offer his arm. "I am Perhaladon an Trodaí, Prince of the Black Woods. I hope you will forgive me if I forgo the pleasantries and get right down to business. I have invited you here today to announce my intention to court you, if you would be so gracious as to entertain the thought."

She looked at him squarely, noting that he was taller than her, and tall for an aelf, though not unusually so, with high, narrow ears and almond-colored eyes. His eyes seemed to be set at an odd angle, even for a Black Aelf. The high cheekbones and narrow, smallish nose actually worked with his eyes, giving him a cat-like look. He had combed and curled his jet-black hair into a grand pompadour, seemingly just waiting for a crown. His almost human, pointed goatee was to be the only thing out of place.

The scent of blacknut sat heavy on him. It had an almost musky quality about it, with pepper and rosebud hints. The aelf valued the blacknuts for their oil, if not their bitter, dense meat. However, the time to grow the trees made the oil quite rare and the Black Aelf restricted its sale. There were less than a hundred trees growing outside the Black Woods, half of those in the Great Forest itself. The High Aelf had two which Fairwind had climbed as a youth. There had been extraordinarily little of the oil produced, most of the nuts left where they fell in order to regrow the Black Woods.

Fairwind blushed, actually quite flattered by the blunt, unemotional request. Many told her of her beauty, comparing her hair to strands of polished gold, or likening her eyes to the sky on a cloudless summer day, but no one had ever truly courted her. Not once since she left home and began studying as a mage. She blamed the traveling for some, but most she blamed on Sir Braxlo.

He is handsome, if in a non-standard way for an aelf.

"What is your intention, courting a daughter of the realm?" She began the questions taught to her many years ago.

"Marriage, Your Highness." Perhaladon began. "To foster peace and tranquility among the aelf and demonstrate we are all one." As he spoke, he motioned her to her seat, took his, and waved the servant girl to pour the wine. Braxlo moved the chair between them, standing in its place.

"And what is your intention in courting a daughter of the High King?" she continued.

"Friendship, Your Highness. To foster peace and tranquility between our two kingdoms and strengthen the fellowship between our people."

She sat back and tasted the wine. Cold to her tongue, the spices in it made it a refreshing respite against the heat of the day. She thought she might have tasted mint but wasn't sure. "And what is your intention in courting this baineann?"

Judging by his reaction, this took him a little by surprise. As a princess, she should have used banphrionsa, but instead, she used the word for girl. He could have continued the customary answer anyway, but she hoped for something a little more sincere.

"Love, Your Highness. My apologies if I overstep, but I have sought out bard songs about your exploits for some time now. I met you once when you visited the Black Woods. A lad of twenty, I had not yet even stood for the Deasghnáth Pasáiste. But my father let us serve the guests at the feast. I remember your beauty and your kindness that day."

"Well," began Fairwind. "Let me see if I can remember which one you were." She reflected on the trip many years ago. The Black Woods were almost all fresh growth, the trees young and vibrant, singing with the wind. She remembered thinking how large and open the great hall was. The branches of the majestic trees had not yet enclosed the space, leaving a great opening in the center where starlight came in.

And her first time drinking High Aelf wine. She had waited patiently for the boys pouring the wine to come around again, not wanting to seem improper. She almost asked for more when a young aelf, one of the noble sons she thought, came over to her with a golden pitcher. He looked up and asked her if she would like some, and she nodded. Then he...

"Oh, my!" she exclaimed and looked at Perhaladon, and burst into laughter as he smiled back at her. "You are the boy who spilled the wine on my dress!"

"Not just your dress, I recall, Your Highness. I seem to remember drenching you with an entire carafe." He smiled sheepishly, then stood straight and looked her straight in the eyes, his face slowly lightening to a pinkish hue. "You, despite your shock and embarrassment, used a spell to clean yourself, then convinced my father to let me stay, as no evidence remained. It was then I fell in love with Fairwind Duine Fionn, High Aelf princess, and ninth in line to the High Aelf throne. I fell in love as only a young boy could upon seeing the most beautiful aelf in the world, then having her do him a small kindness." Then, getting down on one knee, he took her hand, bestowing a kiss on her open palm. "I fell in love deeply and completely. I come to court you, in order to see if the princess I fell in love with might somehow fall as deeply in love with me."

Fairwind sat dumbstruck. He had strayed far from the standard response. She had intended to draw something closer to his actual intentions; however, she had not expected this. She looked at him again and saw the earnestness in his eyes. Then, closing her own eyes, she repeated the words she had learned long ago, words she had not thought she would use for decades to come.

"Perhaladon an Trodaí, Prince of the Black Woods Throne. I, Fairwind Duine Fionn, give you permission to send notice to my father you are courting me. I shall make myself available to you to convince me of your sincere intention." Then she looked at him, "I will be in Foresight for the period of the Jubilee." Smiling and batting her eyes a bit, she added, "You have until Jubilee ends."

II

The Wyvern's Aerie

25th of Frendalo, Year 1124 AGW

Alliandre rode Aeris over the drawbridge through the Northern
Gate. Not much had changed in the last year. Young children, most of
them boys, gathered just inside the gate, calling out to guide travelers
to the best tavern in town. Or the best inn, or the best stables, or whatever else a traveler might look for; "best" being whoever would pay the
urchin for bringing guests there. Alliandre snarled at the first boy who
approached, and the others, staring at the imposing man on the giant,
odd-looking warhorse, gave him a wide berth. He knew if he let the
crowd of children press too close, there would be something missing
from Aeris' barding when he checked at the stables. He knew one of
these urchins had likely already run off to inform the local thieves' guild
of his arrival.

Some merchants would give the children a dolcot if they led a traveler to their business. Sometimes two if they were extremely wealthy
travelers. Unescorted travelers would notice much more missing from
their purses by the time they left the city. For this reason, the urchins
usually had a bit of a queue. The orphanages run by the guild charged

one or two dolcots a day, sometimes three, if there were a lot of travelers in and out. But they monitored to make sure all the children earned enough to stay, and the dolcots got them decent food, beds, and clothing. If the kids earned a little more from other means, there were always treats and toys they could buy with their earnings.

He noticed a young, dark-haired girl in a dirty linen dress. She couldn't have been much over seven or eight, constantly getting pushed to the back of the group by the bigger boys as they all jostled to get some traveler's attention.

"You there, young lady, come here now," he bellowed while pointing at her.

Timidly, she walked over. Alliandre turned Aeris to face her, and the stallion lowered his head and snorted right as she walked up. Her advance stopped as the hot, wet air sprayed across her face, smelling of oats and grass and slightly sweet fruit. A flow of tears fell from her eyes while her little knees trembled. "Tell me your name," Alliandre demanded.

"M-m-Marion," she forced out.

Shaking his head with a small smile, he continued in a much lower tone, "Do you know where the Wyvern's Aerie is?"

She looked up, "Ye, y, y, yes ma my L-l-l-ord" she stammered, trying to hold back her crying.

"Very good!" he said, his tone even softer still. "But I am not a lord." Holding up two coins, he whispered in a conspiratorial tone, "I have one dolcot for you now, and I have a malnot for you if you take me there with only three turns."

Marion's eyes lit up. She got her courage knowing she would be receiving coins. Then she thought for a moment. After a brief pause, she looked up and said, "I only know a way with four turns, my lord."

"I am not a Lord, so you may call me Alliandre, and four turns it is." Then he threw the smaller coin to her, nodding approvingly as she caught it deftly in her hand.

She led him straight through Oldtowne, then through Low-towne, turning twice, going across one of the bridges to Hightowne. The bridges were the only way to get to Hightowne. When they built the city, they diverted part of the river to flow around Hightowne, Castletowne, Portstowne, and Jorges Landing. Partly to make sure they had plenty of water, but also to isolate it and make it more defensible in case of attack.

They posted guards on both sides of each bridge, and the guards at this end moved to intercept Alliandre until he raised his shield, displaying the coat of arms. He expected the captain would have informed the guards of their arrival in town, and sure enough, both guards stood briefly to attention and saluted. "Good day, my lord!" they both called out, followed by, "Welcome to Hightowne."

"Well met, my friends," replied Alliandre, "but I am not a lord." Alliandre almost growled the last part.

Across the bridge, they received the same response. One guard even bowed deeply to Marion, offering her a piece of candy as she walked by, saying, "and for you, my lady."

"I am not a lady," Marion shyly growled, imitating Alliandre. But she reached out and took the offered candy, anyway. The guards smiled and saluted the young girl as she walked away.

Once in Hightowne, she thought before continuing straight down four streets and turning to her right. Alliandre kept going straight when she turned. When she realized Alliandre was not following, she turned and ran back. Eventually, she caught up. They turned down a long, winding street several blocks later, traveling several more blocks until, rounding a long curve, he saw the sign three blocks down with a silver wyvern rampant on a sky-blue field with both legs grasping the edge of a golden nest. "You would have had to make another turn had you turned back where you wanted." Smiling, he threw down another coin.

"My lord," she exclaimed when she looked at it. "This is not a malnot, my lord."

"I am NOT a lord!" Alliandre said in his most lordly sounding voice. "But keep it and find a proper lord and ask him to take you in. Tell him it is your ward fee."

He watched her tuck the coin into her boot and run off. He hoped she did as he said, but either way, he would make sure Erich spoke to the guild in case she went back to the orphanage. Whether the orphanage or she found a lord in Foresight, she would be off the streets either way. And one havnot would not make or break him.

He dismounted and laid Aeris' rein across the weathered hitching post. He had no reason to tie the steed up, as Aeris would not move from the spot until Alliandre returned. He also did not worry about him being stolen. In fact, it would be amusing to see someone try. Again. A doorman got off his chair and began walking over to him. "Would you call the stableboy?" Alliandre asked politely. "Send him in to get me, but do not let him touch my mount." Tossing the burly man a dolcot, he walked through the heavy door into the busy tavern.

Smoke from several pipes wafted through the air, and the smell of stale redleaf and roasting meat fought for dominance. The sound of a harp and several flutes came from a small stage on the far side of the great room, drowned out by the conversations of the people scattered at tables throughout. Several chandeliers and immense windows on the southern wall made the room bright, if not exactly cheery. Tapestries depicting myriad beasts and battles, along with several coats of arms, covered the walls. Clean, if rather plain rugs sat beneath each table, keeping the noise from echoing and building on itself.

He nodded toward a familiar aelf woman sitting at a table alone, picking at a plate of fruit and cheese. He walked past a table with a score of paladins eating and drinking and ignoring everyone else. At the bar, a grizzled old man with one arm stood talking to a foppish-looking knight. One of the paladins for the Order of the Wren, judging by his crest. Behind the bar, the owner, a late middle-aged human woman with an ageless face and long black hair still seemingly untouched by gray, stood cutting up some sort of roasted meat and scooping it into trays.

***

Sir Roger noticed the man in the red armor enter the hall. He looked dressed for court, although the sweat soaked in his long hair told him he had been outside for some time. Probably a traveler, and well off by the look of him. Not a lot of dust, despite the dryness of the weather, so he hadn't traveled far, or he had changed after he came into town. The stranger looked around and walked the perimeter of the room.

"Ye'll get mutton when ye pay for mutton, ya freeloading wee man-ling. Now get back to yer friends."

"I must protest, Sir Andras," Sir Roger quietly continued, turning his attention to the barkeep once again.

As a paladin, it would not be fitting to get angry or raise his voice. Sir Roger set out to be the finest paladin in the order. He took his vows and training seriously. Newly raised to the order, he had been the best in his class with sword, spear, and lance, and followed the rules and traditions of the order to the letter. Slightly taller than the older tavern keeper, he had reddish-blond hair, blue-green eyes, and an attractive, but not too attractive, face. His body had not quite filled out to his height, but he had grown far sturdier than the bean pole little boy abandoned at the order ten years prior.

"You of all people know the paladins have taken a vow of poverty, and in return it is the obligation of the citizens of all kingdoms to provide food, drink, and housing at their request." He spoke calmly, quoting the Palladium Contract signed by all the human kingdoms and orders. They continued the week-old argument of theirs, and while Sir Roger knew he would not prevail, he hoped one day the barkeep would break down and give in to the tradition. If not for him, perhaps for future paladins.

Besides, he didn't have the two malnots for the mutton and wine. As the most recent knight to be raised to the order, he became the almoner. The almoner could carry only three dolcots, to eliminate the chance of mistaking his coins with those of the order. He suspected the orders also imposed it to discipline the new recruits to the vow of poverty.

"Ye've got food and ye've got drink. And we have given ye all our attic to stay in," Andras scolded, three fingers raised to Sir Roger's face.

"But if ye urnae paying, ye get the stew and tea. If ye want mutton and wine, ye pay like everyone else."

Then Sir Roger noticed the new arrival come up behind the old man. *Funny,* he thought to himself, *for such a large man in armor, he moves more quickly and quietly than I would have suspected.*

"Hey stumpy!" he heard the man say, then his eyes grew wide as the man drew a sword from his back, striking the bar owner with a sharp thwack! "Quit chatting with the children so I can get something to drink."

Before Sir Roger could even react, Sir Andras had pulled his cudgel from his side and swung it around, just missing the tall stranger.

"You will have to do better than that, old man," the stranger taunted. "In my youth, the greatest swordsman alive taught me the sword."

Sir Roger drew his sword, moving to interpose himself. "Hold your sword, knave. By the order of the king, there are to be no weapons drawn in the city." He moved his sword and blocked the stranger's next blow. A lightning quick blow to his leg surprised him.

Thwack!

He noticed the stranger's blade remained in the scabbard, and the strikes were with the flat of the scabbard. Still, his leg burned. His plate mail would have easily stopped the blunt blow, but it was up in the room. However, his thick leather cuir bouilli tassets and the heavy padding should have stopped the blow as well. Instead, he paused, momentarily paralyzed as the muscles in his thigh spasmed in pain. He retreated slightly, putting his weight on his back leg, then waited for Andras to tie up the man's sword and swung again. He knew the man's armor would stop the sword, so he had no reason to hold back.

Thwack!

Sir Roger found himself down on one knee. Somehow, the red-armored ruffian had deflected his blow and struck him on the shoulder before he even realized his own sword had not hit home. The brute struck again with the flat side of the scabbard and again his cuir bouilli pauldrons, chain shirt, and thick gambeson should have stopped the blow. But as before, he may as well have been wearing linens. His arm hung limp, completely numb, the force of the blow catching him by surprise. It felt like a tree had fallen on him. He stared incredulously at this beast who had forced him down, even while fighting Sir Andras.

Who is this man? he thought to himself. He had not yet seen Andras lose a fight with his cudgel. Many fights had occurred in the Wyvern's Aerie, despite it being in the river district. Anytime men, alcohol, and women were put together, you could plan on a fight. Andras frequently complained the young nobles were the worst. They believed they could always get away with anything, since they were the son of so and so, the scion of this duke or that earl. But Sir Andras always sent them away with a life lesson.

But now Andras strained to block the blows raining down on him, not landing a single blow, despite several attempts. The sword and cudgel were blurs. Slowly, the stranger maneuvered Andras' right side to the bar, then moved to get around to his left side, where his stump provided no protection. Ignoring the searing pain, Sir Roger raised his sword arm and lunged forward again, attacking the man from behind and from his left.

Thwack!

Sir Roger saw the man spin toward him after he committed to his lunge. The man parried his blow, then parried his follow up. The red-armored man spun back, flipped his sword, and smacked Andras on his stub arm again. Then he spun again, swinging the sword back to strike Sir Roger in the side. He saw all this, able to do nothing to prevent it. It all took less than a second, and the blow landed squarely on the side of his steel breastplate. This time, the man had not used the flat of the scabbard. Sir Roger's breath came sharply, wheezing from his left side.

"Awright laddie, dinnae kill the boy." Andras set the cudgel down on the bar and turned to face the stranger.

Sir Roger noticed Sir Guillermo, his banner commander, approach them. Sir Guillermo addressed the man in red armor. "I apologize for

Sir Roger interfering in your affairs, my lord. He is new to the order and still has much to learn. Which is why I let you thrash him for so long." Sir Guillermo then turned to Sir Roger. "You should offer this man penance. I will not have our order in a blood feud with the likes of him."

Realizing his mistake, "My lord, I offer penance to you. Please, let me know what I can do to make amends," Sir Roger pleaded.

"I will consider the beating I gave you to be penance enough." Then, with a broad smile and an outstretched arm, the stranger teasingly admonished him, "Now bother me no more." Sir Roger clasped his wrist as Sir Guillermo nodded his agreement. As they turned to leave, the man in the red armor added, "And I am NOT a lord!"

As he and Sir Guillermo headed back to their table, Sir Roger noticed the barmaid coming over, armed with a large wooden spoon. Curiously, the stranger seemed cowed by the raven-haired lass who barely reached his shoulder.

"Alliandre Del Nileppez Drol Hulloc, shame on you attacking Sir Andras. I would think you had been raised by centaurs."

"Yes, Your Highness." The stranger replaced the scabbard and bowed deeply, only to receive a sharp rap on the back of the head with the wooden spoon. Sir Roger heard the spoon handle crack with the force of the blow.

Alliandre lifted his head and arms to defend himself, but she continued, "If you think you can just barge in here and rough up Sir Andras, you have another thing coming."

Another blow landed on the top of his head, rendering the spoon into two pieces, and the stranger surged forward, grabbing the barmaid around the waist, lifting her clean off the ground. Sir Roger prepared to intervene again when he noticed the barmaid crying. But she actually hugged the big man. Confused, he glanced over at Sir Andras and noticed the man smiling, his good hand reaching back and holding the hand of the woman behind the bar. Andras smiled up at him, then shook his head and casually mentioned, "He is an old friend of ours."

A young man running into the tavern interrupted their hug. He ran up to Alliandre and announced, "I am from the stables. I am here to gather your horses, my lord."

"I am NOT a lord." Alliandre scolded the lad, getting tired of having to remind everyone, and himself, of his greatest failing. Then he followed him out, returning after several minutes with a small grin. He quickly resumed talking to the barmaid and Sir Andras.

***

Sivle and Erich entered the city at a leisurely pace. When the inevitable throng of children surrounded them, Erich flashed his fingers, tossing some coins. The greedy urchins nodded after picking up and distributing the coins, waiting for the next travelers to come through. The well-worn cobblestones showed the age of the road, except where fresh repairs stood above the rest. Street sweepers must have been busy in the afternoon, as the streets were free of dirt and droppings. Rules required riders to clean up after themselves, which usually involved providing a small coin to one of the children. To save the coin, many waited until their mounts had deposited their droppings outside, not too near the gates.

The sun hung still visible in the sky, but it would be dark in an hour, and they were glad to have made such good time. The pink and violet hues in the western sky were just now appearing. "It is already getting a little chilly, is it not?" queried Sivle.

"Haha, like you can tell," teased Erich. While Sivle's armor wasn't as resistant to heat as Alliandre's, it resisted cold marvelously.

"Which is why I asked," Sivle laughed back. "I tried making small talk since you seem to be distracted."

"I am just wondering where Robin is. He and Lolark were supposed to meet us five days ago." Robin and Erich had been friends a long time. They had grown up together, and Erich had even gotten Robin into the Thieves Guild after he had been there, but Robin had gotten bored and taken up spell casting years ago. They rarely saw each other anymore, and Robin had missed the last reunion a year ago. Of course, that might be because of the feud he had with Alliandre.

"I am sure he is fine. Unless he crossed a guild somewhere, or one of the orders, there isn't much he cannot either defeat or escape." Although accurate enough, it could be said for any of them. The main reason they enjoyed traveling together, they could usually go wherever they needed, unmolested or able to get out of any trouble.

"Crossing a guild or an order is exactly what concerns me. He has always overestimated his abilities and is always trying to prove himself." This was also true. Robin's feud with Alliandre began when he tried to appropriate one of Alliandre's swords, just to test his newly learned spell to remove enchantments. But while Alliandre did not have Sivle's or Erich's intellect, he also wasn't stupid and had taken precautions. Now, while Alliandre and Robin remained cordial, neither one of them would stick his neck out for the other. To make it more uncomfortable, the only words they spoke to each other tended toward snide comments or petty remarks. It did not make for entertaining traveling.

"He is probably already in the city, and just didn't want to leave the luxuries of the Golden Palace."

Both laughed as Erich replied, "You are probably right. We will find out tomorrow. Drullock has us going to the Aerie, so we better get our things inside and our horses stabled. Last one there buys the ale!" Erich spurred his horse. Sivle followed hard, though he knew he knew he would lose. The lean black stallion Erich rode ran much faster than the giant brown courser Sivle rode, though Sivle had a few tricks.

They rode through the streets at a breakneck speed, the sound of the iron hooves on the cobblestones making quite a racket. Sivle's brown courser, Highlander, had massive shoulders and flanks, but Sivle didn't breed him for speed. Erich's black banium, Night Flash, had been bred for speed. They were the most popular breed for the races which took place in the various kingdoms. While not as tall as other horses, they could outrun all other breeds. Erich had paid a king's ransom for the foals of two of the greatest champions in the annual races at Alduon.

Night Flash had even won the races at Foresight two years ago, with Erich riding.

They came to the bridge where the guard tried to stop them, but Night Flash rode by before the guards had gotten into position. The guards broke to each side when they saw Highlander bearing down on them. The guards on the other side of the bridge were better prepared, but Erich reigned in Night Flash and cast a quick spell, holding them motionless while he rode between them. He released the spell once past, hoping the guards would stop Sivle. One guard turned and threw his spear at the fleeing rider. He threw too late to catch the speeding horse, and Sivle used the moment to veer off to his side and ride past.

They came to the last turn. Despite Sivle lagging far behind, Erich kept up his pace. He heard Sivle shout some mystical words, and Night Flash slid past the turn, unable to stop on the suddenly slippery surface. Erich got him turned around, made the turn, taking himself out of Sivle's sight for a moment, as Sivle made up much of the distance. Erich reached into a pouch hidden behind his saddle and threw some sharp caltrops down onto the road to slow Sivle down once he turned the corner. He regretted it came down to a dirty trick, hoping Highlander wouldn't actually step on them. He loathed injuring a fine steed, gambling it would merely slow his friend's progress. Highlander seemed almost to expect such a subterfuge, and artfully danced over the sharp, four-spiked devices. Two score paces away from the Aerie, Night Flash came to an unnatural stop, almost throwing Erich over the top.

"Chwala la hudd," Erich commanded, to no effect, as Night Flash stood, still as a statue in mid-stride. "Chwala la hudd," he tried again after taking a few moments to recover.

Sivle galloped by, passing Erich when Night Flash lurched forward again. Erich pulled a set of bolos from his side and threw them unerringly at Highlander's hind legs. He also felt a little bad about the bolos, there being a real chance of injuring the horse, but Highlander broke all the cords with his stride. Even so, he had to slow down as he adjusted his gait to his momentarily impaired legs. It proved to be just enough for Night Flash to surge ahead. Erich pulled off a galloping dismount from the horse just as a boy came out from his perch next to the door.

"Are y-you with the Alliandre guy?" the boy asked Erich as Sivle came riding up.

"Why yes, lad," Erich gave a great bow as Sivle reigned in Highlander and dismounted. "I am Erich of the Black Woods Shrine, high priest of the Forest Spirits."

"Um, well, my lord, he wants to see you immediately, my lord." He looked nervous, but he pulled out a piece of linen with Alliandre's seal, and Erich reached out a hand to take it. "I am to take your horses to the stables and your things to your rooms."

"We are much obliged, young man. I am sure my friend Sivle has a turot for you to show our gratitude." Handing him the reins, he hurried inside.

The boy's eyes went wide, and he looked at Sivle in disbelief.

Sivle gave an irritated glance at Erich, fishing a turot from his pouch and handing it to the lad. Not actually a boy, but a young man of fourteen or fifteen. His sandy blond hair in a bowl cut around his head, except for a patch on top where he tied it in a large topknot. He had the broad shoulders and thick forearms of someone who shoveled charwood and pounded on horseshoes all day, his shirt gray from the ash of a forge. But his hands and face were clean, and his brown boots and trousers looked like they weren't more than a couple of months old.

He knew the boy's father would be quite happy with him this evening. But handing out turots usually attracted unwanted attention. Erich would probably keep the local guild thieves away, but there were many members of foreign guilds who would be in attendance at the Jubilee, and not all of them would know of Erich's reputation.

"Are there more coming, sir?" the young man asked Sivle as he grabbed Highlander's reins.

"Yes, a Knight Errant of Dragonsbane and an aelf princess. Do you have room at the stables?

"Of course, sir. The big man told me to secure an entire barn for you. He said his horse doesn't like being closed in, so there is plenty of room."

"Make sure you wash, brush, and feed all the horses tomorrow morning then."

"Yes, my lord," the boy said as he grabbed saddle bags and other gear from the horses.

"And if I find out you accepted any coin from the others, or talked about it to anyone, I will come and take the turot back!" Sivle knew he wouldn't actually take the turot back, but it would be best to at least try to evade the scrying of thieves. Then suppressing a grin, he muttered to himself, "I picked the wrong group to travel with if I want to keep from being noticed."

Sivle walked into the Wyvern's Aerie, first noticing Alliandre at the bar, talking conspiratorially with Erich while drinking a tankard of something. When Alliandre saw Sivle, however, he quickly motioned him over. He finished speaking and turned from Erich and handed a large tankard to Sivle as he walked up. Curiously, Erich turned and left, all but running out the back door.

"What was that all about?" Sivle asked.

"Just a favor. A small one, but it is fairly urgent," Alliandre replied.

"May I get you something to eat, my lord?" the barmaid asked as she walked up.

Sivle turned and spilled his drink from the fierce hug she gave him. Bowing, he spoke to the barmaid. "Your Highness, it is fantastic to see you. It has been too long since we last stopped in."

"Yes, it has been," she scolded, and pointing at Alliandre, "and this lout didn't even have the courtesy to say hello before he began roughhousing with Sir Andras. He probably bruised his arm the way he kept hitting it so."

"I believe Sir Andras can take care of himself." Sivle chuckled. Besides, after the long, uneventful ride, Alliandre probably needed to let off a little steam. Looking around at the paladins, he continued, "I am kind of surprised he didn't pick a fight with them instead."

"He did, sent one to the chirurgeon," said a familiar, gruff voice from behind the bar. "All while beating my stump raw." Andras smiled at Sivle and set out a large platter of mutton, lamb, and sausages between the two men. "It is guid to see you two. Marion, dear, why don't you take a bit of time to get reacquainted. Vanessa just showed up. She can take the tables for a while."

The barmaid smiled, gave Sivle another hug, then shyly stepped between them, putting her arm around each, leaning her head against the tall, red-armored man.

*** *

Mirandel sat, still picking at her meal. She and Arielle were extremely old friends. She had hoped they would have a chance to catch up. But no sooner had Arielle brought her food and sat down than a banner of paladins entered. Arielle hurried to serve them up, just finishing when a familiar face walked in. She thought of calling young Alliandre over, but he moved purposefully. Sure enough, he glided behind his old teacher and tapped him on his arm stump. Several seconds of chaos ensued, but Arielle headed toward her again with a fresh pitcher of wine.

"I am so sorry, my dear Mirandel. I asked Vanessa to take care of things, so we should have some time to talk. It is so good to see you again."

"Arielle the Beautiful. It has been a while, at least several years, I believe. I so missed you and wanted to stop by during the Jubilee. I have so many questions for you about the comings and goings here, but first, I have news of your son William."

Arielle almost let out a small gasp. She had three sons, Gabriel, Nathan, and William. Gabriel had died during the fall of the Southern Kingdom, standing at the side of his father until the end. Witnesses said he held back the first wave of Golden Aelf when they broke through the gates, falling during the second wave. Nathan had died during an excursion with the Knights of the Golden Chalice in the Great Vreen War when the vreen ambushed their banner. Despite grievous wounds, Nathan and three others held the vreen back while the remaining survivors escaped. When they recovered his body, he had sustained over thirty-five wounds, a dozen of them fatal. And now her youngest, still inside her when she escaped the fall of the Southern Kingdom, trained as a paladin in the same order.

Mirandel continued, "It seems they put young William in charge of a tribune of the younger squires during a recent march to scout the Darklands."

Arielle winced. The Darklands were an almost perfect circle of light-less land, a hundred hursmarcs in diameter centered on the lost city of Vista, her former home. The Knights of the Golden Chalice were the closest order to the Darklands and sent out many missions to scout and investigate the magically darkened territory. Many had never returned. Slowly, the order had reported back. The lands were untouched, but the darkness had killed every living thing. No light, mundane or magical, could pierce it for more than a few paces.

"During the march, just after crossing the White River, they encountered a large force of vreen. The paladins set up to engage them, splitting into two spears, each containing ten full banners. They left the squires in reserve, along with the men-at-arms. A great battle ensued. Sir Vendir White Beard led the charge of the first spear, while Sir Khudahar the Bear moved the second spear to the flank of the vreen. He charged into their side, and the battle went decidedly against the vreen. About this time, a second force of vreen appeared, charging up the hill out of sight of Sir Khudahar. Their force intended to catch his spear from behind. William immediately took action."

Mirandel counted out on her fingers. "First, he sent a squire to Sir Khudahar to warn him of the threat to his rear. Then he lined up the squires and prepared them for a charge into the new wave of vreen. With only three banners of squires and the forty or fifty men-at-arms, it would be a suicide run. Despite being outnumbered over ten-to-one, William said the delay would give the paladins time to crush the other force and regroup to attack the new mass of vreen. He rode to the vanguard position, raised his sword, then thrust it forward to order the charge. Leading his men, he charged straight across the field, driving into the side of the bewildered vreen."

Putting her hand down, she leaned in, lowering her voice. "Unbeknownst to William, the men-at-arms held the rest of the squires up, but they did not reach William in time, and he did not hear their cries to return. Everyone watched in horror as he drove his lone warhorse through the vreen, slashing and turning, getting slowed as he crashed into a crowd of them as they tried to turn and stab at him, then charging forward again. Vreen fell left and right to his sword and his horse's steel shorn hooves. Again and again he spurred his horse onward, until he had made it through the entire force."

She continued, "He rode for a small distance and turned on top of a small rise. Over forty vreen had fallen, and many were closing ranks and turning to meet this unexpected foe. Others kept on marching, while still others were turning as if to engage another wave from the hilltop. William looked for the other squires but did not see any fighting among the vreen. Grimly, he bowed his head and pressed his sword against his breast in honor of his fallen comrades."

Mirandel, always the skilled storyteller, held her hand to her own chest, mimicking the salute, before continuing.

"Now keep this in mind. At this point, the vreen ranks were disorganized. They no longer had an organized force to charge, and William could have stopped. But he didn't. He charged AGAIN!"

Mirandel almost shouted that last word, throwing her arms up in a gesture which seemed to say, "What was he thinking?" pausing for effect before continuing.

"This charge turned out remarkably similar to the last one, except he lost his sword and had to turn to his mace. Then he lost his mace, relying on his axe. But amazingly, he made it through again! This time, he rode forward and immediately wheeled his horse around, charging through the same lane he had just created. He almost made it through a third time when the vreen pulled down his horse and he disappeared into a throng of the nasty creatures. Now, all the vreen were focused on him. They all turned to face him. Somehow, he landed on his feet, still fighting with only an axe and shield. The vreen swarmed him, eventually pulling him down."

Pausing again for effect, Mirandel noticed the horrified look on Arielle's face, the blood draining from it. Only then she remembered she was not telling the story to an audience at court, but the boy's mother. Quickly she rose, putting her arms around her dear friend.

"No. He lives, he lives. Honest." Holding Arielle's head against her breasts, she abbreviated her tale.

"The rest of the squires and men-at-arms charged into the mass of vreen. Most of the vreen were facing William and never saw them. The squires cut through them, killing five times their number in the first pass. One squire grabbed William and got him on his horse, carting him away from the fight. Meanwhile, Sir Vendir and Sir Khudahar, having routed the primary force, arrived to hit the reserve force again. The vreen had turned to focus on the squires. Charging into the flank, the paladins rode through the entire force, killing or wounding most of them. Those who could still run, scattered to be run down. In the end, only a few score vreen escaped."

Releasing her friend, Mirandel returned to her seat, taking a sip of wine before continuing. "There is much more to tell, but I will be brief, though it pains me to do so. In the end, they only lost three squires to injuries, and half a dozen horses. Sir Vendir and Sir Khudahar promoted William on the field of honor. He is now a full Paladin of the Order of the Golden Chalice. From this point on, we shall know him as Sir William the Indomitable. When you see him, you will not recognize him. He has grown a full beard, although it is so fair and fine, it hardly befits his courage. He has also filled out so much I almost mistook him for young Alliandre there, if Alliandre were a foot shorter."

Both women laughed, as they often teased William about his short stature. He actually stood above average height, albeit much shorter than most paladins. Arielle laughed, the color quickly returning to her face.

The two talked for quite a while and went through several pitchers of wine and another fruit plate when Arielle stopped and whispered, "Uh oh. Looks like the other six have arrived. Erich just walked in."

In the door walked a tall, hawkish looking man clad entirely in black. His long black hair held back with a black cord, and his pointed goatee looking freshly oiled. He walked straight to Alliandre. The two spoke, Alliandre moving in close and lowering his voice significantly. He spoke for a few moments, then Erich nodded, snuck a quick glance at the barmaid, and clasped his fist to his chest with a big grin. Then he headed for the back door.

"And here is Sivle, right behind." Arielle motioned at a man in blue armor matching the armor worn by Alliandre in all but color.

Sivle moved up to the bar. Alliandre quickly handed him a flagon of ale before Marion arrived to give him a big hug, spilling his drink. They exchanged pleasantries before she stepped between them and put her arms around each of them.

"It reminds me so much of when they were all in the Court at Vista," Mirandel said softly. "Of all the things that went wrong that day, keeping those three together may have been the best decision you have ever made."

"Perhaps. I just wish Alliandre would accept the fact Marion is no longer a princess of the realm, and he is no longer just a lowly, commoner orphan, and court her. She is twenty-three, and if he does not move soon, he may lose his chance. I am not getting any younger and the requests to court her are growing."

"He believes it will humiliate her in everyone else's eyes. Everyone has had this discussion with him," Mirandel replied.

"I know." Arielle sighed. "Marion loves him too, or I would marry her off to form an alliance. Before she becomes as old and haggard as her mother."

Arielle smiled at her, and Mirandel looked closely and noticed the deep laugh lines and crow's feet etched in her friend's face. Arielle remained beautiful, despite being in her sixties. In her younger days, many confused her with the High Aelf maidens. Kings and noblemen from all over the great realms courted her. Even aelf and dwarven lords vied for her hand. Her raven hair still shone, although Mirandel noted a small band of silver flowed out of each temple. Only a few hairs now, the only sign of aging her hair revealed. Her blue-green eyes still twinkled with the fire of a great intelligence, and the drive built the Southern Kingdom into the greatest human kingdom at the time. Her lips were still full, her teeth still white as snow, but her flawless skin showed some weathering. Still fit from hours working on her feet each day, if one looked closely, the telltale signs of aging revealed themselves in her neck and hands.

It reminded Mirandel again of the brief lives of the humans. An aelf may live over eight or nine hundred years, but the humans were unlikely to live to even eighty. In fact, while most aelf began their adult training and education around thirty, most humans were likely to have already mastered their professions. At fifty, when aelf began to practice in their chosen fields, humans were likely to have already passed their skills and businesses to their children.

Mirandel herself had lived over nine hundred years. Her hair gray and her skin growing translucent. Though slower than in her youth, she could still get about. She would not be adventuring in the Great Chasm, for sure. Still, she looked like she could have been Arielle's mother. But here sat Arielle, also in the twilight of her life, serving drinks and food, running an inn, raising money to pay an army to retake her kingdom so she would have something to pass on to her daughter and remaining son.

Mirandel thought of the song she would write when Arielle retook the Southern Kingdom or died trying. She had been friends with Arielle for decades now, and they talked often about Arielle's obsession with regaining her throne. It consumed their conversations in the years immediately after the fall.

Mirandel responded with a bit of sarcasm, "Yes dear, you look like you are ready for the grave any minute now." The two women smiled. "Don't worry, you have many years left in you, I think. You will get your kingdom back. To help, I have brought a small gift." Mirandel reached into her bag, pulling out a small pouch.

"It is the whole of my collection. What use do I have of them now? These are Turpin Agates. They will fetch a great price for you when you are ready to raise your army. Hopefully, you can use the money to hire one of the great palladium orders to fight for you."

Arielle let out a small gasp. Legend said when a dragon cried, the water would evaporate as it fell, and the minerals in the tears were all that reached the ground. Tear-shaped and incredibly beautiful, they were the rarest gems in the world. A single one could fetch several havnots, and feeling the pouch, there appeared to be several dozen inside. It would certainly be enough to hire a full phalanx from one of the orders. Maybe even two from one of the poorer ones.

"Thank you, my friend. It is humbling to receive such a gift, knowing there is nothing I have ever done to deserve it, and nothing I can ever do to repay it." She rose and gave Mirandel a long hug. "Thank you even more for the news of my son. It is good to hear he is well, and he is following so closely in his brother's path. He will make a fine king someday."

"Excuse me though, my dear Mirandel. I think I should get back to work. Please tell me you will stay here tonight. Alliandre has reserved the entire third floor, but I have the 'King's Room' all set up for a special guest."

"Of course," Mirandel replied. "Who knows? I might even pull out a lute if the wine inspires me."

***

Ariandel had barely ridden into the city when a throng of children approached and asked if she needed directions to an inn or a stable. She held up a dolcot and asked one of them to guide her to an inexpensive inn. One of them darted forward to lead her, while the rest crowded around her. Leaf Dancer snorted and kicked at several of the young humans, so they gave her a wider berth. She followed the young urchin down several streets when she realized she still had Fairwind's dress on.

"Oh, my!" she exclaimed involuntarily. Everyone had left her at the gate. She had gotten a little confused at what she should do, being left on her own. She felt it only right to return Fairwind's gown. "Do you know where the Wyvern's Aerie is?" she asked the boy leading her.

"I think I do," the child replied, then sizing her up, continued, "but it will cost another dolcot."

She looked suspiciously at the ragamuffin. As she was at his mercy, she agreed. He walked back the way they came, then led her uneventfully up to a bridge going over a river in the middle of the city. Two guards moved to block their way, but upon seeing her, they immediately separated and bowed.

"Do you need an escort, Your Highness?" they asked, looking over the young lad suspiciously.

"Your Highness? Oh, I believe you have mistaken me for Fairwind, a princess of the High Elves."

"Well, you are displaying the royal colors, my lady," one guard responded, a bit confused. "We were told you would be coming this way. However, if you wish to travel incognito...?"

At this, the young lad coughed and spoke up, "Your Highness, if I could get my coins now, I will let the guards escort you."

Looking down at him, "I am not Fairwind Duine Fionn!" she stated again. Then turning away from him and addressing the soldiers on the bridge, "But I am on my way to meet her and I would be grateful if one of you men would take me to the Wyvern's Aerie. I guess you could say I am a friend of hers." She tossed one small coin to the boy, surprised at how fast he disappeared.

"Follow me, my lady." one guard replied and began a fast walk across the bridge. The smell of wood fires and meat roasting in the many inns, taverns, and homes in the area began to get stronger. The buildings were mostly brick and stone in Foresight, due to the distance from any forests, but she noticed the building materials had become much more refined on this side of the bridge.

When they arrived, she did not notice any of the horses out front, but she saw a post for tying them, and a teenage boy sitting nearby. As she approached, he hurried to help her down, even offering to carry her bags inside as well. She reached for a dolcot, but the boy refused. "No, Your Highness. I can accept no money from you."

"But I'm not... Fairwind" she finished, as the boy had paid her no mind, rushing in with her bags.

She entered the tavern, immediately noticing the two men in the dragon armor chatting at the bar with a barmaid. *Probably terrorizing her,* she thought to herself. *Poor lass.*

With their helms removed, she could see they could not be more different. The brute stood tall and muscular, with light brown hair close cropped on the sides, but flowing back from the top and down to his shoulder blades in the back. He had piercing blue eyes, and his smile was actually almost endearing, with bright white teeth against olive skin. Seeing him from a distance, his massive physique became quite obvious, with broad shoulders and a large vee narrowing to a solid waist. His thick neck indicated a musculature as impressive as his height, as he towered over the barmaid and the one named Sivle.

Sivle contrasted him in every way. While not thin exactly, he had nowhere near the size or heavy musculature of the fighter, barely coming up to Drullock's chest. Even the barmaid stood almost a hand's width taller. Sivle had the same intense blue eyes and bright white teeth, but his dark brown hair seemed more in line with his swarthy complexion. He smiled less frequently, though, much more serious than his giant companion.

Between them stood the barmaid. A full head shorter than the brute, her long black hair and tanned skin made her dark brown eyes seem almost supernaturally black. Curls fell down around her face, the rest of her hair tied in a long braid, which occasionally peeked out from behind her waist. The slenderness of her frame provided a stark difference from the two armored men. Her smile never left her face, only growing wider to indicate when she found something humorous. Her entire face took part in her smile. Her arms were around both of the men, and if Ariandel had not known better, she would have thought they were siblings, but there were no familial similarities between them.

A long table filled with paladins and dirty plates filled a table near the bar. It appeared several paladins finished their meal as they headed to the back stairs.

She looked around for Fairwind, but she did not see her, just another older aelf woman chatting with a human woman. The old aelf had a glass of wine and the remnants of a plate of food in front of her. Ariandel walked over to a table toward the back and sat facing the door to wait for Fairwind to appear. The older aelf and the human woman hugged, and the human walked back around the bar. The aelf cast several glances her way, then gave her a long stare. She looked back at her, a little uncomfortable, until another barmaid thankfully interrupted to offer her some wine.

"How much?" she asked.

"Five dolcots for a glass, a malnot for the chilled pitcher."

Ariandel thought hard. She had little to waste on frivolities until she could write some scrolls, but the wine looked delicious. The beads of water on the pitcher were joining and ran down to the small silver plate the girl carried it on. "It looks quite nice, but I think I will just have some honeyed water if I may. Or mead if you have it."

"Leave the pitcher and bring another, please." The older aelf spoke as she walked up. "I will gladly cover it."

Surprised, Ariandel looked at her and tried to refuse, but the older aelf shushed her. "It will not be free to you, dear. In exchange for the wine, I want to hear... the story." The older aelf waved her hands grandly, emphasizing the last two words.

"What story?" asked a puzzled Ariandel.

"What story? Why, my dear, what other story is there? I want to know how a young aelf from the Silver Bark Woods finds her way into the Wyvern's Aerie, all the way in the Central Kingdom, wearing the gown of a High Aelf princess?"

"How could you possibly know whose dress this is?"

Ariandel became concerned she had become embroiled in some trouble. The woman examined her closely now, then sang a small ditty while waving her hand toward her. After she was done, the elderly aelf pulled out a small mirror and held it out. Ariandel looked in the mirror for several seconds before she noticed, embroidered in the red collar of her dress, the signet of the High Aelf king and queen glowing with a silver blue light. It had not been there before. Then she realized something which gave her an even bigger shock. Her head began swimming, and the last thing she remembered before she fainted was saying, "You just sang a spell."

***

Ariandel awoke to someone pouring small drips of water into her mouth. Looking up, she saw the red-armored brute once again cradling her head in his arms.

"We really have to stop meeting like this," he said without a trace of humor.

"Get off me, you oaf!" she screamed as she pounded him with her fists. She thought of casting a spell, then her head spun again as she remembered what originally caused her to faint. Rolling off him, she slowly got to her feet, using the time to collect her composure and her thoughts. Looking at Mirandel, she spoke deliberately. "You. Sang. A. Spell."

"Pshaw," Mirandel scoffed as she waved dismissively at Ariandel.

Sivle simply looked at her and said, "Unlearn," before turning to Mirandel and giving her a broad smile.

"Oh child," Mirandel said, touching him fondly on the cheek. "You were always my favorite student. If only I was eight hundred years younger."

"Oh Mirandel, if you were eight hundred years younger, you wouldn't bother with a poor half-aelf mage apprentice." Both of them chuckled, as if at an old joke.

"But you, my dear," Mirandel turned to her again. "Do not think for a moment this drama is going to get you out of telling me the story."

Ariandel looked between them. "Ya... you... you're... Mirandel Amhrán Amhrán órga, the Battle Bard of Mystic Pass," she blurted out. "And you," Ariandel looked at Sivle directly. "You weren't lying." Then she thought a little longer, shook her head to clear it, saying, "So honestly. Who are all of you?"

"All in due time, dear, but first things first, you owe me a story, and I intend to get it."

With the excitement over, Sivle and Alliandre walked back over to the bar. Mirandel sat Ariandel down, poured her a glass of wine, and then took out a scroll, quill, and ink jar and prepared to write. Then she poured a glass of wine for herself, and noticing Ariandel's empty glass, poured another for Ariandel. Then she began.

"First dear, tell me your name and a little about yourself."

Ariandel took another long drink of the wine, feeling it warm her stomach. She was also feeling the first glass going to her head. She told her story slowly and quietly to Mirandel. At times, she was quite animated. At other times, she spoke like she was confessing a great crime. She went on and on, until the sun had well set, and all the paladins had left. Others had come into the tavern, filling the tables. Mirandel wrote everything down, even laughing at one point when Ariandel's voice rose almost enough for the people at the bar to hear while she gestured wildly at Alliandre.

Ariandel continued for another ten minutes, until she ended with, "...and then I came in here, to find Her Highness Fairwind Duine Fionn and return her dress."

Mirandel sanded and blotted the bottom of her second scroll. Looking up at Ariandel, she marveled. "That is quite the adventure you have lived. Thank you for your story and for telling it to me in such detail. Truly, I am grateful. Sadly, however, I fear I have sat here too long. I have a prior appointment I am late for. Please give my best to Her Highness when you see her. I do so wish to have met her again, but I must be going." Setting a handful of malnots on the table, she continued, "This is for the wine, and please get yourself some dinner. It is so kind of you to indulge an old aelf so."

Mirandel packed away her writing accoutrements and left. Several minutes after she had left, Ariandel realized she had not asked Mirandel if she would be interested in training her. She swore under her breath as she realized she had missed the chance to be trained by one of the greatest battle bards alive. Maybe only a small chance, but still.

She pouted for a moment, then noticing the malnots on the table, called the serving girl over. When her dinner arrived, there were still eight malnots on the table. She insisted the serving girl keep them, although it would have more than tripled her current money supply. She was sure Mirandel had not meant it for her. It would be awkward keeping it. She was halfway through her dinner when the door opened and the fighter in black, Braxlo, she remembered, came in, scanned the room, and then held the door for Fairwind.

The moment Fairwind entered, a hush began spreading across the tavern, all faces turning to her. Braxlo led her straight to a table on the far side of the bar where Sivle and Alliandre had seated themselves. Erich had joined them as well, although Ariandel had not noticed him come into the tavern. Seeing her, Fairwind smiled brightly, motioning for her to join them. She shook her head no, but after Fairwind sat down, she whispered to Braxlo, and he came over to invite her formally. The way he stood by her chair, Ariandel realized he would not leave until she gave in. Quickly standing, she allowed him to escort her to the table. Everyone but Fairwind stood as she arrived, but the only seat was next to the oaf. She hesitated, then again declined the offer. Everyone looked at Alliandre, who looked aggrieved, but spoke up with a huff.

"All of you?" he asked, glaring at the table. Then he turned to Ariandel, made a sweeping bow, and said, with the courtliest voice he could muster, "Milady, I apologize for the gruff and ungentlemanly way I treated you earlier. My behavior was uncouth, and undeserved by you. I humbly apologize and beg your forgiveness. I will aspire to better behavior in the future." He rose from the bow and stared at her for several seconds.

Fairwind cleared her throat. Ariandel wondered why everyone looked at her so expectantly. "Oh!" she blurted out, realizing what they were waiting for her. Regaining her composure, she turned to Drullock and replied, her voice only a tiny bit severe. "Very well. I forgive you. I expect your behavior in the future will more closely resemble a member of court, rather than a barbarian from the western reaches." Then, changing her tone to one of perfect courtesy, she added, "By the way, I am Ariandel Spéir álainn, of the Silver Bark Woods." Then holding her hand out for him, she added, "It is a pleasure to meet you, Drullock." Alliandre turned as red as his armor as the rest of the table burst into laughter.

***

Vanessa left the Wyvern's Aerie with a much lighter step, possibly owing to the much heavier purse she carried. Her fiancé, Vandion, would be so happy to see the stack of malnots she had made. The knights, paladins she was told, had not tipped especially well, except one. He cast longing glances at her whenever she walked by. But Marion had told her the paladins could take no wife while in the order, and he was young enough to have many years of service ahead of him.

The men in the red and blue armor seemed to be friends of Arielle and Marion. Their party had been more than generous. None individually as generous as the young aelf who had joined them, but plenty of silver had been laid down to cover the copious amounts of wine, mutton, sausage, and ale the group had devoured. Even though Vanessa protested, Arielle scolded them to show their appreciation to the "young serving girl they worked like a slave." Then they threw more silver out to the table.

She had spent much of her time with their party, but their tips were all in malnots. She wondered if they even bothered carrying dolcots at all. She had heard of travelers so wealthy they did not bother with the small coins, but she had never imagined she would meet one. Now, it seemed, she had met six all traveling together. She thought about what it must be like, but she decided she had no way of knowing. She had never even had two malnots at the same time before. But now she thought she had over a score of them. She might even have enough to let Vandion finish his surprise for the Aerie.

III

The Thing About Paladins

26th of Frendalo, Year 1124 AGW

Sounds of swords clashing woke Ariandel from her slumber. The clanging of swords indicated a great battle coming from the next room. Not knowing any better, she looked around for Fairwind, but she was alone in the spacious chamber set aside for the two females. Fairwind had furnished the room luxuriously, complete with changing screens, soft chairs, and a small couch. She cautiously opened the door and noted the sounds did not seem to get any louder, so she got dressed and ventured down the stairs to the dining hall.

Erich was lounging in a corner, fiddling a malnot over his fingers and back. He was still wearing the same clothes as yesterday. On a closer inspection, the jacket had a different weave pattern. Looking closer, the shirt was definitely a different patterned silk, with a low collar which tied at his throat. She wondered just how many black pants, shirts, and coats he owned. The shoes were different as well. Instead of the black riding boots, he had a low-topped boot which appeared to lace up the side. They had a low heel, and seemed to be made of a supple leather, almost like the hide moccasins the Common Aelf wore.

The dining room was already full. A small group huddled around the window to the courtyard, with one man taking bets. She figured the fighting was coming from there. A fire blazed in the fireplace to her right, the heat providing respite against the morning chill. She went over to warm herself. She had put on a plain green skirt made of woven cattail silk with a matching shirt made of coarse cloth. She had made both of them herself years ago. Over the shirt, she wore a yellow knit shawl with the pattern of a jaguar decorating the back. Silverwood buttons joined the two corners, which were draped down to her narrow waist. She had not taken the time to braid her hair, instead she pulled up the sides and secured them with delicate combs of polished silverwood, inlaid with silver panthers. The young barmaid, she never got her name, was hurrying around serving platters of eggs and bread and sausage and great mounds of bacon. As she walked by, the smell hit her, a growl coming from her stomach, despite all she had eaten last night.

Erich stood beside her. She had not noticed him leave his spot and walk over. She was leery of him still. She remembered when he first appeared standing over her, even though she was alert for someone approaching, which was creepy. Also, how he always observed his surroundings, even when speaking directly to you, was always unnerving. As was the way he seemed to blink around when you were not looking at him. She wasn't sure she wanted to be alone with him, although he had been a perfect gentleman the night before.

"Fairwind said to tell you, 'Good morning,' and you are welcome to stay with her for the duration of her stay in Foresight. She regrets she had to leave early, but she received a summons this morning."

"A summons?" she queried, more than a bit surprised. "Who would dare send a summons to a High Aelf princess?"

"Her father." Erich seemed to be up to something, but he continued nonchalantly. "She rushed back home this morning as soon as she received the summons. It seems her father has received a Togra Chun Páirt. She is being courted."

"WHAT?" Erich grinned broadly at her, as she tried to get over her shock. "I thought you have been acting conspiratorial, Lord Erich. Do the others know?"

"All but Sivle. Fairwind was having firstmeal with me, Lolark, Braxlo, and Drullock when the summons came. She no sooner finished eating when the summoner took her there," he pointed to a small open area immediately in front of the fireplace, "and created a portal to take them away. She asked me to make sure you received her invitation. She seems to have taken a liking to you. Maybe because she has been traveling with just us men since Dragonsbane Castle." Glancing over her shoulder, he asked, "What do you have for me?"

"What do I have? Nothing, I just... oh, my!" Ariandel jumped out of her boots as another man reached his hand across her body. She had turned her back toward the space in front of the fire just a few seconds before. Startling her, someone was there handing some sort of scroll to Erich. She noted the strange symbol and came to the only conclusion she could. "You are a thief, aren't you?"

She did not know whether that should frighten or outrage her. He seemed much too flamboyant to be a common thief. He also wore a holy symbol around his neck, but it made sense to her. She wondered how she had not noticed until now.

"Please, milady. Such a baseless accusation." His face took on the look of someone quite offended. "I'll have you know I am a high priest of the Black Woods Temple. One of a few humans even allowed in the Black Woods, actually. A friend of all aelf and defender of the sacred truce."

The serving girl, who had just brought a tray of bread, porridge, and fruit to a table, interrupted him with a slight nudge. "He prefers the term rogue, milady. He claims he does not steal, but I would watch your valuables." She smiled brightly, and continued with an exaggerated curtsey, "My lord Erich. Can I get you anything else this morning?"

"Oh no, Your Highness," Erich replied, with just as exaggerated a bow, "You have done quite enough already." They rose from their respective prostrations, smiling at each other. Then she was gone again.

"Why do all you call her 'Your Highness'?" Ariandel asked. She remembered last night, no one, not even the oaf, referred to her otherwise.

"Because she is Marion the Virtuous, daughter of Arielle the Beautiful, and Tristan the Bold, king and queen of the Southern Kingdom. First in line to the Southern Kingdom once they recapture it."

Ariandel's jaw dropped. Then came back up as she realized he must be joking. "Working in a tavern? I don't believe you."

"Her mother, Queen Arielle the Beautiful, owns the tavern. That's her behind the bar. Sir Andras Anarawd, their Master of Arms, is the bartender. And watchman. And a better man with the sword has never lived." Erich paused, letting her absorb the information, then continued, "They fled here after the fall. King Henry the Great granted them this building as a home, which they turned into an inn. They have been raising money to hire an army to take back the Southern Kingdom ever since, but time is growing short. In over fifteen years, they have not raised even half of what they will need. The chests which Drullock and Sivle brought will certainly get them closer. It may still be several years away I am afraid, but Arielle is getting no younger."

Ariandel thought for a moment. She had heard the queen had escaped Vista, but few stories about her life were known after she had gotten out. Ariandel assumed she had remarried to a nobleman somewhere, similar to Queen Elizabeth in the Northern Kingdom. Although in Elizabeth's case, she was the original regent, and so remained queen after the death of her first husband, Richard the Hunter. Ariandel tried hard to remember all the lessons she had received regarding the human kingdoms, but they escaped her. Besides, they ended years before the fall of the Southern Kingdom. She had not kept up on human history since then.

Then the barmaid was there again. "Cara Ríoga, may I get you something for firstmeal? Her Highness, Princess Fairwind, informed me you were her lady-in-waiting. I am to make sure you are well attended. She inquired of Lady Mirandel to ask if she would be interested in training you. Fairwind had to leave for the Great Woods, but she will give you the answer this evening when she returns."

Ariandel sat somewhat dumbstruck but regained her composure

quickly. "Yes, Your Highness, a small firstmeal would be delightful. Perhaps some of the fruits I saw earlier?"

"And some bacon," Erich added. "You cannot call it firstmeal if you do not have some of their bacon. They are actually quite famous for it. They make enough to feed an army. Or to raise an army."

"We are actually famous for it," agreed the barmaid. "Please do not call me Your Highness. Alliandre and Sivle do, only because we grew up together. Fairwind, Braxlo, Erich, Robin, and Lolark picked it up, but I do not need another patron referring to me that way. It is quite embarrassing. Just call me Marion."

"Agreed!" Ariandel smiled back as Marion gave her a genuine smile of relief. If she were honest with herself, Ariandel was relieved as well. Also, a bit nervous. If her parents discovered she met two princesses and addressed them by their first names, they might disown her. But she had not grown up in court, so she was sure she would slip up eventually if required to follow the formalities. "Thank you for your kindness."

Marion left again, so Ariandel thought to question Erich once more about the scroll, noticing Erich has already hidden it from sight. "What was on the scroll you received? I am sure you read it while we were talking."

A corner of his mouth betrayed a hint of a smile, but Erich showed no other reaction. "A favor Drullock had asked of me. It can wait until he finishes playing with his swords."

Erich nodded to the noise coming in from the courtyard, then escorted Ariandel to an empty table. He sat silently, saying nothing else. A minute later, Marion returned with two plates. One plate of fruit and soft cheese, another mounded with bacon.

"Do you mind?" Erich asked, pointing his nose at the bacon.

Ariandel nodded she did indeed mind, smacking his hand as he reached for the plate. He pulled his hand away before it reached the plate, then turned around and left. Only when she looked at the plate again did she realize several pieces missing. "I thought you didn't steal," she said, but when she looked up, Erich was no longer in view.

She finished her meal. The clanging of swords still echoed through the halls, so she went out to see the reason for the commotion. A crowd of paladins and knights stood around a melee circle raised about a foot off of the ground in a great fenced-in field. On it, Braxlo and another giant man sparred against Drullock. The giant was easily the largest man she had ever seen. Standing at least a full head taller than even the ogre, Drullock. She thought he might be a hill giant, but his armor indicated a knightly order.

Fascinated by the rhythm and the intricate footwork and movements, she sat on a bench to watch. Though she rooted for the powerful stranger to crumple Drullock's helm into his skull, the brute seemed to be exceptionally good with his swords. He eventually defeated the two of them based on the congratulations he received. Then another joined the fray. Three against one, surely, Drullock would lose. Mesmerized by the giant stranger and the mock battle being played out in front of her, she sat watching until the sparring ended. The oaf had not lost, receiving many slaps on the back. The giant removed his helm. Turning, he surprised her with the most handsome face she had ever seen. For a human, at least. Her heart fluttered, and she blushed.

The men began talking, the conversation turning serious until they began laughing. By the color of his face, it appeared to be at Drullock's expense. The laughter grew until Drullock stalked off. The rest of the men continued their conversation without the brute. She tried to think of some way to introduce herself to the tall stranger, but the men finished their conversation and packed their gear, leaving before she had a chance. She promised herself she would meet this giant somehow.

***

Lolark could hardly believe it. He had sparred with Alliandre less than a year ago and could win three or four of ten in their duels. Today he had been hard pressed to win even the one.

Then Braxlo joined him two to one, and together they managed only four victories. Now, with Sir Nelson Stormbringer, a former master and commander of the Order of the Silver Cross, joining them three against one, Alliandre had already won three of five. The four of them danced around. Though surrounded, Alliandre darted in and out, his two swords moving almost faster than Lolark could follow, blocking and parrying the blows raining down on him.

Braxlo had become a sword master before Alliandre was born. Both Lolark and Sir Nelson had been the Master of Arms for their order at different times. Yet the three of them were hard pressed to land a blow and spent more than half their time defending blows from one of the blurred swords. Lolark had fought alongside Sir Nelson frequently during the various wars. Likewise, Braxlo and he had a long history of fighting together while adventuring. Though they worked to coordinate their attacks, Alliandre dodged or blocked all their blows. Sir Andras sat on the side, calmly calling out advice to his former pupil.

Alliandre rewarded Sir Nelson's rush forward to attack by extending his sword to clang against Sir Nelson's helm. Several minutes later, Alliandre maneuvered his sword behind Lolark's shield, striking the giant man's left elbow with a quick stroke. Within seconds, Lolark winced in embarrassment as a sharp jab to the breastplate removed him from the fight. Braxlo battled alone for two minutes more before he, too, conceded defeat. The trio won three of the next four bouts, ending the duel with a draw.

Lolark's ears rang from the clamor. They had been dueling for over an hour. Sweat drenched their clothing and armor. As he unbuckled his armor, Lolark rubbed the sore spots where there would be bruises in the morning. Alliandre may have one or two, but he seemed in good shape. Even when Alliandre conceded, Lolark doubted Alliandre had taken a solid hit.

All four of them had been using dueling blades, of course. These were thicker than standard swords, with the edges grounded dull, and a squared-off point. Likewise, the combatants all wore only the cuir bouilli armor and plain helms, so they would feel any solid hit. Lolark had a natural advantage because of his size and strength, but it mattered little when someone was as skilled as Alliandre had become.

"You have improved greatly, my friend. Or have you managed some enchantment you have not revealed? I take it you plan on fighting in the Grand Melee next week."

"Yes, I do. No enchantments, though. I went to the Brass Helms Keep last year and trained under Sword Master Alexander Del Hauptman. He tortured me with endless drills and handicapped me to improve several of my attacks, and even more of my blocks and parries. There were always three or four or five opponents rotating in and out so they were always fresh. To top it off, he made me use two massive sword breakers, so even these dueling swords seem light in comparison. Day and night for ten months I trained, until the time came to ride for Dragonsbane to meet everyone. Which reminds me, why didn't you meet us there?"

"Trouble in the Great Chasm. We lost another squad nearby. The grendlaar are increasing their activity. Sir Tristian ran across a large force, moving to the northwest. Over ten thousand, he estimated, if they haven't cut the size of their banners. One of his knights counted a hundred and ten grackles in the horde. I led a spear to investigate, but we found only dusty tracks and tatters of cloth in the grendlaar's abandoned camps, though we searched for over a week. Hopefully, the grendlaar returned home."

Alliandre whistled at the implications. The grendlaar seemed to arrange their military in a similar manner as the knightly orders. Their primary unit seemed to also be a spear, comprising ten banners, similar to the orders. Except they had a hundred screaming grendlaar in their banners, a grackle leading each banner. Which is why, when counting grendlaar, the grackles were counted and multiplied by a hundred. At any rate, while a human spear contained over two hundred men, a grendlaar spear was over a thousand strong.

"Let's hope one of the larger clans moved in on one of the smaller clans then."

"It won't matter," Braxlo called out with a grin. "With the way Alliandre fought today, we could just ride Her Highness over to the other side and the grendlaar wouldn't stand a chance."

Alliandre flushed red, then turned and quietly sheathed his dueling swords. General laughter rolled through the courtyard and grew louder when Braxlo spoke up again. "But once he made it to her, he would just put his hands behind his back and follow her like a little puppy dog, so all would be for naught."

Grabbing the rest of his gear, his face growing even more red, Alliandre walked calmly through the double doors to the dining room, then stalked up the stairs to his room.

Sir Andras broke into the middle of the group and faced down Braxlo. "Tell me, you who claim to be his friend, why are ye always tearing his arse up so? Since yer spirits-cursed bastard friends refused him knighthood at Dragonsbane all those years ago, for no guid reason as far as I have ever been told, he knows he will never have the rank to court her. It is a deep wound he carries, knowin' those he respects the most do not feel he is worthy of nobility. And, by extension, not worthy of her. And you, in front of all these other noblemen, none of whom are worth even half of him, have tae salt the wound."

"Begging your pardon, but it is a wound of his own making, Sir Andras," Braxlo replied, his voice raising with his ire. "Tell me the queen would not jump for joy and throw away all precedent if he asked to court her. And Marion as well. He is the only one who does not think he is worthy. Maybe a bit of arse tearing will make him get out of his own way and he will pose the question to her."

Lolark put a huge, gauntleted hand on Braxlo's shoulder, gently speaking to him. "You and I both know that would dishonor her greatly, at least in his eyes. He could never do it." Looking around, Lolark raised his voice. "Despite his lack of tact or discretion, his disregard for laws and protocols, you all know Alliandre has the noblest heart of any. At least any I have ever met." He looked at all of them, his expression saying, "including all of you." "In all our years knowing him, has he ever failed to do what is right, despite the cost to himself? Have you ever known him to be second to battle? Ever? Has he ever turned down a request for aid from anyone, rich or poor, noble or otherwise? So, I ask you again, Braxlo, in all the time you have known him, has he ever failed to do what is right?"

"No," admitted Braxlo stubbornly, still not willing to give in. "But most of the time, you have to paint a cursed picture of what is right before he will recognize it. And I tell you, my friend, nobleman or not, he and Marion together is what is right."

All their heads nodded in agreement.

"But that is not what is actually bothering you, is it Braxlo?" Lolark looked him squarely in the eye. "I fight the same battle, my friend."

"I don't know what you are talking about," Braxlo argued.

Lolark sighed and looked around at the group of elder knights and paladins. "Alliandre is following the dream we all had when we were young. We had our glory, while his is still ahead of him. Our skills are in decline, while he improves every day. It is a hard thing to get old and put down the sword. Even harder to hand it off to the next generation."

Braxlo began arguing but stopped. He looked away, unable to hold eye contact with Lolark. Grunting something unintelligible, he went over and began packing up his gear.

***

Sivle slept late, then rose and began his prayers. Best to be in the proper state before visiting the Great Temple in Foresight. He finished his prayers and pulled a purse from the chest under his bed and peeked in. A hundred havnots, his annual tithe. Of course, he was assuming he could get an audience. The current high priest, Mariotteo Del Malcolm, was one of the foremost scholars of the Forest Spirits, despite the rambling, non-scholarly prose to her work. Her theories had caused many in the Great Forest Temple to pull their hair out, taking years of life from the Leathdhéanach, the highest priest in the Great Forest Temple. But many, if not most, of her theories were sound. Though Sivle did not like to admit it, she had bested him during many theological discussions. But this was not the source of his dislike of her.

Unfortunately, she was also petty, arrogant, and vindictive. Sivle had a run-in with her several years ago over a young acolyte the high priest treated as her personal slave. She had always felt entitled to the same privileges as one of the great lords. There were men and women such as this in every organization, and occasionally it worked out well for the slave. However, Sivle considered it an abuse of the significant power assigned to the high priest. Sivle called it out and insisted on an investigation. This resulted in a demotion for Mariotteo Del Malcolm, sending her to serve at the Great Temple for several years.

She considered it the same as being sent to prison. She became just another acolyte to the Leathdhéanach, which galled her greatly. She bided her time there, saying the correct things until securing her release. As luck would have it, two years later, she returned as high priest to the temple at Foresight. From what he had heard, her banishment taught her little. Though she was much more careful about who she selected as acolytes, and how she treated them in view of others, there were still rumors.

Sivle walked the half hursmarc to the temple. On the far side of Hightowne, it was the most imposing building in the quarter. Grown from living trees, it overflowed the block the priests grew it on. The trees which formed the outer walls were massive after so many centuries, with a canopy towering fifty feet over the next tallest building. Vines wove across the walls, forming living tapestries, creating the illusion the subjects on them were moving as the wind blew across them. As he came into sight of the door, he drew out his holy symbol and blessed it.

The door opened as he approached. He entered and walked across the foyer to the hallway. Pulling a pure white robe from a hook in the hallway, he went into an alcove and changed. From there, he went directly down the hall to a large chamber to cleanse himself. Bowing as he entered the chamber, he began his chants as he moved beside the massive metal tree in the center. This was the sanctum of the temple. A statue of the Great Tree made of wood interlaced with iridium stood in the middle. As he knelt before it and reached out with his symbol, he could feel the power course through him. He cringed as the pain grew, knowing he was in for an ordeal. It had been a year since he had cleansed. There had been much to be cleansed for in the last year.

Beads of sweat formed on his brow. A rivulet ran down his chin, the sweat soaking through his robe. Despite the increasing pain, Sivle continued his chants, holding his holy symbol firmly against the silver tree. The sweat turned pink, then red, as blood soaked through. A pool formed around him before running to a drain around the base of the tree. The tree was glowing brightly, and Sivle knelt there several minutes before the sweating subsided and pain receded. When it ended, he removed the holy symbol from the tree, setting it on a stand made for that purpose. He removed the robe, folding it before setting it on the floor and kneeling beside it. An acolyte appeared, about ten years old by the looks of her, with a water bag. She poured it over him while he washed the sweat and blood away.

The acolyte then brought him a new robe, bowing her head. She picked up the soiled robe while he returned to the changing room. His cleansing completed, he took another hallway down to the office of the high priest where an older acolyte sat at a table. Sivle announced himself.

"I am Sivle Si Evila Drol Revo. I am here to speak to the high priest, report on my activities, and receive her blessing."

He then sat down to wait for his audience with the high priest. The acolyte left to announce him, returning after several minutes with an uneasy expression on his face.

"It elated the high priest to hear of your visit, Lord Sivle. A critical matter currently occupies her. She will see you as soon as she finishes."

"I have no intention of interrupting the high priest. I intend only to pay my annual tithe and receive her blessing. Please inform her I shall wait until she finishes."

The acolyte went to relay the message, then returned to continue his studies. He occasionally looked up, an uncomfortable look on his face, saying nothing until the time came for lunch.

"Lord Sivle, I must fetch the high priest her midday meal. Is there something I can get for you?"

"The Forest Spirits will sustain me. I have cleansed so I shall fast until I have received the high priest's blessing."

He knew testing his willingness to wait provided a means of ascertaining his discipline. He had made acolytes wait for him in the same manner.

"As you wish, my lord. Please excuse me." The acolyte left Sivle alone in the small chamber.

After a short while, the acolyte returned, announcing, "The high priest is still occupied." He then returned to his work making copies of a pile of scrolls. Probably the "Decrees of the Early Years," he thought as he remembered the many copies he had made as a child in Vista. Curious, he started a conversation with the acolyte.

"What are you working on, son?"

"The high priest's letter on the 'Decrees of Creation,' Lord Sivle. I am making copies to distribute to visiting priests during Jubilee."

Sivle was a bit taken aback. The "Decrees of Creation" was heretical to many of the aelf nations. It would rile the visiting aelf priests if she passed them around. What could Mariotteo Del Malcolm be thinking unless she wanted to deliver a poke into the eye of the Great Temple. "May I see one, son? To read while I await the high priest, if it would please you."

The boy hesitated, then shook his head, refusing his request. Sivle had stood and walked over while pleading his case. He read the scroll laying open on the table. The first thing Sivle noticed was the date, earlier in the year.

An inquiry into the 'Decrees of Creation' and the supporting decrees.

Compiled this second of Canton, year 1124, AGW.

Máistir Urnaí Mariotteo Del Malcolm Drol Habisuee, High Priest of Foresight.

The scroll then began the actual scholarly portion, which would describe how she arrived at her hypothesis: the aelf were not the first race, even perhaps the fourth. The acolyte removed the scroll before Sivle could read further. Sivle's mind raced. He was not prepared to accept this at the moment, but that could be his own bias against Mariotteo. Something about it pulled at the back of his mind, like a memory he could not recall. He could feel his calm lifting, so he put it out of his mind and resumed his prayers while waiting for his audience.

More hours went by until the sun was below the horizon. The acolyte left to fetch dinner for the high priest. Again, Sivle declined any food. It would do no good to give Mariotteo any grounds to deny him his blessing, so he sat patiently. He found the delay an opportunity to practice his patience and calm. He chanted to himself a long requiem commonly delivered in the month of Alkadolo. He finished it and looked at the Acolyte. Several more hours passed. The moon was halfway to its zenith. The acolyte looked even more uncomfortable when Sivle asked him to please let the high priest know he was still waiting. He tried to protest. Sivle insisted, sending the acolyte off quite flustered.

The boy came back and with a trembling voice announced, "My apologies, my lord. The high priest forgot you were here. She has retired for the evening. She notes she is quite busy, but perhaps you can return in a few days."

Sivle smiled at the lad, replying, "I shall return in a few days."

***

Victor had slept in. Once he got up, he checked on Mortimer. His friend was still unconscious, yet still among the living. Leaving Mortimer to get the horses, he went outside. With Jubilee coming, the stables would be full. Walking briskly, he headed out, hoping one might pay for some spare horses. The four horses they had recovered looked like good ones. If he could get three turots each for them, he would have enough to heal his friend. The cloak was enchanted, so he was going to keep it.

He arrived at the stables and found the horse master there. "Good day, my lord. Are you looking for some extra horses for Jubilee?" he called out across the horse barn.

"One blasted minute, man. Can't you see we're trying to get this cursed shoe off?

Victor couldn't. All he could see over the gate was the man standing, looking at a fidgeting horse. He waited patiently until the man finished, dusting his apron as he came over.

"What have you got there for me then?"

"Just a few horses which were left to me when my father died," Victor lied. "They are farm horses, but good riders too, I think."

"They don't look like farm horses to me. Not big enough to do any proper work."

"I kept the big horses. But I thought with Jubilee I might get some money for these. I was hoping for five turots each." *Always ask for more than you want.* Mortimer had taught him that lesson a long time ago.

The horse master realized the negotiation was on and put on his best bartering face. "Five turots? I can't even sell a farm horse for five turots. I can give you two for each."

"How about three each? With the Jubilee, surely there will be a good market for solid horses."

"Maybe. Tell you what, you look like a pleasant chap, and I am sorry to hear about your father, so I will give you ten turots for the lot of them. But that is as high as I can go."

Victor thought about the offer and looked the man in the eye. He couldn't tell if he could actually go any higher. "Done!" he said and held out his hand. The horse master clasped wrists with him, motioning him to follow him to the house a short distance away.

Horses sold, Victor walked straight to the shop owned by a mage under whom he had studied. Despite not having parted on the best of terms, he knew the mage would be willing to sell him some wares. The shop was in Hightowne, though. The guards stopped everyone who was not a nobleman, or at least a wealthy merchant, from crossing the bridges. However, he knew a few ways around the bridges. An hour later, he knocked on his old mentor's door.

His teacher opened the door and let him in. An older man, he appeared to be the stereotype of the crazy, absent-minded mage. From the pointed cap with the stars and moons on it, to the long blue robes and the pointed shoes, he looked like the mages in the troubadour shows. His belt held a small pouch, ostensibly for spell components, and a small wand. Victor did not know a single mage who used a wand, but Hubert always had his with him. His long gray hair flowed down and seemed to merge with his beard. Hubert had trimmed neither in years. Victor was familiar with the act, deciding to go along with the performance for now.

"Ah, Vincent. How are you, dear boy? What can I do for you?" The old man grabbed his arm and pulled him into the shop. Victor noticed Hubert look behind him, then lock the door once they were inside.

"Master Hubert, it is Victor, and it is good to see you again. I am looking for a potion to heal a friend of mine who has been terribly hurt. He is literally on death's doorstep. Do you have something which can heal him? I have a few turots I have saved the last few years."

"Certainly, my boy. For you, I would be happy to give it to you for free if I could. I still have rent to pay, though. Still, I should have a healing potion for you. Let's see, where did I put the healing?" The old man tottered around the shop, opening drawers and cabinets. He circled the shop twice, taking several minutes to do so, shouting out, "Alice! Alice, where are my healing potions?"

A small black cat came down from a cabinet and jumped up on a rack near the old man. He reached over and picked up the cat and then spoke to it. "That's my good girl. Do you remember where we put all the healing potions?" He rubbed the cat, then held his ear to it as if listening to it speak to him.

"Oh, that's right, they did, didn't they? I had almost forgotten. Thank you, Alice. I don't know what I would do without you."

He put the cat down and turned back to Victor. "I am sorry, Virgil. A messenger from the guild came by and bought up all my healing potions for the Jubilee. They go through them like fine wine during all the jousting and what not. Terrible business, all that fighting. Then they just pick up and all go drinking after. I have never seen the point. Now, my boy. What can I get for you?"

"Healing potion, Master Hubert. Are you sure you don't have any?"

"Of course, I have healing potions. Just let me remember where I put them." The cat meowed loudly again, and the old man stopped. "Are you sure, Alice?" Then he turned back to Victor.

"The guild bought them all. Whatever do you need a healing potion for? Are you going on an adventure?"

Slightly frustrated, Victor tried to remain calm. Tiring of Hubert's game, he raised his voice just a little. "My friend, Mortimer. Almost dead. I have money." He held out a handful of turots.

The old man's eyes narrowed, thinking for a moment, then he jumped back into character. "Your friend. I remember now. But I am out of healing potions. The guild came and took them all, you know. I have a Life's Breath potion. That will help your friend. Just made it this morning. Best I can do on short notice, sorry." He opened a cabinet door, reaching in and pulling out a small vial. "This will be twenty turots." He moved over to Victor, holding one hand out, palm up, with the vial in the other. Victor did not want to get into a bidding war with him, wearying of Hubert's antics, so he fished more turots from his purse and counted them out into the old man's hand. No sooner had he hit twenty when Hubert pulled his hand away with the coins and opened his other hand to give the vial to Victor. Taking it, Victor quickly left.

The Life's Breath potion would ensure Mortimer did not die, but it would be days before he was up walking again. A healing potion would have healed his wounds as well. Now they would have to heal naturally. It might take weeks for Mortimer to regain his health.

***

Alliandre was still in a foul mood when he cleaned up and came down for his midday meal. He should be far past getting upset over Braxlo's teasing, as he knew his friend meant no insult. Alliandre had known Marion for as long as she had been alive. He remembered holding her when she was born, playing peek-a-boo with her as a baby. Playing hide and seek with her in the castle at Vista, remembering how she had cried when she could not find him, thinking him utterly lost. When he showed himself, she ran and hugged him for several minutes. After that, he always selected the hiding spaces she was likely to check. He still could not stand to see her sad, spending as much time at the Wyvern's Aerie as he could spare. Lately, it seemed to be all for naught.

Leaving the Central Kingdom at twelve, after their escape from the Golden Aelf attackers, he promised Marion he would become a knight, return, and marry her. For an orphan to become a nobleman, this was the common way. Some merchants purchased their rank. He certainly had the wealth to purchase a title. However, it took generations before other nobility recognized their titles. Others attained knighthood because of their actions in battles, but in the multitude of battles and victories he had taken part in, his status as an orphan cursed him. He had one more chance, which was to win the Grand Melee. Tradition was when unknighted warriors won, the king would bestow knighthood upon them. As soon as he won the tournament, he would fulfill his oath.

He came down the stairs and noticed the din of a tavern full of noisy patrons. He saw Erich standing near the courtyard door talking to Braxlo. Lolark had evidently left with Sir Nelson. A banner of paladins, the same ones from when he arrived, sat at the same long table. He looked for an empty spot to eat, away from Braxlo, when he noticed Erich approaching.

"Did you raid my closet, or are you still upset?" Erich jested as he handed Alliandre a scroll.

"What do you mean?" he asked, realizing then what he was wearing. His black boots, shined to a high sheen, were over black pants with a dark burgundy stripe down the out seam, and a black gambeson containing the same dark burgundy pinstripes over his burgundy shirt. Over it all, he wore his black cloak. To be fair, there was a lot of gold trim on his shirt cuff. The buttons, too, were all polished gold. Regardless, the overall effect was pretty similar. The thought about what he was wearing broke his mood a bit. "What is this?" he asked Erich, holding up the scroll.

"The favor you asked. The young girl did indeed return to the orphanage. However, I asked the patrons to find a reputable merchant or tradesman who might accept her as a ward. They were aware of a full baron who was willing to take her. I made sure he was reputable and checked him out myself." Erich gave a small, exaggerated bow, obviously quite pleased with himself.

"Reputable?" Alliandre asked, a bit of suspicion in his voice. "Meaning what, exactly?"

"Meaning he does not associate with the guild. I thought you would appreciate that. He also has a daughter about her age, and a younger son. The scroll is from the guild master, describing his lands, holdings, and other particulars, for your approval. We will not send her there unless you approve, but I promise, she will have a wonderful future with them."

Alliandre tucked the scroll into his belt pouch, then grasped Erich by the wrist and looked him straight in the eye. "Thank you." He was about to say more when he saw some gentlemen leaving a table and instead walked over to take their spot.

Erich followed him until he sat, then continued to the door, but not before whispering, "You owe me."

Alliandre groaned, then turned to make a retort, stopping as Erich was nowhere to be seen.

He looked around for Marion, finding her standing off to the side, waiting for him to finish his conversation. She had a tray with ale, mutton, and bread. He rose as she approached, setting the tray in front of him.

"Good day, Alliandre. I missed your duels this morning. I trust they went well. You seemed upset when you came in." She spoke as though making small talk, but stood a bit too close to him, her hand raised to his shoulder.

He reached up and set his hand on hers. "It went well enough. I was upset because I am still a boy, overly sensitive concerning certain subjects."

"Sir Andras told me. I'm sorry your vow to me brings you such embarrassment."

"It is not my promises to you. It is my failure to fulfill them. But I *will* win the Grand Melee.

"As this will be the first time you will carry my favor, you had better."

She gave him a small wink, patting his shoulder as she continued her duties. Following her with his eyes while she went out of her way to stay in his view, she disappeared behind a table of young lords laughing and shouting at one another. He ate his food in silence, his mind focused on the melee and what more he could do in the next nine days to ensure he would win. Rumors were how there were already almost four hundred entrants, many of those hoping just to make the first cut. He knew there would be many skilled fighters there, as there had not been a Royal Grand Melee in years. But Alliandre would be better. He had to be. He had done nothing the last two years but train for this.

He had even won the Grand Melee in Castle Iron Keep last year. The duke who hosted the event was so impressed that he requested the knighting, but the Iron King declined. The orphan curse followed him. This Jubilee, however, would be different. King Henry the Great was a friend of his, thanks to Alliandre fighting with, then saving, Prince Lucas during the Great Vreen War. If Alliandre won the Grand Melee, there was no question that he could fulfill his oath.

Finishing his meal, he laid a single havnot under his plate, then left to find an armorer to repair some dents and scratches in his armor. He also needed a new gambeson. He wanted to be at his best, as well as to look his best, for Jubilee. He should probably apologize to Lolark as well. He had struck him quite hard several times earlier. Lolark he was so large that sometimes Alliandre had to swing extra hard in order to move fast enough to strike and get back out of his reach. At least, that is what he told himself.

***

Drullock walked down the stairs, glancing over at him and Erich, then turning to head the opposite way. Erich excused himself, moving toward Drullock. Braxlo took the chance to go to his room and clean up, not wanting to be in the room with Drullock. Once in the room, he stripped down and used a bit of the balm Sivle had prepared. Several blows Drullock caught him with made Braxlo wonder if he was wearing the girdle Sivle enchanted to enhance his strength and endurance, but Braxlo knew better. If there was a better fighter around, Braxlo didn't know who it might be.

He supposed he could be nicer to him, but Drullock had an arrogance all his own. It galled Braxlo, because Drullock was as good as he thought he was. Actually, maybe even better. Some part of Drullock still thought of himself as a poor orphan boy, affecting his confidence. And Braxlo knew part of him resented how good Drullock had become and wanted to bring him down a notch. Particularly after the thrashing Drullock had given them.

He cleaned and repaired his dueling armor while he waited for the stench from Sivle's salve to fade. Fairwind usually cast a minor spell to repair his armor, clean his clothes, and otherwise keep him looking like a great lord, but she had left early this morning. Planning to compete in the Grand Melee, he wanted to look his best. After this morning, though, he was reconsidering. He used to pull out three or four bouts in a duel with Drullock, but today, he and Lolark together were lucky to reach that.

Finishing the repairs on his armor, he went down to eat. Looking around, he saw Drullock had left the Aerie, so he went to sit at the bar and tried to catch Marion's eye.

"I dinnae think ye would like the food ye would get from her today, laddie." Sir Andras came over from the door and moved behind the bar. "She is none too happy wae ye. Best to give it some time. Alliandre may have cooled off, but Marion will hold on to it all day."

Braxlo smiled a bit. He should know better than to run Drullock down in the Aerie, or in Foresight at all, for that matter. "I don't suppose you know who tattled on me, do you?"

"When Alliandre stormed upstairs, she became curious. She asked me, and I couldnae do but tell her the truth. I am sworn to service to her family after all." The burly man shrugged his shoulders and continued. "The queen has some chickens which just came out of the oven. Would ye like one of those, or the mutton?"

"I will have the chicken, please. And some roasted roots if you have any. And a mug of the mead you had last night."

Sir Andras left to get the food together, and Braxlo turned as some boisterous men entered the tavern. A banner of paladins from Lolark's order, the Order of the Silver Cross. No doubt Lolark had recommended the place to them. He thought of the old joke, if you gave something free to a seamstress, she would return with a new dress for you. If you gave something free to a shoemaker, he would return with a new pair of shoes for you. If you gave something free to a paladin, he would return with twenty more paladins. "Well," Braxlo thought, "Sir Andras will soon show them why not a lot of paladins come here for the free food."

Laughing to himself, he turned and waited for his food to arrive. Hearing the paladins pounding the table, calling for service, he noticed Marion calmly walking over to them. Paladins were usually a good lot. They were brave and honest men who had taken vows of obedience and poverty to their order. Their vows of poverty meant they turned over to the order everything they earned or otherwise obtained. In exchange, their order covered all their living expenses, along with a small stipend each month. In most orders, life was good.

They had the best horses, food, weapons, and armor. While each banner slept together in the same section of the barracks, the individuals each had their own space surrounded by seven-foot-high walls, affording them some privacy. Each room also had a desk in front of the opening, with the openings staggered so you were not staring at your banner-mate while working. Each paladin also had his sword stand and his armor stand with his cuir bouilli, breastplate and half helm. They kept his full plate and his other weapons in the armory, keeping his horse's barding and saddle and other accoutrements in the quarter-master storehouse next to the stables.

Their vows of obedience meant paladins were expected to follow all orders, upholding the code of chivalry above all else. This was the chief difference between the palladium orders and the knightly orders. Knights required the sponsor of a regent. Therefore, the regent could command the order to perform certain duties. Outside of those duties, an individual knight could insist on payment to perform any other actions requested of him.

A high priest raised paladins to the order, requiring no regent. All negotiations to hire paladins had to go through the Master and Commander of the Order. Once hired, a knight may flee against over-whelming odds. They expected paladins to cheerfully charge the hoard. Needless to say, hiring a knight, or an order of knights, was far less expensive than hiring a similar number of paladins. The life expectancy of paladins was also much lower. Still, half of all paladins made it to their retirement after twenty years of service.

The Palladium Council had oversight of the palladium orders. Seventeen of the most recognized master and commanders comprised the Council, negotiating with kingdoms and other factions, and adju-dicating complaints and grievances against the orders. They could also commit all the orders to an action, as they had during the Great Vreen War. Long ago, in the time just after Jerome Nileppez began knighting the first men for the Freehold of Dragonsbane, they had negotiated the Palladium Contract.

This contract required all nobility, citizens, and guilds in the signa-tory realms to provide food, housing, horses, armor, or other aid as required, to any paladins who requested it. In return, the palladium or-ders would mediate differences between kingdoms, enforce agreements and contracts, and patrol the roads to prevent brigands or attacks from vreen, grendlaar, or any other manner of creature. While all observed the spirit, both sides often parsed the letter of the contract. The Wyvern's Aerie parsed it strictly by the letter.

Braxlo's food arrived and he began eating. As always, the roots were perfectly roasted, a bit crisp still, but hot and tender. They cooked the chicken till the skin was brown and crispy, the meat inside so moist and tender a knife was not even necessary. Whatever seasonings the cook John used were a secret to him alone. Braxlo had eaten in the courts of several kings and had yet to taste anything as delicious. He dipped another piece of chicken in the sauce which accompanied it, washing it down with a long draught of the sweet mead.

A raised voice disturbed his breakfast, accompanied by a fist pounding the table behind him. Looking over, the commander of the Banner was standing, apparently dressing down Marion. He waved his gauntleted finger in her face, even tapping her once on the sternum. Braxlo noticed Sir Andras retrieving his cudgel. Deciding to make some amends with the princess, Braxlo crossed the distance to the table and laid his hand heavily on the shoulder of the commander.

The commander wheeled at him, almost catching him with a clenched right fist.

"Whoa now, friend," Braxlo calmly said as he barely dodged the blow. "What seems to be the problem where a noble paladin such as yourself would raise his voice to a serving girl? Not to mention attempt to strike a knight of Dragonsbane."

The name "Dragonsbane" made the commander pause. He took a breath, regaining his composure.

"My apologies, Sir Knight. It was this lass' refusal to honor the Palladium Contract which caused my ignoble actions. I am terribly sorry for my actions against you. I was not aware you were a knight, as you wear no crest, but I offer penance to you."

"I require no penance. As you stated, I am wearing nothing to identify myself as a knight. In truth, I am a Knight Errant, not an active member of the order. However, you may wish to offer penance to the lady you have dishonored."

"Me? Offer penance to a serving girl who refuses to honor the Palladium Contract? That will not happen. Not today, or any day."

Sir Andras had arrived, but before he could speak, Braxlo took a step forward, putting himself nose to nose with the commander.

"Allow me to introduce myself, Commander. I am Braxlo the Brave. Perhaps Lolark the Luckless has spoken of me. I am sure I will be dueling with him tomorrow, as I did this morning, and please let me assure you I will vouch for the Wyvern's Aerie. They have always followed the Palladium Contract. In fact, a banner of the Order of the Wren resides here under the contract as we speak. If you have a complaint, perhaps you should bring it to Lolark. I am sure he would be happy to resolve any problems his order has with the Aerie."

With the mention of Lolark, the commander's face flushed red, and he turned to Marion, babbling an apology. However, Sir Andras stepped in front of Marion, holding his cudgel up to the face of the cowed man.

"Ye should know ye were speaking to Princess Marion of the Southern Kingdom. I know you lads come from the Great Chasm, but here in Foresight, yer order carries no more weight than any other of the orders. Which be none. As I am sure Her Highness told ye, we will give ye yer food and drink, but it will be what we decide to serve ye. If ye want to make orders of us, you lads will have to pay like the rest of our customers."

Braxlo saw the blanched expression on the commander's face, and an idea came to him. Turning to Sir Andras, he reached into his pouch, pulling out a few turots.

"Sir Andras, as these are members of my good friend Lolark's order, I am sure they meant no insult to Her Highness, or the Wyvern's Aerie. Please accept these and allow me to pay for their meal, the finest you have."

Sir Andras looked at Braxlo with a puzzled expression. But he took the turots and glared once more at the commander. The commander bowed to Andras. "My apologies. I shall report my actions to Sir Lolark and will accept any penance he requires."

"That is unnecessary, for I have a penance for you after all." Looking at Marion, Braxlo continued, "For your penance, I request only that you bring your banner here at sunrise to challenge the man named Alliandre Del Nileppez Drol Hulloc to a duel. Your banner against him. And invite Sir Lolark to observe and inform him as to the reason. Then your honor shall be clean." Knowing Alliandre would not refuse the challenge, Braxlo smiled to himself. *Alliandre may hurt some of them, but hopefully they can teach him some humility.*

Marion looked over at Braxlo with a suspicious frown, then turned and walked away. But when the commander agreed, Braxlo heard a chuckle from the princess.

***

Vanessa arrived at the Aerie at her normal time. She looked around to see if the group from the previous night were present, but unfortunately, though the tavern was full, none of the group was there. Sighing, she went around the bar to put on her apron.

"Good afternoon, Your Majesty," she said as she bowed to Arielle. She wasn't sure why she bowed, but everyone else did, and Arielle was always so kind to her she didn't mind. She was fortunate to have this job, as she made enough money to supplement the farm. The Aerie paid her taxes, and often Marion would give her part of her tips when the night was slow. She was so happy her uncle had brought her here and said a good word for her to the queen.

"Good afternoon, Vanessa. Thank goodness you came in today. The tavern is full. It is all Marion can do to keep up." Arielle carried over a large platter heaped with venison and a small roast of what looked like boar meat. "Please bring this to the long table in the back."

She carefully grabbed the platter and carried it back to the table. Walking to the middle, she sweetly asked the gentlemen to move aside, standing they quickly complied. One of them even reached across and grabbed the platter and set it down for her. She quickly glanced around to see if any glasses needed refilling, but there were two pitchers of ale on the table, the men doing a good job filling their own glasses.

By the end of the shift, her feet and arms were sore, and she had seen none of the party from the night before. She had a modest pile of dolcots, as well as a single malnot. "Is every night during Jubilee going to be like this?" she asked Marion when they had a break.

Marion let out a small laugh, then replied with a wink. "It will be good early on, while all of them still have full purses. Once they set up the Grand Market, they will spend their money there. Most who stay at the Aerie will have plenty left over. The number of knights will probably go down, replaced by paladins."

Truth be told, Vanessa could not tell the difference between the two until after they left. The knights usually left several coppers on the table. The paladins would leave one, two at most. The ones who had the stew and lukewarm tea often left nothing. She had asked Marion how to tell them apart, but she had not understood the differences between devices and symbols and crests. It was an unfamiliar language, and she didn't care to learn it right now. She had figured out not to linger at the tables where she brought stew, though.

She would watch Marion flirt and wink and smile at the knights, and wished she felt comfortable doing the same. Marion had her long black hair pulled up and tied with a ribbon in the back, her bangs bordering her face on top, with a long lock of hair hanging down in gentle curls from each temple. Her white blouse tied up at her neck, not a glimpse of her breasts was visible. But the outline was clear from her brocaded corset on the bottom. The golden necklace nestling snugly in front outlined a clearly generous bosom. Her skirt reached just above the floor, swaying back and forth as she walked. Every once in a while, the pleats would fall in place perfectly to outline her backside, particularly when she bent forward to place a platter or pitcher on the table. She did nothing lewd or tasteless, yet she showed off her feminine wares while covered from neck to ankle. Marion was a princess, Vanessa knew. She imagined she had grown up with education and training on all facets of attracting noblemen.

If Vanessa were to wink at a knight, she was sure he would take it the wrong way, forcing her to fight off his amorous attentions. Besides, she was quite happy with Vandion, even though some knights gave her appreciative looks and whistles. But Vandion was kinder to her than anyone she had ever met, and she had promised to marry him in the spring. They would complete the project he was working on, then save their coins from the harvest and her job and have a splendid wedding feast during Frescao, right after the planting. She wanted to have the wedding during Jubilee. He deferred, noting the harvest time would be remarkably busy for him, while she would be extremely busy at the Aerie. The costs would be much higher for everything as well. He had been right, of course.

Just as she was leaving, the man who dressed all in black came in. He had not taken two steps inside the door when Andras called across the hall to him. "Lord Erich, would ye be kind enough to walk young Vanessa home tonight?"

"Oh no, Sir Andras, that isn't necessary," the young girl assured him. "Besides, I am meeting someone just across the bridge, so I will be fine." She left quickly out the door.

She would walk through Hightowne, and once she crossed the bridge, Vandion would be there, and they would ride the rest of the way home. Besides, the man in black gave her a bad feeling. Nothing he had done, but he seemed shifty and would disappear into the crowd whenever he got up. She left alone, looking back to be sure he wasn't following, then headed home. She passed all the shops shut or just shutting down, and other taverns with people still going in. Just two days before Jubilee. While the inns and lodges were filling up, the tavern halls still had room. The noblemen and ladies were happy to go out and hobnob with visiting nobles, and even the occasional adventurer.

A man began following her after she passed "The Crooked Rooster". She turned toward the bridge, waiting for him to come around the corner, which he never did. Another time, two young men crossed to her side of the street ahead of her and walked side by side, blocking the side of the narrow street. When they got closer, they seemed to remember something, running back across the street. Then she was at the bridge. As expected, Vandion was waiting for her.

"How was your night, sweetheart?" Vandion asked as he pulled her up behind him.

"Busy, but I made good tips, even another malnot. How about your day?"

"I scrounged around the old blacksmith forge and found some iridium dust. That will save us a lot. I bought the wires and built the frame. About one more turot and we will have enough to get the rest of the things I need."

"A turot? Are you sure? It will take me months to earn a turot."

"Perhaps not. I went through the fields. They are looking much better than last week. The beans and wild root are ready to harvest. Other crops are coming in." He pulled a pear from his pack and handed it back to her. "And the pears are already falling. Did you serve the new people tonight? Or did Marion take the big spenders?"

"She is not like that. They did not come in tonight, not a single one of them, until I was leaving. But Marion said they would be down for firstmeal if I wanted to come in early tomorrow. I thought about it, but I wouldn't have time to get the housework done, so I told her I couldn't."

"That is good. You need your rest anyway; you have been so tired lately."

She hugged him tightly. She had been concerned he would be angry with her for turning down the offer. But he always thought of her first. She was so fortunate to have found him.

***

When the serving girl declined an escort, Erich shrugged his shoulders and looked the question at Sir Andras, who waved him to follow anyway. Erich waited a count of ten, then followed the serving girl out. He returned just over a quarter hour later, taking a seat at the bar. Sir Andras looked at him, asking, "Well? She made it home safe then?"

"Not sure. She was telling the truth when she said she was meeting someone. A half-aelf on a well-trained roan. Kind of puzzling after I thought about it."

"Thank you for following her." Arielle walked out of the kitchen. "I pulled a hen out of the oven for you. I know how much all of you like my hens." She walked back toward the kitchen to get the hen, while Sir Andras came over.

"What do ye mean, puzzling? Speak plainly, laddie," he demanded.

"Well, I would guess they could sell the horse for at least a hundred turots, yet here she is working, making a handful of dolcots a day. He seems well off. They seemed quite cozy, so why make her work? He does not seem to be the type of gentleman I would recommend. I cannot figure out what the swindle could be. It just feels like one to me. However, it might just be my suspicious nature."

They both smiled at his last comment. They knew Erich throughout the kingdoms. Every guild gave him information and kept their guild members from interfering with his business while he was in town. In exchange, he passed on information, delivered messages, and refrained from killing the guild masters. There were rumors he had done just that when he left Tristheim. The guild masters had given him an ultimatum – stay with the guild or go to prison. He left Tristheim. They arrested him a few hursmarcs out of town the next day.

Erich was in prison for less than two days when all the guild masters mysteriously died in their sleep. They found Erich the next morning in his cell, seemingly still imprisoned. Later the same day, the new guild masters decided their predecessors had been wrong to keep him there and released him. When they returned his possessions, they found they included several personal items from the deceased guild masters.

Sir Andras spoke up first. "I will ask her about him tomorrow. She is a sweet lassie and has been a big help here."

"That she has," the queen replied as she returned with the hen, "so it would be wrong to go spying on her. But I trust your instincts, Erich. We will keep a watchful eye on her while she is here."

Lolark came through the door, along with Drullock, who was

carrying a large pack on his back. They made their way to the bar, Marion stopping them halfway. "I have a table ready for you over here." She led them over to a table set away from the others, next to the kitchen. They had set out a massive throne-like chair for Lolark. Erich joined his friends as Lolark and Drullock moved over to the table. Erich sat across from Lolark while Drullock took his large bag up to his room. When he came down, he walked over to the bar to chat with Marion and Sir Andras.

The smells of roasting meats wafted into the room as Arielle came in with a pan of roasted chickens and a ham surrounded by onions, carrots, and turnips. She set it down in the middle of the table, hurrying back into the kitchen. She returned moments later with another tray, this one with several pitchers of wine and ale. One more trip, and she placed flagons and crystal glasses in front of each chair, eight in all. Lolark cast a questioning eye at her. She only shrugged in reply as Drullock returned to the table. They all began filling their plates, eating while it was hot.

Braxlo came in after a bit. He looked magnificent, with a brand-new cloak, boots, and a new scabbard which appeared to be made out of obsidian. By the large pack on his back, he had gotten his armor repaired as well. He waved while heading up the stairs to the room, returning later with the scabbard still on. Erich passed him a pitcher, asking, "Braxlo, my friend, was the beating you received from Drullock this morning so bad you needed a new sword?"

Lolark and Erich laughed, Braxlo hanging his head in mock shame. "I will admit I spent quite some time repairing my cuir bouilli. I had to bring my plate mail to Master Gunther to be repaired." Then his face brightened as he held his new scabbard up. "But while waiting for Fairwind, I came across a vendor whose wagon lost a wheel just inside the gate. When he saw me, he stopped what he was doing and pulled this off his wagon."

He laid the scabbard on the table. To say it was black was an understatement. Not just black, but different textures of black. The body seemed to absorb the light, while the locket and chape appeared to be polished so when the light hit them right, they shone like polished boots. The finial, even more polished, until it seemed to be reflective, had images flashing across it as they turned and passed the scabbard around. They made the stud on the back of the locket of the same material as the body, the effect tricking the eye into thinking there was a hole in the scabbard instead of a notch to attach it to a sword belt.

"Why, thank you, Braxlo, this is a most generous gift," Erich teased as he pretended to attach it to his hip. "You have a good eye."

Braxlo pretended to lunge for Erich, instead grabbing his plate and pulling it the two seats over. "Tell you what, my friend Erich," he said between bites, "tomorrow I will duel you instead of Drullock. If you win, you can have it." Lolark laughed out loud. Erich didn't duel. He was certainly deadly, but not in the same way Braxlo or Lolark were deadly. If he wanted someone dead, they would find them dead, with nothing to connect Erich to the death. The one time anyone could remember Erich dueling a knight over some forgotten insult, Erich left with ten severe bruises to go along with the great bruise on his pride. After that, he refused to duel.

Drullock walked back over to look at the new scabbard as well. "Nice" was all he said as he handed it back to Erich before sitting down in between Erich and Lolark, two seats away from each of them.

"Do I smell?" Lolark joked, raising one of his enormous arms and sniffing loudly at his armpit.

"Not any more than Erich, which is why I sat between the two of you."

"Come on, Alliandre. Sit next to your old friend Lolark." Lolark reached a long arm around Drullock and began pulling him closer. A short tussle followed, with Lolark easily manhandling the smaller man. "Not so tough without your fancy girdle, now are you."

"Tougher than you with a sword, if those bruises I gave you this morning are any sign."

Lolark pulled Drullock in, wrapping both arms around him in a great bear hug. He kissed his cheek sloppily until a hard wrap on his head interrupted him. Looking up, Marion was there, wooden spoon in hand. "Sir Lolark, I would think a paladin of your reputation would have learned better than to pick on someone so much smaller and weaker than you."

"Oh, save me, Princess Marion. This ogre is trying to take me away to his lair." Drullock brought the back of his hand up to his forehead in mock despair.

As Marion cocked the spoon back, Lolark relented. "I thought the dashing knight saves the princess, not the other way around." Immediately after it came out of his mouth, he regretted saying it, but Drullock took no offense.

As Lolark let him go, he replied, "Since I am just a poor orphan boy, it is perfectly appropriate." Then, standing and sweeping Marion into his arms and swinging her into a deep dip, he finished, "My heroine." They stood there for several seconds, their faces just inches apart, looking into each other's eyes. Lolark, Braxlo, and Erich looked on expectantly, hoping they were just about to kiss, when Drullock quickly straightened up, a blush reddening his face as he stepped back. Raising the knuckle of Marion's hand to his forehead, he bowed, "My apologies, Your Highness, I meant no disrespect."

"Silly boy," Marion said as she leaned in and gave him a kiss on the cheek. "We were just playing, there is no disrespect in having some fun." Then, walking away with an exaggerated wiggle, "I am just a simple tavern wench, after all."

They all smiled, watching her as she disappeared behind the bar.

The entire tavern hall was silent. Everyone seemed to be entertained by their antics. Then Sivle entered the room, glancing around before holding the door for Fairwind. He made a big show of escorting her in, sending a teasing look over to Braxlo as they crossed to the stairs. Sivle returned a few moments later without Fairwind. He looked haggard, sitting between Erich and Alliandre before grabbing a plate and scooping a chicken and some vegetables onto it. Before he said a word, he tore off the leg, taking an overly large bite.

"Hi everyone. How are all of you doing? Sorry I am so late." Drullock mimicked Sivle as he poured his friend a glass of wine.

"I was furious at Braxlo earlier, but I grew up and am fine now. Thanks for asking, Sivle," Erich responded in a perfect imitation of Alliandre.

"I am fine as well," Lolark chimed in, copying Braxlo's low, gravelly voice. "Drullock gave me a beating earlier, so I bought a shiny new toy to make myself feel better."

Alliandre spoke with Erich's slow drawl, "I just hung around all day sneaking up on people and running errands, because that is all I am actually good at."

Braxlo, not sure who he should mimic, just asked, "Where did you find Fairwind? I waited for her at the front gate like we agreed, but she never showed."

Sivle swallowed, then spoke. "She had a traveling companion. He is stabling his horse right now. We might need another seat." He looked around and counted the eight seats. "Hmmmm."

Everyone but Sivle turned to the door as a well-armored half-aelf with purple tinted eyes came into the tavern. Sivle looked at their expressions, grinning, then shoved more food into his mouth. The unknown visitor just stood at the door, waiting patiently for the next several minutes. Fairwind came down the stairs, accompanied by Ariandel. As she moved to the table, the visitor moved across the tavern hall, meeting her just before the table.

"Hello everyone. Look who I found in the room, writing scrolls." Everyone stood as Fairwind stepped up to the chair between Lolark and Braxlo, pointing Ariandel to the chair on the other side of Lolark. Ariandel began moving, but slowly. As soon as she came down and saw Lolark, she could do nothing but stare at him. She shuffled behind his giant chair, looking up at his golden hair, the same color as Fairwind's. She got around him when the giant gracefully stepped behind her, holding her chair.

"And who is this fair maiden, Fairwind? One of your ladies-in-waiting? How rude of you not to introduce us to her."

"We met her on the road to Foresight, Lolark. If you had bothered to meet us as we planned, you would have been introduced already.

ALLIANDRE RISING - 99

But no matter. Ariandel, meet Sir Lolark the Luckless, Paladin of Paladins, Master and Commander of the Silver Cross Order at Castle Silver Cross. Lolark, meet Lady Ariandel Spéir álainn, Cara Ríoga, of the Silver Bark Woods. Mage of some renown and my new student." Then she gave Ariandel a wink, whispering across Lolark, "It turns out Mirandel is otherwise occupied."

"It is a pleasure to meet such a beautiful representative of the Silver Bark Woods." Lolark gave her a sweeping bow. "I trust we will see much of one another if you are training under Her Highness."

"I would enjoy that, Sir Lolark. I saw you fighting earlier today against Drullock. I could not follow who won and lost, but your skill with your great sword is impressive. Your technique mesmerized me." Many of them smiled while her own face grew warm with embarrassment.

"Thank you, my lady. I am glad you are not familiar with the art of the sword, as," he paused, then continued, "Drullock soundly thrashed us." Smiles around the table again, and Sivle even snickered. "It was all Braxlo and I could do to keep him from sending us to the priests."

Ariandel sat as the rest of the table turned to Fairwind, who swung her hand toward the newcomer.

"This is Prince Valian Tríúa Rugadh, Cosantóir Ríoga. Lord Marschall of the Great Aelf, Knight Protector and brother of King Drake Fíor-oidhre."

"Well met, Your Highness. We welcome you and news from the Great Forest." Lolark gave a deep bow, raising his glass. "To the Great King of Kings. May the spirits protect him and his sons." It was the standard toast to the king. Erich watched as Braxlo quickly poured a glass of wine for the prince once Lolark began his toast. Everyone responded, "To the Great King. May the spirits protect him and his sons."

Prince Valian emptied his glass, giving a quick bow to Lolark. Holding his glass to Braxlo to refill, he replied, "Thank you, Sir Lolark. It is good to see there are some humans who keep the tradition alive. May I return the favor?"

"Please, Your Highness."

"To the Kings of the Human Realms. May they forever live in brotherhood with the aelf." Everyone repeated the toast and Prince Valian held his glass to Braxlo once again. With the introductions over, Fairwind sat, the rest of those still standing following.

"Prince Valian," Braxlo asked him as he filled the glass for the third time, "what brings you to Foresight. Surely you did not abandon your post just to attend the Jubilee?"

"Not at all, Sir Braxlo. I was carrying a message from the Great King to all the aelf kings. While speaking with King Aedengus Duine Fionn, I had a chance meeting with Her Highness." He turned and gave a small bow to Fairwind. "Of course, she enchanted me again with her beauty. However, the real reason I was happy to meet her is I have heard she travels with one of the great human swordsmen, Alliandre Del Nileppez Drol Hulloc. I was hoping for an introduction to find out if he is as good as his reputation."

"I can assure you, Prince Valian," Braxlo said with a smirk, "he is one of the best swordsmen I have ever crossed blades with. Please come to the courtyard tomorrow morning. If I am not mistaken, he is dueling a banner of paladins from Sir Lolark's order."

Lolark looked at Braxlo askance. "Now I understand the message today. I take it you had something to do with that?"

Braxlo looked at him with a wounded expression, "I only did what I thought necessary to uphold the honor of Princess Marion the Virtuous after your commander decided it was within his rights to dictate her responsibilities under the Palladium Contract."

Lolark rolled his eyes. "So that is what it is about." Looking at Drullock, he continued, "Were you a witness to this?"

Drullock shook his head. "This is the first I have heard of it. But I guess fighting a bunch of paladins will be a good workout."

Erich chimed in, "It is too bad you were not here this morning, Prince Valian. You could have watched the mighty Alliandre best three sword masters at the same time. Now, mind you, they were all quite aged."

"It was a draw as I recall," replied Lolark, "though if you think them so old, perhaps you would like me to arrange for you to duel the oldest one." This brought laughter from around the table.

"Touché." Erich smiled as he feigned a wound to his heart.

Marion came up with more hens and ham. Seeing Prince Valian, she bowed quickly before leaving. She returned with more pitchers of ale and wine, then faced the prince and gave a deep bow. "Hello, Your Highness. It is a pleasure to see you again. Welcome to the Wyvern's Aerie."

Prince Valian stood and walked over to Marion. "Your Highness. The pleasure is all mine. Your beauty remains unchanged from when I saw you during the wedding of Queen Elizabeth the Widower."

"And you are even more charming than you were that day. Perhaps you would allow me to accompany you on the dance floor during the Royal Ball next week."

"To my great sorrow, my duties take me elsewhere. I promise you, when you return to the Southern Throne, I will come and spend a week dancing and celebrating with you."

"I will hold you to that promise. As you made it in front of a paladin, a master and commander no less, you cannot get out of it. Even the King of Kings will have to release you from his service." Bowing deeply again, with a fond smile and a playful wink, she left to continue her duties. The prince followed her for a bit with his eyes, then returned to his seat.

"Speaking of the King of Kings' service, how is the Great King?" Erich asked. "With an aelf as the only remaining heir, I suppose your job is all the more difficult."

"Why would you think that?" Prince Valian asked.

Erich paused. Everyone knew of the prophesy of the aelf. No aelf would serve as King of Kings until the bond between the human king-doms and the Great Aelf king were as strong as the bonds between the human kings. But the human kings were bonded by blood. He tried to answer tactfully. "I merely allude to the assassination of the princes all those years ago. If there were nobles among the aelf willing to kill the two children, surely, they might try to remove the king before something happens to his son, or he has more children."

Prince Valian laughed. "That would be quite the feat. The king never leaves the palace. Since the death of his sons, he has become paranoid. He distrusts everyone, but the humans most of all. It was humans who killed his sons if you recall."

"Voldarians, yes. But they do not act on their own. Someone hired them, and there is no reason for humans to see the prophesy fulfilled," Erich said. "This leaves the aelf themselves."

"Rumors, I assure you." The prince laughed, then grew more serious. "And Queen Reaganel Dílis Mór assures everyone the prophesy is still in effect. I am unsure how she knows, but she is quite adamant."

"She would know," Erich conceded. Prior to her being raised during the Comórtas le Haghaidh Banríona, her knowledge of the spirits had been unmatched. Even by the Leathdhéanach.

The conversation turned to less grim topics, and they ate and talked until it was late, the other patrons leaving. The troubadour on the stage began packing his lute away. Erich used the moment to inform the group of his efforts.

"As we were all here, except Robin, I submitted a request for an audience with the king. He has agreed to meet us tomorrow afternoon." Then he turned back to the table and sat. The conversation turned to meeting the king and to the tribute they had brought to honor him.

The prince got up and turned to Erich. "Lord Erich, I have a message and a gift for the king and queen as well. I planned to request an audience tomorrow, but if you would allow me to join you in your audience, I would be in your debt."

"Of course, Your Highness. I believe he has set aside the entire afternoon for the Party of the Seven. We would consider it an honor to share our time with you."

The prince stood, announcing, "I fear I must take my leave of you. I regret the brevity of my visit, but I must go to slumber early if I am to witness this Alliandre Del Nileppez fight a banner of paladins at sunrise."

"Speaking of paladins, it looks like the Order of the Wren has shown up." Erich pointed at the group of knights who had just walked in. Most of them seemed to have already had their fill of food and drink, but they went to the long table near the bar they were fond of and raised a cheer for the Aerie. Marion soon came out to take their orders. As she walked up, they settled down, politely asking her for ale or wine. Even Sir Roger made no argument as he ordered just a beer with his last dolcot.

"What has gotten into them, I wonder?" Lolark asked rhetorically.

Once they received their drinks, the paladins began a slow song about the Battle of the Blue Lake Bridge. It was a well-known song, prominently featuring the Order of the Wren. Deservedly so, as a single spear held the bridge for nine days against four or five times that number of Black Aelf during the long-ago war between the aelf and men. While they held the bridge, Drake Del Nileppez marched his knights two hundred hursmarc and reinforced the position just as the last banner of The Wren prepared to die, the aelf delivering one last charge. The aelf were so discouraged at the reinforcements, they retreated across the bridge. Less than thirty paladins survived, all of them suffering serious wounds. It was the beginning of the end for the aelf. The humans would march slowly and inexorably toward the Great Forest after that day. To this day, the reference to a "Wren on a Bridge" referred to anytime warriors stood prepared to defend to the last man or someone was in a hopeless position.

"Sir Andras!" a raised voice called above the din. Alliandre was on his feet in a split second, recognizing the voice calling out. Across the hall, Marion was in the grasp of a brawny-looking man in fine clothes with a small dagger hanging from his belt. His bright red shirt matched Drullock's armor in color, with yellow ruffles decorating the collar. His arms poked through the middle of his bright orange coat, the coat sleeves dangling from his elbows. Tucked into high yellow leather boots were red pants, matching the shirt.

He was struggling to give Marion a kiss with one arm around her back, the other firmly grabbing her shapely rear. Sivle saw Drullock's eyes flash. In a moment, he was in motion. He reached over to grab Drullock, barely catching his sword belt, then holding on for dear life. Erich and Lolark, recognizing the danger as well, struggled to rise to interpose themselves. "Let Sir Andras handle it," Sivle commanded him.

Sir Andras was behind the bar. He grabbed his cudgel, but he was too late. Before he even got around the bar, the table of paladins rose and moved into formation, surrounding the two as they struggled. Marion had her left arm lodged against the man's throat, preventing him from getting too close. He was not as tall as Alliandre, but much more heavily muscled than Marion. Slowly, he was forcing her head toward his. He moved his hand from her bottom and grabbed the back of her head. She raised her knee to his groin, but he skillfully pivoted his hips, taking the blow on his thigh.

The paladins, at their commander's shout of "Ready arms!" drew their swords. This got the man's attention. He turned Marion around and held her to him, his left hand wrapped around her torso, firmly grabbing her right breast as his right hand reached toward his dagger. Several swords appeared at the man's throat, kidneys, liver, and back. Tips pressing just hard enough to cause the man to freeze, slowly he removed his hands, first from the dagger, then from Marion. The situation ended, Marion turned and punched the man, staggering him.

Then she turned to Sir Andras as he arrived. "He was just drunk. He meant nothing by it."

The commander of the paladins grabbed the ruffian. "He assaulted a princess of the realm! The punishment is death!"

Several "Ayes" sounded from the other paladins.

"Here at the Aerie, we follow the laws of King Henry the Great," Sir Andras said as he struck the man once with his cudgel, knocking him senseless. Sir Andras grabbed the unconscious man from the commander and dragged him outside. Everyone heard the bell outside ring, alerting the town guard there was a problem at the tavern. Sir Andras returned several minutes later, giving a nod to the paladins. "Thank you, laddies. I'll be buyin' the next round of drinks for ye."

A loud cheer went up among the paladins. They quickly finished their drinks before calling out for more. Meanwhile, with the excitement over, Drullock went over to Marion, then escorted her back to the kitchen.

As the night wore on, several patrons got up and left, until it was only the Party of the Seven and the paladins in the bar. Sivle and Drullock excused themselves after Drullock returned, eyes dark and angry. Fairwind and Braxlo spoke, deep in conversation, with Erich occasionally interjecting. Ariandel was in heaven, with Lolark explaining in great detail the vagaries of dueling.

Erich, who had finished the wine while everyone else was engaged in their conversations, tapped the table with a mug. "It is time for bed, ladies and gentlemen, but before we go, I would like to propose a toast. To the Party of the Seven. May neither distance nor pride ever separate us."

"To the Party of the Seven!" everyone repeated as they raised their glasses.

"Thank you, Erich," Lolark nodded as he spoke. Then he turned to Ariandel. "My Lady, it has been a pleasure. I am sorry if I have bored you with my explanation of our craft. But if I have to watch Alliandre pummel on my paladins in the morning, I want to be rested. I hope you do not mind if I excuse myself." Then, looking at Braxlo, "I hold you responsible for any injuries they sustain tomorrow."

Ariandel asked to no one in particular, "But as I understand it, isn't he fighting an entire banner at once? Surely, he is the one who should worry about an injury."

"No, my lady," Lolark said sadly. "Half of the banner are sword masters. The rest are fine swordsmen and women, but Alliandre is far better. He and I dueled last year, and even since then he has improved significantly. He is undoubtedly better than any of my order, much less the banner Braxlo has condemned. They are newly raised, lacking experience fighting together. It will surprise me if they win even two bouts out of ten."

"A hundred turots says they do not win a single bout," Braxlo challenged.

"I will take that bet," said Erich. "Even Drullock cannot go against twenty without losing one bout."

"Done. Thank you for the money, my friend. The paladins do not stand a chance. Particularly when I convince him the honor of our lovely Marion is at stake." Braxlo smiled at Erich, turning to Lolark. "How about you, my honorable friend? Going to bet against your paladins and dishonor your order?"

"Not at all. It is a penance; one which I hope they learn a fine lesson from. There is nothing I would like more than to see the new commander learn a bit of humility. I only hope Alliandre does not injure any of them."

Ariandel spoke up. "You all make this Alliandre sound as if he is some sort of supernatural swordsman. I think I shall get up early as well, if it is acceptable to you, Fairwind. I should like to meet this Alliandre."

Everyone looked at each other with a confused look, then slowly all of them began laughing.

IV

⚜

News for The King

27th of Frendalo, Year 1124 AGW

The morning began early for Alliandre. Sivle woke him and Braxlo well before dawn, the three of them going down for first-meal. Sivle dressed in his priest's garb. The same garb as the night before, however, it appeared newly cleaned.

Alliandre and Braxlo wore high boots, long pants, and a loose shirt. Each also carried a large pack with their cuir bouilli armor and dueling helms. Braxlo's coat was black, of course. As a Knight Errant, he could choose any of the colors of the natural dragons, and each stood for his chosen profession. White for knights who still served their order. Red for those who went into military service for one of the kingdoms. Gold for nobility, blue for court, green for civilian life, whether it be as a merchant or farmer or some other trade, and black, for sell-swords. Most knights who became adventurers chose the black or green.

Alliandre hoped to finish firstmeal early to get down to register for the Open Melee Tournament. As he was not a knight, he would have to place in the top tier of the Open Melee before he could sign up for the Grand Melee. He didn't think he would have any problem there. Most of the entrants were town guards or soldiers hoping to impress an order enough to sponsor them as a squire. Winning the Open Melee was not likely, but if they made it to the last few rounds, they might get a sponsor.

It was expensive to become a squire. The squires, or their sponsors, provided their own armor, weapons, horses, barding and suitable attire to wear if invited to the order. Hence why the sponsoring of a squire was a portentous event. This is also why the palladium orders were so much larger. They provided everything, but most of what the paladins earned they turned over to the order. When a paladin left, they took nothing with them but their arms and armor and any money they had saved.

The three friends walked down to the dining hall, deserted except for two cleaning women, Jean Marie and Diana. They could hear John banging pots in the kitchen. Sivle greeted the two women cleaning the stone floor and said a few words, waving his hand. At once, a circle of light appeared on the surrounding floor. He pointed his hands, fingers extended at the center of the circle, then slowly raised his hands. As he did so, the circle expanded outward, eventually moving up the walls and onto the ceiling, cleaning and polishing the stones. It even brightened and polished the wooden beams. As it passed over the tables and chairs, moved to the side for cleaning, it had the same effect, cleaning and polishing the stained wood until they looked brand new.

The ladies looked in awe, bowing to Sivle. They picked up their mops and brushes and buckets, taking them back to the kitchens. Braxlo and Alliandre grabbed one of the large tables to move it to its place on the floor. Then they began moving the rest of the tables as well. Sivle began moving the chairs. The cleaning women came out to help Sivle with the chairs and soon they had set up the hall, looking as good as when it was first built. The women bowed down to him, the older addressing him. "Thank you, Lord Sivle. It is always nice having such a great lord stay with us. Please let us know if you would like anything."

"Just some food, Diana, as soon as John can get something ready. Dueler's firstmeal for those two, but I am fasting this morning."

"I'll be taking a full firstmeal," corrected Braxlo. "I am not dueling, so I will not be missing your bacon."

Alliandre thought about the bacon as well, then figured he could have his morning meal after he finished beating on paladins. He didn't know why, but the thought made the corners of his lips twitch upward. He pointed at the big throne they used for Lolark, then he and Braxlo moved it into its position, facing the fire. He thought about warning the cook about all the paladins arriving soon, then figured Lolark would handle any issues the Aerie encountered with his order.

Two minutes later, he had fruit and cornbread laid out before him. Diana brought a mug of morning beer along with it. "John just pulled this cornbread out of the oven for you, Master Alliandre."

"Thank you, Diana. We appreciate the good care you take of us in the morning." Alliandre laid a turot on the table for her and smiled as she refused.

"Oh no, milord. The queen would not be happy with us taking coin from you."

"The queen takes coin from us, and we will not be taking advantage of our friendship. Please take this and we will say nothing to the queen."

Alliandre and the morning ladies performed this ritual every day. It went the same with Sivle as well, although most days Sivle did not come down until mid-morning. By the time he had finished his prayers and memorized any spells he thought he would need, he often missed the morning meal entirely. Today, before he left to see the king and queen, Sivle needed to receive a high priest's blessing. The high priest in Foresight would not see him, so he planned to visit the temple at the Great Chasm. It would cost a scroll, but he could rewrite it tonight or on the morrow. Besides, perhaps he could catch two fish with one hook.

***

Alliandre finished his meal about the time Braxlo received his. He sat quietly, contemplating the upcoming duel. Fighting twenty-one men at the same time wasn't easy. However, only half a dozen could approach at once, so he was confident he could handle them, particularly if they sent their best fighters first. Hopefully, they were inexperienced, and would approach him with a shield wall. A problem would arise if they decided on mixed weapons, using two lines with pole arms or spears in the second line. Then he would have to break the lines and constantly flank them, continually watching his back.

He understood Braxlo had offered this penance for their interpretation of the Palladium Contract, although he was unsure why. Sir Andras always made it quite clear where the Wyvern's Aerie stood. Unless one of them had attempted to manhandle Sir Andras, but then why was Sir Andras not pounding them into Tristian Mutton? He raised the question while Braxlo was putting a thick strip of bacon in his mouth.

"By the way, Sir Braxlo, how is it Sir Andras is not fighting this banner of paladins? Surely you do not think he is up to the task?"

"My good friend," Braxlo said between bites, "Sir Andras had not yet arrived, forcing me to intervene."

"Then why are you not fighting the paladins?"

"Because the banner commander was dressing down the lovely Princess Marion. Being quite offended, I, of course, immediately interjected myself. After moments of consideration, I thought you would prefer to mete out their penance."

"Dressing down Marion? In what way?" Alliandre knew he was being maneuvered, but the thought of someone raising their voice to Marion enraged him.

Braxlo coyly continued. "Now, my memory is not perfect, but I seem to recall him wagging a finger at her, maybe even tapping it against her lovely chest."

"Braxlo, will you help me with my armor, please?" Alliandre rose from the table, grabbing his pack as a scuffle seemed to come from the door.

"Wait yer turn ya shite bastards. There's plenty of time before yer beatin', and ye better be polite to yer betters if ye dinnae want one before Alliandre gets ahold of ye." The kerfuffle settled itself shortly. A banner of Silver Cross paladins came through the door, led by Sir Andras escorting Marion and Arielle. Prince Valian, following the paladins in, came over to sit with Braxlo and Sivle. Lolark arrived soon after the Silver Cross paladins.

As the sun began coloring the clouds in the east, Alliandre went outside with Braxlo. The Silver Cross paladins followed him out. Fairwind, Ariandel, and Prince Valian joined them soon after.

The dueling grounds were not a fancy affair. A wooden fence in a rectangle twenty paces from center to the short side, sixty to the long side. On the near end, a raised circular field thirty paces across, cleared of grass and covered with small pebbles. Duels and training took place here, with benches just outside the fence for onlookers. Outside the circle were boxes framed with timbers for the combatant's spare shields and weapons, and for the second to stand. They replaced any shields or weapons damaged during the bouts.

There were ten bouts to most duels. Both contestants wore steel helms and breastplates, with cuir bouilli armor over the rest of their bodies. The dueling swords, dulled and blunted, were heavier than a normal sword to prevent excessive injury. Still, injuries occurred during duels, even between equally matched combatants. For this reason, tradition demanded a chirurgeon be present. With paladins taking part, this was unnecessary, the paladins being able to treat most injuries. Sivle came out, addressing Alliandre. "Alliandre, I hope you will forgive me, but I have pressing business I must attend."

"Go, my friend," Alliandre responded. "I will not need your services, and there will not be much entertainment in this bout today."

The commander of the Silver Cross paladins stepped up to the square, announcing his challenge. "I, Commander Sir Anthony the Rash, challenge Alliandre Del Nileppez Drol Hulloc to a duel against the fourth banner of the twenty-second spear of the Order of the Silver Cross." Alliandre announced his acceptance of the duel. The commander turned to Braxlo, asking, "Sir Braxlo the Brave, do you accept we have met the terms of your penance?"

Sir Braxlo came forward. "I affirm you have met the terms of my penance. You have upheld the honor of the Silver Cross. I shall marschall the duel and appoint Sir Lolark as the second for your banner."

"What!? He's the brilliant swordsman, Alliandre? But his name is Drullock. I thought you said he was a barbarian!" Everyone turned at Ariandel's outburst. She looked around, quite embarrassed with everyone was looking at her, many of them smiling or laughing out loud. Alliandre glared at her, then at Braxlo.

"I swear, I never said you were a barbarian," Braxlo assured him, his hands up in mock surrender. The smile on his face belied his apology, though.

Embarrassed, Ariandel turned to leave. Fairwind caught her arm and stepped in front of her. "You will not want to miss this. You will get to see Drullock defend the honor of his princess. Besides, it wouldn't hurt you to get to know Prince Valian better."

Ariandel protested, then, seeing Lolark standing there, relented. "I guess I can wait and see how he does against Sir Lolark's paladins."

Lolark bowed and moved to the square where the knights had laid down their gear. Braxlo allowed the knights to line up, turning to Alliandre. "Since the barbarian Drullock, I mean Alliandre, is at a disadvantage, he shall choose the armaments for the duel."

Alliandre stared daggers through Braxlo, but then simply called out, "Dueler's choice." He did not want the paladins to have any excuses for the beating he was planning for them.

"Very well," Braxlo continued, "Combatants, draw your weapons and meet at the edge of the field."

"Shield wall," Sir Anthony called out. The twenty men and women in his banner grabbed their swords and shields, moving quickly to line up on the field to his left. Alliandre stepped back to his position.

"Beeeeeeegin!" Braxlo yelled dramatically as he waved his sword in circles in the air before dropping it.

In two ranks, the paladins pushed forward in unison. Sir Anthony was confident they would win if they were disciplined. They had crossed to the center of the circle when Alliandre charged.

"Brace!" Sir Anthony called out. The line of paladins planted their feet and prepared for the impact. Alliandre picked his target well. Alliandre hit dead center, sweeping the sword thrusts from the few paladins he was within reach of, before driving his shoulder squarely in the center shield. It knocked the young woman back, out of position. Alliandre opened a hole in the line with three quick slashes and a thrust. He performed a crossover, getting behind the left side of the line. He side-stepped down the rear of the formation, taking out a half dozen of the paladins as they attempted to turn to face him. He dueled the two rear paladins on the end, constantly circling away from the rest of the banner. Sir Anthony called out orders organizing his banner, but they were down to ten men, Alliandre still pecking at the edge.

Two more went down. With eight men left, the shield wall was pointless now. Sir Anthony gave the command, "Encircle". His paladins smoothly moved out to surround Alliandre, but not before he took another out of the bout. They fought for a minute longer, Alliandre whirling, pivoting, and lunging until only Sir Anthony remained. Sir Anthony had been a sword master for years now. He had dueled with some of the best paladins in the order. But Alliandre moved incredibly fast, running through combinations and strokes faster than he could recognize and react. He tried a viper strike. Alliandre swept aside his sword. Then, with a three-strike combination, drove down the shield before sending a crashing blow straight to the shoulder of the commander.

"Hold!" Braxlo called out. Alliandre stopped the blow heading toward the paladin's head.

Sir Anthony got up slowly, favoring his left shoulder. The sword had created a gash in the cuir bouilli, despite the dulled blade, leaving the shoulder sitting at a strange angle. Alliandre had seen enough combat to know the collarbone was likely broken, if not smashed. Braxlo helped Sir Anthony over to his box. Lolark helped set the bone, then laid his hand over the shoulder, murmuring a few words. Sir Anthony smiled his thanks.

No sooner than he had stood, Sir Anthony gave the command to his paladins. "Shield wall, spears."

Each man and woman went to their packs and pulled out a spear before racing back to the line. Braxlo repeated his command, "Combatants, draw your weapons and meet at the edge of the field." Then, after the men got into formation, "Begin!"

The second bout went much like the first. The spears gave more range than the sword, but once he was behind them, they made it more difficult to turn. Sir Anthony gave the command to surround Alliandre much sooner, leaving a full dozen to surround him. Alliandre was humming a children's song as he broke their spears, methodically taking out one paladin after another, again leaving Sir Anthony to the last. This time, Sir Anthony got his shield on his sword a bit, the blow only denting his helm a little. He bowed his head, acknowledging the hit, the warriors returning to their positions.

Staggered shield, half moon, boar's tooth, vreen hoof. Sir Anthony tried every formation he could think of, but Alliandre seemed to have mastered a counter to all of them. Twice more, Lolark had to lay hands on Sir Anthony, once on one of the other paladins. For the last bout, Sir Anthony changed to a modified wave attack with mixed weapons. For a moment, they pressed Alliandre back. But by now, Alliandre had identified the weaker members of the banner, maneuvering them to force the more skilled swordsmen to expose themselves in order to protect them. One by one, he took them down until he faced Sir Anthony alone once more. Then, for the first time during the duel, he spoke.

"Sir Anthony, I am Alliandre Del Nileppez Drol Hulloc. I defend the honor of the Southern Kingdom." He performed a thunder hammer, risky but effective if landed, splitting Sir Anthony's shield with his right sword. Sir Anthony dropped the worthless weight, changing to a two-handed grasp of his sword.

"I will tolerate no disrespect of the kingdom or its rulers." A spin and double blow to the sword moved it out of position. Following immediately with a thunder strike from the right sword, he struck Sir Anthony's left arm. Painfully, the paladin moved it behind his back, attempting to defend himself with just the one hand holding the sword.

"And I will kill any who would presume to lay hands on any member of the royal family. Especially Her Highness." He punctuated the last statement with a quarter spin to his right, pinning Sir Anthony's sword with his left sword, followed by a half spin to the left where, using all his strength and momentum, he delivered a crushing blow straight to the side of the helm. Despite the dulled edge, the force of the blow crumpled the steel helm, driving the metal through the padding into the jaw of Sir Anthony. He crumpled like a rag doll, blood flowing from underneath his helm. Alliandre returned to his square while the paladins gathered around Sir Anthony's motionless body. Removing the helm gingerly, several paladins placed their hands on Sir Anthony. Eventually, he stirred, remaining unconscious. The bruised and disfigured jawbone indicating his injury was far more serious than their ability to treat. Lolark walked over to Alliandre, a scowl on his face.

"Was that necessary? He was newly raised and already knew he had slept with the grendlaar."

"Yes. It was. I am just a barbarian, after all."

"Is that what this was all about? One comment from some aelf maiden who you don't even know makes you ready to kill a man?"

"I meant it when I said I will kill anyone who lays hands on them." Looking straight into Lolark's eyes, "Anyone." Reaching into his pack, he drew one of his scabbards and turned back, walking purposefully toward Sir Anthony. Lolark, seeing what he was doing, reached over to grab him. Alliandre expected it. A quick hip throw sent Lolark crashing to the ground. Alliandre walked over to the group, forcing his way to Sir Anthony. Unsheathing the sword, he placed its tip against Sir Anthony's throat.

The paladins rushed to get their swords as Alliandre spoke just the command word, "Shlàinte".

The sword glowed. A moment later, Sir Anthony's eyes fluttered, the bruised side of his face returning almost to normal. He looked up at Alliandre, who extended his arm. He clasped wrists with Alliandre, allowing Alliandre to pull him to his feet. "Well fought, Sir Anthony.

But, be fairly warned, next time you so much as look crossly at Her Highness, we will not be dueling in cuir bouilli."

Alliandre turned to Braxlo, giving him a small bow before returning to Lolark. "The barbarian comment was kind of funny, actually. She spent two days with us and didn't know my real name." He chuckled as they walked back into the tavern.

Lolark put a massive arm around Alliandre's shoulders, pulling him in. "We shall make sure she knows it now, my friend. We will make sure everyone knows it."

***

Sivle went back up to the room, gathered some items together, and meditated for a few minutes, clearing his mind. He took out a scroll, reading the stamins on it until a portal appeared. He stepped through, vanishing from his room.

He appeared immediately after in a small hallway. Hooks sprang from the wall, a single white robe hanging on them. He pulled the robe from the hook, taking it into a changing room. After changing, he went down the hall to the cleansing chamber. Bowing as he entered the chamber, he began his chants as he moved to the wood and metal tree in the center. Similar to the one at the temple in Foresight, albeit less than half the size, it served the same purpose. Kneeling before it and reaching out with his symbol, the familiar tingle began. Cleansed the day before had its benefit; the discomfort was short-lived. Sivle continued his chants, holding his holy symbol firmly against the silver tree until the cleansing was complete. Removing the holy symbol from the tree and setting it on the stand, he removed the robe, folded it, and set it on the floor, kneeling beside it. An acolyte appeared, or possibly a priest apprentice given his age, to help him cleanse himself.

The acolyte brought him a new robe. Bowing his head, he picked up the soiled robe while Sivle returned to the changing room. After changing, he walked to the office of the high priest. A young priest was sitting at a table, and Sivle announced himself.

"I am Sivle Si Evila Drol Revo. I am here to speak to the high priest, report on my activities, and receive their blessing."

"Welcome, priest. The high priest is aware of your presence. He is preparing the ceremony as we speak. Would you care for some water?" The young priest held a carafe and a glass out to Sivle.

"No, thank you. I appreciate his haste in preparing, but I have prepared myself for a fast after the cleansing."

The priest bowed, leaving the carafe and glass on a small table. He left through a small archway, returning shortly after. "The high priest will see you now."

Sivle followed him to a small temple lined completely in boards of different patterned wood. One board for each type of tree in the Great Forest, including one of the Great Tree itself. It was the same in each temple. In the center, a stand held a fallen twig from the Great Tree in stasis within a spirit jar. Next to the stand, an old aelf stood. His hair more silver than the holy symbol around his neck, his skin was almost translucent. Still, he stood with the grace and dignity of a king. His robes were the typical brown, with green sleeves and a sky-blue stole. On his head, however, a small golden cap designated him as the high priest. Hanging from his neck was a large silver pendant with the image of the Great Tree orbited by the ten Forest Spirits.

Prostrating himself before the high priest, Sivle and the priest began chanting. The holy symbol around the high priest's neck glowed as he laid his hand upon Sivle's bowed head. Light moved from the pendant to his arm into Sivle, causing a halo to surround them both. As the halo of light faded, the priest spoke.

"Arise, Sivle Si Evila Drol Revo. You have received my blessing. Go forth to serve the Forest Spirits, protect the Great Tree, and serve all the beings in the land."

"As the Great Tree shades all around it, so shall I strive to protect all who are within my reach."

The two began another chant. When they completed it, the high priest left, retreating to a small shrine in the northernmost wall. Sivle rose to his feet, following him there.

"Most blessed priest, thank you for your blessing. Alas, I have one more task, which is to submit my tithing to the temple."

"This is not your temple, priest. Submit your tithe to your own temple as required."

"I submitted myself to the high priest at my temple. Because of circumstances beyond her control, she cannot see me for several days. This delay will put me past my tithing day. Therefore, I request this temple receive my tithe so I may avoid penance."

"I see," said the incredibly old aelf. "This would have nothing to do with any personal differences you have with the high priest there?"

"No," Sivle said, almost truthfully. "She asked I return several days hence. I have only until tomorrow to pay my tithe. As the law requires, I have gone to the next closest shrine to receive my blessing and pay my tithe."

"As the law is written, so it must be upheld. I accept your tithe."

Sivle opened his purse, pouring the hundred havnots into the tithing tray in the shrine. The high priest's eyes grew wide as he saw the maximum tithe deposited at his small temple. Bowing to Sivle, he spoke. "May the spirits continue to smile on your path, priest, and may your faith in them bring you good fortune."

"May the spirits smile on this temple, providing for the needs of its priests," Sivle replied with the response he learned as a child. Bowing again, he left the temple.

Once outside, he walked along a small path until he reached the edge of the Great Chasm.

***

Ariandel was pouting a bit as she followed Fairwind back into the tavern. Prince Valian had spoken to her several times, making small talk during the duels. But she had embarrassed herself again with her lack of knowledge of the fighting. She could not follow all the moves as he explained the differing formations and techniques being applied, nor the benefits of each weapon. She was sure she had offended him when she mentioned how she had always preferred the mastery of the mind required for use of the spirits over the mastery of the body required for swordplay. It was then Fairwind reminded her Prince Valian was the Lord Protector of the Great King, and one of the greatest swordsmen alive. Lord Erich spoke up to soften her embarrassment, noting the more physically fit a priest or mage was, the better they could channel the spirits. Similarly, only through the study of the techniques and forms could a swordsman truly become a master.

Apparently, the oaf was a master. Even the prince seemed impressed with his knack for picking apart the banner of paladins, avoiding their coordinated thrusts and strokes while carefully maneuvering them into positions where he could pick off one by one. "He often targets the most skilled among them first, always saving the commander for last before going after him with a reckless fury. It exposes his weakness," he told her.

"Which weakness is that, Your Highness?" Erich asked. "He seems to display no weakness I can discern."

"Hubris, my lord," the prince explained. "He goes to great lengths to hit the females straight down on the head, certainly much lighter than he hits the men. Also, he passes several opportunities to take out the commander early, choosing instead to keep him for last, when he then believes he can inflict great pain on him. Clearly, he assumes he is talented enough to defeat them despite handicapping himself in this way."

"I would call it confidence, Your Highness," Erich continued, "and chivalry where the ladies are concerned. With Alliandre, chivalry is not uncommon. And with all due respect to your skill and knowledge, his assumption appears to be correct."

"That it is. Today. But he would benefit from someone who would defeat him to give him some doubt in his abilities."

"Perhaps you would do us all the favor of bringing some humility to him, then. We would all appreciate it, believe me," Erich added, several around him grinning in agreement.

"I have not dueled in ages. If I am to be honest, I am not sure I could defeat him in such a manner. His size and strength give him a distinct advantage in the dueling circle. He seems to have trained specifically to win in this environment, while I have trained to defeat opponents who do not wield dulled weapons."

Erich laughed. "It sounds like you are conceding defeat, then. Perhaps we can arrange a blood duel if that is more to your liking."

This brought a smile to the prince's lips as well. "You are correct, Lord Erich. I could not defeat him in the circle. I may not fare as well as the paladins. But in a blood duel, I believe he would find me a much more dangerous opponent. Perhaps I could even teach him the lesson I believe he needs? But unlike him, I possess the humility to acknowledge even there I may fail. I am not sure we have seen him at his best."

They went back to commenting on the duels, Braxlo and Erich yelling taunts or encouragement to Lolark, who sent the same disgusted look to both of them. Ariandel thought she might at least give her condolences to Lolark when the duel was over, but Lolark didn't seem the least bit bothered. Even after Drullock flung him to the ground before holding a sword to his banner commander's throat in a cowardly act. Made worse as he had already knocked the man senseless. But Lolark and the lout left the circle together, smiling and talking.

The duel over, Fairwind grabbed her arm and whispered, "We will eat, but then it is time to begin your studies." With a little wink, "Have you learned to combine fire and earth yet?"

The duel was all but forgotten, and she didn't even taste her first-meal. Earth and fire. She had wanted to learn it with her last instructor, but he insisted she not try anything so advanced until she was ready. Truthfully, she suspected he was not capable of combining them himself. She finished eating before changing to her simple woolen robes, noting Fairwind did the same. Although, Fairwind's woolen robes were much more elaborate and well-made than hers. They also appeared to have several hidden pockets in them, as she pulled spell components seemingly out of thin air.

They spent the rest of the morning practicing the stamins combining fire with earth. "You must crawl before you walk," Fairwind had told her. After she could make a small pile of dirt burn, they moved to gravel and larger clumps of dirt. She found this combination difficult, even more so than fire and water. A bit of air spirit added to the mix would make water burn, but the mix of earth and fire had to be quite exact. Depending on the type of dirt, the mix was different entirely. You had to weave the spirits together in a certain way, and tightly, to hold them together so the earth did not burn out right away. Ariandel had scorched both of them badly when her thrown pebble exploded just a few steps from her. Fairwind could throw hers a score of paces, even skipping it across the ground, before exploding. They kept working on different drills with the size and composition of the earth until she could send a blacknut-sized clump almost thirty paces before it exploded. Fairwind declared the training for the day over, and they went in for lunch.

Ariandel was ravenous after several straight hours of casting, and she finished three plates of mutton and sausage and bread and cheese, almost before Fairwind had finished her first plate. She noticed their empty pitcher of wine, but she couldn't remember Fairwind drinking any. Her hunger now sated, she thought about her lessons.

"Your Highness," she began.

"Just Fairwind, please." Ariandel blushed a little at the reminder but continued.

"Fairwind. If we added aether spirit to the earth, wouldn't it hold the blast, allowing us to send it much further? Similar to the way we combine aether spirit and fire spirit to make our fire blasts."

Fairwind leaned in. "I commend your thought process, but it is not a simple thing to do. You must master this step before you add another. Many mages have died or become seriously injured combining aether, fire, and other spirits. Aether and fire combine well, as do aether and other spirits alone. But aether is a jealous spirit. It does not like to share with too many other spirits." Fairwind leaned back, smiling, then confessed, "Which is a fancy way of saying I have not yet mastered it, so I cannot teach it to you. Lord Sivle could, though, as he has mastered techniques to coax all the spirits to his will. But for your safety, I suggest you master earth and fire before you attempt to add aether."

Fairwind smiled again, lifting the wine pitcher teasingly before commenting, "It appears we are out of wine." She raised her hand for the serving girl. "We have time for another pitcher, then I have to get prepared for our audience with the king and queen. You can spend the afternoon contemplating your lessons, or whatever you like to spend your time doing."

"Writing scrolls, Your, I mean Fairwind. I was hoping to write enough to pay for my training." Then, upon looking at her scorched clothing, "And a new robe now."

"Fret not, my dear. I will train you as Lord Sivle has trained me. I will charge you only for the components we use and the damages you cause. So far you only owe me for some stones and dirt, some spark stone, and, of course, a new robe. But you can pay me afterward."

"Thank you, my lady. I shall endeavor to be your best student."

"That will be easy, my dear, as you are my first."

After the wine arrived, they chatted about other things until Fairwind finished her glass and left Ariandel alone to finish the rest. Ariandel considered the training, running through the stamins they had used. She thought the tightness of the weaving was where she had the most difficulty and was trying to think of ways to improve. She had finished the wine when Marion interrupted her thoughts.

"May I get you some pastries, my lady?"

"I'm sorry, I am not a lady, Your Highness."

"Just Marion, dear. Remember our conversation? And you are Cara Ríoga, are you not?"

Ariandel nodded.

"Which makes you a lady, does it not?" Marion said, giving her a little bow.

"Oh dear, I guess you are right. Well then, Marion, since we are not using titles, you may just call me Ariandel."

"Very well, Ariandel. Would you like some pastries?" Marion smiled sweetly, then turned her head as Fairwind and the others came down. "One moment, please."

Marion went over to the bully and gave him a low bow, then jumped up to hug him around the neck, planting a kiss on his cheek. "My hero!" she said with an exaggerated swoon. "Erich told me how you defended my honor. Sir Anthony even came back afterward and apologized again."

Hopping down from his arms, she continued, "He gave me a purse full of malnots for the paladins' meals, then asked I serve him stew and tea as penance to me for his disrespect. I told him he had fulfilled his penance, but he was insistent on it."

"Well then, perhaps venting my anger on him did some good." Alliandre grew serious as he changed the subject. "When we return from court for dinner, perhaps you could join us?" Alliandre bowed, blushing a little at the request, but Marion only gave him another kiss on the cheek. "If we are not too busy, I would spend the entire evening with you. Don't count on it, though. Jubilee is tomorrow, so we will be full, but wait just a moment."

Marion ran to the kitchen, returning with a tray of pastries. She brought them over to Erich, Fairwind, Lolark, and Alliandre. With a final wink at Alliandre, she turned to bring them over to Ariandel.

"Here you go, please have as many as you would like." Marion held the tray in front of Ariandel, still looking at Alliandre.

"May I ask you something personal, Marion?" Ariandel asked as she selected a pastry with spring berries in the center.

"Well, it depends on what it is?" Marion dropped her gaze, moving around to the corner of the table.

Ariandel blushed. She did not want to offend another royal, but she continued, "It is about Drullock," she said directly.

Marion continued around the table, standing across from Ariandel. "He doesn't like to be called that. Sivle never should have shared that with them."

"But I just don't understand what you see in him." Ariandel had said it more bluntly than she had intended, but it was out.

Marion stared at her for a few seconds, then sat down. "OK, first, tell me what you dislike about him so much."

"Dislike about him?" Ariandel was incredulous. "Where do I start? He is arrogant, rude, uncharitable, and a bully. He pulled a blade on a paladin even after he had knocked the man senseless. He abandons helpless, wounded travelers and even when he helps, leaves you even worse off than you were." She planned on continuing, but Marion's frown had turned into a small grin. "What are you smiling about?" Ariandel asked sharply. "Do you approve of the way your apparent courtier, Drullock, treats people?"

"First of all," Marion said somewhat crossly, "his name is Alliandre Del Nileppez Drol Hulloc. I could never say Alliandre when we were young. All I could do was mumble and finish with Drullock. Sivle picked it up because he thought it was funny. By the time I could speak, everyone called him Drullock. Since we left Vista, he hates it when others call him that. He may treat you better if you referred to him by his actual name."

Ariandel protested. "I actually just learned his name was Alliandre today, so that is NOT my fault."

"Never matter," Marion interrupted. "That apple is off the tree." Then she leaned forward, her tone softening. "Ever since I can remember, though, he has protected everyone smaller than him. When some of the older kids at court would pick on the younger kids, he was there to make them stop. When Sir Andras began him with the sword, which was at seven, I am told, he was dueling with the squires within a year. He became a squire himself at nine, the youngest ever in the Southern Kingdom by several years. At eleven, he was training the new squires and even some of the younger knights, being bigger than most of them. In all that time, he never picked on the younger or smaller squires, and he always found time to play with me and the younger kids, despite this often forcing him to stay up late to finish his chores and duties."

Sitting back, she continued, "Then the Golden Aelf attacked. I was almost seven, and he was twelve. They sent the squires to gather the women and younger children to get them to safety. Sir Andras came for my mother, my brother Nathan, and me after the main gate fell. Alliandre came back after getting the others through the tunnel to make sure I was safe. Then aelf pursued us. We fought them at our backs the entire way. Sir Andras was magnificent, but they wounded his arm in the fighting, forcing him to fight with one sword. Alliandre dropped his shield to pick up Sir Andras' dropped sword, fighting side by side with him the entire way through the tunnel. When we got out, the other squires and the wounded knights stepped up to defend the queen, but there were only three aelf left. They quickly captured the aelf and brought them with us to the Central Kingdom."

Her eyes filled with tears from the remembered pain, but she bowed her head a little and finished her story. "I was terrified, but Alliandre stood watch outside my tent every night. He was still there, standing guard every morning as we hid from the aelf. After three days, King Henry's soldiers found us, escorting us to Foresight. They gave my mother, along with Sir Andras, Nathan, and me, refuge here in Foresight. Sivle, who had been a priest in the temple in Vista, transferred to the temple here, while Alliandre went to the Freehold of Dragonsbane to become a knight. After five years of being a squire, they turned him down a third time and dismissed him from the order. Sir Andras himself sponsored him, and it incensed him. It was because of his 'character' was all they would say," she continued.

"And here we are today. So, you ask me what I see in him? I see a boy who ran back into a castle he knew was overrun to help us escape. I see a boy who stood awake for three straight days, so a little girl wouldn't feel frightened. I see a man who will do whatever it takes to keep his promises, and I see a man who has always stopped to help those truly in need. Despite all this, he was told by the knights he used to worship, the knights of an order his many-great grandfather led, he was unfit to be one of them. Still, he does nothing but try to act with honor."

Marion lifted her head and looked Ariandel straight in the eye. "So, regarding the things you dislike. Is he arrogant? He is quite modest, actually, when you consider how good he is. You say he is rude. I say he is just direct. You can blame that on Dragonsbane. But he has never been uncharitable, or a bully. He used his sword to heal Sir Anthony, his wounds being beyond what the paladins could heal, and I have never heard of him abandoning anyone, especially the wounded or helpless."

"He abandoned me," Ariandel defiantly spoke up.

"Yes." Marion smiled. "I heard your story. Highwaymen attacked you while you traveled near the Great Chasm. They wounded you, along with your horse. You had no healing, and he stopped. He made sure you were OK, giving you a jar of Sivle's ointment. This treated your most serious wounds, along with your horse's, yes? Doesn't sound like he abandoned you to me."

Ariandel sputtered a bit. "You make it seem like he was a knight in shining armor. He wasn't. He was rude and obnoxious and obviously looking down on me because I had the temerity to be wounded."

Marion cut her off. "He should not have stopped at all. He had a job to do, which was ride to Foresight to make sure there were no problems when the rest of the party arrived at the gate. He was to alert the guards and the king they were all coming. Then he had to secure lodging and stable for the horses, especially the enormous monster he rides. But he stopped and made sure you were OK, did he not?"

"Well, yes," Ariandel admitted, "but when I asked for healing, he just looked at me with disgust."

Marion raised her finger at Ariandel, "He gave you healing, did he not?"

"Well, yes, I guess," Ariandel spat out reluctantly. "But a thimble of good it did me. It exhausted me and my horse. Four hours later I could not ride; my horse could barely stand. He knew that would happen the entire time."

"He probably did," Marion conceded. "But it was what he had, and it kept you from dying. He also knew Sivle and the others were behind him. Perhaps you should try a little gratitude and see if it doesn't change his attitude toward you." Marion got up from the table, giving Ariandel a small smile while picking up her tray of pastries, then continued to the other tables.

Ariandel considered Marion's words. Maybe from his ill-bred perspective, he was trying to be helpful. But she could not bring herself to like him.

***

Erich was the first to arrive at the castle gates, casually watching the alert guards eyeing him suspiciously. The gate was a simple wooden structure, but Erich knew they suspended an iron portcullis behind it, ready to drop with the pull of a lever. There was a line of what looked like silver stones across the opening. Erich knew these were glyphs spread across the cobblestone walkway to the castle. No doubt anyone attempting to pass by the guards would be in for a painful, probably fatal, surprise. Erich smiled. Anyone trying to get into a castle through the front gate deserved whatever they got.

Fairwind arrived with Braxlo, Alliandre, and Lolark. The five of them stood outside the gatehouse for several minutes when Prince Valian arrived as well. With all of them there but Sivle, they announced to the guard they were there for their audience with the king and queen, waiting patiently while a page ran to announce their arrival. "I wonder where Sivle is. It isn't like him to be late," Erich commented.

"He needed to get the high priest's blessing and pay his dues," Alliandre offered. "He left before we dueled this morning. I expected him back hours ago."

"Isn't that the same high priest he had removed several years ago?" Fairwind asked, smiling broadly, "She made him wait all day yesterday. Maybe he isn't coming."

"I suppose that is a possibility," Erich answered, "but since he has the gift for the king, perhaps we should give him a few minutes longer."

Several more minutes went by. Alliandre and Erich were getting genuinely concerned when a portal materialized in the middle of the street. The guard jumped out of his boots, calming down once he realized it was not an attack. Sivle walked through looking a little disheveled, but otherwise none the worse for wear. The residual static made his hair stand out from his head. Playfully, Fairwind smoothed a single lock into place, ignoring the rest. "There, much better."

"You are in a rare mood, Your Highness," Sivle responded, chanting quickly, and smoothing the rest of his hair into a hasty pompadour. "You must have had a good day training your young friend."

"I did. She picked up the lessons quickly. Even wanted to add aether to earth and fire. I thought perhaps later this week you could teach the both of us how you do it."

"I would be happy to do so, Your Highness," Sivle said with a small bow. "But it will have to be tomorrow, or after the Wizard Tournament. While Alliandre may be our odds-on favorite for the Grand Melee, I plan on entering my fire missiles into the Wizard's Tournament. I need to write several more scrolls."

"What about your fire stones?" Fairwind queried. "Trust me, they are much more impressive."

"I had only just figured out how to make them work when I showed them to you. The stamins are extremely complicated. It would take me too long to write enough scrolls to enter them. I have written just one, on my war scrolls."

"Tomorrow afternoon, maybe?" Although Fairwind posed it as a question, everyone knew from experience he had better prepare to train her and Ariandel after lunch on the morrow.

A banner of guards appeared, the commander approaching the party. "Lord Erich, I am Sir Victorious. The king has requested I escort you to the Throne Room. If you and your guests would please follow me." He then gave a deep bow, waiting for the group to return it.

Sir Victorious and his banner were not the normal, ornamental knights usually assigned to escort visitors. Most members of court received only a pair of knights, even large groups rarely receiving more than a handful of knights with polished armor who looked the part of a noble warrior. Not to say they were not warriors, as palace duty was often a reward for exemplary duty or feats of some repute.

But with Fairwind, an aelf princess, the king was apparently leaving no chance for insult. Sir Victorious' polished armor shone. Erich could tell the armor, as well as the sword, mace, and axe hanging from his belt were enchanted as well. So, too, the armor and weapons of all the other knights. Their tabards had the Silver Castle of the Central Kingdom on a green field, with the three stars representing the three great human kingdoms on the gold chevron below. The gold chevron was made of actual gold thread woven into the fabric. Erich considered whether they had an enchantment to keep them looking so fine. He smiled when he thought what escort the king would have sent had he known the Crown Prince of the Great Aelf Kingdom accompanied them as well.

They arrived at the main keep and the banner walked alongside the visitors, two of them turning and assuming guard positions every few paces until Sir Victorious stepped forward to open the door. Stepping inside, he announced loudly, "Your Majesties, the Party of the Seven, and Prince Valian of the Great Aelf." Evidently, he had recognized the prince.

Erich led the way in, followed by Prince Valian. Then Fairwind accompanied by Braxlo. Lolark came next, followed by Sivle and Alliandre. They walked to a line several paces away from the king and queen on the throne and bowed deeply.

The king and queen stood and walked toward the group. "Arise, friends. Come, let us sit." The king pointed to the side where he had chairs set with small tables. He hugged Prince Valian, then shook hands with the remaining guests, hugging Alliandre last. "Prince Lucas could not be here, but he sends his regards. He should arrive tonight or early tomorrow morning. He expressed his desire to see you, Alliandre, hoping you will have the chance to train him again."

"Thank you, Your Majesty. Please send him my regards as well." Alliandre bowed again, then added, "I regret my training kept me away for so long."

"Yes," the king continued, as they walked over to the chairs. "I understand you registered for the Open Melee. Know I would be happy to add you to the Grand Melee rolls as well. There is no need for you to prove yourself in this kingdom."

"On the contrary, Your Majesty. I will let no man claim favor or intervention when I am knighted, as I hope you will do when I win the Grand Melee."

The king clasped Alliandre's wrist. "If I thought you would accept, I would knight you here and now." Raising his voice, "and in front of a royal prince and princess, as well as a council paladin, I swear to you I shall knight you on your victory in the Grand Melee."

Everyone raised a cheer. Well, everyone but Prince Valian and Erich, who both delayed by pouring wine into their goblets. "Just what his bloated head needs," Erich stated under his breath while Prince Valian looked at Alliandre from behind his glass.

They sat reminiscing on their adventures since each of them had last seen the king and queen. Erich passed over several scrolls from various nobles throughout the land who had heard he was traveling to Foresight. He often transported messages for a small fee. In every instance, he delivered the messages with the seal on the documents unbroken. It was uncommon for him to arrive in a city without several scroll cases to deliver. It was also uncommon for him not to know exactly what they wrote on them, unbroken seals notwithstanding.

Prince Valian arose, bringing out a small chest. "Your Majesty, I came to deliver a gift from the Great King, along with a message from the Great Queen." He opened the chest. Inside sat a wooden crown encrusted with blue gems. The wood itself was ingrained with silver and golden streaks throughout, the streaks forming the structure of the crown itself. "I bring a crown for Prince Lucas, made from the wood of the Great Tree itself. Enchanted by our artisans, it will provide wisdom and health to whoever wears it. It is by this gift the Great King hopes to ensure the bond of friendship we have known for so long." Prince Valian brought the crown over to the queen, handing it to her, then handed a scroll to the king.

"Prince Valian," the king stood, embracing the prince. "I hope the Great King knows we shall always honor our bonds of friendship. Our oath to never war against the aelf nations again is as strong now as when my great many times over grandfather swore it when they brokered the truce. Let us never again make war upon each other. If any other kingdom makes war upon an aelf kingdom, we shall raise our armies and defend them. As we have during the Great Vreen War, and even the Grendlaar Wars so many centuries ago."

The two separated, the prince speaking again. "We have full faith in the human kingdoms, having spent so much time among you. However, we fear the message in the scroll may interfere with our relations. Please know the Great King has reasons he cannot divulge. I assure you he wishes nothing to come between our friendship. With this, I have messages to deliver to several more kingdoms. I hope your Majesties will forgive me if I cut my meeting short. I promise you again, I intend no offense." The king looked askance at the prince, embracing him again while ordering Sir Victorious to escort him out.

Sivle rose to address the king. "Your Majesty, we have a gift for you as well," he stated, pulling a small pouch from his belt. Opening it while saying a few words, he reached his arm in, up to the shoulder, before pulling out a small, wide dagger. Handing the dagger to the king, he continued, "Please accept this as a small token of our friendship. Alliandre gave me the idea, hoping you find a use for this."

The dagger handle was almost as long as the blade. It looked more like a sword handle than a dagger handle. An exquisitely jeweled pommel with an intricate wire wrapping covered the ebony handle. The cross guard sporting two small langets which locked the dagger in the sheath. The sheath looked to be entirely iridium, featuring a gold throat, locket, finial, and chape. The king turned it over in his hands several times before drawing the blade. Much to everyone's amazement, the blade was much longer than the sheath. The king finished drawing it out, ending with a full long-sword in his hand. He swung it several times in the air before replacing it. "What a marvel this is. When it is in the sheath, it weighs far less than when drawn." Thanking Sivle and the others, he ordered more wine.

***

They talked until late in the afternoon, when pages came in informing the king of other business. "My friends, thank you for coming to see me. I regret my duties must take me away. But one last piece I do not want to forget." He pulled a small purse from his coat, tossing it to Alliandre. "I appreciate you paying my guards. The captain felt the need to pass it up. It made its way to me, so I am returning it."

Alliandre weighed the purse in his hand a moment, then tossed it back to the king. "Please return it to the captain to distribute it to his men. With Jubilee tomorrow, I have the feeling they will earn it."

"If you have a moment, I have one last inquiry." Alliandre grew serious, and everyone else grew quiet. "There was a man picked up from the Aerie last night after assaulting Her Highness. I was wondering what was to become of him."

The king's expression faded, a concerned look crossing his face. "Duke Del Mornay's son, yes. I am afraid, Alliandre, as he is a duke's son, despite his intoxication, we will flog him and put him in the stocks. However, Princess Marion herself has requested his punishment not be severe." Everyone saw Alliandre's expression turn from serious to angry as the king continued. "He is fighting in the Grand Melee; you can express your displeasure then."

Alliandre bowed. As he stood, he looked resigned to the young Del Mornay's fate. "If it pleases Your Majesty, advise him when you release him, he should not go near the Aerie again." The king merely nodded in reply.

With the audience officially ended, they walked outside the keep, exchanging hugs and clasped wrists. The queen whispered a few secret words to Sivle before Sir Victorious escorted them to the front gate. Outside, they began their walk back to the Wyvern's Aerie. Alliandre, whether from excitement or hunger, rushed ahead into the Aerie to look for Marion.

***

The Aerie was full of people. Several banners of paladins and knights filled the dining hall. Three men sat at their table, one of whom even sat in Lolark's throne-like chair. The other serving girl came over and gave him a shy smile. "My lord, I can seat you at the bar if you wish. You can wait for your table to empty or request them to leave."

Alliandre just scowled at her, then bowed. "I am not a lord, my dear." He straightened, trying to put on a pleasant expression before continuing. "I will ask the gentlemen at our table to vacate it, as we will have need of it soon." Giving another small bow, he strode purposefully past her to the table. Three men of obvious means sat evenly spread out, so he approached the one in Lolark's chair. They had moved it to the opposite side, back to the fire, facing the rest of the hall. Erich always insisted on sitting with his back to the fire; Lolark, liking to be as far away from Erich as possible, therefore chose the opposite side.

The man in the chair reminded him of Erich in some ways. He had black hair, a hawkish nose, and dark, brooding features. He wore silks and dark velvets like Erich, but with an excess of ruffles and embroidery. He also had a small scorpion claw and stinger tattoo peeking out of his collar, designating him as a member of the Voldair Thieves Guild. Obviously of low rank, as any competent assassin would not be drawing this much attention to himself.

The other two looked like henchmen or guards, both wearing black gambesons with gold buttons. Not quite a uniform, but both looked of similar quality and wear. Both were blond, with faces which would be quite attractive in the dark. The one to his left had a branding scar on his left hand. It was unclear what the brand had been, however. *So, either a criminal or an ex-slave,* he thought. The other across the table had a nose which he appeared to have broken several times. Broken nose noticed him come up, placing his hand beneath the table. Alliandre assumed it was for a dagger, hoping it would not come to fisticuffs.

"Good evening, gentlemen. I am Alliandre Del Nileppez Drol Hulloc. I am sorry to displace you, but it seems you are occupying our table. You appear to be finishing your meal. I hope you will give it up, as we are here now."

"You look mighty few for a 'we,' my friend." The obvious leader of the trio stood up. "The barkeep told us he reserved this table, but if we wanted to, we could wrangle with you over it when you arrived."

"We have arrived, but I have no desire to wrangle over the table." Alliandre forced a tight smile. "Allow us to take care of your dinner this evening. You can go spend your money on wine and ale at the bar."

"You keep referring to yourself as a group. However, while you are a big fellow, I think perhaps you should wait for your friends to arrive."

"Perhaps you should look over to the door, my friend." The black-haired thief jumped as Erich appeared behind him to his right, laying a hand on his shoulder as he began speaking. "See the man who looks like this chair is too small for him? He will not care you moved it, but since you moved it into my spot, I am a bit put off."

The leader turned with a sneer, quickly regaining his composure. "Who might you be? You are obviously the one in charge here. What if we wish to dine longer?" Turning his back to Alliandre, he used his few inches of height on Erich to intimidate him. His sneer disappeared and his ruddy complexion turned white as Erich answered.

"I am Erich the Black. No one is 'in charge' of the Party of the Seven. We each do as we please. We all would like to sit down and eat now. Thank you for leaving."

Few people knew of the Party of the Seven in Voldair. Anyone not involved in any of the major conflicts of the last dozen years may have never heard of them. Erich was another matter. After Tristheim, The Voldair Guild recruited Erich. There were few from the guild there who did not know his story, and his name. The three men quickly rose from their chairs before vacating the tavern, avoiding Sivle, Braxlo, Fairwind, and especially Lolark, as they left. Alliandre and Erich moved the giant chair across the table, just getting it set, as Marion came out of the kitchen. She saw them and turned back in, emerging seconds later with a bucket and rag.

"I am sorry, Alliandre," she said as she began clearing and wiping down the table, giving him a small smile. "It looks like dinner together is out of the question. Perhaps it will settle down later." She finished the cleaning, giving a bow to everyone. "I will go check on your food. Sir Andras got some fresh turkeys; they should be just about done. He roasted a pig too, serving it earlier. Soon it will be mutton and sausages for everyone, so eat fast." Turning sharply, she ran back into the kitchen.

***

Beauregard walked up to the house he had visited previously, knocking on the door. Within a minute, Victor answered. Seeing Beauregard, he quickly opened the door, hurrying him inside. "Hello Beauregard, what can we do for you today?"

"More like, what can I do for you today? I sold the armor. It turns out it was worth more than I thought. I wanted to see how much you received from the sword and cloak to square up with you."

"The cloak was worthless, but it was better than mine, so I kept it," Victor lied. "I sold the sword for fifty turots, I think mainly for the gem. I had to spend half to buy a Life's Breath potion for Mortimer."

"Life's Breath, spirits bless him? How is he?" Beauregard put his best concerned face on, pulling a small vial from his pack. "Here is a potion to heal him. Please, take it, and tell me what happened."

"What happened is we ran into spellcasters." Vincent grabbed the vial and hurried to the back room with it. He walked over to his now conscious friend, placing the vial in Mortimer's hands while guiding his hands up to his mouth. Within moments of drinking it, color flooded back to Mortimer's face as the burns from the fire and ice faded. Looking once at Victor and Beauregard, he rolled out of his bed.

"Thank you, Beauregard. That is your name, isn't it? I feel much better, much better indeed." Mortimer hugged both men, then questioned the newcomer. "That wasn't just an ordinary healing potion. I feel energized, almost better than I did before I left."

"It was a strong healing potion, yes," Beauregard told him. "Once I heard you needed Life's Breath, I just gave you the strongest healing potion I had." It was the only healing potion he had. He had one other potion for invisibility he kept for emergencies. He hated wasting the potion, but he could get more. "Besides, I want you healthy, as I have a task for you."

Both of them eyed him a bit suspiciously. "I don't know," Mortimer said, "the last job we did with you didn't work out so well."

"Whatever do you mean?" Beauregard put on his best offended face. "When I left you, you had gained a cloak and sword and dagger, neither of you having to do any work. Is it my fault you got ambushed on your way back to Foresight?"

"It wasn't on our way back," Victor said carefully. He told him of the two riders they had encountered and the spells they both threw back, despite both of them riding what looked like warhorses.

Beauregard asked several questions regarding the two riders, their clothing and appearance. He wasn't sure who the first one was, but he was positive the second was Drullock. The two were lucky to have survived the sword's Ice Cone. He wondered if Drullock had mis-aimed the blast. If he had been riding hard, it was possible, but not likely. Maybe the rocks had provided them some cover.

"That was a tough break," admitted Beauregard. "But there is no chance of that here. I just need you to cast a spell on a fighter during the Open Melee. I have quite a large sum of money on him losing. I will pay you each twenty turots to cast a dual spell on him together, so it is not detectable. I also need you to be enchantment judges, so you can flag him if he tries to have anyone dispel it."

Beauregard took a small purse out and poured out the contents onto the bed. He pulled two havnots out and handed one to each of them.

"This is for the armor. Bad luck on the sword and cloak. I thought for sure they had enchantments. The armor sure did."

He counted out twenty turots, placing them in two piles next to two scroll cases which looked like vreen bone. They were as valuable as one of the golden coins.

Picking up one case, Victor opened it up. "A concealment spell, huh?" So, this is to cover the other.

Mortimer picked up the other scroll case. Opening, he read the scroll carefully. "This looks like a fatiguing spell. This will certainly cause him trouble in the melee. But he will know someone enchanted him, will he not?"

"Not if you cast the concealment spell at the exact same time. You will need to practice. I put five spells on each of them. If you can do it in less, you can keep the scrolls." Beauregard gave a deep bow.

"Why don't you cast one of them? I would think it would increase the odds tremendously."

"Mortimer, if he sees me anywhere, he will know something is up. Besides, I will have to have an alibi, won't I?" Beauregard shrugged his shoulders, picking up the stacks of coins. "I came to you because we worked so well together before. If you don't want the extra turots, I can find someone else. Not much skill required to just read scrolls, after all."

Victor put his hand on Beauregard's arm, stopping him. "Mortimer was just covering all the details. You wouldn't want to hire people who didn't consider all the angles, would you?"

Beauregard put his thoughtful face on. "Now that you mention it, that is exactly why I want you. I guess we can sit and plan this out carefully and I will answer any of your questions."

They spent the rest of the evening planning, even drawing a map of the Jubilee grounds, and the likely spots Drullock would set up. Planning the approach, where they would come in, and where they should be when they cast the spells. Mortimer added backup contingencies and plans for unforeseen events which were as unlikely as a dragon attack. By nightfall, they agreed on a straightforward plan. Beauregard let them add all the contingencies they wanted as long as they were comfortable. Leaving Victor's house, he headed to the Golden Palace to relax. He needed to write some more scrolls. With Jubilee tomorrow, he had some more plans he needed to set in motion.

V

Jubilee Begins

28th of Frendalo, Year 1124 AGW

Alliandre rose at his normal time, dressed, then began rousing Braxlo, Erich, and Sivle. Smelling bacon already, he thought maybe he could talk with Marion before the tavern got too crowded.

Everyone dressed in their finest today. Even Sir Andras wore a fine golden tabard, silk and gold thread intertwining in the pattern. Arielle wore an ornate golden gown, two fists of wyvern claws holding each sleeve to the bodice. The Southern Kingdom's wyvern clutching a golden nest adorned her blue corset. The long skirt fell just above tripping height, revealing shoes with scales of silver reflecting the light, twinkling as she walked. She had styled her hair in braids along her temples, meeting at her neck before cascading down to the middle of her back. Combs, carved to resemble a wyvern's head, holding everything in place as she bounced around the already half-full tavern.

Alliandre looked around for Marion, but she was nowhere to be seen. Sitting at his spot at the table, he noticed it was still as they left it last night, albeit much cleaner, with a dozen pastries already decorating its center. Catching Arielle's eye, she smiled, nodding to him while continuing on her rounds. She reached the table, putting her hand on Alliandre's shoulder, which even with him sitting was as high as her own.

"What a dashing figure you make today. It will upset Marion knowing she missed you this morning."

"Is she alright?" Alliandre asked, concern creeping into his voice.

"Of course. The Jubilee Court is being selected this morning. She wanted to look her best." Laughing now as Alliandre stared at her, she continued, "The selections are in an hour. If you hurry and eat, you can be there to cheer her on."

Alliandre's face lit up. He did not know Marion was on the list of maidens to be selected as Jubilee Queen. He wolfed down sweet cakes and ham and bacon, nodding his thanks as Arielle brought a basket with more food. Inside were loaves of bread, cold mutton, ham, bacon, and cheese, along with a jug of mead, two flagons of wine, and assorted fruit. Not caring how ridiculous he looked carrying the femininely decorated basket, he bowed deeply and laid a single havnot on the table, then turned and left before she could protest.

He practically ran out of the tavern, heading to get Aeris. Stabled for days, he knew the magnificent beast would like some exercise. He hurried to the stables and threw the doors open. The stable master pointed at a large barn door.

"The beast is in there," he said with a frown. "We fed him well, but he refused to go to the pasture. It has been all oats and hay."

"Thank you, milord," Alliandre replied. "I should have warned you he would not budge from where I left him."

Alliandre went to the door, pushing it open. Sure enough, Aeris was standing right where he had left him. Droppings behind him, the remains of a hay bale, and a cleaned-out bowl of oats littered the ground in front of him. The stableboy cleaned his saddle, barding, and other gear, placing them on a stand which had not been there when he dropped Aeris off. He quickly put on the blanket, saddle, and caparison before leading Aeris from the stables. Pulling a malnot out of his pouch, he tossed it to the stable master as he walked the great beast outside.

Once outside, he mounted Aeris, then began a slow trot. He would have liked to go faster, but like-minded travelers packed the roads in the city, dressed in everything from jeweled silks and velvets to simple cloth and leather. All of them brightly colored. All of them in his way. The sheer size of Aeris, along with the thumping of his hooves on the ground, turned many heads, those same heads quickly moving aside, clearing his path. Once he made it to the gates, he broke into a gallop off the main road and headed to the fairgrounds.

It only took Aeris a minute to travel the short distance to the seats built for Jubilee. Alliandre left Aeris at one end of the rail where other tied their horses, laying the rope across the end post. Tossing a coin to the young man tending the horses, he said, "Do not touch him, or let anyone else touch him, please."

The boy, about sixteen, the youthful body filling out, caught the coin. Bowing, he replied, "Yes, my lord. Thank you, my lord."

"I am not a lord." Alliandre tired of reminding people, but accusations of impersonating a nobleman were embarrassing. Better to always be on record denying it.

He headed toward where the wealthy merchants and nobles sat. The king reserved space for them. The turot fee was outrageous, but were it a havnot, the seats would still be full. As it was, it was early enough there were still several empty seats. He rushed up and stood in line, trying to count the empty seats and the people in line ahead of him.

He had just reached the front of the line, handing the gatekeeper his fee, when two royal guards stepped up to him. "Master Alliandre, if you would follow us, the prince has asked you to join him."

He recognized one knight from their audience the day before and bowed deeply. "I am deeply honored the prince would accept my presence. Please, lead the way."

He reached the king's box just as trumpets blared, announcing the start of the activities. He took a seat at the back of the open pavilion, three rows behind the royals, and sixteen seats to their right. Prince Lucas turned and nodded. Alliandre returned the nod with a smile.

The first event at every Royal Jubilee was the selection of the Jubilee

King and Queen. The king's advisors selected twenty-four young, single nobles of the realm from all applicants. Marion, at twenty-three, was the oldest of the ladies there. She was also the most beautiful as far as Alliandre could see. Of the young men, two stood out to him. One of them wore the same coat of arms as Earl Del Comaste Drol Seville, the mayor who greeted him at the gates. The other had flaming red hair, rare outside of the Northern Kingdom.

The young Del Comaste, standing well over six feet tall, had a blacksmith's physique. It was accompanied by his jet-black hair, which only highlighted his steel-gray eyes. Like most of the young men, he looked to be about eighteen, carrying himself with all the poise and confidence one would expect of a lord from a noble house. A brightly jeweled dagger hilt rose from the scabbard on his left side, the same place Alliandre carried one of his swords. The red-haired youth standing next to him was the same height. Lean and long-limbed, his waist came to the same height as the waist of the taller mayor's son, his hands hanging inches lower.

The men and women stepped forward to introduce themselves to the judges looking on, making notes on sheets of parchment. Alliandre kept one eye on Marion the entire time, while evaluating those he thought were the top picks. He knew much more than this went into the judging, but this was a chance for the Jubilee crowd to meet the candidates and pick their favorites. Once the introductions finished, each of the candidates performed with an instrument, or sang, or both.

When they finished, the judges met, selecting the top six from each group. These would be the royal court for Jubilee. The judges bid each of the twelve return for questions, mostly related to politics in the Central Kingdom, but also on their accomplishments and goals. Each of them had several minutes to get through the questions, ending with the final young lady, when asked what her goal in life was, providing the answer of the day as far as Alliandre was concerned.

"What I would like most to become," the young woman stated slowly and thoughtfully, "is the queen of the Central Kingdom! I love you,

Prince Lucas!" Then she exaggerated blowing a kiss to the royal booth, sent a wink which was just as exaggerated, then sauntered to the side as the crowd laughed and hooted.

The judges left to deliberate while jugglers and acrobats performed for the crowd. They returned some ten minutes later, having selected three knights and three ladies-in-waiting. Marion was not among the ladies, indicating she was the queen or one of the two princesses. Alliandre was sitting on the edge of his seat when they announced Marion as the first princess. Disappointed, he sat back, unable to stop glaring at the judges. Marion was all smiles. Her prince, the red-haired youth. They proclaimed the Del Comaste boy, Gerard was his name, King of Jubilee, announcing an olive-skinned brunette as his queen.

Everyone from the king's pavilion went down to congratulate the court. Prince Lucas saw him and came straight to him, wrapping him in a massive bear hug.

"Alliandre!" he yelled as he lifted the much bigger man. "It is good to see you, my friend. Mother and Father told me I just missed you yesterday. I almost went to the Aerie, but I had duties to attend to."

"I was sorry you were not there as well. But we will have a drink together later and catch up." Alliandre focused his attention on the prince, but in the back of his mind, he wanted to console Marion. "Maybe after the parade is over?"

"It will have to be after the luncheon, my friend." The prince, only three years older than Marion, explained. "We will be in the parade, then we have to host the new royal court this afternoon at the Royal Luncheon. I will have some time after the luncheon, if you don't mind one of the tent vendors."

"As long as I am with you, my friend, it can be last year's ale on the back of an oxcart." Alliandre smiled fondly, remembering when they returned from battle years ago, having that for their first drink. They continued until most of the king's party had congratulated the new court and filed away. The two men clasped wrists, the prince walking over to meet the new court.

Disappointed for Marion, he went down to see her. She ran over as soon as the royals finished greeting them, giving him a hug. "I am so happy you made it, Alliandre. I'm sorry I said nothing earlier, but I didn't want anyone to influence the judges."

"I would have never done that," Alliandre protested.

"No, but Erich would have." She held a finger up to his lips as he began protesting, then continued. "Now I can say I won this all on my own."

"But you didn't win, even though at least you are still a princess." He tried his best to sound encouraging, but she just laughed at him.

"Silly, this isn't a duel where only one person wins." Her smile broke the scolding tone, and she explained further. "Making the court means I will get to meet all the dignitaries here at Jubilee. And the king and queen, the real ones, are generous with the gifts they give the royal family and their retainers. Best of all, it shows the other nobles in the kingdom accept me as one of their own nobles, not a refugee from a fallen kingdom, deserving of only pity." Grabbing him by the arm, she pulled him toward the others gathered in the field. "Come here, I want you to meet Ferdinand."

She led him over to the red-haired boy and bowed. "My Prince, please allow me to introduce to you Alliandre Del Nileppez Drol Hulloc, my friend and a former citizen of the Southern Kingdom."

Alliandre bowed as well, and as the prince rose, Marion continued. "Alliandre, please meet Ferdinand Del Broussard Drol Franos, son of Baron Jacque Del Broussard and Baroness Julia Del Franos. They control the Northwatch Barony in the northeast of the Central Kingdom."

"A pleasure to meet you, Lord Del Broussard," Alliandre said as they clasped wrists.

"The pleasure is all mine, Lord Del Nileppez. I have heard stories of the Southern Kingdom, and how few of the court escaped, although you must have been quite young."

"I am not a lord." Alliandre tried to keep the anger out of his voice.

"Just an adventurer who is hoping to be elevated so I can properly court a certain princess." He smiled over at Marion, and she blushed a bit, then grabbed his hand again. "And yes, I was but twelve."

"Alliandre, I have a favor to ask," Marion said. Looking over at Ferdinand, she continued, "If it is alright, Lord Ferdinand, we need horses and a driver to pull our carriage in the parade. I would love it if you and Aeris could do it."

"My dear Marion," Ferdinand protested. "I have brought two of our biggest draft horses for this eventuality. There is no need for your friends to tire their horses by pulling the carriage through town."

"But you have not seen Aeris," Marion assured him. "No one will have a more impressive team. We will only need Aeris."

"I am confused. Who is this Aeris?" Ferdinand knew the answer as soon as he finished the question. "Oh, you named your horse Aeris. My apologies. But the carriage, while open at the top, is actually quite large, with two footmen along with the driver. I fear Marion has not much experience with carriages if she thinks one horse can pull it."

Alliandre ignored the young man's last comment. "I am afraid even if Aeris were inclined, wouldn't it seem to put you above the queen? Besides, Marion, this is your day. You do not need me getting in the way." Alliandre smiled down at Marion.

"Nonsense," Marion grabbed both of their arms as she added, "Ferdinand can look at Aeris and then he can tell me what I know about carriages."

Begrudgingly, Alliandre led them to where he had left Aeris. A small crowd had gathered around the creature, waiting to see who would claim him. The young man tending the horses was shooing the people away, anxious at seeing several children trying to pet the beast. Once Aeris came into sight, Ferdinand's jaw dropped. As they got near, and he saw the actual size of the monstrous animal, he addressed Alliandre.

"What kind of animal is he, er she?" He asked, still unable to take his eyes off Aeris.

"He, and I do not know. I found it struggling in the marshes east of the Copper Leaf Woods, and it seemed to bond with me. It was just a young colt. As he grew, I broke him in the saddle, training him as my warhorse." Ferdinand was about to ask how Alliandre mounted him when Aeris bent his forelegs, lowering his chest to the ground. Alliandre reached to grab the pommel, stepping into the stirrup with his left foot. He swung his right leg back and over the high back of the military-style saddle to get situated.

"You have got to pull our carriage, Lord Alliandre. Please. The rest of the court will be so jealous." Turning to Marion, Ferdinand bowed slightly. "I apologize for doubting you, My Princess. This Aeris is the most amazing beast I have ever seen." Aeris snorted at this, Alliandre swearing his eyes actually twinkled.

"I am NOT a Lord!" Alliandre said again, then patted Aeris on the cheek as the magnificent beast stood. Turning Aeris back toward the end of the fairgrounds, he continued, "If we are going to embarrass ourselves, Aeris, we might as well get to it. Your Highnesses, please lead me to the carriage."

The new royals were among the first groups in the parade, making them travel all the way across the fairgrounds, into the tent city where the parade began. They lined the royal carriages up, gold first, for the queen and king, then two silver for the two sets of princes and princesses. The remaining three were blue, red, and yellow.

Footmen stood at each side of the carriages, dressed in regal finery. They wore ruffled collars flowing out from jet black velvet coats with long tails. Their pantaloons bloused just above the tops of their knee-high stockings, which matched the color of the carriage. Black leather shoes, shined to a high gloss, completed each outfit. Workers painted their names on a large sign, while stablemen attached two great leather-brown horses to their carriage harness.

"Hold there, my good men. We will need to adjust the harness for a single horse." Ferdinand bowed to the men, who returned the bow. Seeing Aeris, they began adjusting the traces for a single horse.

The problem came in finding a collar which would fit Aeris. In the end, they rigged some straps, attaching the traces through the saddle and securing them to a strap around the chest. Both men were extremely nervous as Aeris snorted, striking his hoof up and down, but Alliandre stepped to his head to calm him. Marion even found some fruit from the basket Alliandre had brought, offering it to Aeris. He ate it while nuzzling Marion with his broad, long face. Once they finished, Alliandre began helping Marion into the carriage.

The footman on Marion's side stopped him, grabbing Marion's arm while coolly reminding Alliandre, "Your job is to drive. We are the Royal Footmen."

Marion cast a nervous smile to Alliandre as the man assisted her into the carriage before taking his place on the narrow side rail where he would stand for the entire parade. Over a hursmarc in hard shoes. But as the man had said, they were Royal Footmen; they did not get their position by being fragile. Coming from the royal guard, proven in battle. Too old for normal military duties now, their loyalty to the crown earned them a life in court and relative ease. Alliandre merely bowed and replied, "Of course, my lord, my apologies" as he climbed up into the driver's seat. Then he passed the basket back to Marion and her prince.

Up ahead, Alliandre watched the actual royal family in their carriage, preceded by a spear of knights of the royal guard. Following them came various members of court accompanied by a troop of infantry. They moved off slowly, no one moving any faster than the heavy infantry could march, reminding Alliandre why he hated traveling with an army. Then it was their turn. With the command of "Aeris, Dance," the carriage moved forward.

The parade lasted the better part of two hours, winding through the tent city from the southeast where the fairgrounds were, around the city walls, before entering through the Western Gate, continuing through the city and across to the Eastern Gate and back to the fairgrounds. Through it all, Aeris sharply brought up his hooves, waited a moment, then put them down again like a circus horse prancing around the ring. He gave no sign he was pulling a fortress stone worth of weight behind him.

***

Vanessa woke herself exceedingly early in the morning, earlier than Vandion, even. She quickly stoked the fire, putting water on to boil. She filled it extra full, making sure it did not boil dry before Vandion arose. Putting on a new woolen skirt and a fine cotton blouse Marion had given her, she looked at another gift, a beautiful green silk corset with a silver rampant wyvern on the front. Unable to lace and tie it tight in back, as her arms would not reach, she was sure Marion would tighten it when she arrived at the Aerie. Black leather, low-heeled boots finished the outfit. She was happy she and Marion had the same foot size, as her plain leather shoes would have looked quite odd with the other finery. She threw on her cloak and left for the Aerie.

As early as it was, the tent city around the city proper was abuzz with activity. Vendors were cooking and building stalls to sell their wares, a few people already moving among the tents with carts stacked with food or pots or any number of items for sale. The sky was not even reddening in the east; she hurried to make it to the Aerie before it did. Arielle requested she work from sunup to midnight during Jubilee, meaning she would only get a few hours of sleep each night. Arielle also promised she would make a year's worth of tips during Jubilee. She had not believed it until she had served the party staying there. Another meal with them and she would have a year's worth of tips just from their group. Yesterday's tips had included a malnot as well, from a patron who had slapped her rump. She looked over to Sir Andras, who sighed but came over and chastised the man.

Marion often just slugged the men who bothered her too much. As long as they kept their gropes limited to her arms and waist, Vanessa usually just brushed them away and said nothing. Sir Andras made sure anyone who got too grabby ended up with a lump on their head. Vanessa was used to the occasional hand on her arm, but she drew the line with slaps and grabs. And Sir Andras seemed as protective of her as he was of Marion.

She made it to the gates, stopping to check in with the guards.

When she stated she was heading to the Aerie, the guard asked her if she wanted an escort. A young guard walked with her all the way to the bridge to Hightowne. There was a small stream of people coming in and leaving the city, and she thought she would be safe enough from there. Arriving at the Aerie, she noticed a small crowd had already gathered. Hurrying to the kitchen to get her apron, she returned in time for one of the party, the half-aelf, to ask where Alliandre was. "I just arrived," she explained while taking his order. Walking back to the kitchen, she noticed him leave to look for Alliandre outside.

More of the party arrived as she was bringing the half-aelf his food. Vanessa's heart fluttered, elated she was here for their table. They came and ate, leaving a small stack of malnots for her. She could hardly contain her excitement. Now she was sure Vandion could complete the surprise. Her excitement lasted the entire day. Not even some of the extra touchy patrons could ruin her mood.

Arielle came up to her during a lull after firstmeal. "You are radiant today, my dear," the tavern owner declared. "Is there any news we should know about? Perhaps something about the boy you have been seeing?"

"How did you know about that?" Vanessa asked quietly. She had told no one at the Aerie about Vandion. Sir Andras would insist on meeting him, probably scaring him away.

"My dear. I used to be a queen with hundreds of spies. Do you think you could keep something like a courtier from me?" Arielle gave her a wink and continued. "It is all right. Your personal life is your own. We are all happy for you. What does he think of you working so late at night here?"

Vanessa thought carefully. If they already knew about Vandion, what else might they know? She would hate to have worked so hard on her surprise. "He doesn't like it. He said I should find an inn or tavern closer, or one that is not open so late. However, none hired me except you. But if we have a good crop this year, we may have enough for me to quit the Aerie and stay home." This was not totally true, but close enough she didn't consider it a lie. She wanted to paint Vandion in the best light possible.

Arielle looked at her. Vanessa thought the former queen could tell her last statement wasn't exactly true. But the queen just hugged her, saying, "Remember, you are like family here. Sir Andras knew your father and grandfather. Your friend is always welcome here. We would love it if you would bring him by sometime so we could meet him."

Vanessa scowled. "I am not sure Sir Andras wouldn't frighten him away."

Arielle laughed. "Sir Andras can play quite the ruffian, but if your friend cannot handle him, perhaps his love isn't strong enough when the truly scary things happen. Like children, for instance." Giving her another wink, she nodded to several paladins coming through the door. "Back to work. I will take these. Perhaps the next group will be merchants."

***

Sivle came down and looked for Alliandre in the tavern. Not finding him there, he went to the dueling grounds. A crowd was watching two duelers go back and forth, but Alliandre was nowhere to be seen. Trying the kitchen to no avail, he walked back into the dining hall to find Braxlo, Fairwind, Erich, and the aelf girl Ariandel seated at the table. He agreed to train them this afternoon, but he intended to be finished in time to attend the Bard Competition. With Mirandel performing and judging, he was looking forward to it running well into the night.

Erich, looking at him oddly, asked, "Surely you are not attending Jubilee dressed like that? You look more suited to be crawling through the mines at Silverhelm."

"I have to use another scroll today, following up on something I found yesterday. Part of the reason I was so late to see the king. I will be back for lunch," Sivle assured Fairwind.

Sitting down, he helped himself to a pastry. Soon after, the serving girl arrived and brought his tray of food before taking everyone's order. Finishing first, Sivle went up to his room, opened a scroll, and after a short incantation, disappeared through a portal. Reappearing at the temple he had visited the day before, this time, he did not go inside, instead retracing his footsteps to where he had found turnips growing on a ledge the day before, assuming grendlaar would gather them. He sat meditating for some time before two grendlaar appeared.

Immediately, they attacked with their farming implements. Sivle used a small telekinesis spell to send their weapons flying from their hands. "I have no wish for war. I wish to speak to your leader. Please, go fetch him."

The grendlaar hesitated a few moments. Seeing Sivle still sitting, making no hostile actions, one ran off while the other went down a crevice to pick up the tools. After retrieving them, he began working the ground, removing weeds and ripe turnips, his eyes rarely leaving this strange half-aelf. Several minutes later, the sun rising almost an eighth of the way across the sky, a full banner of armored grendlaar arrived, surrounding Sivle on both sides.

"Ollphéist a shealbhú," Sivle said, freezing a great number of the grendlaar in place. "I mean to bring no war," Sivle added as the few grendlaar still moving freely cautiously approached. Sivle interlocked his hands, speaking again. "Lucht leanúna lasrach." This sent gouts of fire from his fingers, leaping out at the approaching grendlaar. The grendlaar jumped back after being scorched, many of them seriously. Then a grackle came around the corner.

"Enough aelf," he commanded. Sivle let the flames go. "What do you come here for, if not to steal and make war?"

"Stories," Sivle replied.

Confused, the grackle approached, eyeing Sivle closely. Wearing no armor, Sivle carried no weapons either. But the grackle had seen he could cause substantial damage with the spirits. "Release my subjects, so they may return to their families," he commanded again.

Sivle looked at the grackle square in the eye. "As you command," he said, dropping his hold on them. The grendlaar, released from their paralysis, began attacking again.

"Stop!" the grackle admonished them. "Return to your homes. Report to my brother I am here. Catch this one's scent. If I do not return, hunt him and his family to avenge me."

Several of the grendlaar approached Sivle with noses forward, gaining his scent. They chittered excitedly to the grackle, jumping up and down while pointing at Sivle. "Enough!" the grackle shouted, sending the grendlaar scurrying back whence they had come, including the two farmers.

"You are brave aelf, to come here alone and unarmed." The grackle sat down within arm's reach of Sivle. "What stories do you hope to hear?"

"Legends," Sivle replied. "Legends of long ago, when the grendlaar arose."

"Those legends are lost, aelf. Your kind, and the humans, destroyed them long before my kind arose to lead the Mtumwa."

"Then tell me about your kind," Sivle replied, taking a pen and ink and blank parchment out of his pouch.

"Those stories belong to us. Why do you wish to know them?" The grackle wasn't exactly hostile, but Sivle could tell he suspected some trap.

Sivle thought for a moment, then answered. "I wish to understand how the grendlaar came to be enemies of the aelf and humans. An acquaintance met two grendlaar who didn't seem to act the same as normal grendlaar. It reminded me of some things I found long ago in the Great Chasm. If what I suspect is true, perhaps we can bring peace between the grendlaar and other races."

The grackle thought on this for a while, eventually standing. "I will find an elder to discuss this. Stay here. I will return shortly."

Sivle rose as well, bowing. "I am named Sivle. I will wait for your return, but I have to leave when the sun is at its peak." Then he reached his arm out toward the grackle.

The grackle, grabbing Sivle's wrist with a crushing grip, simply replied, "I am called T'Whorase. I will return when the elders decide to come."

He returned an hour later with two clearly older grackles and a dozen armed grendlaar. Looking at Sivle, who had risen from his seated position, he made the introduction. "Aelf called Sivle. This is Itelizi and Ityotyosi. They are two of the elders of the Kumalo clan."

Sivle bowed deeply and spoke when he rose. "Elders of the Kumalo clan, I am honored you agreed to talk with me."

"We know you, Sivle Wea wa Roho," the elder named Ityotyosi interrupted. "You have killed many of the Mtumwa and the Mabwana wa Mtumwa. Why do you invade our lands now?"

"I wish to learn your history from before we came to your lands in the Great Chasm, before war between the grendlaar and other races began. I wish to find some way to bring peace with the grendlaar." Sivle was sincere in this last statement. He had long said if they could turn the grendlaar into allies, they could fully explore the Great Chasm, bringing its riches to the world.

"And why should we reveal our history to one who has destroyed an entire clan?" It was Itelizi who questioned him now.

"I admit I have been an enemy of the grendlaar," Sivle began.

"Mtumwa." Ityotyosi interrupted him again. "Your word 'grendlaar' is a slur on our people. An aelf demon from the past who preys on children. We do not prey on children. Nor are we demons."

"My apologies, elder." This was the first time Sivle realized the grendlaar had their own name for themselves. It made sense, but in the five hundred years since the Great War, the only times anyone had ever gone to negotiate treaties with the grendlaar, they had not returned. "While I have fought and killed many... Mtumwa, I believe the aelf and human nations have misunderstood the Mtumwa. I tire of the violence. I want to know why the Mtumwa attack our cities and our explorers in the Great Chasm."

The elders spoke together for a while, their language a guttural, rough language with many sounds with which Sivle was unfamiliar.

Similar to some of the bird calls with their clicks and whistles, they continued until the older grackle raised his hand and began speaking to him again. "Three millennia ago, the Mtumwa lived throughout the land. We hunted, built farms, and had built great clans. We traded with the vreen and centaurs and dwarves. We stayed out of the woods, because the aelf hunted us there, but they never made war on the Mtumwa. Then the humans came. They negotiated treaties and broke them, then negotiated new treaties which they broke. Then they made war on the Mtumwa, driving us from our lands. They killed our elders, destroying many great clans. They forced us to hunt at night and live in caves and tunnels. Now, they invade our homes, killing our women and children and sending metal-clad men to make war on us. So, when they come into our lands, we kill them. But we are like the grass, and we will one day take back our lands, despite what the Wadogo tell us."

Sivle considered this for a while. The humans had lived in small towns and cities. As they grew greater in numbers, they expanded their lands through treaties. He could understand how, from the grendlaar perspective, they could construe the renegotiations as violations of the treaties. But human lives were brief compared to the other races. Similar to grendlaar, which sometimes lived to sixty or seventy, humans rarely lived to a hundred, sixty considered old. As he thought about it, no one had ever investigated how long grackles lived.

"How old are you, revered elder?" Sivle asked.

The elders conferred again before Ityotyosi replied. "I was born two hands of years after the War of Devastation. What you call the 'Great Grendlaar War'." As he spoke, he raised his hands with ten long, clawed fingers held up.

Sivle's eyebrows rose noticeably. If grackles lived that long, as long as dwarves, it meant they had almost certainly developed advanced societal functions. Sivle knew they organized themselves along clan lines, and these clans warred against each other from time to time. However, with the grackle lifespan, they should have much more sophisticated societal organizations.

"And what clan do you belong to?" Sivle asked.

"I belong to the Kumalo clan, which tributes to the Ulundi clan, which tributes to the amaHlubi clan, which tributes to the Great Hlubi clan Chieftain Isipongo." The grackle conferred with the other elder for a moment, then continued. "In this way, we organize the great clans to provide protection and to train our Mtumwa."

Another thought struck Sivle. He addressed his question to the younger elder. "You criticize the humans for making war on the Mtumwa, but don't you often make war upon each other?"

The elders shook their heads together. "No," Ityotyosi replied, ignoring Sivle's direction. "The Mtumwa only attack each other to train or demonstrate their new position."

"I do not understand," Sivle stated. "We have observed large gatherings of grendlaar marching toward lands we know belong to other clans."

"Yes," Ityotyosi replied with a sigh. "When a Mabwana wa Mtumwa raised an umndeni, we consider them a chief. When they can muster a kikosi, they may go and tribute to another chief or clan, thus gaining their protection. When they can raise a kikosi kubwa, they can tribute to a larger clan, and they can accept tributes of kikosi. Likewise, when they can raise a jeshi, then they can tribute to a great clan chieftain. Whenever they tribute to a larger clan, the clan's chieftain must march a similar number of the tribute units to the tributing clan. They then join the tributing soldiers with his soldiers and march back."

"When a clan chieftain dies, the new clan chieftain must allow his clan soldiers to experience battle at his side. It is then we attack the humans or another clan until the spears are bloodied so they can assess the mettle of their Mtumwa. Then the clan returns. But the Mtumwa have never warred against each other."

Sivle's mind raced. Depending on the sizes of the units, this drastically changed how people had assumed the grendlaar organized their clans. "I apologize, revered elders, but I am not familiar with those terms. How many of the Mtumwa are in a kikosi?"

The two elders talked again in their strange language. Ityotyosi spoke again. "We disagree about whether to discuss our forces. This is all we will tell you. A chieftain controls a hundred Mtumwa in his umndeni. A kikosi comprises ten Mabwana wa Mtumwa and their umndenii. Ten kikosi make up a kikosi kubwa. In this way, ten kikosi kubwa make up a jeshi."

"I apologize again, but I am unfamiliar with the term Mabwana wa Mtumwa." Sivle thought he knew, but felt it was better to ask.

The two grackles looked at each other. Then Ityotyosi stood up and placed both hands on his chest. "We are Mabwana wa Mtumwa."

Sivle struggled to keep his mouth closed. Doing the math, there were a thousand grendlaar in a kikosi. What the humans had always referred to as a spear. There were ten thousand in a kikosi kubwa, and a hundred thousand grendlaar in a jeshi. Humans were aware of over twenty clans. Then again, perhaps they were mistaken. To think there were over two million grendlaar soldiers in and around the Great Chasm was enough to frighten anyone. To Sivle, the idea was inconceivable. "And how many jeshi does the Great Chieftain Isipongo command?" he asked.

Without hesitation, Ityotyosi declared. "Isipongo only controls five jeshi. But he is one of the smaller great chieftains. Of the thirty-seven great chieftains, twelve control at least ten jeshi."

Sivle whistled. "Great spirits!" he exclaimed. "How many Mtumwa are there?"

Ityotyosi motioned Itelizi to rise. Once they were both standing, Ityotyosi declared with a small smile, "We are like the grass." He grabbed the arm of the other elder before turning to leave.

***

The next group were indeed merchants, leaving Vanessa a pouch full of coins by the time the lunch crowd had left. Excitedly, she noticed the two aelf women sitting together with the knight dressed all in black. If the rest of them came in for lunch, tipping as generously as at firstmeal, she could get Vandion what he needed for the surprise. Perhaps buy him a new cloak as well. She walked over to them.

"Hello, my ladies, and Sir Knight. What can I get you?" She stood between the two aelf women. The fighter had never touched her, but it was a habit by now.

"Where is Marion?" the older aelf asked her. Although it was hard to tell age with aelf, the younger looked about sixteen, and the older not even as old as Marion. Vanessa knew from stories both were probably older than the grizzled fighter.

"She was competing for Jubilee Queen," Vanessa spoke softly, not wishing to spread it too far. "Arielle told me if she does not return this afternoon, she won. If she returns, then we will all act like she was on an errand." Vanessa tried to remember the older aelf's name. She thought she was some sort of aelf noblewoman, but no one had taken the time to explain who these visitors were, only the fighter Alliandre and Marion were a couple, only not. Alliandre and the half-aelf were friends of Arielle from when she was Queen Arielle. Vanessa, deciding to ask, hoped she wouldn't be insulting them. "If you do not mind my asking, with Jubilee here, everyone has been so busy no one has told me who you are or how you know the queen."

The warrior in black stood and reached out his hand. Vanessa initially pulled back, before noticing he had only extended his hand, not attempted to grab her. Slowly, she reached her own hand out, placing it in his palm. He bowed to hold it to his forehead before speaking. "I am Braxlo the Brave, Knight Errant of the Freehold of Dragonsbane." He rose, letting her hand fall, waving his hand toward his companions. "I am the sworn protector of Her Highness, Fairwind Duine Fionn, princess of the High Aelf, and an accomplished mage. Accompanying Princess Fairwind is Ariandel Spéir álainn, Cara Ríoga. As she is Fairwind's Cara Ríoga, she is under my protection as well." Finishing the introduction, he gave another deep bow.

"And how do you know Queen Arielle?" Vanessa asked, a little shocked at the sudden gallantry the fighter displayed. Looking at her, he merely shrugged.

Fairwind replied to her. "We have only met her at the Aerie. It is Sivle and Alliandre who know her best." Fairwind thought for a moment. "We met her only a half score years ago, when we first began traveling together. What a party of misfits it was. Sir Braxlo and I had met Sir Lolark." Pointing at the massive throne-like chair to her left, she added, "he is the one they built that chair for." Smiling, "Lolark was traveling with a mage of the Red Crest Magistry, Lord Robin. He was friends with a priest he knew named Erich, who was friends with another priest named Sivle, who grew up with Alliandre in the Southern Kingdom as wards of the Throne. Sivle, Alliandre, and Marion all played together growing up, until the Golden Aelf invaded and took over their kingdom."

Fairwind smiled up at Vanessa, asking, "Does this clarify things?"

"Vanessa smiled back. Not really. I gather Alliandre and Sivle are friends of Arielle. You are friends with Alliandre and Sivle, so you all come here."

"Very good," Ariandel told her. "Except I am not friends with any of them," then casting a glance at Fairwind, "maybe Her Highness, but I am definitely never going to be friends with Drullock, or Alliandre, or whatever his name is." Saying it with a smile, Vanessa wasn't sure if she was serious or not. With the introductions finished, she began taking their orders.

"Will anyone else be joining you?" she asked Fairwind.

"Sivle had better be," Fairwind said tartly. "He is to train both of us this afternoon, and he had better not be late. As for the rest, who knows. We are all planning to attend the Bard Competition this evening, but Erich was talking about attending the Artistry Competition exhibits this evening."

"It is a Thieves Guild meeting," Braxlo added helpfully.

"Sir Braxlo, you know as well as any that Erich is not a thief. Any association he may have had in the past with the Thieves Guild is left in the past. He is a respectable, landed nobleman." Fairwind seemed quite stern, but Braxlo just smiled.

"Yes, Your Highness. It is as you say." His smile continued, though, and Vanessa caught the barest smile from Fairwind as well.

"None the matter," Fairwind continued. "I think us ladies will have the hens and roasted roots. Perhaps a pitcher of wine as well if it isn't too much trouble." Then she looked over at Braxlo.

"I will have a hen, with some of the roasted venison I smell cooking. Some roasted roots along with a loaf of the corn cakes John makes so well. And a flagon of mead." As Vanessa left, he twisted back to add, "Might want to bring a large pitcher of the mead instead." By the time she returned, Sivle arrived as well, picking food off of Braxlo's plate, to the annoyance of the big fighter. The four ate their lunch quickly before leaving for the dueling grounds.

After they had left, Vanessa made several trips to the pantry with a string to make some measurements for Vandion. Almost discovered twice, she got the measurements, tucking the string with the knots inside her coin purse. Arielle let her nap in the afternoon, one of the morning cleaning women working instead. She slept, dreaming of riding with Vandion in a magnificent carriage. She could hear the hooves thundering on the ground.

Pounding on the walls woke her. Quickly going into the bar, she found two noblemen pounding at a mousekin crawling on the wall. Looking like mice, they were actually insects which delivered a nasty bite. Vanessa wondered how it got here. They were more common in the western plains and savannahs. Neither man was successful at hitting it with their wooden canes. Sir Andras came up and knocked it once lightly with his wooden mace, squashing it.

Looking at the two nobles, he scolded them. "You two dandies couldnae take a wee sleeping baby. Look at the dents in me wall now. Take yer fancy walking sticks and go before I have tae teach ye not to go poundin' on polished silver bark. But ye better pay yer bill first, or I'll make yer heads look like the wee bug there." Carefully, he scraped the bug into a napkin, emptying it out back. The two nobles, shame-faced, paid their tab and staggered out. Sir Andras shook his head. "If ye canna hold yer drink, ye shouldnae be drinkin' at noon."

As long as she was up, Vanessa figured she should get back to work. She grabbed her coin purse, smiling to herself as she rubbed the wound string between her fingers. It was time for the evening meal. Vanessa grabbed her apron, hoping the party would be in again. She went over to Arielle. "Have you heard anything from Marion?"

Arielle smiled broadly as she shook her head back and forth. Then, Arielle leaned in and whispered to her. "Do not tell anyone from the Party of the Seven, only Alliandre knows. I am sure she will want to tell them herself. She will be terribly busy the rest of Jubilee, so I hope you can work like this every day. I promise you it will be worth it."

"I shall do whatever it is you command, My Queen." Vanessa gave a small curtsey, but Arielle's smile left her.

"Never address me that way." Her face was still pleasant, but her tone made it clear she meant every word. "You are a subject of the Central Kingdom. King Henry and Queen Persephone have been quite generous in allowing me to stay here, but this is their kingdom." Arielle's tone softened, and a small smile returned to her face. "If you wish to pledge fealty to the Southern Kingdom after I have liberated it, I will make you a baroness. But please, never say that again, even in jest. There are too many ears and eyes that would love to make trouble for us."

"Yes, my lady." Vanessa was on the verge of crying. Arielle gave her a hug, before getting ale for three knights bawling loudly for more. Vanessa dried her eyes, going back in the kitchen to put on her apron.

***

Ariandel had never attended a bard competition as large as the one scheduled for later in the afternoon. If her training didn't go any better, she still might not. Sivle first instructed them to prepare a spirit shield, only turning the edges outward. This proved to be more difficult than she expected. Even if it was not perfectly square, as Sivle's was, it was still as good as Fairwind had managed.

Next was levitating small clods of dirt in front of the shield, blending aether spirit to the earth spirit before adding fire. Sivle explained aether was volatile when adding to two spirits already combined, while fire and air were two which added on top nicely. Still, when she bound the earth in aether and tried to add the fire, the result was an impressive explosion, sending her toppling backward despite the shield. Fortunately, Fairwind fared only a little better, sending her dirt clod almost two paces before it too exploded.

"Very good ladies," Sivle told them. "Now, just be more delicate with the fire spirit. Ariandel, you are forcing it into the seams and folds you left. Try coaxing it, rather than just stuffing it in." Turning to Fairwind, he smiled. "You know what you did wrong, don't you?" he asked.

Fairwind nodded sheepishly. "I left far too much room in my first weave, hoping to make it easier to add the fire spirit, but it just made the whole thing unstable."

The next try wasn't any better. On the fifth try, she got the dirt clod to hold long enough to throw it. It went as far as Fairwind's first attempt. They had scorched the ground in front of them, and one of Fairwind's attempts had traveled about ten paces, still burning on the ground. Ariandel wiped the sweat from her eyes, levitating another piece of dirt.

"Hold off a moment please, ladies." Sivle began creating a thin line of aether. Then he created a line of air and began twisting them together. They twisted around each other for about a step before dissipating. He added another line, this one of fire, to the other two. The three lines constantly moved out from his hand about a step, weaving in and out of one another like a hair braid, but never touching.

"Practice until you can move them out a full step. Start small, though. If they touch, they will react." He watched as Fairwind and Ariandel began, then turned to leave. "While you practice, I shall get us a snack. This level of constant casting is draining. I don't want you to hurt yourself because you are weak from hunger."

In a few minutes, Fairwind had hers out a full step, practicing another minute before she stopped, turning to watch Ariandel. Ariandel let the weaves touch for the third time, gasping as a mini jet of flame spewed from her hands.

"You are doing fine," Fairwind assured her. "Move your body with your hands, don't do it all with your fingers." Ariandel tried again, getting them an arm's length away before they touched.

Sivle returned with a platter of bread, cheese, and some pears. Ariandel did not know where the pears came from, but she was glad for them. He also brought a large silver pitcher of wine. The three of them rested and ate before trying the exercise again. Ariandel eventually moved the braid of spirits a good stride out, and Sivle let her try the flaming dirt again. "But first, always create a spirit shield."

Carefully, Ariandel created her spirit shield, forming it into a box before flattening the sides to create an outward facing curve. Levitating a small clump, about the size of a child's marble, into the air, she carefully wove earth and aether around it. Like the exercise they had done earlier, she left a small amount of space in place to weave the fire spirit through. Carefully, she threaded the fire spirit around and through the other two until it came around to where it began. Then she cast it down toward the far fence line. It went almost five paces before it exploded.

They practiced the rest of the afternoon, Sivle explaining how to change the weave to hold longer, how much fire spirit needed to be added, the thickness of aether spirit, or any of a hundred tips and tricks she had to consider for each try. But, as the afternoon ended, she sent the dirt to explode exactly on a small mound of stones Sivle had placed thirty paces away. Fairwind was working on larger clumps when Sivle declared the lesson finished. "We will want to clean up and get ready if we expect to catch Mirandel singing tonight."

**

Sivle led the group down to their seats near the stage. They had reserved booths for noblemen and women, while the commoners sat far to the side or behind the nobles. Prince Lucas gave them to Alliandre earlier, even providing a seat for Ariandel. Alliandre intended it to be for Marion, but she was sitting with the other royal court members, just behind the judges.

Dozens of bards stood in a long line behind a hastily constructed fence, ending at a large pavilion set up with a small stage opening to the fairgrounds.

Alliandre arrived minutes before the competition began, more than a little drunk, towing an even more drunk prince along. They parted ways as Alliandre went to his seat, noticing Sivle placed him next to Ariandel.

Alliandre bowed to her and spoke, "My Lady Ariandel, so pleased you could attend on such short notice." Whispering to Sivle as he sat, "If she faints again, you get to catch her. Every time I help her, she gets upset with me." Alliandre grinned broadly, Sivle rolling his eyes.

"What took you so long? You were to meet us at the Aerie an hour ago," Sivle whispered back.

"Marion needed me, or rather Aeris, to pull her coach during the parade," Alliandre explained. "Afterward, I had to do my own errands. Then I met Prince Lucas at one of the ale vendors. He said his ale was the strongest in the human kingdoms, and I think he may be right. Sorry, I lost track of the time."

Sivle was about to chastise him when a man walked across the stage. He was wearing golden tights tucked neatly in short, bright green leather boots which perfectly matched his green ruffled silk shirt. Over the shirt, he wore a purple velvet vest with satin-rimmed pockets and large gold buttons, unbuttoned to display the ruffles on the sleeves and down the front. A short, floppy hat completed the ensemble. Anyone seeing him could be forgiven if they thought he should be at a jester competition. In truth, Lord Pembroke Del Wren, Baron of Chasmwatch, was the king's own jester, and a competent bard to boot. He was also the king's most trusted advisor and a mage of exceptional talent. Raising his arms to quiet the crowd, he spoke in a voice clearly enhanced by air spirit. "Ladies and gentlemen, noble and common. They have given me the great privilege to introduce the judges and the contestants for this evening's competition. Our first judge is Sir Tristian Del Moor, Paladin of the Wren, Lord and Commander of Wren's Keep."

A portly man in cuir bouilli and a steel breastplate came from behind the side of the pavilion, waving to the crowd as they applauded politely. His tabard had a stone tower, surrounding a shield displaying a green field with an argent wren on a bend azure. He came over to Lord Pembroke, who said a few words while waving his hand over him. When Sir Tristian spoke, his voice was amplified so even those in the back heard him clearly. "For some time now, the bards have inspired the fighting men and women of the kingdom to heroic deeds. Their songs have brought courage, strength, and even healing to our soldiers, knights, and paladins. Tonight, I will judge the impact of their words and music on our hearts and minds." Giving a small bow, he jumped off the stage and stood before his chair.

Lord Pembroke spoke again. "Our second judge tonight comes from the Copper Leaf Woods. We are pleased to have her. Although only three hundred years young, she is already renowned as a troubadour and songstress, singing for over a dozen kings and queens in the last year alone. It is my pleasure to introduce to you Lady Sumangil Amhrán Éan."

An aelf appeared from the side of the stage opposite where Sir Tristian had entered. She also came up to Lord Pembroke, who seemed to speak and wave his hands over her before she spoke. "Bards use their song and their music to inspire and encourage. Practicing and perfecting their talents before using them to enchant the spirits to do their bidding. Tonight, I will judge their musicianship and presentation." She then stepped to the edge of the stage, where Sir Tristian helped her down to her seat.

"Our third judge needs no introduction. We would be terrible hosts, though, if we invited her without asking her to perform for us." Lord Pembroke sauntered across the stage. "May I present to you the greatest living bard, Mirandel Amhrán órga."

On the stage, a single aelf sat with a lute. Black boots went to her knee, below yellow satin pants tucked inside. A green blouse with large golden buttons peeked out from behind a gorgeous lavender bustier. A shawl of lavender and green covered her shoulders, adorned with birds set in emerald and sapphire.

Cries of surprise went across the crowd. Mirandel had not performed for a large gathering in years. As the curtains opened, a wave of thunderous applause cascaded over her. She brushed her fingers over the strings of her lute, waiting for the applause to die down before speaking.

"I am happy for the invitation to play for you and judge the competition of the many fine men and women who pursue this calling I have dedicated my life to." More applause. She strummed her lute again to quiet the crowd. "I am grateful my work has touched so many, and I hope you all are just as touched by my words today. It has been twenty-eight years since assassins took the lives of the two younger Prionsaí Ríoga, leaving only a single remaining heir to the Great Aelf throne. I think the event is overdue for a song."

Mirandel Amhrán órga began playing a slow up and down melody on the lute. Sivle had never heard it before, which probably meant it was one of Mirandel's newer songs. When he had trained with her a decade ago, he listened to her entire repertoire at least twice. Enchanted with her voice, the weavings of air and aether and fauna went forth as she sang. She had a voice which was soft and sultry, yet she could turn it brassy and loud at the drop of a hat.

When she began singing, the words washed across the crowd, and they stayed quiet until her last note.

A prophesy older than the aelf longest aged,
Was delivered to all, as the great battle raged.
Men dropped their swords, and the aelf dropped their bows.
To mourn all the noble lives whom they owed.

Cry with a mother and mourn with a queen.
An evil unlike what before we have seen.
Eyes flashing violet, she wailed, and she cried,
The assassins had taken the great banríon's pride.

For hundreds of years then had peace served us well,

But hatred and faithlessness remained with us still.
Never more clear to us now, I must say,
As the Prionsaí Ríoga deaths showed that sad day.

Cry with a mother and mourn with a queen.
An evil unlike what before we have seen.
Eyes flashing violet, to the spirits, she called.
Assassins have stolen the future of all.

There is not one living who can chronicle now,
Who hired the assassins, the why or the how.
The queen's eyes flashed violet from all of her pain,
The killers have never been heard from again.

Cry with a mother and mourn with a queen.
An evil unlike what before we have seen.
Eyes flashing violet, she schemed, and she planned,
'Till the bounty and sentence were known through the land.

The aelf nobles cheer for the Corónú to start,
For this, some were willing, to break a queen's heart.
An aelf is the only Prionsa Ríoga at last,
But the queen has her allies, friends, true and fast.

Cry with a mother and mourn with a queen.
An evil unlike what before we have seen.
Eyes no longer flashing, with violet or tears,
She patiently waits through the passing of years.

The aelf nobles cheer for the Corónú to begin,
But perhaps the aelf nobles will pay for their sin.
An aelf is the only Prionsa Ríoga, it seems,
But visions of her dead sons remain in her dreams.

Cry with a mother and mourn with a queen.
An evil unlike what before we have seen.
Eyes no longer flashing, at peace in her home,
Just hope that your name has not made her tome.

Mirandel stood and bowed as she finished the last notes. Walking to the edge of the stage as Sir Tristian rose to help her, she simply stepped off the edge and gently floated down to her seat beside him. Sivle, watching her closely, noticing her stumble, and her paleness. Lady Sumangil Amhrán Éan rushed to help her.

"Are you ill, my lady?" Lady Sumangil asked.

"It is nothing but my many years, their effects escalating as they grow," Mirandel said softly as she stood up to face the crowd and wave. "Nothing the spirits can do for this old body."

Slowly, the applause began and grew until Lord Pembroke had to shout, despite the enchantments carrying his voice. It was several minutes before Lord Pembroke could silence the crowd, but after several minutes he took control again. "Our first contender this year is a young aelf from the prairies west of the Copper Leaf Forest. May I introduce to you, Arnelor Croí Íon."

The curtains opened as Lord Pembroke stepped to the side of the stage. Seated was an aelf who was the spitting image of Lolark, if Lolark had pointed ears, slanted eyes, and was two feet shorter. His voice was velvet smooth, and he used it perfectly to sing a short song about a knight who saved a town at the cost of his own life. A common tale, but his telling of it seemed to move even Alliandre, although Sivle was sure it was because his friend was still drunk.

The evening passed as the bards brought the crowd through a range of emotions and moods. Excitement as Brannagar Del Húrphen sang about the daring raids of the Copper Aelf paladins during the Great Vreen War. Sadness as Russielle Croí Iasair recounted how two young humans found love, honor, and a tragic death joining a river caravan traveling up to Voldair. Master Rene Del Ossur brought everyone to their feet, singing a song describing the eventual victory in the

Grendlaar War half a millennium ago. Sir Roanoake the Terrible re-counted the siege of Stein Virki, describing the loss of all but ten of the defenders before winter snows drove back the attackers. Then, Alanalle of the Dale was introduced.

With the lanterns illuminating the stage, the first thing Sivle noticed was her golden-tinged skin. Dressed in a green dress trimmed with golden leaves on purple vines and snow-white epaulettes on her shoulders, she brought with her a small harp. Softly at first, then harder, she plucked the strings until her voice rang out, surprising everyone. She began with a recount of the Great War, and the terrible toll it took, particularly on the Black Aelf, but even more so on the Golden Aelf. She told the story of desperate battles they had, losing almost an entire generation of elders to the human invaders. Then she began sing-ing about the decision to uproot the mountains and the great magic they had discovered to do it, which took the lives of all involved in the casting.

The harp changed its tone as she began feverishly plucking the strings. Then she told of the years of preparations until the Golden Aelf were strong enough to take back their lands and more. The slaughter of the Paladins of the Golden Chalice and Gold Keep and the invasion of the Southern Kingdom. The heroics of the Golden Aelf army, who, though betrayed by the Great Aelf, persevered and took the Southern Kingdom. Slowing down, she sang next about the peace and prosperity which the Golden Aelf enjoyed today and finished with a warning to all those who thought to make war against the Golden Aelf again.

When the last notes of the harp faded, the crowd was silent. Sivle looked around. Everywhere, people looked around in shock. Several people began whispering, a few hisses heard in the back. Then the king stood. For several seconds, the crowd became even more silent until the king began clapping. Slowly at first, the rest of the royal party joined in. Soon, most of the crowd was giving polite applause, with a cohort of Black Aelf paladins standing and cheering enthusiastically. Sivle looked over at Alliandre with a concerned look. But Alliandre was searching the royal party for Marion. If he saw her, he gave no sign.

The longest song of the evening occurred when Lord Jacob the Carpenter sang all three parts of Baron of the Finger Bands, a well-known song about the Third Millenia BGW (Before the Great War). Challenging him was the old, crusty bard, George the Martinet. He began the first part of the epic Melody of Frozen Water and Flame, thankfully stopping after the first part, Leisure Sport of Royal Chairs. When the crowd gave a standing ovation, Sivle thought it may have been because he refrained from continuing the seemingly never finished song.

The rest of the evening was much the same. Gawander the Lark, hailing from Foresight, ended the competition with a song about being raised in the "greatest city in the known world," bringing everyone to their feet. Afterward, all the bards got back on stage together to sing an old song about the valiant Prince Lucas of the Central Kingdom. It recounted how Prince Lucas and a man-at-arms held out against a spear of vreen, causing the vreen to withdraw in humiliating defeat.

Sivle recognized it as the encounter where Alliandre had saved Prince Lucas' life. The vreen grievously injured Prince Lucas on the last day, and Alliandre had already used what healing he had. Alone, against over a hundred remaining vreen, he defended the mouth of the cave. When the vreen withdrew, Alliandre carried Prince Lucas for three days through the mountains, until he could heal him. Days later, the prince discovered several arrows and bolts had penetrated Alliandre's armor. Despite two of them oozing blood the entire time, Alliandre had healed the prince instead. When he told their tale, Alliandre omitted the prince falling, in fact reversing their roles in the telling. Prince Lucas had never forgotten it.

It was a rousing song, punctuated with a refrain which matched any drinking song found in the taverns. With that many bards playing and singing, the energy in the air was palpable. Sivle thought it might overwhelm some, but he danced and swayed with the tune, both energized and euphoric. Looking around, it affected the rest of the crowd the same way. Several were standing and singing along, though Sivle could not hear them over the bards. He looked at the royal booth, noticing Prince Lucas staring over at Alliandre, who gave a small salute in return. At the finale of the song, explosions and burning lights filled the night sky.

In the end, Sir Roanoake took the golden harp awarded to the winner. They awarded Russielle Croí Iasair a silverwood Lute for the runner-up. The judges named Fortuna Del Regga the best new bard, giving her a scholarship to train at the school in Foresight. The crowd applause named Gawander the Nobleman's Choice and the queen herself presented him with a royal invitation to play for Their Majesties and guests at the Royal Ball. The invitation also included a bag with fifty turots.

Sivle watched as guards led the new royal court to the stage to meet all the bards. He caught sight of Marion there. He looked over at Alliandre, who had already caught sight of her. Alliandre waved to get her attention. It was not to be, so after a while of mingling with old acquaintances, they made their way back to the Aerie.

VI

❧

Training Day

29th of Frendalo, Year 1124 AGW

Vanessa skipped to the Wyvern's Aerie. Vandion gave her a ride as far as the bridge. The guards remembered her from the morning before, knowing she worked at the Aerie.

"Milady, would you like an escort to the Wyvern's Aerie?" the nearest guard asked.

"Thank you, but that is unnecessary. I am sure the streets are quite safe." She waved at Vandion as he rode off, gazing at him for several seconds. She loved the way he pranced his horse when she was not on it. He always rode slowly, at an even gait, when she was riding with him, ensuring she stayed on.

"If it would please you, milady." The guard approached her and bowed. "Sir Andras will usually let us fill our wine sacks and give us some bread and cold meats when we escort one of his beautiful staff to the door. It has been a long night, and we are on for several more hours still."

Vanessa blushed. She was not used to being flirted with. The guard was clearly flirting; however, it was only because he wanted her to accept the escort. Sir Andras did always hand out a cloth of food to the guards when they came on business to the Aerie. She looked at him, bowing politely, flirting back. "In that case, it would be an honor to be escorted by such an, um, a dashing guardsman as yourself."

They exchanged introductions as they walked. He regaled her with his exploits so far as a guardsman. "I entered the Open Melee. If I do well, perhaps an order will select me as a squire." Turning bashful, he surprised Vanessa with a request. "It is customary for a fighter to carry a favor from a lady. Would you have a favor I could carry for luck?"

She blushed, politely declining, mentioning Vandion several times. He was quieter then, only perking up when she asked if he would like her to ask Sir Andras to train him. He went on and on about how Sir Andras did not train anyone, and what an honor it would be. Vanessa didn't understand the excitement. Sir Andras was quite old, over sixty she thought. He had not fought with a sword in over fifteen of those. But the guard, Jason Si Gladahar, seemed overjoyed.

They made it to the Aerie without incident, with Jason accompanying her inside. Already, the tavern was full. Vanessa went directly to Sir Andras, who appeared to be in the same clothes as he had worn the day before, the guard following close behind her.

"Sir Andras," she began. "This young guard has escorted me from the river bridge. I was wondering if I could prepare him a basket, as you often do."

Sir Andras looked at her askance. "Ask John to prepare him a guard sack and fill his wineskin with the morning beer." Then, with a small bow to the guard, "Thank you, laddie, for seeing her here safely."

"One more thing, if it would please you to do me a small favor?" Vanessa all but batted her eyes at Sir Andras, as she had seen Marion do when she was imposing on his goodwill. "He entered the Open Melee Tournament. I all but promised him you would give him a lesson or two." She bowed her head in apology at the last, then raised her head and added helpfully, "He can come as soon as his shift is over and would wait until you can take a break."

Sir Andras scowled at the young girl. "I cannae do that, lassie. I am sorry, but I made an oath to train only those soldiers who swear allegiance to the Southern Kingdom. This young laddie has already made an oath, and I won't steal soldiers from King Henry." Seeing the look of disappointment, he thought of a compromise. "I'll tell ye what, lassie. When Alliandre comes down, I will ask him to train the laddie. Have him come by after his shift. Now, give me his wine sack."

Jason looked confused but bowed to Sir Andras anyway. "Thank you, my lord. I have not heard of this Alliandre, but I would be in your debt for any help you can provide." Sir Andras had already turned and walked away, and Jason turned to Vanessa. "Do you know who this Alliandre is?"

Vanessa gave him a knowing look. "He beat a bunch of paladins yesterday, that's all I know." Jason's eyes grew wide as he checked Vanessa's face to be sure she wasn't joking. When Sir Andras came with his sack and wine skin, he bowed, thanking him again before leaving.

Vanessa looked up at Sir Andras, smiling sweetly. She was even more excited to get her surprise set up for him and Queen Arielle. She went right to the pantry, opening her pack, and as Vandion had taught her, laid iridium wire on the floor carefully in a precise pattern. Sprinkling some powder Vandion had given her, she covered the wire so they would not notice it. Looking at the ground closely, she made sure she had hidden it from casual sight.

The first part done, she hurried to the kitchen to prepare the rest. Pretending to clean the floor, she laid out another set of wire in the same pattern. It was more difficult with all the activity, but she usually helped scrub floors when she began her shifts, so she hoped no one would suspect. She had just finished sprinkling the powder over the last section when Arielle called over to her.

"Vanessa, dear. No need to clean. Diana and Jean Marie have already cleaned this morning." Smiling over the counter, she continued, "I think someone from the private rooms has come down. You may want to get to them before Diana does."

***

Sivle rose an hour before dawn, roused the others, and came down to find the tavern full. Seeing their regular table empty, he sat down. The serving girl, Vanessa, hurried out to him, arriving shortly after he had gotten himself settled. She seemed like a sweet girl, and she was in unusually high spirits this morning.

"Good morning, my lord." She began with her normal greeting. But then she hurried on to offer him the special firstmeal Arielle always had prepared for them. "John has sweet cakes with spring berries this morning, along with fresh eggs from the hens. Of course, we have our bacon, and Her Majesty has put together a special firstmeal for your party. Will others be joining you this morning?"

"The rest will be down shortly," Sivle answered. "I have an errand to run, so I suppose if you bring everything out, it would be easiest for you. If you have any of the mace bean tea, I could use some today instead of the morning beer."

"Certainly, my lord. I will have it right out for you." Vanessa rushed back into the kitchen, passing the request to John, the cook.

She wondered when he slept or did anything else. He seemed to always be in the kitchen. She had never made the mace bean tea, as almost no one ordered it. It was a dangerous drink; only those with a robust constitution could drink it. As soon as she asked for the beans, though, Arielle took over, explaining she knew just how Sivle liked it. The tea finished brewing. As she brought the steaming pot out, John let her know the first sweet cakes were ready. Setting the tea out quickly, she hurried back for the cakes and a plate of bacon fresh from the stovetop.

Alliandre came downstairs soon after she delivered the last platter. Erich came down a few minutes later. Braxlo was the last, following behind Fairwind and Ariandel like a sheepdog herding chickens. The ladies were chatting about something, Braxlo rolling his eyes quite frequently. Once they were all seated at the table, Fairwind addressed Sivle.

"Would you be so kind as to make some time this afternoon again for us, please?" Sivle groaned internally at the request as Fairwind continued. "We both feel we would benefit from another lesson."

"Yes, my lord," Ariandel added enthusiastically. "I practiced the drill you taught us last night. I think I am on the verge of mastering the three spirits together. Your skill at teaching is quite impressive. It almost makes me happy Mirandel was not available."

She lowered her eyes just a bit at Sivle, the flattery so obvious he had to stifle a laugh. But Fairwind once again delivered the request with the intent of a royal decree. He wasn't obliged, but he had nothing better to do this afternoon.

"Fine," he simply said. Then, after rethinking his day, "But it will have to be a bit later. I am going on a bit of an adventure again this morning." Seeing Ariandel's eyes light up, he quickly added, "No, you cannot come along."

"Do you need any help with..." Alliandre asked, stopping as his attention shifted to the door. Marion entered the tavern with her prince, Lord Del Broussard, beside her. Following her came King Henry and Queen Persephone, along with the rest of the new royal court. Prince Lucas came in, accompanied by an older man and woman Alliandre had never met, dressed in bright yellow, orange, and red. Golden feathers adorned the woman's bodice, arranged as a fan supporting her covered bosom. Her yellow skirt stopped just above her ankles to reveal bright red shoes with orange laces.

With the presence of the king, all the patrons rose from their tables, bowing until the king acknowledged them. Spreading his dark purple cape with his arms, he commanded the tavern crowd. "Sit, everyone. We are here at the invite of our new princess, Lady Marion the Virtuous. Please, sit back down and continue your meal." The patrons sat back down, but all eyes still faced the door.

***

Alliandre had just finished his first plate of food when King Henry entered the Aerie, along with the entire Jubilee Royal Court. Happy to see Marion, he rose to greet her.

Lucas came straight over to Alliandre, clasping wrists with him.

"I am sorry to do this to you, my friend, but I need you to leave for a few minutes." Prince Lucas looked deathly serious. Alliandre looked at him questioningly.

"What troubles you, my friend? I have already met Marion's prince, Lord Del Broussard. He seems like a delightful fellow." Holding his hands up and open, he continued, "You will have no trouble from me."

"He is not the guest I am worried about, my friend," Prince Lucas replied. Sighing, he reached up to grab Alliandre by both shoulders. "There was an incident here a couple of days ago where a young lord assaulted Marion."

"Yes, I was here," Alliandre said with a nod. "Fortunately, a banner from the Order of the Wren was here and handled the situation. Your father explained he was to be flogged and held in the stocks for a few days then released."

"Yes. He was," Prince Lucas paused, "but no more. He is the son and heir of Duke Randolf Del Mornay of the Western Watch. Duke Del Mornay controls almost a tenth of the Central Kingdom's armies, supporting twenty full banners of paladins at Wyndgryph Keep as well. Not to mention the five hundred Wyndgryph knights, which he also supports in the name of the king."

"How does that concern me?" Alliandre asked.

"It means," the prince lectured him, "the Duke and Duchess Del Mornay came all the way from the Western Watch to plead for leniency for their son, which my father has granted. They are here now for Sir Rodney to apologize to Marion and Arielle and make restitution. In return, Arielle and Marion will grant their forgiveness so they can put this behind them without a loss of honor."

Alliandre's eyes flashed dark as he moved to the door. Soon, Sir Andras appeared beside him. "Settle down, laddie." The old knight laid his hand across Alliandre's chest. From the time he was a small child, it had been the signal from his mentor he was at a rubicon he should think carefully about before crossing. "Without the support of the nobles, the king cannae rule the kingdom. King Henry needs the duke to maintain the western border. Like it or not, King Henry is granting the wee shite clemency, laddie. None in this house shall contest it."

"So, we have two sets of laws and punishment then." Alliandre looked at Sir Andras directly. "When I was young, they taught me there is only one law. For a ruler to be just, all the laws must apply equally."

"Aye, laddie, ye learned yer lessons well. But the real world isnae so perfect. This is a sacrifice ye must make when ye are king. Ye accept a small wrong in the short term to preserve the kingdom. He did no lasting harm to Marion, and the laddie received a knock on the head and time in the dungeon to dissuade him from repeating his behavior again. Now, the laddie is going to apologize. The duke will give Marion a small gift as an admission his son was in the wrong, and we will all forgive and forget. All of us."

Alliandre looked at Sir Andras, his eyes flashing again. While not exactly pushing either Sir Andras or the prince aside, Alliandre strode past them toward the gathering crowd. "It had better be one hell of an apology."

Walking to the door, Alliandre arrived just as the king had finished his introduction of Duke and Duchess Del Mornay, along with the new royal court. As Arielle instructed Diana to escort the newly crowned royals to a private dining room, the king interjected. "Princess Marion. Could we bother you for just a moment, please?"

Marion looked a bit concerned, but curtseyed and replied, "Of course, Your Majesty."

Addressing Marion, Arielle, and Sir Andras, the duke spoke up. "I understand a couple of days ago, a young nobleman drunkenly assaulted Princess Marion. I am sad to say the lout was my son, Sir Rodney." Turning to the king, he continued, "I will do what I can to see he is on his best behavior from here on." Turning directly to Marion, he went on, "Your Highness, please accept my apologies for my son's behavior, and accept this as a small token of our contrition."

The duke stepped aside; the duchess stepping forward to his spot with a small chest, which she handed to Marion. Inside sat a small tiara and matching necklace made of solid gold, with generous amounts of rubies and sapphires decorating them. "These belonged to my great-aunt, and I hope you will accept them, and our apology, in the spirit of building a long and lasting friendship."

Marion curtseyed to the duchess and spoke as she rose. "I am honored by such a magnificent treasure. I assure you I bear no ill will against your son. I have witnessed too often the effect drink can have on otherwise kind and honorable people."

Arielle was about to speak when the duke stepped forward with his son in tow. A lump still rode high on his head where Sir Andras had hit him. The young knight, though bleary eyed, was dressed in new clothes, wearing a jeweled long sword at his hip. The duke spoke as they approached. "Queen Arielle, Princess Marion, may I introduce my son, Sir Rodney. I believe he has some things he would like to say as well."

The young lord bowed his head slightly, addressing Marion. "My Lady, I apologize for getting drunk the other night and clumsily displaying my attraction to you. Whether it was the drink or the blow to the head, I remember little of the night. I am told, however, I behaved badly and I am deeply sorrowful. Particularly if I have offended you. I should have remained sober and requested the right to court you formally before taking liberties with you." His apology finished, bowing his head slightly again, he turned to leave, stopping only when his father grabbed his tunic. With a great sigh, Sir Rodney turned around and stood next to him.

It wasn't much of an apology, not even addressing her properly, and Marion cast a questioning glance at the duke, who merely shook his head and rolled his eyes. Marion curtseyed again, addressing the duke. "I accept Sir Rodney's apology in the spirit it was given, Your Grace." Then turning to the king and queen, "Your Majesties, if I may excuse myself, I am supposed to be entertaining the royal court this morning." She went to the kitchen with the chest, returning moments later.

Meanwhile, Alliandre stared long swords at Sir Rodney. The knight, catching his glare, smiled. "Father, I think there is one here who does not accept my apology."

The duke looked over at Alliandre. Alliandre could feel Sir Andras at his back, along with Prince Lucas, who placed one hand on his friend's shoulder and stepped in front of him.

"Duke Del Mornay," the prince said, bowing, "may I introduce Alliandre Del Nileppez Drol Hulloc. He was raised in the court of the Southern Kingdom and fought alongside me in the Great Vreen War. He is a great friend of mine, and of the Central Kingdom."

The duke bowed, but his son spoke out. "Just a friend of the Central Kingdom? Then he is not a subject of Their Majesties?" Turning to his father, he continued, "Oh, so then this must be the poor commoner soldier who Prince Lucas had to protect in the Great Vreen War. He glares as if he wishes to challenge me. Perhaps the king would allow me some exercise this morning."

"I serve the Southern Kingdom," Alliandre stated matter-of-factly. Waving his hand over toward Arielle, he added, "I serve Queen Arielle the Beautiful." Seeing Marion returning, he added her as well, "And I serve Princess Marion the Virtuous. If you wish to duel, I have my gear upstairs."

"There is no need. I have a sword. You have a sword. Why not just handle this here and now. Or stop glaring at me like a mongrel dog trying to stare down a wolf."

The king stepped forward and interposed himself between the two. "They have settled this matter. There will be no duel. You may meet in the Grand Melee if you choose to and settle your differences then. Am I understood?"

Sir Rodney just laughed. "Woof woof, little dog. You should thank the king for saving your life. If it were..."

"ENOUGH!" The duke grabbed his son, yanking him back and around. "It is your life we are trying to preserve here. Leave and do not enter this place again. If you wish to be duke someday, you will avoid any altercations with the Southern Kingdom from now on."

The duke then shoved his son to the door, hustling him out to the street. The duchess turned to Arielle and bowed, then to the king and bowed, speaking gently. "I am terribly sorry for the behavior of our son. I think after my elder sons died in the various conflicts, my husband spent too much time training him with the sword, depriving him of training in diplomacy and chivalry. I suspect his time with the Wyndgryph knights has not helped either."

Looking straight at Alliandre, she bowed, addressing him directly. Alliandre could see the tears welling up in her eyes. "Please do not harm my son. Lady Arielle knows what it is like to lose a son, and I have already lost three. This is our only remaining heir. I beg you to let him live long enough to learn some wisdom." She then bowed again before leaving with the king and queen.

The excitement over, the noise in the tavern soon reached its previous levels as Alliandre and Prince Lucas walked back to the table. Marion walked quickly to the back room, not even saying goodbye. Prince Lucas slapped Alliandre on the back as they walked and said, "I have not tasted the Aerie's bacon in a while. I hope you don't mind if I stay for firstmeal."

Alliandre looked at him suspiciously, wondering if there was another surprise, then clasped him on the shoulder. "As long as you are buying the morning beer, you can stay as long as you like."

**

Sivle left the Wyvern's Aerie immediately after firstmeal. The eastern sky began to lighten with the coming sunrise. He needed to use a flying spell today, having used all but one portal scroll. Deciding to use it to get back from the Great Chasm in case a quick exit was needed, he walked through town and out the Eastern Gate before casting his spell. Once he was airborne, the city disappeared behind him quickly. He could only hold the spell so long as he could concentrate on generating the weave to stay aloft.

His trip to the Great Chasm was uneventful. Only twice did he have to change course to avoid grendlaar forces. As he neared the chasm, the hills became larger, requiring him to twist around much more than he had planned. Almost half a hursmarc out from his destination, his concentration faltered, forcing him to land. He chose the downslope of a spur, landing gracefully in a quick walk, gradually slowing to his normal pace.

He had walked halfway there when he once again noticed a large group of grendlaar marching into a cave hidden in the side of a hill. He would not have noticed the cave if he had not seen the grendlaar entering. A couple of spears worth, or kikosi, he remembered. By the packed and trampled earth, Sivle suspected there were many more. He marked the cave on his map. Once he finished, he slowly crept away from the cave, continuing to the Great Chasm.

Arriving at the temple, he went inside, first making himself invisible, then silent. These were both done with air and aether spirits, which he had mastered long ago. Though air and aether were the easiest spirits to weave together, they were also the hardest to hold together. He had practiced these for so long; he was confident they would last long enough for what he wanted to do. Moving silent and unseen, he waited for an acolyte to go outside, following her out and down a short path. From there he turned toward the Great Chasm, while she followed the path around to a small grove of trees.

Soon he was back to where he had met with the grendlaar elders. Seeing no one immediately about, he wandered in the direction the grendlaar had come from. Occasionally, he saw small gardens hidden among the vegetation. He had not noticed them before; the plants were hidden among taller vegetation with similar foliage. Only when you knew what to look for did they become obvious. Anyone casually noticing them would probably just attribute them to wild growth, but Sivle had seen the grendlaar hoeing the soil and harvesting them. He knew they were no accident.

He thought of his own keep in between the Black Woods and the Great Chasm. He, Erich, and Alliandre controlled tens of thousands of blocks of farmland. It was on the edge of what had been the Black

Woods a thousand years ago. Only Erich's status with the Black Aelf prevented the aelf from overrunning the lands. The presence of the Black Woods was also a deterrent to grendlaar raids, along with the constant population of mages at Sivle's school and fighters training under Alliandre's cadre. Stone walls surrounded almost a tenth of the land, raised by Sivle years ago, leaving tens of thousands of blocks of land open and unused.

One of the chief sources of revenue for their keeps was the trade of produce from the protected farms. Sivle couldn't help but wonder how much more revenue they could bring in if they could trade with the grendlaar. It was a question for another day, however, as currently he was more interested in finding where the grendlaar lived to assess their numbers. If they numbered even a tenth of what the grackle elders had implied, the world was in for a rude awakening. Coming around a bend, a squad of grendlaar soldiers drilling in a small cave surprised him. The wind rushing through the caverns had covered the sound of the commands being spoken, and the grendlaar moved silently as they swung their spears at imagined enemies.

Sivle watched for a short time until one of the soldiers put his nose to the air. He chittered excitedly, placing the entire group on alert, sniffing and probing for the unseen enemy. Moving quickly downwind, Sivle crossed the cave mouth. While the grendlaar could not see or hear him, he still had to walk on the loose stones. Several rolled away as he crossed. The grackle drilling the grendlaar came over, swinging his sword in broad arcs. Sivle chose discretion, continuing down the path, leaving the chittering grendlaar behind.

Farther down, he came across another "garden," with two grendlaar tending what looked like spring berries. They carefully plucked the ripe berries while leaving the others to finish ripening. Spring berries were a delicacy in most places because the hearty bushes liked thin, rocky soil. Many merchants sent excursions to the Great Chasm to gather them, often transplanting the entire bush to replant it in one of the mountain ranges. But the particularly touchy plants were difficult to cultivate. Many of the transplanted bushes died within a few days.

After wandering for several hours, he noticed several grendlaar emerging from a cave. Letting them pass upwind, he waited several minutes before cautiously approaching the opening. No sound came from within, so he cautiously entered. Pulling a light stone from his pack, he explored the cave from front to back. Pretty nondescript as caves go, the opening was just a few paces across; the cave going back almost a score of paces. Oblong in shape, he looked for some sign of it being occupied, but other than a few torch sticks, it didn't seem to be used. He was just about to leave when something caught his eye.

He wasn't sure what was wrong, but the back wall of the cave did not seem quite right. He searched along it, looking for a seam or a crack, but there was nothing. Then he noticed it. The light from his stone cast shadows over the uneven surfaces of the stone walls, but not on a certain section of the back wall. Scrutinizing it, he closed his eyes and walked into the wall. He passed through the wall into a brightly lit hallway. The walls were not quite polished stone, but what he saw was clearly not a natural tunnel formation, either. The arched ceiling had light stones set in sconces hanging from a center beam.

He walked along the hallway for a few minutes, when doors appeared. Not daring to open them, he stopped at each and listened for sounds of activity. Hearing none, he continued down the hall until it opened into a grand hall. He could see hundreds, if not a thousand or more grendlaar at stone tables, eating and drinking, but the hallway was silent. Walking through the opening, the sound of it hit him like a fire blast. Guardedly, he walked around the perimeter of the great hall, looking for another exit.

The hall must have been several hundred paces across, taking him several minutes to get even halfway around to the other side. Passing an opening where grendlaar were carrying out platters of food, the smell of roasted roots and vegetables carried across the air. Some even smelled like some sort of cooked meat. A fountain in the center was used to fill pitchers with water. He hurried past, dodging the grendlaar carrying the trays and platters out and returning with the empty dishes on small carts. He was nearing a great double-door when a small voice behind him surprised him.

"You don't belong here. What are you doing sneaking around our dining hall?"

Sivle looked behind him at a miniature man. Smaller than the grendlaar even. Dressed in a white woolen shirt over brown woolen pants, with little leather moccasins covering his feet, dark dust covered his entire outfit. The man was looking directly at him, his scowl and stare showing he was waiting for a reply.

"I am exploring the grendlaar home," Sivle said, "I mean no harm to any here, but I fear if I am seen, there will be trouble. I am..."

"We know who you are and your many names. Sivle Si Evila, Clan Slayer, Kóngsson, Spiorad Mór Fíor-oidhre. You are not welcome here. The Na Oibrín are under our protection." The small man waved Sivle back the way he had come, his expression not of someone willing to be disobeyed.

"If you would wait to dismiss me, I would like to talk to you about building a friendship with the Na Oibrín." Sivle hoped to stay but knew he would have to leave if the little man insisted. "An acquaintance of mine had a discussion with Gron-gohlotsch, which made me realize the error in the way we have made war on the Na Oibrín."

"Gron-gohlotsch is a fool." The little man seemed less angry, but again waved his hand. "From the time after the great cataclysm, the Mór-Oibrín have done nothing but kill the Na Oibrín. And you, Kóngsson, you and your raiders have killed more than any. Or do you not remember?"

"It was a war," Sivle replied. "I wish we did not have to kill them, but they attacked Silver Cross Keep, ravaging the settlements in the area."

"That is the Mor-Oibrín's side, I suppose." The little man grabbed Sivle's hand, pulling him back the way he had come, continuing his lecture. "The M'Pande clan had farmed and gathered that land for centuries before the Mór-Oibrín came to it. When the Mór-Oibrín came, they attacked the families without warning. The Mór-Oibrín knights hunted the Na Oibrín, so yes, the M'Pande defended themselves. Then you arrived with your butchers and wiped all that remained of the clan. They were kind and gentle people, with no skill in war. But even when they surrendered, you did not let them free, but turned them over to the knights, who tortured and killed them in the end."

Sivle thought back, reflecting on the last battle. The paladins and knights of Silver Cross Keep had fought an unending stream of grendlaar for months. Whenever they defeated a war party, usually several thousand strong, another would attack somewhere else. Lolark had called on Braxlo and Alliandre for aid, and the entire party arrived to help. Sivle, Fairwind, and Robin had used great walls of fire to trap an especially large group of grendlaar in a deep, cliff-lined valley. Then they used fire and ice blasts to decimate the ranks. Sivle used an earthquake spell to disrupt their formations, but it caused an avalanche from both sides, which buried all the grendlaar in the falling stone. The remaining two thousand grendlaar tried to break out, but Alliandre, Braxlo, and Lolark, along with a spear of knights from the keep, prevented them from escaping. The few hundred grendlaar who survived surrendered. They were marched back to the keep and executed.

Sivle thought about the grendlaar he saw in the hall. They looked almost like children. Ugly, flat-faced, beady-eyed children, but children, nonetheless. Far different from how they looked brandishing spears and charging. Stopping, he pulled back on the hand leading him.

"I wish to make some amends for our actions. We did not know the history of the Na Oibrín and did not think to look at the conflict from their side. The Na Oibrín have always attacked humans, so we did not investigate or try to negotiate. But I think the time for peace has come."

"If the Mór-Oibrín kept their treaties millennia ago, there would be no need for negotiations for peace. Now, I am afraid even if the Ter Oibrín could trust the words of the Mór-Oibrín, they will not. It is all we can do to keep them fed and housed now the land above the ground is denied to them." He waved at the grendlaar filling the great hall. "Their numbers diminish as their food sources are taken from them. There are Ter Oibrín who wish to unite the clans to take back the land from the aelf lands to the Black River. They believe they can overrun the armies of the Mór-Oibrín. But we know of all the lands beyond and know the Mór-Oibrín would ultimately destroy our servants entirely."

Sivle took this opening. "Then why not try for peace? If I, a Clan Slayer, can ask for peace, surely that will hold some sway over the Ter Oibrín."

"It would only embolden them." The little man shook his head sadly. "They would see it as an admission of weakness at this point. I am afraid we must delay the inevitable as long as we can. But perhaps you can do one thing."

Sivle nodded his head up and down. "Whatever I can do, I will do."

"Very well. When next you wage war on the Na Oibrín, and we know there will be a next time – After you have defeated them, send them home with food and blankets and livestock. Show them your wish for peace. Maybe then, some will change their hearts and negotiate for peace. But be warned. Do not make a peace which you cannot keep. The Ter Oibrín have long memories. For their entire existence, they have had the promises made by the Mór-Oibrín broken. Now, since you do not appear to be leaving, I shall have to force you to leave."

"I will leave now," Sivle said. The next moment, he was standing at his keep with the little man beside him. A bit disorientated, Sivle just looked at him and asked, "How?"

"Is this not where you and the red giant live? I have brought you home safely, as I ask you to do with my people."

"I see." Sivle tried to think of something to make the little man stay. "Let me make one more gesture of friendship, then. I will command my men to fill up several wagons with crops and a score each of pigs and sheep." Pointing at a field just outside the fence line, he continued, "They will arrive there at sunset. Take them back to the Na Oibrín and let them know from this point forward, Sivle Si Evila Drol Revo will refrain from fighting the Na Oibrín, unless they first attack me."

The small man nodded and turned to go.

"Wait," Sivle called out. "What is your name, should I want to talk again?"

"I am named Krom-gohlotsch. I sincerely hope we do not meet again." He then disappeared without so much as a wave of his hand. Sivle spent the rest of the morning arranging for the wagons to be filled, and the livestock left out. He also included several rams and boars, in case the grendlaar could breed animals. Then, with the preparations made, he went to his library to gather several more scrolls before using a portal to return to the Wyvern's Aerie.

***

Alliandre and Prince Lucas finished their firstmeal and stayed drinking in the tavern when the serving girl came up, a member of the town guard in tow.

"Excuse me, my lord," she began.

"I am not a lord," Alliandre exclaimed, almost by habit.

"I apologize, milord." She looked to Alliandre like she had been trying to raise her courage to speak, and having done so, was unsure of what to say.

"Well, girl, spit it out." Alliandre shook his head at the harshness in his tone, but the apple was off the tree, as Marion liked to say.

"Yes, milord." The girl swallowed once, then began again. "Sir Andras told me you might give this young man some training in fighting since he escorted me from the bridge this morning. He signed up for the Open Melee, wishing to become a squire. I told him what a mighty warrior you are, defeating all the paladins the other day. Sir Andras told me you wouldn't mind giving him just a few lessons." It all came out quickly and jumbled together, but she smiled sweetly when she had finished, with just a slight flush coloring her cheeks.

Alliandre stood and looked the two of them up and down. "Sir Andras!" he called out.

Sir Andras came over and immediately apologized. "Aye, sorry laddie. I forgot to ask ye, but Miss Vanessa asked me if I would give the laddie some lessons. I cannae do that ye know, but I told her you would." Sir Andras looked unapologetically at his protégé. "It might do ye some good to train again. Ye always were the best trainer I had."

Alliandre looked at the young man again. About seventeen or eighteen, he had probably been in the guard less than a year. A full head shorter than Alliandre, he had a stocky build, with legs slightly out of proportion to the rest of his body. His sword hung from his left hip, with the scabbard tight against the leg so it didn't bounce around. The sword looked clean enough, and the rest of the uniform was in good repair. "What is your name?" Alliandre asked.

"Jason," the boy squeaked. Clearing his throat, he began again. "Jason Si Gladahar, sir."

"Tell you what, my friend," Prince Lucas spoke up. "I will be his sparring partner, and you can give us both a lesson."

Alliandre glanced at his friend, then back at the boy. "Since the prince has commanded it, I guess it would be seditious of me to deny the order. Come with me." Turning briskly, he left for the dueling grounds.

Prince Lucas merely looked at the lad. Seeing his hesitation and excitement, he prodded him on. "Well son, are you always this slow when given a command by your teacher? GO!" Jason charged to catch up with Alliandre, with the prince sauntering behind, smiling the entire way.

Alliandre was true to form. It had been years since he had trained the squires at Dragonsbane. Even longer since he trained the squires in the Southern Kingdom, but old habits die hard. He first led Jason and Prince Lucas through some basic drills, evaluating the skill level of the young man. Steadily increasing the complexity of the drills, he added more sword strokes and parries. After each drill, he would explain how Jason could improve, repeating the drill until Jason had mastered it. The boy was a quick learner and a natural with the sword. It was a shame he wasted his skill in the guard.

The guards' responsibility was security in the city, not fighting a war. They trained in the basic skills of carrying, swinging, and stabbing with a sword. But as the king restricted who carried weapons in the city, it was unlikely they would ever fight anyone else with a weapon larger than a dagger. For this reason, they focused on containing and peacefully resolving a situation rather than fighting. If they encountered an armed assailant, the guards would blow a whistle or run back, getting the more experienced officers to deal with it.

The sun was high overhead and on its journey down by the time Alliandre gave the two a break. After refreshing themselves with the water and mead Vanessa had thoughtfully brought out, Alliandre declared it was time to put the drills to use. It was then they realized Jason had no cuir bouilli to spar in. A call to Sir Andras brought out some paladins of the Order of the Night. Though Alliandre had never heard of them, they had their cuir bouilli armor with steel breastplates and helms. Between them, they patched together a set which fit Jason well enough. With the crisis solved, Alliandre began. Setting both of them on opposite sides of the dueling circle, he raised his sword and commanded them to begin fighting.

Prince Lucas charged the boy. At the last moment, once Jason had raised his shield, he pivoted behind the shield, catching Jason with a sharp blow to the back of the head. The paladins who had come out clapped and cheered. The prince turned to Alliandre with a big smile when his own helmet rang from a blow which stunned him. Looking up, Alliandre appeared none too pleased.

"This is not a duel, Your Highness." Alliandre gave a curt bow, then continued. "The purpose of this exercise is to allow young Jason here to practice the drills he has learned, not to demonstrate what a great warrior our noble prince is. Please refrain from using any techniques we have not drilled on yet."

Prince Lucas returned the bow to Alliandre, then bowed to Jason as well. "My apologies, milord Jason. I will endeavor to be a better wooden dummy from here on out." Then he flashed a big smile at Alliandre while returning to his position on the edge of the circle. Jason also returned to his position, a puzzled look on his face.

"Begin," Alliandre said when both were in position. As the two men circled, Alliandre calmly called out the names of the drills they had performed. Despite pulling back his speed and aggression, the prince still defeated Jason each time. However, he labored more and more as the day dragged on. After several hours, Prince Lucas announced it was time for him to go. Looking exhausted, but also disappointed, Jason knelt on one knee, thanking him. Standing, he looked at Alliandre.

"I guess this means we have finished." The disappointment showed in his face, but he bowed deeply, "Thank you, Sir Alliandre."

"I am not a Sir," Alliandre reminded him again.

"My lord Alliandre," a paladin interrupted. "I am Sir Tristian the Light. If it would please you, it would honor me to spar with your pupil."

"For the spirits' sake, I am not a lord," Alliandre repeated. He hadn't planned on spending the day training. The morning and half the afternoon had already passed. However, as he thought of the week ahead, this was truly the only day he had free. He wished to observe the other martial tournaments to evaluate the competition he may face in the Grand Melee. The Sword and Shield Tournament in particular.

The winner would be his chief challenger in the Grand Melee, assuming he made it. The Jousting Tournament as well, although it was not uncommon for someone to be more skilled on horse than they were on foot. Certainly this would be true of the Open Joust, where, like the Open Melee, the knights did not complete. "Very well. Let us get some food, and we will continue after we have eaten. A round of drinks on me."

A cheer went up among the paladins, Jason beaming as they went inside. Alliandre spoke to Sir Andras, who sent Diana outside for a brief time. Vanessa brought them food and drink, Alliandre paying with a single turot. They ate and drank until a small man came in with a string and a scroll. He measured every aspect of Jason, often whispering a discussion with Alliandre, who gave him a small purse of coins. With his business finished, they returned to the dueling grounds.

The rest of the banner joined them, cheering for Jason and Sir Tristian. Alliandre stopped the sparring many times in order to train Jason in further drills. Each time he did so, the paladins joined in as well. By the time the sun was easing toward the treetops, Jason had done so well, Alliandre had been training advanced techniques, including assassin's block, otter dive, and sand snake strike. Drills went on for another hour until Alliandre announced the training completed for the day.

"Come back the morning of the Open Melee Tournament," he told Jason as the young boy left. "It will hardly do for you to go to the tournament with no armor. They will provide you some, but it will be piecemeal and ill-fitting, as this is, hampering your movements just like today."

"But milord, I have no money to pay for armor." Jason looked a little embarrassed as he continued, "I have been saving, but I had hoped to get noticed by an order to avoid paying for it."

"It is your reward for being such an attentive student." Alliandre smiled and reached out his arm to the boy. Dumbstruck, Jason clasped wrists with the much larger man and then turned to go. Alliandre was still smiling as he returned to the bar to get some ale. Training was thirsty work.

"Aye laddie, you seem a lot more relaxed now ye got to turn your attention to something positive." The old barkeep handed him his glass but kept a hold of it while they locked eyes. "It was a hard thing ye did this morning, and dinnae think we dinnae know it. But everyone agrees it was the right thing to do today. And if ye fight him in the Grand Melee, be tryin' not to kill him, or even hurt him too bad. We dinnae want to cause grief to King Henry, now, do we, laddie?"

"No, we don't," Alliandre agreed. He tried to raise his ire again at the insults they had forced him to ignore earlier, but he just couldn't. Whether it was the time passing or just fatigue, he recognized the duke's son as a spoiled and pampered man whose life had been filled with everyone telling him he was a skilled knight. When put to the test, it would likely be heartbreaking, as those tests were commonly fatal.

"To your health, old man!" Alliandre said, raising his glass before draining it.

***

Ariandel was getting frustrated, but it was good frustration. Fairwind had asked Sivle to explain how he made multiple fire stones. He agreed, but he met them at the Mage's Academy, rather than the Aerie. In hindsight, it was a good idea, affording them more privacy, while protecting the Aerie from errant spells.

After having the three of them raise spirit shields, he picked up a rock, tossing it in the air in a short arc, then catching it in his other hand. Then he tossed it up again, catching it back in the hand in which it had started. Then he picked up another stone, throwing first one, then the other, catching them in the opposite hands. Next, he picked up a third rock and began juggling the three rocks, commanding Fairwind to add more rocks until he had eight rocks rotating up and down in front of him. Then his hands stopped.

Air spirits wove in and out, continuing the motion of the stones. One after another, each stone broke into four smaller stones, rotating as one. Slowly, Sivle wove aether and fire in while tightening the arc in which the stones traveled. He cast it out. The stones flew as one to the far end of the grounds, separating and exploding in eight small diamond patterns, forming an octagon of fire and stone, cratering and scorching the ground below.

Ariandel sat speechless. Fairwind, however, was not so enthralled.

"That is all well done, Sivle," she complimented him. But then her tone turned to scolding. "But you need to teach us how to do it, not just show off your talents."

"Yes, Your Highness," Sivle said as he bowed. "The first thing you need to learn is how to juggle the stones."

He began throwing stones up at each of them to keep in the air. Fairwind managed the three he gave her, but their arc was flailing, requiring all of her concentration. Ariandel, on the other hand, struggled with two for quite some time. By the time she managed to keep a third in the air for more than a few seconds, she was sweating, her breathing becoming strained. Fairwind mastered the three stones but could not keep a fourth stone up for more than one arc.

They practiced juggling for several hours until both could keep the four stones up through several cycles. Then Sivle showed them the stamins for the air spirits. This proved much harder. Ariandel understood she wanted the air spirit to carry the stones in the pattern they had while she was juggling, but the coordination required for weaving the spirit was much more difficult than merely moving her hands. Likewise, Fairwind was having difficulty, although she was better at it than Ariandel. Sivle was willing to keep the training going, but fatigue had set in. Both Ariandel and Fairwind chose to quit for the day, returning to the Aerie to eat.

"Tomorrow, I expect you to continue this lesson," Fairwind stated without a hint of a request in her voice.

"After mastering four stones, I can teach you the next steps." Sivle smiled broadly, holding his arms out and shrugging. "Only after you have mastered four without thinking, can I show you the stamins to add aether and fire. My guess is this will take you some time, but please reach out when you are both ready."

VII

Warrior's Code

30th of Frendalo, Year 1124 AGW

Alliandre went down to the tavern hall early, finding his way to the bar. It was still at least an hour and a half before sunrise, but he could not sleep. The martial tournaments began today, and he wanted to study each potential adversary he would face. There wasn't much to be gleaned from the shield wall. However, once a formation was broken and reverted to hand-to-hand combat, the skill of the combatants could be evaluated.

Only a few others were in the bar; Diana and Jean Marie were providing what fare they could. John had just arrived to fire up the ovens and cooking fires, so Alliandre went behind the bar, pouring himself his first morning beer. Warm and flat, they added spices the night before to counter the staleness, and a bit of mead to sweeten it. He didn't know the recipe, but he often missed it when he wasn't in Foresight. They served it until the keg ran dry, then it was back to the real beer or ale.

Marion came in, skipping over to him immediately. His mood instantly brightened. He stood, waiting for her customary jump into his arms. Since she could walk, she had always greeted him that way, but today her jump seemed half-hearted.

"Have I offended you, Your Highness?" he asked, quite worried he had.

"No, silly," she replied. "I was just thinking how upset you must be with me."

Alliandre tried to think. He could remember nothing Marion had done which would cause him to be upset. He hugged her tight, setting her down gently in front of him, clasping her hand, staring directly in her eyes. "Truthfully, I cannot think of anything you have done which would cause me to be upset." Still staring at her, he waited for her to explain.

"Sir Rodney the Magnificent," was all she said.

"You were the one who was wronged. Why would his lack of honor and his fate of an inglorious death upset me?" Alliandre said it without emotion, almost as if his death were a foregone conclusion.

"You cannot. I thought that was clear. And also why I am afraid I upset you." Marion looked at him with damp eyes, hoping for him to say something to calm her fears. Something to prove to her he would take no action against the duke's son.

"We will meet in the Grand Melee," Alliandre said with surety. "And I will humiliate and punish him for his actions."

Marion looked up at him, not sure if she believed him. "And that will be his inglorious death?" she asked.

Alliandre shook his head. "Even if it does not come at my hand, it will come, believe me. I have seen too many knights so sure of themselves they will rush headlong into any battle, against any odds. So sure of themselves that the thought of death never crosses their minds. Until the day comes when death greets them." Smiling at her, he tilted his head slightly. "Many have accused me of the same thing." Straightening his head again, he continued, "But I have always understood death awaits every man who enters battle. I have been fortunate to have lived this long, but I rush into battle knowing it may be my last day. Sir Andras taught me that when he first gave me a sword."

Marion looked up at him. "But we, including me, forced you to let him insult you and stand by. I was so ashamed, I had to leave." Tears were now actually dropping slowly from her eyes. "When he called you a mongrel dog, I was so ashamed of myself for forcing you to endure it. I am so sorry, Alliandre." Sobbing softly, she wrapped her arms around him.

Holding her gently, Alliandre took a deep breath. He could feel the anger of the moment rising again, quickly settling it. Speaking softly, in as calming a tone as he could manage, he said, "It was what you had to do. What the king had to do. It would do me well to become more practiced at enduring insults rather than always insisting honor be maintained." Stroking her head softly, he added, "I would bear any insult if it meant you would regain your throne. If you needed me to be a court jester, I would dress in green and purple and wear a block of golden cheese on my head for you, only to see your smile."

Marion giggled. She separated from him, smiling up at him. "I may just hold you to that." Hugging him again, she pulled up a seat next to him. "Which reminds me, wait until you hear what Ferdinand said about you and Aeris."

***

Braxlo came down to the dining hall to see Drullock and Marion talking and laughing while eating what must have been the entire stock of the Aerie's bacon. A massive platter of it sat in front of them, along with a bowl of what looked like cooked eggs. Seeing the seat next to him was open, he sauntered over to sit down, helping himself to the bacon as he did. Surprising him, Drullock passed him the bowl of eggs as well, even pouring him a glass of the morning beer. It wasn't Braxlo's favorite, but he wasn't about to interfere with Drullock's good mood.

"Good morning, Your Highness. Good morning Drul, um, Alliandre. You both seem in extraordinarily good spirits today." Popping a piece of the bacon in his mouth, he scooped some eggs onto a plate which Diana has just placed in front of him.

"Would you like some ham steak, Sir Braxlo?" Diana asked.

"Please!" mumbled Braxlo, past the half-masticated bacon in his mouth.

Drullock turned to Braxlo, replying to his greeting. "Good morning, Braxlo. Lady Marion was just telling me about her experience so far as a princess in the Jubilee Royal Court."

Marion blushed a bit, but nodded. "I am afraid my prince and I have created a bit of a firestorm."

Braxlo was interested now, but it didn't stop him from taking a mouthful of eggs and washing them down with a swig of the beer. Swallowing quickly, he asked, "Your Highness, what could an innocent, endearing young lady like yourself have done to sow any controversy?"

"It wasn't me exactly," Marion began. "As I told Alliandre, it was my prince who set it off. After Alliandre pulled our carriage in the parade, our queen, Lady Andi Del McDowell, became upset, making some not so flattering statements regarding Alliandre. So, my prince, Ferdinand Del Broussard, apologized, saying he was dreadfully sorry, but his princess only had one retainer, and he couldn't help it his mount was the most impressive beast in the known world."

"Doesn't seem too outrageous to me," Braxlo commented. "Seems like a diplomatic answer."

"Indeed," Marion agreed. "But then Lady Andi added 'the fact Aeris is blue is quite appropriate, don't you think?' which irritated Ferdinand, since blue is the color of one of the ladies-in-waiting, not a princess. So," she paused for effect, "he added 'the green livery of her driver, along with the green caparisons on her horses pulling her gold carriage are quite appropriate for her selection of queen as well.'"

Braxlo almost spit out his drink. Green and gold were long recognized as the colors of courtesans. This is why court jesters and bards and other entertainers always added purple to distinguish themselves. "And how did Lady Andi respond?" Braxlo asked.

"She insisted her king defend her honor and challenge Lord Ferdinand to a duel. But everyone knows Lord Gerard and Lord Ferdinand are great friends, so Lord Gerard suggested perhaps each of us ladies could choose a champion, and they could duel it out. Lady Andi insisted it be a blood duel, selecting Lord Gerard's father, who was there with them. Earl Comaste happily agreed."

Pausing again, Marion tried to suppress her laughter. "When I told them my champion was Alliandre Del Nileppez Drol Hulloc, he turned white. Then he told Lady Andi he was sorry, but regrettably, her honor was beyond defending."

Both Alliandre and Marion laughed again, as Braxlo chuckled at the thought of the poor Earl Comaste having to disappoint his son's queen. Alliandre would not have seriously hurt him, but anyone who had ever met Alliandre, or even seen him in passing, would have to be supremely confident to risk a blood duel over such a trivial matter.

"That isn't even the best part," Marion blurted out between giggles. "Last night at the queen's dinner, everyone presented her with gifts, since she is queen." Putting on an innocent face, she continued, "We gave her a set of gold-embossed silverwood combs, set with emeralds." Smiling broadly, she finished while trying to withhold her laughter again. "After she received each gift, as is customary, she had to display them. When she put on our gift, she looked again like she would have been more comfortable at the Golden Palace."

All three laughed again, Marion excusing herself. "I must get going, however. King Henry is hosting us at the palace this morning to meet the representatives from each of the aelf kingdoms. Then this afternoon we get to meet the representatives of the dwarven kingdoms. Tonight, we will host the winners of the Shield Wall Tournament at the palace." She got up, curtseyed to Braxlo, and leaned in to give Alliandre one last hug. Then she walked out the door, holding it open as Sir Andras walked in.

***

Fairwind and Ariandel came down the stairs, discussing the training for the day. Rather than practicing the drills Sivle had taught them, Fairwind wished to work on some air spells. She knew from experience gaining mastery in one spirit helped you when trying to combine it with others. Air was the easiest spirit to master. Which, according to an incredibly old joke, was why even bards could use it.

Fairwind noticed Braxlo, walking over to him and Alliandre. As she came over, Sir Andras set up two settings for them next to Braxlo, then hurriedly got glasses for them.

"Good morning, gentlemen," Fairwind addressed them as she arrived. Both Braxlo and Alliandre rose and bowed to her before giving their own greetings. "Sir Braxlo, I thought for sure you would be at the Sword and Shield duels this morning."

"It is the Shield Wall Tournament today, Your Highness," Braxlo corrected. "Drullock and I were just finishing our firstmeal before going to scout it. Is there anything you need before we leave?"

Smiling at Sir Andras, who had just arrived with a silver pitcher of wine mixed with citrus juices, she shook her head. "I am sure Sir Andras is up to serving us this morning. We plan to train all morning. If you could come by at noon, His Highness, Perhaladon an Trodaí, has asked me to dine with him this afternoon. I would like you to attend as chaperone."

"It will be as you command, Your Highness." Braxlo bowed again. He and Alliandre left the Aerie soon after, a pile of malnots decorating the bar where they had been sitting.

Fairwind and Ariandel were finishing their firstmeal when Sivle and Erich came down the stairs together. Sivle walked straight over, while Erich wandered to the far side of the table.

"Good morning, Your Highness. Good morning, Lady Ariandel." Erich bowed to each as he greeted them, taking a seat on the other side of Sivle.

"Good morning, Lord Erich," Fairwind replied. "I was just telling Lord Sivle we would not need his services today, but I would ask a small favor of you."

Erich looked a bit surprised, and warily agreed. "Whatever you command, Your Highness."

"It is just a small thing," Fairwind assured him. "I would like you to find out what you can about His Highness, Perhaladon an Trodaí, Prince of the Black Woods. I want to be sure his intentions are sincere, though I have no reason to doubt them."

"It will be as you say." Erich bowed again.

"Thank you, Lord Erich." Fairwind now turned to Sivle. "As I was saying, I am going to give Lady Ariandel some lessons myself this morning, weaving the air and aether spirits together. I think it is safe to say we will not be needing your services today."

"Good to hear," Sivle replied. "I have scrolls to write if I am to get my entry to the Spellcaster's Competition completed. I fear I will have to write scrolls all night. However, if you are working with air and aether, may I offer a small exercise?" As she nodded, he raised Fairwind's glass into the air, spinning it. Slowly at first, soon it was creating a whirlpool in the liquid inside. Adding aether, the sides of the glass became frosted until the wine and juice inside turned to slush. Setting it down gently on the table, he gave a small bow.

"It is harder than it looks," Sivle assured them. "Once you have mastered it, you can use it to practice your control."

"As always, Sivle, you amaze me with your insights. We will certainly add this to our training today. In fact," she said, turning to Ariandel, "if you are finished, Lady Ariandel, we can go now." Grabbing the pitcher and goblets, Fairwind walked out to the dueling grounds.

Once they were settled, Fairwind looked excitedly at Ariandel. "My dear, you do not know what great fortune it has been to train you. Lord Sivle is always generous with his time and his magics, but I think he has taken a liking to you."

"What makes you say that?" Ariandel did not get the same feeling from Sivle which Fairwind was sensing. "He only addresses you and seems disappointed in my skills."

"Nonsense. You would not know because you have never worked with him before." Shaking her head vigorously, Fairwind assured Ariandel. "He does not offer tips unsolicited. Nor does he show off. But in the last two days, he has twice now tried to impress you with his skills. If you strum your harp correctly, you may have him singing your tune, instead of his own. Think of it. You would have one of the world's most powerful mages at your beck and call."

Ariandel laughed to think of it. She could tell Sivle was a powerful mage, but other than the stones exploding the day before, nothing he had done was any more impressive than many mages she had heard of. Mirandel was certainly more powerful. Toron had trained Sivle, so even Toron had to be far more skilled than Sivle. And Sivle had not shown the slightest interest in her, other than as Fairwind's lady-in-waiting.

At any rate, she was not interested in him. At all. Determined to make her name in the world, she delayed trying to find a mate. She dreamed of meeting a Silver Aelf mage of great power, certainly not some half-aelf bastard, not that she held his unfortunate parentage against him. It was no fault of his that his father abandoned his mother when she was with child. It was a common tale, even among the nobility, maybe even more so. But the nobles could always send their daughters away on a trip, returning to raise their "niece" or "nephew" due to an unfortunate accident to their distant relative.

Fairwind was in good spirits today, though. Moving to the far end of the dueling grounds, they practiced their magic. Fairwind handed her a glass, filling it with wine. "Just to practice with," Fairwind assured her. Sure enough, they practiced the drill Sivle had demonstrated earlier. It was more difficult than Ariandel had imagined. She had picked up hundreds of objects. It was one of the dozen tricks she learned under Toron. However, picking up a wineglass and picking up a wineglass with liquid in it were two different dragons. When the glass held liquid, it required much more control than with an empty glass, lest the contents spill.

Fairwind was quite skilled at picking up the glass. Trying to spin it, she ran into problems. She didn't spill any wine, but Ariandel could tell it was a struggle for her. Ariandel herself picked up the wineglass, but when she attempted to spin it, it tipped over.

"Drink," said Fairwind.

"What?" Ariandel replied.

"If you spill, you have to drink what is left. Motivation to succeed, don't you think?"

So, Ariandel drank. As the morning went on, both of them success-fully spun the glass, despite many mishaps. Ariandel suspected some of Fairwind's were deliberate, just so she could drink some wine. Adding aether and chilling the wine proved an even greater struggle. Fairwind could get the glass chilled, but often ended up freezing the wine solid. Ariandel struggled to chill the wine even a little. Fairwind eventually showed her how she braided the aether into the air spirit, rather than just intertwining them. This allowed the aether to slowly cool the glass.

Next, Fairwind expanded on the drill, showing her how to heat the wine using fire spirit instead of the aether. By the time they stopped for their midday meal, both of them were quite comfortable with Sivle's drill, while also reaching their limit of wine. Entering the tavern to eat, Fairwind excused herself, heading upstairs to change. Ariandel sat at a small table. She jumped as Erich appeared in the chair next to her.

"Will Her Highness be down soon?" the black-clad priest asked politely.

"I think so. She went up to change." Ariandel wasn't sure how to address Erich but decided this was a good time to find out more about him. "Excuse me, Lord Erich. I was wondering if you could help me with something."

"It would delight me to be of any service I can, Lady Ariandel." Al-though Erich said it with a bow and a sincere voice, Ariandel couldn't help but think there was too much sincerity to be genuine.

Nevertheless, she asked her question. "How did you become a priest in the Black Woods?"

Erich paused. He had never discussed his past. He answered slowly. "My parents were killed during the Grendlaar Wars. A Black Woods priest found me and raised me as her own. When I became old enough, I became an acolyte, eventually becoming a priest."

"In the Black Woods? That doesn't seem possible." Ariandel knew the Black Aelf and their disdain for humans.

"My mother was well connected." Erich smiled. "Eventually, after I had performed my service as high priest, I left to roam the world to learn more about the spirits."

"Then you became a thief?" Ariandel was about to correct herself, but Erich smiled again.

"I trained under the Thieves Guild. There is a difference. I do not steal from honest people, nor even most dishonest ones. I also disdain the taking of life, despite my prowess in the art."

Ariandel pivoted. "Then how is it you, a high priest, associate with a barbarian like Drullock, and why do I suspect you are even more dangerous than he tries to portray himself?" She smiled her sweetest smile at him. If the question surprised him, his face showed no sign of it.

"While I am loathe to admit it, there are few I would like to protect my flank more than Drullock. Fewer I would like angry at me." Smiling, he continued, "Though he is tactless, he is actually one of the most honest men I have ever met. While I dislike his straightforwardness much of the time, he truly does not know how to dissemble. I have never known him to lie, and he will take the short end of a deal just to ensure he is not seen to be taking advantage of another."

Ariandel thought on this. "Good qualities I admit, but I would think a man of your standing would not stoop to associating with such a brute, and a common knave."

Erich paused a moment at this. His smile fading, he answered her seriously. "I am not sure. He has saved my life, and indeed our entire party's lives, several times. Despite our differences, together we make a formidable force. He is part of it. I guess it is like a beautiful woman with a mole on her chin. She may despise the mole; but removing it would mar her beauty more than the mole does. For this reason, she celebrates the mole as an essential part of her beauty."

"Alliandre may annoy me, but to remove him from our party would change us to where we would not be the same. So, we celebrate his lack of tact or guile as a part of what makes us who we are. Besides," he added, his sarcastic grin returning, "Sivle is his friend. Even if Drullock were the most incompetent soldier in the realm, I would accept him in order to ensure Sivle was by my side."

Ariandel scoffed. "You and Fairwind act as if Sivle is the greatest mage of this age. I can tell he is skilled, but don't you think you bias your opinion of him because of your friendship?"

Erich turned gravely serious. "Make no mistake, my young friend. I am careful not to do anything deliberately which would make Alliandre upset with me. But I am deathly afraid of something I might inadvertently do to make Sivle upset with me. I have seen him create magics even the aelf bards have never sung about. Several years ago, he cast a spell to shake the ground. Not only did it shake the ground, but it also brought the mountains down. I do not think he even knows it was his strength which caused it, instead attributing it to happenstance."

Shaking his head, he sighed. "Mirandel refused to teach anyone after she realized her power was too great for the world. I believe Sivle has found the secret to that power, not yet understanding what he wields."

"But I have seen nothing which would indicate some secret power. Even when he was training me, he never displayed a hint." Shaking her head, she refused Erich's evaluation again. "I have seen some of the greatest mages in the Silver Leaf Woods. Trust me, he has done nothing to make me believe he is even of their level."

Erich thought a bit, then challenged her again. "And what of Mirandel have you seen which demonstrates her power?"

"Easy!" Ariandel replied instantly. "She sang a spell. Not a bard song, but an actual spell." Crossing her arms triumphantly, she smiled up at Erich sweetly. Her face dropped instantly when he replied to her.

"Exactly, my young friend," he said with an evil smile, "and who do you think taught her to do that?"

***

The two lines of men, six in each row holding shields, faced off against a similarly armed group across from them. Standing behind the two lines were four men with halberds. Standing at the end of each row, a pair of large knights wielded various weapons. The men hurled taunts at each other as the marschall stood between them. A banner on a tall pike rested on the marschall's shoulder.

204 - DANIEL E MYERS

Alliandre and Braxlo looked out at the groups of forty men paired up against each other. There were twenty-four other groups paired the same way, but only one of those groups had the colors of Wyndgryph Castle. Alliandre was interested to see just how good Sir Rodney was. A horn blared from the side. The marschall raised his banner high, dropping it at the sound of another horn, signaling the start of the tournament. Marching toward each other until they were just a few paces away, the two groups charged.

A great crash of shields and swords rang out across the fairgrounds as a thousand men joined in mock battle with each other. Shield walls were the common formation used by the humans, so effective soon the dwarves and aelf even adopted them. The centaurs had been later in adopting it. Realizing their size and mass made it even more effective, they chose larger shields and long spears to reach over their shorter opponents. Few now wanted to face them in formation, trying different techniques to counter their natural advantage.

Alliandre wasn't interested in the centaurs right now. He had identified Sir Rodney earlier, though the knights were all dressed the same. Sir Rodney's size and swagger were all too obvious. Set on the right side of the line, Sir Rodney charged around with his two swords slicing the air, trying to flank the other line. A warrior met him with a great sword, forcing him to slow his advance as the spear-sized blade scythed toward him. The knight stepped forward, forcing Sir Rodney to parry, catching the full force on his own swords.

Sir Rodney locked the great sword in between his blades and guards, trying to run up the blade to his opponent. He released the great sword as a mace came close to crushing his head. Parrying the mace, he stepped back, looking for his partner. His deformed cuisse told him everything he needed to know.

The mace returned to arc at his head, but he parried it easily, side-stepping to put the mace wielding opponent between him and the great sword. The knight with the great sword responded by stabbing over the shoulder of his partner, which afforded Sir Rodney the opportunity to lock the blade once again, running it down on the shield of the man in front. From there, it was simple to release the great sword once again, using his newly freed sword to come down heavily on the helm of the unhappy mace wielder.

The wielder of the great sword pulled away from Sir Rodney's sword. The momentum of the blade had been stopped. The knight backed away to gain some space, but by the time he got the sword's momentum up, Sir Rodney had closed and thrust his sword into the poor man's bevor. Nodding his acknowledgement of the hit, he lowered his sword, turning to join his partner on the side. Six others sat there already.

Sir Rodney now had the right side opened. Looking across his formation, his two knights on the left side had gone down, their opponents controlling the left side. But the wall was holding, three of the Wyndgryph shield men bursting through the line. The halberdiers tried to hold them in, but with no shields in front of them, they were poorly equipped to do more than slow their advance.

Sir Rodney charged the line, hammering the back row, forcing them to turn. This allowed his shield men to flank around the front man to begin rolling up the line. The same thing was happening to the Wyndgryph knights on the other side, but their halberdiers confronted the fighters, allowing their shield wall to shift to prevent being rolled. Within a minute or two, Sir Rodney gave the command to separate. The men of the Wyndgryph knights broke away from their formation to fight individually with almost two-to-one odds, quickly finishing their opponents.

Alliandre was impressed. Sir Rodney acquitted himself well. He noticed the left sword was almost always a heartbeat behind the right sword, something Sir Andras had broken Alliandre of when he was twelve. Most fighters who used two swords naturally had their dominant hand moving slightly faster than their non-dominant hand, creating a small gap in their defense and their attacks to exploit.

The rest of the battles took longer, with the dwarven Hammer Hold knights defeating the centaurs' Kau Pa'uhū knights. Many of the teams were upset with this pairing originally, pitting two of the finest competitors against each other. Then they revealed the Kau Pa'uhū had paid handsomely for the chance to eliminate their rivals early on. Now, they had paid instead for the chance to watch their rivals move on.

With a quarter of the teams eliminated, the field filled with groups again. This time, Alliandre was watching Sir Johan Giant Slayer, of the Stone Brook knights. Sir Johan had also trained at the Brass Helms Keep; Alliandre's training overlapped his by almost a month. Though Sir Johan defeated him nine bouts out of ten before he left, Alliandre had trained for nine months after he was gone. He was interested to see how much Sir Johan had progressed. Sir Johan, armed with sword and shield, stood in the middle of the front line. This would be a formidable shield wall team if he were one of the weaker members.

Initially charging the line, Sir Johan stopped just short, letting the rest of his line catch up before pressing his opponent. Switching to a coffin nail formation, the halberdiers charged the center of the line as the second row of shield bearers slid outward. The halberdiers were vigorous in their slashing and hacking, relying on the six men in front of them to provide protection. Sir Johan and five men surrounding him in the front row fought defensively to give the remainder of the wall time to encircle and roll up their opponents.

On the right side, they forced the end warriors to curl back or risk being flanked entirely. But on the left side, they forced the end knights to turn their shields away from the man next to them, exposing both. Normally, the halberdiers could drift to the ends to protect the flanks, or the outriders could step in. Their halberdiers had moved in to counter the boar's tooth, leaving them out of position. Sir Johan's knights exploited this perfectly.

The weakness of the coffin nail formation was the fact the center of the line was only one man deep. This risked a breakthrough if any of the knights fell. Fighting defensively, Sir Johan and his companions needed to hold out long enough for the maneuver to complete. The halberdiers in the center stepped up as the second line to add weight, exposing themselves to the opponent's halberdiers. Sir Johan was magnificent, Alliandre recognizing several of the techniques he had learned from Master Del Hauptman when fighting multiple opponents. Despite a vicious charge by the Waterton halberdiers, Sir Johan and his line held, losing only one shield and two halberdiers. By the time it broke into melee, three Waterton paladins were left against eight of the Stone Brook knights.

Now that the two mass battles had culled half the teams, the real tournament began. In the remaining battles, the only warrior of note was Sir Ramon the Brash, who held off six Iron Keep paladins, dispatching four of them before first losing his shield, then losing the match. The Iron Keep paladins hoisted Sir Ramon onto their shoulders and raised a cheer for him. The tournament order still being set, Braxlo excused himself. "You will have to scout the rest of your competition by yourself. Lady Fairwind has need of me this afternoon."

***

Fairwind came down in the same dress she had let Ariandel use coming into town. Ariandel thought she had looked like a servant when she had worn the dress. However, Fairwind wearing the dress looked like the High Aelf princess she was. Large curls fell around her shoulders, covering her modest breasts while still allowing their curvature to be accentuated. Long braids wrapped around her head, tucking into each other to create a natural headband to hold the rest of her hair in place. Blue and gold ribbons wove through it as well, a tree-shaped comb made of solid gold with emerald leaves securing the hair on the crown of her head.

"Your Highness," Ariandel said with a bow. Rising, she asked, "Aren't you a little afraid he will recognize it as the dress I wore when we entered Foresight?"

"We separated long before I approached his pavilion, so if he notices, it will tell us something about him, will it not?"

"Very good, Your Highness." Erich bowed as he approached. "I see all those years we spent together were not wasted." He rose from his bow, Fairwind flashing him a small dagger cleverly concealed in her sleeve.

"There are many things I have picked up along the way, Lord Erich. However, I have always believed it best to let the ones who specialize in gathering intelligence do the heavy lifting. Speaking of which, have you learned anything?"

"I have indeed, Your Highness." Erich held a chair for her, then sat beside her. "I am sorry, Lady Ariandel, but this must be a private conversation. I hope you don't mind."

"Certainly not, Lord Erich. I was thinking of lying down, anyway." Smiling at Fairwind, she continued, "It must be the heat, for I am feeling quite faint after our training this afternoon." She bowed to Fairwind once again, then walked up the stairs to the room they shared.

"First off, is the news good or bad?" Fairwind asked.

"Good news overall. Perhaladon an Trodaí is actually a member of the Ath-leasaiche. Quite enlightened as far as you aelf go." Erich waited for Fairwind to nod before he continued. "It is unlikely he will ever ascend to the throne, but he seems to have made some particularly excellent investments in trading companies, cutting himself off from the treasury. Everything you see him with, he has earned."

"Scandalous!" Fairwind joked. She had cut herself off from the treasury years ago. The Party of the Seven had accumulated a literal dragon hoard's worth of treasure in their years of adventuring together. She would have to live to a thousand to have a chance of spending it all.

Smiling, Erich continued, "His servant is also a volunteer from the temple. Evidently, he is quite renowned for his treatment of his servants, rewarding them handsomely for their service. His current servant is from the Iron Keep. Orphaned during the Great Vreen War, she ended up an acolyte at the temple there, moving to the Black Woods temple before being selected to accompany him to Jubilee."

Fairwind sighed with relief. The Black Aelf were known for their antipathy toward humans, many keeping slaves in the Black Woods. Those who did not outright enslave humans kept their "servants" indentured to the point of being slaves. The Ath-leasaiche groups had been forming throughout the aelf kingdoms for centuries, strongly supporting the human-aelf alliance and opposing the enslavement of humans, or even grendlaar. But the Black Aelf resisted longer than most.

Erich paused when Fairwind sighed, waiting for her to speak. Seeing her look back up at him with expectant eyes, he summarized quickly. "The only negative things I could find are he has taken up the human habit of the pipe, and for some reason, he does not eat fish at all. I have compiled a partial list of his holdings, known associates, and cities where he owns homes. You are also the first aelf he has courted, and as far as my sources could tell, the first female aelf he has even been alone with, immediate family excluded."

"Thank you, Lord Erich. I am quite reassured by your report." Sliding a turot over to him, she turned to look for Braxlo. "Now where is my chaperone? I do hope he is not late. Turning to thank Erich once again, she was only slightly surprised he no longer seemed to be in the tavern.

***

Alliandre walked with Braxlo all the way to the vendors before they parted ways. Braxlo to go meet Fairwind, Alliandre, to the nearest mead vendor. He passed a man selling hostra legs – a hostra being a large ground bird. Originally from the lands far west of the Pride River, some enterprising centaur merchant had brought back a bunch for breeding. Thriving in the grasslands the centaurs roamed, the herds migrated with the half-horse men. Many prized their legs for their great size and tenderness when cooked properly. The rest of the bird was less prized. Its undersized wings and breasts sold mainly for soups. Pointing at a smaller one, Alliandre pulled a malnot out for payment. Another ten dolcots got him a tankard filled with a sweet beer from the Silver Lake region. Prices were high in the fairgrounds, but it beat walking back into the city.

He returned to his place near the fence along the fairgrounds. Everyone cleared a path for the giant with two swords on either hip. Missing several rounds, the first match of the main tournament had just begun.

The Copper Woods paladins facing off against the Iron Keep paladins. Both sides locked in battle, neither side with an advantage.

The battle changed quickly when one of the Copper Woods paladins leaped over the shield wall, slashing at his opponents from above. Three halberds met him, forcing him back down on his own companions. This effectively knocked the shield wall down. The Iron Keep paladins were quick to capitalize. In almost no time, they had cleared the entire center of the line, sending shield men dancing among the Copper Woods halberdiers. With their line shattered, they gave the order to separate, but the outnumbered men were in two small groups, surrounded by Iron Keep shield men, still in formation.

Alliandre continued scouting the men from each team who had entered the Grand Melee. Sometimes it was difficult to see each one, at least until the later rounds. He decided by the end of the day there were a few of whom he would have to be careful. Duke Victor the Handsome was one. Younger than his title would imply, he defeated seven of the Pua'a Kua'a centaurs in the Redton knight's upset victory. He also was the last man standing in their loss the next round to the Haku Kāne centaurs.

Alliandre made more mental notes of the combatants he might face, particularly the Waterton paladin who had fought so well against Sir Johan. Planning in his head how he would face each of them, he did not leave the field until the sun was setting. He knew Marion would be busy with her "princess" duties, so he wandered around the vendors for a while before heading back to the Aerie.

**

Braxlo hurried back to the Wyvern's Aerie to get ready for Fairwind's courting. He did not know what was planned, but Fairwind had used her magic to clean and buff his armor until it shone like polished obsidian, reflecting the light in dark sparkles as it moved. Arriving at the Aerie, he went up to their room to find Erich resting. He had noticed Fairwind waiting in the dining hall but began chatting with the priest.

"Up late last night?" Braxlo teased his friend.

"No, Braxlo. Waiting for you, actually." Erich rose from his bunk and walked over. "There is some information related to our princess' suitor which I did not want to bother her with, but I think you should know."

"Tell me as you help me put on my armor." Braxlo threw his bevor over to Erich. "Fairwind is already dressed downstairs and will not appreciate me being late."

Erich, deftly catching the bevor, walked over to help his friend. First Braxlo stripped down, washing up while Erich unbuckled the armor from the stand. Braxlo put on his sturdiest woolen tights and his heavily padded gambeson before Erich came over with his new linen and leather arming jacket. His heavy leather boots completed his undergarments. He decided against the mail hauberk, as he was not planning on engaging in any combat today. Then Erich bent down and began armoring him.

Buckling on the sabaton, he relayed his message. "The Voldair Guild has marked Prince Perhaladon an Trodaí for death. I didn't bring this up to Fairwind, as she would no doubt inquire about it. We do not want the prince to do anything to tip off the Voldarians he knows they have marked him for death. If they find out Fairwind told him, it may put her in danger." Finished with the boot covering, he began attaching the greaves and cuisses. "Being a leading member of the Ath-leasaiche, there are several in his own kingdom who want him dead."

"I have heard of the Ath-leasaiche," Braxlo commented as he handed his other set of leg armor to Erich. He loved it when Erich helped with the armor. He could attach the buckles and straps faster than anyone he knew. He and Drullock could put on most of their armor themselves, but Erich dressed Sivle faster than either of them could dress themselves, usually in time for Sivle to help with Drullock while Erich finished Braxlo up. "There are many in those groups. Why does the prince deserve a death mark?"

"Prince Perhaladon an Trodaí is the highest ranked, and one of the most vocal, members." Finishing the greaves, he made sure the pegs were securely in the matching holes in the cuisses, then ran the strap through the greave loop, tightening the bottom strap. Then he pulled the leg armor up firmly and attached it to the arming jacket. "Some members of the court have hired the Voldair Assassin's Guild to make an example. Be fairly warned." Tightening the final straps, Erich moved to the breast and back plates.

Braxlo stayed quiet, thinking about what he had just heard, now regretting leaving the hauberk on the rack. Erich quickly finished with the cuirass, moving to the plackard, which was already attached to the tassets, faulds, and culet. "I could shadow you if you would like and warn you if there is an attempt," Erich offered.

"No, my friend, that is not needed. But perhaps you can get me some vials to treat poison from your drawer." Braxlo moved around a bit to make sure Erich had tightened the plackard sufficiently. It was perfect, as usual. Although Erich wore no armor himself, he seemed to be an expert at putting it on. Erich deftly put on the couters and guards of vambrace on each arm. It took half a minute to get them secured, and when he finished, Braxlo raised his arms in the air.

"Wear this amulet. It will provide proof against poison for you in case they attack you first." Erich looped a small copper medallion around Braxlo's throat, tucking it inside the breastplate, then began attaching the pauldrons. Braxlo's armor was an older style, with massive pauldrons. Dipping low over the breastplate on Braxlo's left side, it provided another layer of armor over the heart and lungs. On the right, the lance hook was left on, even though it was unlikely Braxlo would be fighting on horseback. Braxlo said it gave him a handy place to rest his hand when not holding his sword.

Erich attached the bevor then held the sword belt around for Braxlo to fasten. He handed Braxlo his shield, which the stoic knight slung across his back. Overall, the knight was wearing over thirty pounds of armor, much lighter than if it had been steel instead of enchanted iridium. Braxlo put on his gauntlets and picked up his sallet. Holding the helm in his left hand, he took one last look in the mirror, nodding to himself. Turning to Erich, he asked. "Could you please do me one last favor, and see to the horses?"

***

Fairwind looked up the stairs again. It had been fifteen minutes since Braxlo had come in and gone upstairs. She knew it took a while to armor up, but it was getting near the time to leave. She loathed being late. It showed a lack of care and attention. She was just about to go up herself when he appeared, resplendent in his magnificent, if monochrome, armor. Nodding an apology, he came directly down to her.

"Your Highness," he said, bowing before her. "I stand ready to do your bidding."

"You made me quite anxious. We barely have time to eat a quick bite before we must leave. It would not be proper to keep my first suitor waiting." She waved at the young serving girl, who nodded and went into the kitchen, returning moments later with a tray holding bread, cheeses, and meats. They stacked piles of each on their plates, eating quickly, washing it down with the wine Fairwind had been sipping. When they finished, Braxlo stood, holding Fairwind's seat as she gracefully rose from the table.

"The horses should be out front, Your Highness."

They walked to the front door, Braxlo setting a single turot on the table before he left. Holding the door open for Fairwind, he quickly scanned the outside of the tavern. Nothing in the street appeared to be suspicious. Holding her hand, he walked her down the few steps to where the horses sat. The saddleless caparison was once again decorating her horse, with the folding tables already in place. He assisted her onto her horse, put away the folding tables, then mounted his own horse and began a slow walk to the prince's pavilion.

The ride was uneventful, neither speaking much until they had passed through the Northern Gate, when Fairwind asked him quietly, "Why so tense, Braxlo? Is there some danger I should be aware of?"

Braxlo looked over and flashed a small grin. "No, Your Highness, it is just Jubilee. I want to make sure the cutpurses think twice before approaching us. I also want to make sure none follow us."

"Fear not, brave Braxlo. I am sure the prince will provide ample security while we are under his banner."

"Of that I have no doubt, Your Highness," Braxlo gave a small bow to Fairwind from his horse, relaxing visibly as the prince's tent came into view. It towered over the nearby tents. Approaching closer, it looked to be a score of paces across. Paladins immediately fell into formation, stopping the pair and carrying a full set of stairs for Fairwind. She dismounted daintily, accepting the hand of the banner commander. By the time she had made it down the stairs, Braxlo had dismounted himself, falling in step behind her.

Walking to the tent, each pair of paladins raised spears with banners attached, one with the great oak tree of the High Aelf, and one with a circle of black nut trees surrounding a black fox, with a smaller great black nut tree of the Black Aelf on the bottom. The banners alternated sides as they walked through the ten pairs of paladins, the paladins crossing the spears as they passed. Arriving at the opening to the prince's tent, the banner commander pulled the opening aside and announced Fairwind.

"Your Highness, may I present Her Highness, Fairwind Duine Fionn, Princess of the High Aelf and celebrated War Mage. Sir Braxlo the Brave, Knight Errant of the Freehold of Dragonsbane, Hero of Formount Pass accompanies her." He stood aside, allowing Braxlo to step forward into the tent. Surveying it quickly, he reached back to escort his ward inside. This was all perfunctory, of course. There was little chance the prince would allow anything, or anyone, inside which would threaten Fairwind. But Braxlo took his duty seriously. He would not let complacency be the cause of harm to her, the one to whom he had pledged his life.

The interior of the tent was sparsely decorated. A small table with two chairs and a chessboard sat on one side. In the center, between two poles, a long table stood filled with various fruits, breads, cheeses, wines, and even a pitcher of ale. On the far side of the tent, the prince had placed large stuffed chairs with small tables next to them beside a small firebox. The prince had been sitting on a large couch.

Rising once they were announced, dressed in simple trousers and a silk shirt, the prince walked quickly over to greet them. Braxlo felt like they had overdressed.

"Welcome, Your Highness. Please come in and make yourself at home." The prince bowed deeply, taking Fairwind's hand as he rose. "I am delighted you could join me today. Would you like some refreshments?"

"Perhaps a glass of wine." Fairwind replied as she curtseyed deeply to the prince. "We did not want to be presumptuous, so we had a light meal before we came, since we are meeting in the afternoon." As soon as she began speaking, Braxlo headed over to the long table, pouring a glass of the chilled wine for Fairwind.

"Anything for you, Prince Perhaladon?" Braxlo asked as he finished pouring the glass.

"I will have a glass of wine as well please, Sir Braxlo the Brave, Hero of Formount Pass." He then paused as if for effect and continued, "But if I may be so outrageous as to suggest we forego our titles, referring to each other by our first names. It will quicken our conversation."

According to tradition, as Fairwind and Prince Perhaladon were equal in status, they could have dropped the honorific without permission. While borderline rude to do so if unacquainted, it was quite common among members of the same court. Fairwind never required it of Braxlo; however, he always used them in public. But for the prince to allow Braxlo to drop the honorific was unheard of, particularly from an aelf noble to a human.

"It harms me none to refer to you by the title your birth and accomplishments have earned you, Your Highness," Braxlo simply said, as he finished pouring the second glass of wine. Bringing the glass of wine to the prince, he added, "I do not plan on speaking much today. After all, this is a chance for you two to get acquainted. Your spies can gather any information you need on me."

With an enormous smile, the dark-haired aelf took the glass of wine, simply nodding.

The role of the chaperone was a simple one. Tend to the needs of those in attendance and ensure those being chaperoned were not placed in any compromising positions. It was common to people un-accustomed to formal chaperones to think Braxlo should have been only concerned with Fairwind. However, while the prince was gracious enough to allow Fairwind to bring a chaperone she trusted, Braxlo was just as obligated to ensure nothing violated the safety and reputation of the prince as he was to protect Fairwind.

The afternoon dragged on, with Perhaladon and Fairwind discussing politics, the state of affairs between the High Aelf and the Black Aelf, as well as the increasing attacks by grendlaar around the Great Chasm. The Golden Aelf came up, and while Perhaladon was sympathetic to the plight of their brethren, he had a strange opinion of them.

"It is my belief," Perhaladon stated after they had been discussing the recent (by aelf standards) attack on the Southern Kingdom, "most of the Golden Aelf want peace, and would quickly return to their homes. However, I believe the leadership has been corrupted. In the last several hundred years, the factions who hate the humans seem to have gained more and more power, silencing the voices for peace."

Fairwind thought about this for a bit before replying. "I am not old enough to have witnessed any changes, save in the last hundred years, but I remember stories of Golden Aelf bards roaming the lands even centuries after the Great War. That does not seem to be the case now, so there may be some merit in your point of view. Still, they refuse even the Great King now. Whether by the choice of the people or just the leadership, I am afraid I cannot opine on the matter. It is an interesting idea. So, you believe if they changed the leadership, the Golden Aelf would rejoin the community of aelf and honor the Great Treaty?"

"I do," Perhaladon said simply. "There have been prisoners captured during their raids of the human settlements decades ago. The few who did not commit suicide have told a grim tale of life in the Sleeping Dragons."

"I have heard those stories. I dismiss most as attempts to gain sympathy to avoid the executioner's axe." Shaking her head, Fairwind considered the possibility they were true. "I have no doubt life secluded like they are has been difficult, but are you sure there is not some embellishment for the sake of their captors?"

Perhaladon nodded his head. "Certainly, there is embellishment. But the stories are consistent across years and lands. I hope to see a reconciliation with our golden-skinned brethren, then perhaps the truth can be divined. But it will not happen with the current leaders. Were you aware they no longer have a king and queen, but a council?"

"I have heard, but I cannot believe it is true." Fairwind had indeed heard the rumor, dismissing it immediately. It was absurd to contemplate a dozen or more aelf arguing incessantly about every facet of the administration of the realm. She had sat through several of her father's council meetings when she was younger. While having the benefit of other's experience and learning was beneficial, at some point someone had to decide on a course of action. Then someone would have to ensure every member of the council supported it. "Just think of the chaos when the council factions begin warring against each other."

Perhaladon smiled, as if he was familiar with this reasoning. "The Palladium Council has existed for a millennium, despite the mix of human, dwarven, and aelf paladins in the council. Yet they have made themselves as powerful as any of the kingdoms."

Then began a discussion of the difference between a kingdom and a distributed set of orders and keeps, and the rotating leadership of the Palladium Council. This turned into a discussion of the differences between the human and aelf orders, and the changes even in the aelf military after recruitment of knights and paladins began, something unheard of before the Great War. Eventually, this led back to the Great War, and the changes in the lands since then, coming full circle to the plight of the Golden Aelf.

Braxlo stood stoically in the background, refilling wine glasses and fetching fruits or bread or anything else his two wards requested. Then the banner commander was at the door of the tent. "Your Highnesses, I regret to inform you your time for this encounter is over. The sun has begun setting. Her Highness will want to leave soon if she is to return to the city before it is dark." Bowing, he left the tent again.

"Fairwind, your charm seems to have hastened the movement of the sun. It seems we had just begun our time together. I did not even get around to showing you the gift I had made for you. If you would allow me now, please join me at the chess table." He rose, stretching out his hand to help her up, then clasping it with both of his hands as they walked the several steps to the chessboard.

Fairwind looked at the chessboard. At first glance, the carved pieces pitted aelf and humans in white against many fearsome creatures in black. A great Tullamore dragon was the "queen" of the beast's side; a fearsome rock troll as the "king". The pawns were all shaped as vreen, with the bishops, knights, and rooks represented by nagas, manticores, and minotaurs. Carved out of wood from black nut trees and polished to a high luster, each piece was a masterpiece sculpture.

Peering closer at the white pieces, a small gasp escaped her. She herself was the "queen," and an excellent likeness of her as well. Perhaladon was the "king," and all the pawns were human or aelf knights. The rooks took the form of majestic trees, one an oak and the other a black nut tree, looking similar enough at first glance they seemed to be the same. Only the shapes of the leaves were different. A High Aelf and a Black Aelf paladin represented each of the knights, with a male and female priest representing the bishops.

The white pieces were all carved from oak, and an oak from the Great Woods as well, evidenced by the traces of silver in the grain. Alternating blocks of the black nut and oak made the board, separated by gold inlays. Silverwood surrounded the board, completed by carvings of mountains and forests surrounding the two sides. It was a priceless gift, requiring many months and skilled artisans to complete.

"I am honored by such a magnificent gift, Perhaladon. Thank you. I did not know anyone knew how much I enjoy playing chess, and I will cherish this forever."

ALLIANDRE RISING ~ 219

Perhaladon raised her hand to his lips, kissing it softly. "Perhaps to-morrow we can play a game, if you are not too busy in the afternoon."

"I am afraid my friend Alliandre is in the Open Melee tomorrow afternoon, and I have promised to watch him thrash others who have done nothing to wrong him. I hope you do not think me forward, but perhaps you could accompany me. We can walk back through the food tents afterward to get a bite to eat. Then we can return for a game, or two." With those last two words, she smiled a small smile up at Perhaladon, giving him a small wink.

Smiling himself, Perhaladon kissed Fairwind's hand once again. It shall be as you say. I will find you at the fairgrounds. Motioning his hand toward Braxlo, "Sir Braxlo the Brave, Hero of Formount Pass, Knight Errant of the Freehold of Dragonsbane, I remove myself from your care and return your ward to your protection."

Braxlo walked over, taking Fairwind's hand and bowing to Prince Perhaladon. Then he walked Fairwind over to the tent door. They had just reached it when the banner commander appeared again, flinging it open. Outside, the paladins repeated their formation of crossed spears, separating the spears as they allowed Braxlo to lead her to where the stairs awaited her. They mounted and returned to the Wyvern's Aerie, barely speaking. All the while, Fairwind had a bemused smile on her face.

VIII

⚜

Alliandre's Ascent

31st of Frendalo, Year 1124 AGW

Vanessa walked alone to the Eastern Gates. Vandion had woken early to harvest what crops he could. She thought she might as well get to the tavern early if she could. Passing the gates, a young man stood, almost as if he were waiting for someone. Nearing the gates, she noticed he carried an old, battered sword, but was otherwise wearing fine brown woolen britches and a clean gray tunic with the city's device emblazoned on the chest. Walking closer, there was something about him which was familiar.

Five paces away, he continued toward her. "Good morning, Vanessa," he said with a bow. "I was hoping you would allow me to accompany you to the Wyvern's Watch today. Your friend Alliandre told me to come by to pick up my gift."

Alarmed at first, she realized it was the guardsman from the other day. Jason, she thought his name was. "It is the Wyvern's Aerie, and Lord Alliandre is not my friend, but he is friends with the Qu-, er, Lady Arielle. Why did you wait for me, and how did you know I came this way?" Looking suspiciously at him, she was unsure about traveling with someone who was stalking her.

Jason looked down, twirling his black boots in the dirt. They were old and worn, but he had applied boot black to them this morning, brushing them until they shone. "You walked from this direction. I thought you must come through the gate here." He looked up sheepishly and continued, "I forget how to get there. The only time I have been there was when you brought me. I was so excited when I left, I forgot the way back."

Vanessa giggled a little, then simply said, "Come along," as she continued through the gate.

The trip to the Aerie was quite awkward. Jason seemed to want to ask her something, but every time he spoke, she would look at him and then he would make some innocuous comment like how chilly it was getting in the mornings, or he would point out some building and tell her who lived there. She supposed he was just trying to make small talk, but whenever she answered, he would give a small reply and then go back to summoning the courage to speak again. She had thought she had made clear she had promised herself already, but she brought up Vandion twice just to remind him. She could take it no longer. With the Aerie's sign a dozen paces ahead, she challenged him.

"You clearly have something you want to ask me, so go ahead. The worst thing I will do is say no, which is highly likely." She stood in the middle of the street with her hands on her hips.

Jason looked at her, then averted his gaze. After several seconds of awkwardness, he looked back at her and began speaking.

"Milady. As you know, I am entered in the Open Melee Tournament this afternoon, and if it would please you, I would like to fight as your champion." The words poured forth like good mead at a grand feast. "I know you said you are betrothed, but it would only be to honor you and you would not need to bestow any rewards on me if I win, which I probably won't, but still. I mean, you could if you wanted to, but only if you wanted to and even then, it would not have to be anything more than a hug." Then, realizing he was vomiting words, he stopped talking and looked at her pleadingly.

"No," she simply said. Smiling sweetly, she pointed at the Aerie's wooden sign hanging across the street. "Well, here we are. Thank you for the escort, my brave guardsman, and good luck in the big fight." She walked into the tavern, leaving him standing in the street looking shocked.

***

Sivle arose in the morning to find everyone but Erich still in bed. Checking the window again, he noted the sun was rising. Usually, everyone was awake even if they were not getting out of bed. Erich had left, probably to search for Robin. The two of them were childhood friends, similar to Sivle and Alliandre, and he could tell Erich was worried. They all wondered what Robin was up to, though it was always best NOT to know what Robin was up to. Erich had a bit of a conscience; Sivle was not so sure about Robin. Robin was not bad, necessarily, but he was always scheming. And he held onto grudges far past the point when they should be forgotten.

Alliandre was in bed as well, which was curious, since he was fighting today. Walking over, Sivle lightly touched his friend.

Alliandre turned his head and smiled. "Just making sure I get my rest, Sivle. I cannot afford to lose in the Open Melee, or I won't get a chance to participate in the Grand Melee."

"Against guardsmen and adventurers, I think you could do this in your sleep, old friend."

Sivle turned to the writing desk in the room, pulling out his prayer book. Facing the rising sun, he began his prayers to the Forest Spirits. Praying to each in order, each getting their due respect, each receiving the pleading for tolerance and for penance for any misdeeds he may have made against them. Fortunately, he had never been sent a penance, but he believed his cleansing each year made up for it. By the time he finished his prayers, he was sweating and exhausted again.

Opening his desk again, he exchanged his book for an old leather case with his scroll making supplies. The previous day he had been quite productive, working late into the night. It was laborious to write the same spell to a scroll. You had to spend the time learning it; only then could you copy the stamins. On a whim, he had written one scroll last night without bothering to relearn the spell.

He had never done that before. In retrospect, he wondered why more wizards didn't do it. It was much quicker than actually memorizing the spell and then transferring the memorized stamins onto paper, though the chance of writing the stamins incorrectly were much higher. But he had invented the spell in the first place, not learned it from anyone. He was so familiar with the stamins, he just had to remember the steps he went through creating it. He thought if one could get good at creating spells, there would be no need to memorize them at all. But when he tried for a second scroll, he realized the lateness of the hour was not aiding him in writing down the stamins correctly. He needed to ensure the stamins were correct.

So, he had gone to bed late last night. Now he could eat and with luck have had enough rest to relearn his spells so he could transfer them to scrolls. He would also have to learn the spells required to enchant an item, as Alliandre had asked for a favor of him. Yawning again, he looked around the room. Seeing Braxlo and Alliandre had not risen yet, he returned to bed, leaving a note for Alliandre to wake him. It was the best hour of sleep he had ever gotten.

***

Sivle awoke to Alliandre shaking his shoulder. Amazingly, he felt quite refreshed from the brief nap. Thanking Alliandre, he got dressed. Planning to spend most of the day writing scrolls, he put on his most comfortable tights and low boots. He found a blue tunic with green brocade on the sleeves.

He checked his supplies once again, then went down to firstmeal with Alliandre and Braxlo. Braxlo actually had a bright green tunic on today. Well, it was more of a dark forest green actually, but compared to the dark clothing favored by the grizzled fighter, it seemed almost cheery. Alliandre put on his thick woolen tights and a brand-new gambeson and arming jacket. Over the top he threw a red tabard with the blue field and rampant Wyvern of the Southern Kingdom embroidered on the front and back. It was unique, as the back side actually had the back of the Wyvern.

Alliandre had it made as a joke for Sir Andras before he left for Dragonsbane, but his old mentor refused it, scolding Alliandre for dishonoring the device of the Southern Kingdom. But Alliandre grew fond of it over the years, wearing it for every tournament. Sir Andras eventually got used to seeing it, and it brought a smile to the queen's face when she would see it, only because she was in on the joke. It was only a few years ago Arielle admitted she herself had embroidered it. None of the other seamstresses in the kingdom would have dared create it.

As they went down the stairs, the tavern was still full of the firstmeal crowd. Sivle had just gotten down the stairs when a young man with a sword bumped him hard. Glaring at him, Sivle noticed the boy didn't seem to even be aware he was there. He thought of saying something when the youngster shouted past him.

"Lord Nileppez, I came here as you asked, waiting all morning. I thought we would practice some more, if you don't mind giving me more lessons."

Alliandre laughed. "First off, young Jason, as I have told you, I am not a lord. Second, nothing you learn this morning will help in the melee this afternoon. You would only tire yourself, risking injury. Better to rest and eat well. Have you had your firstmeal?"

"A little, my lord. Just some rolls and a glass of morning beer, I think they call it."

Alliandre's expression turned flat. "I am still NOT a lord. Just call me Alliandre. Come with us. We will have a good meal to fuel our victory this afternoon."

"But Alliandre," Jason spoke nervously. "Won't we be sluggish and tired if we eat a large meal? My captain always points to how we feel when we engorge ourselves before a long march."

Alliandre smiled again. "It is four hours before any fighting, Our stretching and warm up will rid us of any lethargy we may feel from eating. But the afternoon will be long, and we will not have time to eat once the melee begins. You do not want to be weak from lack of food if you make it deep into the day. I do not wish to countermand your captain, but today you are my trainee, and you will follow my instructions. Or do you wish to remain a guardsman?"

"But the tournament is in three hours, not four," Jason protested.

"Yes. The tournament is in three hours," Alliandre patiently instructed his pupil. It had been too many years since he had trained anyone, but he fell back into uncharacteristic patience. "Then they will introduce the two hundred and fifty entrants. This will take over half an hour. Then they will read the rules. Then we will all draw numbers. Another fifteen minutes will have passed. They will give us fifteen minutes after they draw the last number to get organized and lined up. By then, over an hour will have passed."

Alliandre held up four fingers. "So, as I said, we have at least four hours to get ready. We will eat, then stretch, then get armored. Your first gift, as my pupil, is already in the back room. Master Sorenson brought it by late last night, I am told. Your second gift, which my friend Sivle will have to assist with, is also there. So, sit down and eat and stop worrying about the time for fighting. It will be here soon enough." He held a chair for the young man, then sat down in his customary spot.

Vanessa walked up and glanced at Jason before addressing Braxlo sweetly. "Sir Braxlo, what may I get for you this morning?"

Sivle answered her. "Dueler's firstmeal for these two, I am sure." Thinking about the lateness in the morning, he changed it a bit. "Better add some ham if John has any left. And a plate of mutton would be nice. For me, I would like one hen and the melons and a platter of the roasted roots."

"And a pitcher of the morning beer if there is any left," Alliandre added.

"I am sorry, but we finished the last of it over an hour ago. Perhaps a pitcher of the ale?"

"We will take a flagon of the sweet mead then," Alliandre decided.

"I will have a plate of the sweet cakes," Braxlo added. "And a plate of the bacon along with some ham. And you better bring another flagon of the mead."

"Thank you, Vanessa," Jason added, then sheepishly ducked his head.

"So, Alliandre, what is this gift I am to help you with?" Sivle asked.

"Come with me, I will show you. Hopefully, it will not take you too long." Alliandre stood with Sivle and walked to the back room of the tavern.

***

Firstmeal came, and Jason and Braxlo dug in. Jason had never eaten such good food, or so much of it. "Is this how you eat all the time?" he asked quietly. "These sweet cakes are just like my mom's, but sweeter somehow, without being overwhelming. And this ham is amazing. And the mutton is so tender, nothing like what my mom made. And I have never had mead before, but I love it."

"Careful with the mead," Braxlo cautioned. "It is sweet, but it is stronger than beer. Stronger than some wine, even. You have already had two cups. You might want to stop at three."

"Yes, my lord," Jason said sheepishly. "But I have never eaten so well. Even when the king throws the annual feast for the guard, the food isn't this good. Well, maybe some things are, but not the mutton or the ham."

"How long have you been with the guard, Jason?" Braxlo asked politely to make conversation.

"Three years," Jason proclaimed proudly. "I am eighteen now, and have served my obligation, so I can apply to transfer to an order if they will accept me. Which is why I am hoping to do well in the tournament today. I have given my application to my captain to submit, but I have to do well today. Otherwise, I guess I will have to do two more years in the guards and try again."

"You will do well today," Braxlo told him. "Be careful of whom you fight. Check their armor before you challenge them. If it is bright and shiny, be careful. If it is old and battered and looks like the warrior wearing it is too, leave them alone. If they are wearing piecemeal armor, go after them. If you can find Drullock, stay close and listen to him. He is a pain to deal with, but he knows his craft better than anyone I know."

"Who is Drullock, Sir Braxlo?"

"Forget I said it," Braxlo said. "It is a nickname for Alliandre, and not one he would like me saying in front of you. NEVER call him that if you wish to remain in his good graces. Stay close to Alliandre and listen to him, and you will go far in the tournament."

"Yes, my lord. I will." Jason put another bite of ham in his mouth and savored the saltiness. But it had a sweetness to it as well. It was easily the best meal he had ever eaten.

Soon after, Sivle and Alliandre returned, the fighter grinning ear to ear.

They finished eating, and Alliandre and Jason went to stretch. They had stretched for quite some time when Alliandre declared it was time to get "dressed for the ball." He had Jason wait while he went inside, returning with Braxlo, each carrying a large leather bag. Braxlo set one down in front of him, with the letters J G embroidered on a large patch on the closing flap. Undoing the buckles, inside Jason found a brand-new set of cuir bouilli, with a steel cuirass. It had a steel helm with a visor and chain-mail hanging down over the cuir bouilli gorget. On top sat a leather arming jacket, also brand new. It was much nicer than the armor he occasionally wore as a guard, and even nicer than the armor the soldiers wore on patrol.

Alliandre had Jason stand as he and Braxlo dressed him, starting at the feet and moving up. With both of the experienced warriors working together, it took just a few minutes. As they dressed him, Alliandre explained how the armor fit together. Each piece worked in conjunction to protect him, and the pieces of armor below it. Next came the dueling swords. These were heavier than the sword Jason carried. He had dueled enough to be used to the extra weight, but it surprised him to see there were three of them. The bottom of the bag contained a large wooden shield faced with steel. It was lighter than he expected. As he hoisted it up, he practiced a few of the blocks Alliandre had shown him. "It's so light," he exclaimed.

"It is iridium," Braxlo explained. "Lighter than steel, and just as strong. Plus, if you ever want to enchant it, it will be ready."

"We will have Sivle enchant it before we leave Foresight," Alliandre declared.

"Is this the second gift you talked about?"

"No." Then Alliandre pulled his own armor out of his pack. Jason looked in awe. The red died pieces, shaped to look like scales, fit together perfectly.

Jason watched as Braxlo put on the armor, from the feet up, just like they had done with him. Again, Alliandre explained as Braxlo attached each piece how it protected a certain part of the body, as well as the attachments and pieces of armor below. Watching, it made more sense. He had put on and worn armor before, but this armor was far more complete than the armor he was used to. Alliandre's armor had a bevor instead of a gorget, which fitted with his helm to look like a stub-nosed dragon head, complete with teeth set in a slightly open mouth.

Both of them armored, Alliandre began stretching and moving again to test the range of motion in the armor. In no time, Jason was sweating and breathing hard, but as he complained, Braxlo would tighten a strap or adjust a buckle. Before he knew it, the weight seemed more like he was wearing just a heavy gambeson. He had noticed the captain and other officers had custom-made armor, now he knew why. The benefit of fighting in well-fitting armor gave him an almost unfair advantage, *which must be why Braxlo advised me to pick out people in piecemeal armor to fight.*

Alliandre began running through their drills. Different combinations of blocks and strikes. Slowly at first, but gradually picking up the tempo until they were dueling all out. Alliandre explained how to identify each attack and the proper defense against it. He also reviewed when to block, when to parry and when to dodge, as well as how to identify feints and misdirects. Alliandre had touched on all this during the day they had spent training, but it made more sense to Jason the second time.

Alliandre took off his helm, asking Braxlo to fetch them another glass of the mead. As Braxlo returned with the glasses and a flagon, they toasted to victory before leaving for the fairgrounds.

"Aren't you coming, Braxlo?" Alliandre asked as Braxlo stood with his head down.

"I am truly sorry," the old fighter began, "but Fairwind's courtier has requested she spend the day with him. She intends to watch your victory, so I shall be there to see you. I am afraid I must beg your forbearance."

"Granted." Alliandre came back and clasped wrists. "There is no need to ask forgiveness for putting your first duty above all others. I can manage myself today."

***

Victor woke early, dressed quickly, and walked over to get Mortimer. He and Mortimer were planning on getting to the fairgrounds early to determine where to wait for their mark, as well as decide where to cast their spells.

The grass, heavily dewed from the cool night previous, reminded him of the season, and made Victor grateful for his thick brown woolen shirt and heavy brown woolen pants. He had gone shopping the night before. He looked down and cursed as he noticed the dew soaking his new leather boots. Moving quickly to the lightly traveled road, a wagon going by forced him to dance the side of the road precariously.

He knocked twice on Mortimer's door before it opened. Mortimer peeked out with a smile. "I've been waiting for you, Vic. Are you ready to make some more money?" Mortimer had obviously not gone shopping. He had hidden a dozen malnots in his sleeve, but he was saving most of the remaining money from Beauregard to buy healing potions. For some reason, he had become paranoid about dying.

"Mortimer, my friend, I can feel the weight of my coin purse already." They clasped wrists, then Mortimer came outside, locking the door behind him. They walked along looking like a minor merchant and his servant until they arrived at the fairgrounds. It was still several hours before the melee, but he thought they would get positioned for their spell-casting. Arriving, they walked up to the paladin acting as marschall and reported in.

"Victor Del Drago, sir. We were told to report to be judges in the melee."

"And I am Mortimer Si Brackenwood, Sir. We should be on the list."

The tall paladin looked at the two men, then looked at his list. Finding them, he checked them off and gave them a big smile. "You both have guard experience, good. We are gathering in front of the king's box to explain the rules and what to look for. There is some good ale there too, I am told, but don't leave yourself unable to do your jobs."

Pointing at a pavilion set up on the other side of the fairgrounds, the paladin nodded to them and continued standing, waiting for others to check in.

Mortimer and Victor walked over and got a mug of the ale. They stood and drank their ale, looking over the other judges. Thirty men and women in similar clothing gathered in the pavilion. Victor and Mortimer engaged several of the finer dressed in conversations, remembering their names and where they were from.

About an hour and a half before the tournament, an older knight stood on a small stand at the front of the pavilion. He raised his hand, and within moments, the pavilion was silent. "I am Sir Richard of the Waste, Knight of the Iron Keep, and honored to be the Grand Marschall for today's Open Melee Tournament. Welcome and thank you for volunteering to assist the marschalls in ensuring a fair and safe tournament. To assist you in your work today, each of you shall receive a ring to detect enchantments."

"Each contestant will have themselves checked before the competition. You will also keep an eye out for spellcasters attempting to enchant combatants. We do not expect there to be much of this today, but it will be good practice if you plan on judging the Grand Melee later this week. Remember, every one of you who judges both competitions may keep your rings, and the stamins to recharge them."

A murmur went through the crowd. Sir Richard stepped down from his box and another knight stepped up. He began explaining the rules of the competition, what to look for and how to report a violation. Several times he repeated, "At no time are you to engage or interfere with the combatants, leave it to the marschalls."

As soon the briefing was over, the group crowded around the ale once again. The heat of the day was rising as Mortimer and Victor re-filled their mugs, waiting for the fighters to arrive.

The first ones arrived about an hour later. Mostly adventurers, with a few guardsmen and soldiers now and then. But none in distinctive red armor. The tournament time was approaching, and the red-armored man had not shown. They walked around, in case they had missed him, but he was not among any of the fighters at the fairgrounds. Victor thought maybe Beauregard had been mistaken, when something red flashed in his peripheral vision.

There was no doubt in Victor's mind this was the warrior to whom Beauregard referred. He was taller than all the other gathered combatants, his armor looking like he was dressed in the skin of a small red dragon. Victor got Mortimer's attention. Together they walked over, preparing to cast their spell. The red-scaled man was talking to another warrior in shining, polished armor. The two of them conspired for several minutes, until they clasped wrists, going their separate ways.

Victor gave the signal. As they had practiced, they began chanting their incantations. Before the tall man had gone a half-score paces, the spell triggered. Other than a slight pause in his stride, the big man didn't react. But a minute later, as Mortimer and Victor were testing other combatants, the man stretched and shook his body vigorously. Victor went up to him, pointed at him with his ring, and slapped the patch on the big man's armor, indicating he was free from enchantment.

***

232 - DANIEL E MYERS

"What is your number?" Alliandre asked.

"Seven," Jason replied. "Is that good?"

"Not for you." Alliandre laughed. "Here, I have eighty-three. It is a better number for you. Let's trade."

Not understanding why, Jason exchanged numbers with his mentor, inspecting the new chip. "Why was mine white, and yours is red?"

"Didn't you listen to the rules?" Alliandre chided him, but with a small smile. He remembered his first tournament. The whole time until he clashed swords was a blurred jumble of emotions and people mumbling.

"There are two of each number, one red and one white." Holding his token next to the one he had just surrendered, Alliandre explained further. "We draw them to determine who we will fight in the first round. Better fighters usually like to have lower numbers. Normally, in the Open Melee Tournament, there is no bidding on the lower numbers, but it would embarrass a fierce warrior or someone trying to make a name to have a number over a hundred."

"I see," Jason replied. "So, do we do this every round?"

Alliandre smiled and shook his head. "No. After the first round, you will return to your numbered spot and wait until all the fighters have finished. Then there will be rounds of fifteen minutes where you may challenge anyone. As the rules master said, you cannot challenge anyone already engaged. It is also impolite to confront someone who is clearly waiting to challenge someone else. This is where you need to be alert. Look for someone who is not wearing fancy armor. Or looks like they don't know what they are doing. When the fifteen minutes are up, they sound a horn, then you return to your number. They remove the numbers of the defeated warriors, so your number will move."

Turning and placing his hand on the young man's shoulder, Alliandre spoke in low, reassuring tones. "You will not win this tournament, but the orders will watch once it gets down to the last thirty swordsmen. Make sure you make it there. If you handle yourself well, even if you lose, you may still get an invitation to squire."

"Yes, my lord," Jason said with a small bow.

"I am not a Lord," Alliandre replied with a wry smile.

"You are to me." Voice cracking, he continued, "Only someone of the noblest heart would have done for me all you have done. You don't know me, or my parents, or anything else. Regardless, you sacrificed your time and treasure to help me achieve my dream. If that is not the mark of a nobleman, then there is none. And if you are not worthy to be a knight, I would rather be your servant than to be a knight myself."

A small lump welled up in Alliandre's throat as he tousled Jason's hair. "Helmets on. Grab your gear and get to your number."

The two clasped wrists one last time before walking toward their respective numbers. He got to his spot and began stretching and twisting to get the blood flowing to his unexplainably weary muscles.

"Are you alright?" the warrior next to him asked.

"Nothing, just feel exhausted all of a sudden." Alliandre was getting concerned until a judge came by to check for enchantments on him. They found none, so he set his mind to the task at hand.

***

Jason looked around. Two rounds had gone by, and he was still in it. Less than a hundred men remained. His first battle had gone well, fighting one of the soldiers. The soldier, his own age, was probably seeking the same goal. But the fight lasted barely a minute, with the other soldier feinting, testing Jason's defenses. When the soldier attacked in earnest, Jason dodged aside and easily cut down his now overextended opponent.

The second round was more challenging. He defeated the first person he fought; the man next to him initially. Then the woman on the other side challenged him. Both were better swordsmen. Jason struggled to keep up with their combinations and movements. But they both had piecemeal armor, giving Jason a decisive advantage. Jason noticed the first man had an issue with movement to the right. So he circled to the right until the man stumbled. As he opened his defenses to catch his balance, Jason struck and defeated him with a quick thrust to the breastplate.

Likewise, the woman's armor must have been made for a man. All except the breastplate, which was clearly designed for a female. The pauldrons were not matched for her breastplate, so whenever she raised her arms, they caught on the way down. Jason sent several blows high on her shield, then slammed her shield with his, sticking her shield for just a moment. He used the moment to sidestep around to her sword arm, performing an eagle's talon, which got by her stuck shield, catching the top of her helm.

He looked around and saw his captain coming toward him. He looked around for someone else to challenge, but there was no one near. Sadly, he planted his feet and waited for the officer to arrive.

"I submit my challenge to you," his captain stated as he got near.

"Good afternoon, Captain Del Jorgenson," Jason called out as the captain came near. This stopped the captain in his tracks. "I suppose I have no choice but to accept."

"Do I know you, warrior?" the captain asked.

"I am Jason Si Gladahar, of the First Watch on the East Bridge to Hightowne." Jason bowed deeply. "You submitted my applications to the knightly orders."

"I deeply regret this challenge then, son. I did not recognize you." The older man, in armor as nice as Jason's, returned the bow. "I would have never challenged you this early had I known. Now I fear I may have ended your chances of being recognized. I am dreadfully sorry."

Raising his visor, Jason acknowledged the position his captain was in. Then, remembering Alliandre had told him showing confidence would improve his performance, and only the audacious achieved glorious victories, he smiled his best smile, saluting his captain. "You will only end my chances if you beat me!" Lowering his visor, he charged.

He knew the captain was a better swordsman; the captain trained his patrol of guards every week. The captain's armor, while not as new as Jason's, was still made for him, fitting at least as well as Jason's did.

In addition, the captain had years of service under his belt. Still, Jason charged.

Salamander strike followed by griffin slash followed by eagle's talon followed by vreen horn. Everything he knew, he threw at the captain. For several minutes, the captain fell back, staggered by the onslaught. Jason dodged several counterattacks, then it was his turn to be on the defensive. The captain seemed to be fond of the thunder strike, but Jason could not remember the counter to it, only that it involved dodging.

By the time he remembered to follow the dodge with a sword breaker followed by a falcon's beak, the captain had switched to a shield press with lightning strikes from above the trapped shield. Being shorter than the captain was a tremendous disadvantage, Jason struggling to escape the press. Pivoting, he attempted to step back and immediately lunge forward with an eagle's talon. But the captain, anticipating it, sidestepped the thrust as he lunged forward, catching Jason with a windmill slash to the helm seconds before the horn sounded, signaling the end of the round.

Dejected, Jason looked around. Easily two or three score fighters remained, which meant the orders were not yet paying attention. Dejectedly, tears filling his eyes, he exited the field. As he walked away, a hand pulled on his pauldron.

"Well done, young man." It was his captain, helm off and smiling. "Had I known you were this skilled, I would have recommended you to be a shift commander. Tomorrow, report to me immediately after your shift and we will reassign you."

"Yes, Sir!" Jason said, feigning the enthusiasm he knew the captain expected. They clasped wrists, Jason dejectedly leaving the field. While fighting back tears, he walked over to where Alliandre stood. At least he could cheer on his mentor.

***

Alliandre waited for the opening horn apprehensively. He was feeling a little off; he didn't know if it was nerves or something worse. He was breathing hard despite cutting short his stretching. His movements were slowed, like he had been sparring all morning instead of sleeping in and taking it easy. Perhaps it was something he ate, but the Aerie's food had never made him sick before. There was nothing to be done for it now, as the Grand Marschall raised his sword and, with a shout, began the first round.

His opponent was another adventurer, apparently. Lacquered armor and a curiously shaped oval shield revealed he had been fairly successful at it. Alliandre approached cautiously, laughing as the man yelled and charged him, tripping several paces away and falling painfully as his armor caught on itself and prevented him from gracefully rolling through the fall.

"Hold!" the marschall called out, and Alliandre walked over and helped the man to his feet. Only it wasn't a grown man at all, but a youngish man, maybe sixteen or seventeen. The boy thanked him, getting set again. Alliandre set himself as well and the marschall signaled them to fight again. It went better for the young man; he seemed well suited to the sword. Alliandre sparred for a bit, then caught him in a manticore strike, using both swords in rapid blows, forcing the boy to flail his sword and shield until they were sufficiently out of position that a falcon's beak easily ended the match.

Walking back to his number, Alliandre observed the remaining fighters. He noticed Jason fighting but ignored him. He would move his direction next round, to clear the fighters between them so he could more easily keep an eye on him. Two fighters still dueled, a city guard and one of the city soldiers by the look of them. Equally matched, and equally cautious in their attacks. Circling each other, they engaged in several blows and counter blows, then retreated again. Alliandre watched for a while, but decided neither was a match for him, looking back toward Jason.

Jason stood on his number now, which was a good thing. Alliandre was happy he had made it through the first round. In four or five rounds, the orders would look for potential recruits among the remaining combatants. He flashed a quick salute to the boy, who was not paying attention, then turned as the marschall's horn announced the end of the first round. The soldier had prevailed, the dejected guardsman retreating from the field. The other almost ran back to his number, removing his helm to reveal a mane of dark red hair and a smile that could be seen from the city.

Alliandre grabbed a drink from his water bag, looking to his left toward the stands. He had hoped Marion would be watching, but while there were people in the king's pavilion, none of them appeared to be members of the new royal court. He adjusted the strip of cloth he had fastened to his pauldron. Fairwind and her courtier sat politely next to the king's pavilion, a servant holding a large shade over them. A small table with wine sat behind them, manned by Braxlo, ever the faithful retainer. Looking closer, he noticed a fair amount of yellow over at the king's pavilion. No doubt "wolf" Rodney was scouting him and evaluating his performance.

Once the break ended, Alliandre moved to his right toward Jason, eliminating each man and woman he came across. This served two purposes, which was to move closer to Jason so he could help guide him to the later rounds. It also moved him farther away from spying eyes. He would give as little away as possible to Sir Rodney, but after sending three opponents to the sidelines to watch, a woman a few inches short than he approached him. She nodded, raising one of her swords in salute.

"Hail and well met, Alliandre." The woman raised her visor to speak. "I am Sheena of the Easton Marshes. I met you once during the Great Vreen War, west of the marshes. We are in close proximity to each other, and though I do not wish to leave the competition this early, it would seem we are honor bound to fight."

"There is no rule stating it is so," Alliandre stated, his breath coming heavily to him. Tilting his own helm back to reveal the upper half of his face, he continued, "and though I would hate to end your dreams of winning, I am afraid I must end your dream at some point."

"Then perhaps you will leave me to pass and we can cross paths in the final round." She lowered her visor, walking past him.

"When you are prepared for defeat, come find me. I shall not pursue you before then." Smiling behind his bevor, he raised his sword in salute before snapping his helm back into place. Then he continued toward his pupil.

Two more fell to his sword before the round ended. He saw Jason between two others. Alliandre's legs were trembling with fatigue as he carefully sipped water from his bag. The third round began. A burly man and his apparent partner charged toward him. The burly man was too slow, stopping to watch as his thinner and taller partner issued the challenge. "You there, big man. Come fight me. See why they call me the 'Giant Slayer'."

"I seriously doubt anyone calls you 'Giant Slayer' without silver exchanging hands, but by all means, end your day." Alliandre was smiling again behind his helm.

The thin man kept his distance while circling around. Then he stopped and raised his helm. Alliandre was confused for a moment, then whirled and crouched down as the bigger man's sword clanged off his own. Alliandre unleashed a hydra strike, initiating the flurry of thrusts above the knee and moving methodically up, until the marschall called "Enough!"

Moving quickly to engage the thinner man, he surprised Alliandre when he sprang forward and thrust in a perfectly executed viper strike. Brushing the sword aside, Alliandre began a series of combinations to move his buckler out of position. The man was quite skilled, fighting much like Erich with his constant weaving in and out, and acrobatic spins and leaps. He actually landed several blows, although Alliandre caught them on his swords first, limiting their actual impact. Alliandre could no longer flick the swords to deflect blows. Every movement required a great effort.

The man was definitely a sword master, making Alliandre wonder why he was not already in a knightly order. The man pressed his attack once again, but Alliandre had sparred with Erich for years now. As the smaller man bounded forward in another leaping strike, Alliandre leaped forward himself, more of a long step in truth, deflecting the sword of the agile fighter and catching his shield arm in his own. From there, it was easy to first strike the agile man's sword arm before bringing his own sword crashing down on his opponent's shoulder, ending the bout.

He looked around for Jason, seeing him in a bout with another warrior, a captain of the guard, apparently. Jason fought aggressively, but when the captain recovered his footing and counterattacked, Alliandre almost screamed. Jason continually allowed his opponent to throw thunder strikes. Jason nimbly jumped aside but didn't follow up and exploit the overextended opponent.

The fight ended seconds before the horn sounded, ending the round. A half score seconds longer, and Jason would have survived the round, which meant Alliandre could have kept him in long enough to be noticed. All there was to do now was make sure he crushed the captain's dreams like he could see Jason's were. He watched Jason walk off dejectedly, his opponent walking over to offer some words. He couldn't tell if they were encouraging or taunting. Then the two clasped wrists and Jason left the field.

***

Rodney the Magnificent and several of his banner mates sat in the king's pavilion, along with a half score of other guests. Most of the others were servants or workers in the palace watching one of their sons or friends compete in the Open Melee today. A few, realizing this was the only event at Jubilee where none of the nobles would be interested in attending, took the opportunity to eat and drink at the king's expense. And the food and drink were exceptional.

The Wyndgryph knights, however, were only here for one reason. To see just how good Alliandre was and prepare for him in case he actually advanced far enough to gain an entry into the Grand Melee. So far, he did not impress them. While Alliandre had won all his bouts so far, he had refused to battle one of the more skilled adventurers and had struggled to defeat two of the others, who clearly had skills. One might have even been a sword master, but all Alliandre's blows seemed to be strained, like it already wore him out.

Sir Rodney pointed. "Look, he is fighting a member of the guard. If that is who he was used to fighting, no wonder he struggles so. It is a far different thing to duel one person than to have an actual duel comprising a half score of individual bouts. Any true swordsman learns your tricks."

Waving a small fan, he continued, "These tournaments, with their breaks and single battles, may whittle down the number of combatants quickly. But the best fighters pair off against each other, leaving the chance someone choosing their opponents well can go far with little skill. If they spend their time walking around, or sparring with someone of much lesser skill, they could avoid the fatigue a real duel would entail."

"This is the difference between knights like us and these commoners who get good with a sword," Rodney spoke out to no one in particular. "They have no stamina. Look at how the fool huffs and puffs. You would think he had been fighting all day, yet we aren't even an hour into this."

"Still, my lord," one of his knights commented, "he seems to adapt to the differing attacks. He has also been flawless in his counters as far as I have seen. But you are correct. He coils and strains for every blow. It makes him predictable, and I am wondering how long he can keep it up. Swinging a dueling sword for an hour differs greatly from swinging a real sword."

"How right you are, Sir Mathias. This shall be our strategy, then. Each of you will challenge him in order of seniority and wear him down. You will exhaust him before he gets through half of you. One of you can defeat him, so I won't even have to face him and disobey my father. Then, if he challenges me to a blood duel, I shall end him once and for all and the fault will lie with him."

***

There were only a half score of them remaining now, all of them adventurers of some sort. Already, the orders sent squires out to inquire of several of the men and women remaining. But none to Alliandre. Adjusting the ribbon after each kill, he continued to search the stands, hoping Marion could leave the Jester Competition in time to see his victory. He looked at the others to size them up. One monster, as big as Lolark, also wielding a great sword, but lacking his friend's skill. Still, he had the strength and training to wield the blade. So much so many of the combatants had avoided him. Alliandre thought he should go after him before fatigue took him completely.

Alliandre wasn't aware of it, but he was six behind the leader in total kills, and she had her sights on him. She waited patiently while he finished with the only remaining man using sword and shield. He was unusually agile for someone using a shield, and many times pulled his shield back into position after Alliandre had maneuvered it out. So Alliandre switched tactics, driving the sword out of position instead. Then, attacking the body, he changed the sword's path, taking out the shield arm.

The man winced in pain as Alliandre used much more force than needed, but he had to swing full force on each swing. His muscles screamed like he had been fighting for days, not a mere couple of hours. He would have Sivle check him when he returned tonight, maybe taking a bit of Sivle's concoction a few hours before bed. Then he would sleep like a snow panther in Adimon. Thinking about it, he felt a lot like he did after using Sivle's ointment, even though the judges detected no enchantments on him. But panic was teasing the edges of his mind. The competition was only getting stronger, and he was weakening with each blow.

Quickly dispatching the one-armed swordsman, he turned to the giant, only to have a lithe woman step up. "Come now, red warrior, you seem to be the biggest fish in this little pond. How about we dance? If you win, you can share my bed tonight."

Savoring the brief rest, Alliandre flipped Marion's favor straight, then shrugged. "I have no interest in your bed, so perhaps you would prefer a chance for someone else to gain access to it."

Laughing, the woman struck a pose. "No man has shared my bed for several years. Why upset my wife by starting now? Have at thee!"

She charged with two tri-pronged weapons which Alliandre had never seen before. She spun them and thrust them, as they seemed to have no edge. Each point was dulled, but he supposed they could still do some damage if they got into a seam, so he prevented it from happening. He protected his flanks and, knowing she could not score a strike with a slash, parried the lunging thrusts she made.

More than once, he found one or both of his swords locked in the tines of the weapons. She would often take the opportunity to kick or headbutt him. Normally, he could overpower anyone who trapped his swords this way, but now he struggled to keep his grip on them. Tiring of the dirty tricks, he delivered a headbutt of his own, followed by a straight on kick to her chest. "Hold," the marschall called out as he sent her sprawling onto her back. Once she had risen, she began spinning the weapons again as she approached.

Alliandre had seen enough to figure out a counter for most of her attacks, and as she thrust, he attacked the weapon, driving it out of her hand before performing a quick thrust through the tines of the other to put a nice dent in the shapely steel of her breastplate. Almost immediately, he had to duck the blade of the two-handed swordsman. "Do all you insist on cheating?" he asked as he rose, charging the big man. Nimbly, the man retreated as he let the blade continue around his head.

This was the strength and the weakness of great swords in single combat. They were twice as long as a sword blade and, when added to the length of the wielder's arms, were effective at keeping enemies at bay. The problem was that in their arc, the body was vulnerable. Alliandre deflected the large blade, deciding to sacrifice a sword. Running forward, he caught the blow, slowing down the blade as it ran the length of his own sword. When it reached the hilt, it cut through the guard, broke the sword at the tang, and continued through to Alliandre's cuirass. But the momentum slowed. It barely even made a sound. At least compared to the clang as Alliandre's free sword moved unimpeded to the great helm of the big man.

Alliandre looked up. There were five remaining warriors. None of them appeared to want to fight each other. Alliandre straightened, feeling refreshed. It was as if he had dropped a great weight from his back. Stretching to his full height, he called to them. "So be it then. Which one of you is first?"

A stocky warrior with a bull-shaped helm, complete with horns, charged him with a long sword in one hand, a shorter, wedge-shaped sword in the other. Alliandre circled back as the attacks came furiously, blocking and parrying just as furiously with his single sword. The man knew his business, slashing and cutting with the long sword, while the short sword acted as a shield when needed, keeping Alliandre from advancing too close, until a quick thrust from Alliandre's single sword ended it.

The horn sounded several seconds after, the group returning to their numbers.

Alliandre took a long draught of water before rummaging in his bag for one of his extra swords. It was the second one he had broken. Taking deep breaths, he looked at the remaining four combatants. Two used double swords like his, while one had a long sword and a nasty-looking mace. The other looked like a blacksmith, carrying a mace and an axe. He had promised the tall, statuesque woman he would not pursue her, so he taunted the mace and axe wielder. "Are you hoping to do well today so your father will let you play with proper weapons?"

"These will seem proper enough when they crush your fancy little helm," the other man answered. "You are a little old to still be playing dress up, aren't you?"

The marschall called "Final Round," meaning it would last until there was only one warrior left. Alliandre determined to make it a short round. Getting his second wind, he skipped to the heavily muscled man. As the two charged, Alliandre waited until the last second before performing a viper strike which caught the man on the gorget, lifting him up and throwing him on his back. Immediately, the male fighter with the two long swords stepped forward.

They circled each other, trading blows for several seconds, when Alliandre realized the warrior was doing a variation of a contact drill. He waited until the man performed a strike. Alliandre spun his wrist as he dodged, striking the extended wrist before using both swords in successive blows to drive down the remaining sword of his opponent. One last strike dented the back of the other's helm.

Two left and the sword and mace man fell to a series of thunder strikes. With no shield, Alliandre forced him to raise his mace above his head, falling lower and lower with each blow until Alliandre's sword reached the crest of his helm first. The man cursed, but bowed, retreating from the field.

"So, Sheena of the Easton Marshes, it seems like it is time to end your dreams."

Sheena bowed, raising her sword in salute. "It is an honor to have met you those many years ago, and an honor to fight you today. But I believe it is too late to end my dreams. I have already received offers from two of the orders. Hail and well met, Alliandre. May our future battles be always together."

"May our future battles be always together," Alliandre replied. Then they touched sword tips and began.

IX

❧

The Blood Oath

32nd of Frendalo, Year 1124 AG

Vanessa watched as Diana took the table with some wealthy merchants. She had been stuck with the accursed paladins. It was unlikely she would bring in a full purse unless travelers came back for lunch or dinner. But that meant she would have to work all day, and they were so close to finishing the surprise. She needed only one more good day, and Vandion said he would have enough to finish. When Marion came in, Vanessa groaned. If she were here, she would take the regulars. Sure enough, she went straight to her friends.

Vanessa hurried to get the plate of cold mutton for the two tables of Wrens. Diana had called them the Wrens first. Soon everyone at the Aerie began referring to them that way. The Wrens didn't seem to mind. Indeed, they began referring to their commander as Wren One. Vanessa returned with the platter of meat. Sir Andras had thrown in some cheese as well. Her fawning paladin, Sir Trevor, rose to help her. She smiled politely, and he commented, "You have a beautiful smile."

"Thank you, Sir Trevor," she replied, then hurried to leave to get the platter of hard bread and tea. She didn't know why she felt bad for the young man, but she also knew he was likely just interested in saving the money the pleasure palace would cost. She grabbed the tray, balancing it with the pitcher of tea. Fortunately, the Wrens didn't like the tea, so they drank little of it. They had ordered ale, but they had run out of money until the rest of their order arrived. As she returned with the bread and tea, Sir Trevor rose again.

"Milady, would you sit with me for a moment and talk?" He looked like a sad puppy dog, and she began to leave when he spoke again. "I am sorry to bother you, but you look so much like my older sister, and I am a bit homesick. I won't bother you after this."

Sighing, she looked him in the eye. He seemed sincere enough. "I will chat with you for a few minutes, but if another customer comes in, I have to leave."

"'Tis fair," he stated, then led her to an empty table. This garnered some looks and snickers from some of the other Wrens, but Vanessa paid them no mind. He held her chair for her as she sat, the polished copperwood smooth and shimmering in the light from the chandelier directly above. The tabletop should have been scuffed and scratched from years of use. Instead, it looked like it had been freshly sanded and oiled. She wondered how they kept the tables looking so new. Sir Trevor sat across from her, bringing two cups and the newly delivered pitcher of tea.

"So, did you grow up here in Foresight?" he asked.

"I guess so. I was born here after the Southern Kingdom fell. My father had been a soldier in the Southern Kingdom's army. My mom had been here visiting her family when the aelf attacked. My father had been wounded in the battle and sent to Foresight to be with my mom." Shrugging, she finished. "So, while I have lived here my whole life, my parents were both from the Southern Kingdom."

"How old are you, then? That was a long time ago. When I was just a child."

"I am seventeen now. My mom was pregnant with me when she left Vista."

"Oh." Sir Trevor looked a little dejected. "I am twenty-five and have been a full paladin for over eight years now. My sister was fifteen when

I left home. The last time I saw her, she was only twenty. We were awfully close."

"What was she like?" Vanessa tried to turn the conversation away from herself.

"She was always happy and smiling." His smile turned to a scowl as he continued. "Even though my mother raised us in a pleasure palace in River Watch, Janel could always ignore the fact my mother was a pleasure princess. I know my mother did her best to make sure we had a warm bed and plenty of food, but I still resent how she provided them to us."

"That is terrible. How did you end up becoming a paladin, then?" Vanessa was actually curious.

"One of my mother's customers. She convinced a commander I would make a good squire, promising him a week in bed if he would take me." His scowl had grown as he remembered the large man who had spent a week in their room. "He spent the week before trying to leave without me. My mother protested, causing him such embarrassment that he agreed. I haven't seen her since. I only saw my sister because she is working at the same palace now."

Vanessa could see his sister's profession troubled the young man. No one frowned at the princesses. For many of the urchins, it was quite common. Once they reached puberty, if they had not picked up any trades the orphanage arranged for them, the boys went to the army or guard, the girls to the kitchens. If they were lucky enough to be smart and talented in espionage, the guild would direct them to one of the palaces run by the guild. Depending on their talent and tastes, there were palaces for all castes. Even some taverns had a few "princesses" working for them. The way Marion flirted with her customers; Vanessa had initially thought the Wyvern's Aerie might be one of those types of taverns.

"What happened to your mom?" Vanessa asked, changing the subject.

"She got old, moving to a lower-level palace. One day some merchant came in who liked to get rough, hurting her terribly. After she recovered from her wounds, she left. No one has heard from her since. Not even Janel." He raised his chin and looked her in the eye. "But that is enough about me. What brought you to be working here?"

"My father died in the Great Vreen War, and my mother raised me until she died last year. I had no way to keep my farm and was going to sell it and try to become a seamstress or something. Vanessa paused before mentioning Vandion but decided she had better. My fiancé said he would try to run the farm, so I could get a job. I tried learning to sew, but my uncle said he knew someone from the Southern Kingdom who might hire me as a tavern girl. I was kind of anxious, not wanting to be 'that' kind of tavern girl. No offense to your mother and sister. But Lady Arielle runs a fine establishment. Her daughter is one of the other tavern girls, and Sir Andras makes sure no one acts up where we are concerned."

She paused. She wasn't sure why she was telling him all this, but he had asked, and he had poured his heart out to her. She pointed as another customer came in. Smiling again, she rose. "Sorry, back to work."

"You have a beautiful smile," he said once again.

"So you have told me. Thank you, I will try to let you see it more often." She gave him a small wink, like she saw Marion do often, immediately regretting it. There was no sense flirting with paladins. They had no money.

The new patron came in and sat alone. Looking to be well into her silver years, she dressed flamboyantly in a bright yellow dress and an orange and red shawl which almost covered the ample bosom she was displaying.

"Welcome to the Wyvern's Aerie," Vanessa said in her sweetest voice. "Can I get you something?"

"Yes, dear." The woman wasn't exactly brusque, but she was certainly direct. "I will take your best wine, and I have heard the bacon and sweet cakes here are wonderful. I would like some of each."

"Yes, my lady." Vanessa gave a small curtsey and went to get the order. As she went to the kitchen, Sir Andras stopped her.

"Be careful of that one, lassie." He leaned closer to her and lowered his voice even more. "She looks like she be from Wyndgryph, and we have a wee bit of an issue with them right now."

She relayed the orders to John. Sir Andras handed her a tray with a pitcher and four full glasses on it. She brought it out, setting a glass next to her patron before setting the pitcher down. She had never seen Sir Andras send filled glasses along with a pitcher, but she followed John's advice. "Will there be anyone joining you, my lady?"

Looking somewhat surprised, her guest quickly composed herself. "Why yes, I am expecting the Duke and Duchess Del Mornay any moment."

Vanessa set down two more glasses, turning to return to the kitchen. She jumped, stumbling as Arielle grabbed the remaining glass off her tray before stepping up to the lady at the table.

***

"Lady Hilde, what a surprise to see you here." Sitting down at the only place without a wine glass, Lady Arielle held her hand out in greeting. "It is so wonderful to see you again. I hope this is a social call."

Smiling broadly, the older woman held Arielle's hand in both of her hands. "Relax, Your Majesty. The duke wishes no trouble with you or your family. He invited me here to show there is no ill will. We will dine, hoping we can talk and patch up any lingering..." she paused, searching for the right word, "enmities, shall we say."

Lady Arielle took a quick breath and held it. Speaking carefully, she replied after a moment. "Let me assure you, your fears are unfounded. Sir Andras and I, and Marion as well, do not hold any ill will regarding Sir Rodney. The duke's son is welcome here anytime, sober preferably." She smiled at the last. Then she gave a small nod, rising to leave.

"And the red warrior, Alliandre?" Lady Hilde held Arielle with her tone. "We saw he won the Open Melee and will fight in the Grand Melee. We both know a skilled warrior can easily cause grievous injury with the dueling blades. And we both know Alliandre has considerable skill."

"He has been told not to seek Sir Rodney. I believe he will obey. However, if Sir Rodney challenges him, I cannot say what he will do. He is, mercurial, shall we say." Arielle sat back down, shrugged her shoulders, and took a large sip of wine.

"The duke has forbidden Sir Rodney from challenging Alliandre as well. But I am afraid it doesn't look like it is an order he will obey. The duke is in a difficult position. It is his sole remaining heir; the duchess is too old to bear him any more sons." Hilde shrugged her shoulders, mimicking her companion. Then she, too, took an overly large sip of wine. The two women smiled at each other.

Arielle visibly relaxed, turning to face her table mate directly. "How did you get dragged into mediating this, Lady Hilde?"

"Just Hilde, please." The older woman blushed a little. "I am surprised you remember me. I don't believe I have seen you since your wedding, although you have barely aged."

"Thank you," Arielle replied graciously. "I only wish it were true. And let's just say you made an enormous impact on me at my wedding." Both women laughed at the memory of the well-endowed woman who literally burst out of her corset as she danced with the newly married King Tristan. "But that doesn't answer my question."

Hilde nodded. "No, it doesn't. Truth be told, I am not here in any official capacity. I came to Foresight to enjoy the Jubilee. I met the duke and duchess, and they used the opportunity to invite me to the Aerie before the festivities today. Then they filled me in on all the palace intrigue. They are quite concerned. The duchess has not slept well since they met Alliandre and saw the look in his eyes. Every night she wakes, screaming for her son."

Arielle nodded somberly. She remembered the sleepless nights after she heard of Nathan's death, and the weeks of not sleeping when William first joined the same order Nathan had served. Her eyes, moist at the memory, blinked rapidly as she leaned in. "I promise you this, I will have Marion implore Alliandre to spare Sir Rodney from any serious injury. He is quite temperamental, but I believe he will honor her request."

"Thank you, Arielle," she said sincerely. "I have always heard your beauty was matched only by your graciousness and charm. I can see why my former husband courted you all those years ago." Then, with another smile, "Thank the spirits you turned him down so he could settle for me."

Both women smiled as Arielle refilled their wine glasses.

*　*　*

Marion raced to the Aerie, hoping to catch Alliandre before he left to scout out the Sword and Shield Tournament. She had hurried over to the Open Melee Tournament the previous day, but it had ended before she had gotten there, Alliandre nowhere to be found. She looked around for him in the Aerie dining hall. He wasn't in the dining hall, although several of the others were sitting at their table. She went over to them, sitting down.

"Good morning, Marion," Erich said as they all stood. "I hope you are not here to see Alliandre. He left early this morning."

"I was, actually. Do you know where he went so early?"

Sivle spoke up as he sat back down. "He gave me a sword to enchant for him, but I did not get to it yesterday, so he agreed to restock some of my scroll making supplies so I would have time to do it today. Then he is going to be scouting out the martial tournaments."

Fairwind giggled. "You sent Drullock for scroll making supplies? I hope they are for writing home, not for writing spells."

Sivle looked her way, then shook his head. "He knows more about papyrus and ink than most mages. I have complete confidence in him. Perhaps you would like to enchant the sword for me so I can focus on my final scroll."

Fairwind giggled again. "I am to be courted by Prince Perhaladon. But perhaps you could take the time to teach the technique to Ariandel?"

Sivle groaned, while Ariandel lit up like lamp oil poured on a campfire. "My lord Sivle, I would be in your debt," she said with wide eyes.

Lowering her head and eyes, she followed up shyly, "If you are not too busy, my lord."

Braxlo laughed out loud. "My Lady Ariandel, there is no need for you to make the request. Her Highness has just commanded it. You can be sure it will be so."

The rest of the table chuckled as Sivle protested. "I did not swear an oath of fealty to Fairwind. I am under no obligation."

"No obligation at all, Sivle." Erich patted his friend on the shoulder, grinning. "Why don't you and I just walk around the city today after you get done with your scrolls." This brought a disapproving look from Fairwind, but Sivle just grabbed another piece of bacon.

Sivle looked over to Ariandel. "My lady, if you wish to learn, or at least watch a demonstration, I have a sword and a shield Alliandre wanted me to enchant to harden and resist damage. They are simple enough enchantments, and I have the requisite stamins on scrolls if you have not learned them yet."

"Oh yes, My lord. I would appreciate it very much." Ariandel lit up again, and for several moments, Sivle could not stop looking at her. Ariandel looked over to Fairwind, who gave her a sly, knowing look and smiled.

Marion watched all this transpire with an amused expression. She had known Sivle her whole life. While he often made use of the pleasure palaces, he had never gotten romantically involved. Like many mages, obsessed with the weaving of the spirits, he had few personal relationships. It was probably why the only friend he had outside of her and Alliandre was Erich. But now he seemed to at least notice a member of the fairer sex. She thought about it for a moment longer, then remembered why she was here. "Sivle, do you know when Alliandre will be back?"

"I regret to tell you I do not, Your Highness." Shrugging, he returned to his plate. "If he knew you were expecting him, he would have been finished by now. But you know how easily distracted he is when swordplay is not involved."

She knew indeed. Since she had some time to spare before getting ready for the tournaments, she helped herself to a plate, deciding to chat for a while. She finished eating, but Alliandre had still not arrived. Dejectedly, she rose to go. "Sivle, when you see him, tell him I am sorry I missed the tournament yesterday. I am so happy he won, even though I knew he would. Tell him to look for me at the tournaments today. If he is still talking to me."

Sivle, Braxlo, and Erich rose as soon as Marion stood. Sivle walked over to her. "Your Highness, Alliandre knows your commitments and would not hold them against you. If he is disappointed, it is at the situation, not at you. I am sure he will be excited to see you."

Hugging Sivle, Marion went over and said goodbye to Sir Andras and the serving ladies, even giving Vanessa a small wave. Then she went over to the table where her mother was sitting.

* * *

Randolf Del Mornay and his wife, Rebecca, entered the Wyvern's Aerie, looking around for their friend. They couldn't help but notice Rebecca's old confidant, Lady Hilde Del Triumph, sitting at a table. She had been a wet nurse for Duchess Rebecca when she was young. The two families, friends for over a century. They walked over to her table and then noticed her guest.

"Lady Arielle. How pleasant to see you again." The duke bowed and held out his hand, but his voice quivered. He was relieved when Arielle took his hand and stood.

"And you, Duke and Duchess Del Mornay." Arielle curtseyed. "It is an honor to have you visit the Aerie when not commanded by the king." The words were biting but delivered with a broad smile. The duke looked hesitant until Arielle laughed. It was a laugh of pure pleasure, her head actually tilting back.

"Relax, Randolf," Hilde chided him. "Arielle and I have discussed the situation. We decided to get Princess Marion involved in assuring Alliandre's cooperation in our plan to have your son survive through Jubilee. Now if we can just get Sir Rodney to take part as well."

254 ~ DANIEL E MYERS

The duke looked a little confused, but relieved as well. "I have little hope of that. Rodney returned from the Open Melee Tournament more convinced than ever Alliandre is merely a talented adventurer, unused to real fighting. He plans to have his banner challenge him one at a time to wear him out. If Alliandre makes it through them, Rodney will finish him."

"Then yer son is a damned wee fool," Sir Andras interrupted as he and Vanessa arrived with platters of hens, sausages, and sweet cakes. Sir Andras paused as he set down the platters.

"You need not convince me of the danger my son is in," the duke interrupted him. "I fear they are going to meet, however, and I only hope Alliandre spares him the beating he deserves."

"Tell yer son not to taunt him, and behave like a duke's son, not a wee shite knight who thinks he is king because he wields a sword well."

"Sir Andras!" Arielle scolded him. "You are addressing a duke," then mimicking Sir Andras, "Ye should remember that, instead of acting like a wee shite yerself."

Sir Andras bowed an apology, the duke smiling. "Sir Andras, I appreciate your candor and your sound council."

Vanessa returned with a fresh pitcher of wine and a platter of bacon. After Arielle gestured to her, Vanessa grabbed Sir Andras' good arm, leading him away to the kitchen. Arielle turned to her guests. "My apologies. How about we eat and determine the best plan to ensure there is not a blood feud between our families by the end of Jubilee."

They ate, discussing their plan, each one thinking hard about how to keep their side from instigating an action which would not only cause havoc for their families, but the kingdom as well. In the end, Marion got up from where she was sitting to come over to say goodbye. Seeing the duke and duchess, Marion cringed apprehensively as the duke stood.

Arielle gave her a hug, then motioned her to pull over a chair. "Duke Randolf and Duchess Rebecca have a request to make of you."

"Good morning, Duke and Duchess Del Mornay." Marion curtseyed to both. "How may I be of service to you?"

The duke walked over, taking Marion's hand. "Lady Marion, we have a favor to ask of you, one which you have no obligation to perform for us, and even less reason. We ask out of concern for our son. He seems intent on challenging Alliandre in the Grand Melee."

"Then he will lose," Marion stated as a matter of fact.

"That is a forgone conclusion, my dear." The duke kept her hand, looking her straight in the eye. "What we ask of you is to implore Alliandre to spare our son. Defeat him, but do not injure him. Or worse."

Marion returned the duke's gaze. "I will do what I can, my lord. I believe Alliandre's temper has cooled some, but I will not ask him to make an oath he cannot keep. Once he focuses on the fight, he will consider nothing beyond the moment, and staying alive. At least, that is what Sir Andras has told me. But I will implore him to spare your son."

"Thank you, Lady Marion." The duchess stood and actually grabbed Marion's face, holding it like an aunt upon finding a long, lost niece. "If my son lives, I can assure you and Lady Arielle the support of Wyndgryph Castle," then winking at Arielle, "if you should ever have the need."

***

Alliandre returned to the Aerie to find Sivle in the room with Ariandel, of all people. On the table in front of the two sat the sword and shield he had given Sivle to enchant.

"Here are your supplies, Sivle. I didn't know you were going to delegate the favor." Alliandre said the words with a harsh tone, but his smiling face made it clear he was comfortable with the arrangement.

"Her Highness requested the lesson. As I had to enchant these anyway, I agreed. Fairwind may have done it, but she is busy being courted." Sivle gave Alliandre a smile in return. "Why didn't you get the guardsman some plate mail as well?"

"After spending the day with him, I almost wish I had. He is a good young man. By the way, he will probably stop by after his shift. Do you think your lesson will be completed by then?"

"It will be," Sivle assured him. "I should also mention Marion stopped by while you were out. She was looking for you. She said she was happy you won, and she is sorry she didn't make it over in time. She did go looking for you, though, and you are to look for her today."

"I should have thought of that and not left this morning." The look of dejection on Alliandre's face was clear, but he shook his head, smiling again. "I know where she will be today. I want to scout the nobles anyway. I am sure I can bump into her. I was just on my way there now."

"My apologies," Sivle said regretfully. "If I had not tried yesterday to create my scrolls without memorizing the spell first, I would not have needed the supplies, and I would have already enchanted the sword. And you would not have missed Marion. I am afraid I have let you down, but I will have these enchanted before I work on the scrolls."

"When requesting a favor," Alliandre recited a lesson they had learned as children, "it is contemptuous to also request the timing."

Leaving the room, he raced downstairs and out the door. He considered bringing Aeris, deciding against it in the end. He raced the half hursmarc to the fairgrounds. Some men preparing for the Sword and Shield Tournament were already arriving and setting up. Alliandre walked around the tournament field he had just left triumphantly the previous day, finding a seat beside the king's pavilion where he was sure he could see Marion, and she could see him.

***

Marion looked for Alliandre but did not see him anywhere. She and the court had watched the Archery Tournament, and it ran longer than expected as the winner, Sir Volinair the Archer, and Sir Tulamon Straight Eye loosed a score of arrows apiece at the swinging targets in the final round. In the end, one of Sir Tulamon's arrows was forced from the center circle by the impact of Sir Volinair's shot. Sir Volinair accepted the trophy, graciously handing half of the hundred turot prize to Sir Tulamon.

Now footmen escorted the royal court into the king's pavilion, two rounds into the competition. She hoped Alliandre was planning on coming late, and letting the tournament whittle down the competitors until only the most likely to challenge him would remain. She noticed Sir Rodney and many of his knights were still on the field, as were several of the paladins of Wyndgryph. Though she tried to pay attention to the fighting, even Lord Del Broussard noticed how distracted she was. "I do not see him, my lady. But fear not, if I am any judge of character, he will be here, looking for you."

"I hope so." She squeezed Ferdinand's hand. "I did not realize the schedule we have to keep as royalty was so demanding. I was expecting to spend more time with him."

She settled down, watching the tournament, with Prince Lucas introducing them to the other dignitaries. When it came time to introduce the Duke and Duchess of the Western March, however, the prince paused.

"Good to see you again, Your Grace." Marion bowed as she held out her hand.

"It feels like we were just together this morning," the duchess teased. "I suppose you have not seen Alliandre yet this morning."

"No, Your Grace. I was hoping he would be here."

"Oh, he is, my dear. He is over on the other side of the pavilion." Pointing in the general direction of what looked like a garden of flowers, feathers, and bows, she added, "You cannot see him over those ostentatious hats the ladies of Cairthorn are wearing, but we greeted him when we first arrived. Alliandre bowed politely, no sign he had made any promises concerning Sir Rodney."

The horn sounded, signaling the next round. Marion watched as the Wyndgryph knights separated to eliminate the other competitors. A female paladin took out two of them in quick succession, fighting awhile with a third before defeating him as well. "Lady Nancy Sword Breaker," Prince Lucas, leaning forward, told her. Pointing out two others, "Those two are Sir Allistair the Silent and Sir Thomas Del Aquinas. All of them are on the Palladium Council."

Marion followed the prince's finger, seeing the two paladins chopping through more of the yellow-helmed knights before Sir Rodney

challenged one of them. The paladin fell to a series of combinations followed by a shield press which held him just long enough for Sir Rodney
to sidestep around him, catching the back of his helm with a blow.

The second paladin wielded a golden-tinged sword. Sir Rodney
avoided him, allowing one of his knights to engage instead. When the
horn sounded, Marion noticed several of the Wyndgryph knights were
leaving the tournament field. The more than half score remaining gathered around Sir Rodney, discussing the next round. It was clear they
would not be fighting each other soon.

The prince leaned in again. "It's good to fight as a team, but it looks
like the other fighters have caught on and are targeting them as well.
Live by the sword, die by the sword."

Target them, they did. The Wyndgryph knights fought valiantly, but
none of the other combatants were fighting each other, just lining up to
challenge Sir Rodney's men. Four rounds later, it was just Sir Rodney.
The Wyndgryph knights had given better than they had gotten. More
than a score of the other challengers sat on the side of the field with
them, including the one with the golden sword. Sir Rodney had defeated him in the last round, after dueling with him the entire previous
round.

With the rest of the knights gone, everyone began fighting each other
again until, several rounds later, it was down to Sir Rodney against
Lady Nancy. It became clear why they named her Sword Breaker. She
swung hard on every blow. If the blocking sword was not up to the task,
it would break, leaving her foe to dodge and block with his shield and
the shard of sword still connected to the handle. If skilled, they might
last until the end of the round when they could get a new sword. Few
were sufficiently skilled.

As good a shape as she was in, she was no longer in her youth. She
had been swinging hard for over three hours now. Fatigue was setting
in. Sir Rodney took advantage of this by feinting and thrusting to
encourage her counter attacks and thunderous blocks. They fought for
half an hour, Sir Rodney drawing her sword out of position. He got
behind it to drive a thrust into her shield arm. It was a quick battle

after that as he trapped her sword with his shield so he could deliver a crashing blow atop her polished helm.

Marion groaned inwardly as she thought of how pompous he had been before winning. Leaning over to the duchess, she said as politely as she could, "Congratulations, Your Grace. It was a, magnificent, victory."

Smiling, the duchess nodded. "Thank you, Your Highness. You appear to be as delightful a woman as your mother, spirits bless her." Pointing in Alliandre's general direction, she added, "Now, could you help me rest easily tonight?"

Marion excused herself, walking past the herd of hats. She saw Alliandre circling around to the front of the pavilion. She called to him, and lit up when he smiled and came running, or rather tunneling, through the throng as they rushed forward to cheer for the victor. King Henry and Prince Lucas had already moved onto the tournament grounds, standing with other dignitaries as workmen hastily set up the winner's stand to allow the crowd to see Sir Rodney close up.

When he reached the stands below her, Alliandre climbed up the lattice on the side, vaulting over the railing. Marion carefully eased down the stairs to greet him. "I am sorry I missed you yesterday, Alliandre. I would have so liked to see you on the winner's platform."

"I should have gone over to the Jester's Tournament. To be honest, I was disappointed. Then my guardsman friend and I got to drinking and talking. Before I knew it, the sun was down." Bowing his head in shame, he continued. "I should have known you would come to the Aerie this morning, but I let myself get sent off on an errand for Sivle."

Marion reached up to lift his chin slightly, looking him in the eye. "We both have our obligations. I was disappointed this morning too, but I am so happy to see you now. I cannot wait to give you your reward for winning the tournament with MY favor." She winked at him, giving him a come-hither smile which would have done any pleasure princess proud. "Now come, I have something important to discuss with you."

Nervously taking him by the hand, she led him to the duke and duchess, pulling hard on his arm when he saw them and paused. "Come now. They don't bite. I promised them I would ask you something. I wanted them to hear so there would be no question about it." Reaching the duke and duchess, they exchanged pleasantries, with both congratulating Alliandre on his victory the previous day.

Marion took the opportunity during a pause to face Alliandre. With much trepidation, she spoke, "Duke and Duchess Del Mornay have asked me to implore you to spare their son. They agree anything you do to Sir Rodney is what he deserves, but as a father and mother, ask you spare their last remaining son and heir. I know you have already said you would not challenge him. But he plans on challenging you. They are concerned you will do irreparable harm to him. Or worse. So, I am imploring you, as the one who bears my favor, to spare Sir Rodney of your justified wrath."

Alliandre's eyes flashed with anger at the mention of Sir Rodney again. He looked at Marion and saw the real pleading in her eyes. He thought perhaps she was being put up to this, but she seemed to want him to spare the man who had so brazenly assaulted her. He began mouthing a promise to avoid harming him, but her eyes held his tongue. Her hands squeezed his tightly. Looking down, he saw the white in her knuckles.

With a sigh of acquiescence, he turned angrily to the duke. Despite the red flashing in his eyes, his tone was almost calm and even. "My lord, upon my word, and the love I have for Her Highness, Marion the Virtuous, I give you my blood oath I will do everything in my power to prevent harm from coming to your son, by my hand or any other, until the end of Jubilee." Seeing the duke nod his acceptance, Alliandre paused.

"Know this, however. If he challenges me, I will fight to my utmost. I will not give him any advantage or hold back. But if I have the opportunity to end the combat without injury, I shall." Looking over to Marion, it was his turn to look her in the eyes. "Is that sufficient, Your Highness?"

Marion looked into Alliandre's eyes and saw the red flash of shame and anger from the humiliation she had just forced him to bear. Again. She could not keep eye contact, knowing she had caused him this pain.

She bowed her head, released his hands, and took a half step back. "I am sorry, my love," was all she could say, tears welling up in her eyes. She turned and left. She had been so excited to see Alliandre, but for the second time, she had forced him to humiliate himself in front of everyone, ruining everything.

Alliandre looked at the duke and duchess, the duke smiling and looking proudly at him, and the duchess in tears herself. "Your Graces," bowing slightly, "is that sufficient for your favor?" he asked.

"Indeed, it is, Alliandre. A thousand thanks to you," the duchess replied. "Now, however, I believe you have some talking to do with Her Highness. I would ask you not go too hard on her. She is an amazing young woman."

Alliandre looked over to see Marion walking away, heading to the field toward the Jubilee Royal Court, to congratulate the contestants. Cursing himself, he ran down the stands. With his long strides, he caught up with her before she reached Lord Ferdinand and the rest of the Jubilee Royal Court. Grabbing her around the waist, he stopped her, pulling her close before she turned. Then he placed a lingering kiss on the crown of her head.

"I do not spend enough moments with you to waste them in self-pity. Forgive me my boorish behavior and tell me more about your reward." He forced a smile, and when she turned and he saw the relief on her face, it became genuine.

Craning her neck to look up at him, tears filling her eyes, she sighed. "Since you arrived, I have done nothing but disappoint you, forcing public humiliation and disgrace on you. It is I who needs forgiveness."

Alliandre bent his head to kiss her on the forehead again. "Nothing could be further from the truth. As I told you, it is character building to be forced to accept these things in order to achieve a larger goal. And I will achieve that goal. I promise you." She reached up and put her hand on the back of his neck, forcing him to lift her up. Looking him straight in the eyes, she leaned her head in, lips parting slightly and closing her eyes as their lips moved closer to one another.

"Our thanks once again, Your Highness," the duke and duchess interrupted them. "And to you, Alliandre. Be assured we will root for you in the tournament tomorrow." They had followed Alliandre down and arrived just before Marion attempted to give him their first genuine kiss. Duke Randolf reached his hand out to Alliandre, who set Marion down to clasp wrists with the duke. The duchess reached her hand out as well. Alliandre bowed to kiss it, but she leaned in and kissed him squarely on the forehead, lingering for an uncomfortably long period.

"I have heard your skill with the sword is matched only by your honor as a man," she said as she released her lips. "I thank you with all my heart. I will sleep well tonight."

***

33rd of Frendalo, Year 1124 AGW

The afternoon sun was high in the air as the paladins squared off against each other. Sir Anthony the Rash was determined to go far in this tournament, for no other reason than to erase the humiliation they had suffered at the hands of a single warrior. Not even a knight. Each of his paladins had taken the loss to heart as well, spending the last several days sparring and training. They were determined not to be embarrassed again. They were going up against the Golden Chalice, one of the favorites for the tournament.

Like the Shield Wall Tournament, the Banner Tournament allowed the entire banner to fight each round. However, the Banner Tournament only had one round where the opponent was random. After each round, banners could challenge other banners. Over thirty orders had entered a hundred and twenty banners. The few orders with only one banner sitting out the first round.

Sir Anthony considered the order facing him. Sir Ereg-Drahcir "The Gentlemen" led the order. His squad leaders were Lady Annodam the Lewd, Sir Yenruoj the Escapist, and the brothers, Sir Malcolm the Young, and Sir Angus the Younger. Together they formed the core of a banner which was renowned for their skill and valor. Their least experienced paladin, Sir Edward, Hero of Shereen Pass, was a sword master who had fought in the Great Vreen War. The banner had been together for over seven years, clearly outmatching his own banner, formed only a few months ago and giving Sir Anthony his first chance at command.

However, the fight with Alliandre had taught them something. Even a single swordsman studying the weaknesses and habits of a superior force could still prevail if he were smart about his attack. Sir Anthony got his squad leaders together, discussing the best way to defeat their clearly more talented and cohesive opponents. Together they formulated a bold plan, one which required several of his paladins to fight at a level high above their current skill. If they could pull it off, they could eliminate Sir Ereg-Drahcir's best fighters right away.

The banners lined up. At the sound of the horn, they charged each other. Sir Anthony's halberdiers swung to the side. At the last second, his paladins stopped, forming a single line, instead of the standard two deep formation. This spread their line far beyond the Golden Chalice paladins, allowing Sir Anthony's squad leaders, wielding halberds, to set them into the torn-up ground. As the Golden Chalice attacked, Sir Anthony's halberdiers dropped the heads of their weapons to just a foot off the ground and thrust, disrupting the shields of the endmost paladins in the front on each side. All four went down from swords thrusts from all sides.

His paladins in the middle were fighting furiously on the defensive, trying only to stay alive as the single file of paladins wrapped around the opposing force. The Golden Chalice squad leaders were challenging the ends, but Sir Anthony outnumbered each two to one. The halberdiers had reset their weapons, thrusting forcefully into the bottoms of the shields of the second line. Sir Anthony lost two paladins, but another four of the opponents went down, allowing several of his own men to charge into the rear of their formation.

The Golden Chalice paladins were beset on all sides. As the second line repositioned themselves to avoid being surrounded, the front line lost its support. Three of Sir Anthony's paladins had gotten behind and pressed the attack from the left side. Two more of his paladins fell, but so did Lady Annodam. He lost three more before Sir Malcolm fell, along with two more from the Golden Chalice shield wall. The three paladins who had pierced the Golden Chalice shield wall fell, but not before the Golden Chalice shield wall broke under the attacks from the previously beleaguered center and the halberdiers which added their weight to the center.

They had reduced the Golden Chalice to Sir Ereg-Drahcir, Sir Angus, and Sir Yenruoj, along with Sir Saep the Black-eyed. Sir Anthony still had half his banner, including all of his squad leaders. They formed into a smaller shield wall, advancing. He gave the command for a wave attack, remembering how it had pushed Alliandre back. His men advanced to attack and fall back, allowing the next in line to press the attack. One by one his men fell, removing Sir Yenruoj, Sir Angus, and Sir Saep before it was only Sir Anthony, and Sir Vladimir the Wolf with three others against Sir Ereg-Drahcir.

Sir Ereg-Drahcir tore them apart. Clearly the equal of any on the field, Sir Ereg-Drahcir danced and thrust and went through combinations of blows and parries at dizzying speed. Sir Vladimir fell to a viper strike which came out of nowhere while Sir Ereg-Drahcir was engaged with Sir Anthony. Sir David and Lady Selena fell to successive eagle's talons. Sir Jasper fell to a frog tongue strike thrown while Sir Ereg-Drahcir retreated. Sir Anthony fell a minute later to a viper strike, which actually had sufficient force to send a fragment of his visor into his left eye. His vision blurred, he acknowledged the hit, dejectedly leaving the field. Sir Ereg-Drahcir returned to his banner as well. Then, one by one, each walked over to the defeated banner and saluted them.

In the end, the Golden Chalice proved too much for the rest of the banners as well. In all their battles, only Sir Anthony and the paladins of the Silver Chalice reduced them to even a quarter of their strength. Sir Lolark brought over a stack of turots, one for each man, assuring them the order would pick up their tab at the Aerie. Sir Ereg-Drahcir made the unprecedented act of coming over with his banner at the end of the tournament.

"Sir Anthony," the older paladin addressed him, and then his banner, "and the rest of your stout warriors. It is a shame we met in the first round, as you are the first in years to challenge us. We raise our swords to you." Each of the victorious paladins raised their swords in salute once again.

X

Revelations

Fairwind awakened Ariandel early the next morning. "We want to get an early start today. We will work on Sivle's drills, then go watch the Spellcaster's Competition," Fairwind explained.

"A day of drills doesn't sound too exciting. Will we get to practice the fire and earth again?" Ariandel's tone betrayed her excitement at getting to train more.

"Certainly. But I want to make sure we are prepared to have Lord Sivle train us again tomorrow. After tomorrow, Alliandre will certainly force Sivle to watch the Grand Melee. And then we will drink and celebrate Alliandre's victory; or drink and commiserate with Alliandre's defeat. Either way, there will be no training. The following day is the Royal Ball and all the preparations for it. No training that day, either. Then I suspect I will have to give Prince Perhaladon an answer, for we will leave soon after."

Fairwind left a small message for Braxlo on the outer door before going down for firstmeal. It surprised her to find Alliandre and Erich already there, both finished with their firstmeal. The two men rose as the ladies approached, Fairwind thanking Erich as he moved and held her chair. Drullock moved to do so as well for Ariandel, but she rushed to the other side of Fairwind, sitting before he could reach her chair. Rolling his eyes, he sat back down in his chair, reached across with one of his long muscular arms, and grabbed another pastry from the middle of the table.

Ariandel reached for one as well, snagging one with spring berries. The buttery pastry was still warm, as was the spring berry filling. She closed her eyes and luxuriated in the dichotomy of the dry, buttery, and chewy texture of the pastry mixed with the moist, sweet, and tender meat of the fruit. The flakiness of the pastry left large flakes on her lips as she chewed. She artfully caught the pieces one by one with her tongue, adding them to the flavor explosion inside her mouth. She let a small "Mm mmm" escape, catching Erich smiling at Drullock when she opened her eyes. Drullock averted his eyes, staring at his own pastry without expression.

"I'm sure you wish you could get that kind of reaction from a woman," she said to Drullock with a small grin.

Drullock immediately smiled, turning to Erich. "Ha! You buy my drinks all day!" Turning to the serving girl, he raised his arm to get her attention. "A flagon of the Silver Springs mead for us, please."

Erich groaned, casting a disappointed eye at Ariandel. "He bet me today when he saw you for the first time, you would skip the pleasantries and go directly to some disparaging remark. You just cost me a fortune." Still, he smiled after he said it, adding, "And two cups, please," as Vanessa came over with the mead.

"Serves you right for making a wager on a mage," Fairwind told him. This was a common saying among adventurers. Many knights and paladins did not think highly of most mages' fighting abilities, betting against them returning from great battles.

Erich moved next to Drullock, grabbing a pastry of his own as he went by the platter. Fairwind was scraping the last of the eggs and the sausages onto her plate, but there was not much of either left. When Vanessa returned with the cups for the mead, Fairwind requested a traveler's firstmeal for her and Ariandel. Ariandel swallowed hastily and added, "And more of these pastries, please." Fairwind cast her own disapproving glance, then nodded to Vanessa.

As Vanessa set the cups down, Marion appeared. She gave Alliandre a big hug from behind. He practically tipped over his chair, turning in it before returning the hug. "I didn't know you would be here this morning. Don't you have to be at the joust?"

"I have plenty of time. I wanted to see you this morning before I get dressed."

"Perhaps then you would like to see me drink Erich under the table before you leave. All at his expense, of course," he added, winking at her.

Filling the glasses, she looked at Alliandre and Erich. "If you have ever wanted to kiss me, drink." She laughed as they both grabbed the glasses and drained them. She refilled them, Erich continuing, "If you have ever chosen to train rather than visit a pleasure palace, drink." She put down the flagon as Alliandre drained his glass, the two friends going back and forth as Fairwind and Ariandel finished eating. Finishing her firstmeal, Fairwind declared, "We are ready to train. Marion, would you be so kind as to bring some more wine out to us?"

***

Sivle counted the scrolls for the fourth time. Then, for the fourth time, he compared each scroll to make sure were exactly the same. For the fourth time, all fifteen scrolls were identical. This was surprising since he made four without re-memorizing the spell. Placing them in the scroll sack, he securely latched it, adding a sealing spell to make sure they stayed in place. Perhaps he was overprotective, but this was a spell even middling mages could learn and cast and would be a magnificent spell to protect forces against vreen and grendlaar.

Comfortable they were complete and secure, he went down to firstmeal. Only Alliandre and Erich were eating. Erich was seemingly in Alliandre's good graces, which surprised Sivle. Marion was standing between them with a pitcher, serving them as they finished their glasses.

Sivle walked up, discovering the reason for their friendliness. They were having a drinking duel. The slurred speech showed it had been going on for quite a while. Marion looked at him as he approached, but she merely shrugged.

"If you have ever killed someone who thought you were a friend, take a drink," Alliandre slurred. Erich grabbed the glass and drank.

Erich replied right away, "If you have never killed someone before demanding they surrender, take a drink." If Sivle's memory was correct, they were at the end of their rehearsed lines. He stepped forward as Alliandre chugged his glass.

"If you have ever given me cause to end your existence, take a drink," Sivle challenged both of them. Both looked at him. Both looked at each other. Erich thought before hastily setting his mug down, spilling most of the contents. Sivle looked at the drunken "priest," rolling his eyes. "You are much better at lying when you are sober."

Alliandre looked at Sivle with a pained look in his eyes. "Many times I have failed to be there for you, my friend," Alliandre slurred. "If you slew me now, I would not blame you." Drunken tears formed in his eyes as he slammed his drink, Erich reaching over with a supporting hug.

"How can the both of you be this drunk before firstmeal is over?" Sivle asked the two of them.

"They chose the Silver Spring mead over the morning beer," Marion explained with a grin. "I kind of like the two of them like this. Erich is much nicer, and Alliandre actually displays some emotion. They are about to get out of control if history is any sign."

Sivle gave her a disapproving grimace, then ordered the two of them back to the room to sleep off the effects of the mead. Marion bowed, rising with a grin. "What may I get for you, Lord Sivle? I must advise you, I must leave soon to attend the Open Jousting Tournament, so please order quickly."

"I would ask you to have John serve whatever he believes I would like. I have a big day myself and need my energy."

Smiling and giving him a hug, Marion whispered in his ear. "Sorry, but they asked for it. And everything I have put Alliandre through, I did not want to disappoint him. Besides, it is always fun to see them drunk."

Smiling as they separated, Sivle chastised her. "I would have appreciated their support today. As it is, they will be worthless until dinnertime."

"Yes, they will." Marion gave another wicked smile before returning to the kitchen. Soon after, she left the tavern. Vanessa brought him a platter heaped with bacon, sweet cakes, eggs, and a full pound of what looked like freshly grilled ham. Sivle sat back and looked at her. "Should I be expecting guests?"

"This is what John said I should bring, my lord," the serving girl said with a bow and an uneasy voice before she turned and returned to the kitchen.

Sivle began digging into the feast of food before him. Before he knew it, Braxlo had joined him. He looked over at the grisly fighter. "And what is our fair princess up to today?"

"Training her Cara Ríoga," Braxlo said between bites of ham and bacon. "She has given me the day off."

"Then perhaps you would like to join me at the Spellcaster's Competition."

Braxlo appeared to consider the offer. "My friend," Braxlo began diplomatically, "I have been in Foresight a week, and have not had a chance to visit any of the palaces. I thought today I might take a tour. Who knows when Fairwind will change her mind?"

Sivle did not know if he was disappointed or relieved, but he was nervous about the competition and yearned to have someone join him. Not that he could win. Several things worked against him, primarily the fact that the spell he entered was not complex. It just combined spirits in a way no one had done before. Also, it was a war-mage spell.

The Great Vreen War ended five years ago. The last grendlaar uprising over thirty years. Scholars who were much more interested in nurturing magic and enhancing the natural elements had taken the Mage's Council over. Not one of them had ever cast a spell in combat.

Sivle had cast spells in anger, and he knew from his study of history there would be more wars in his lifetime. Granted, he would live for several hundred years because of his aelf parentage, provided he wasn't killed prematurely. However, never in the twelve hundred year history of the realms had there been a peaceful century.

Despite this, Sivle could not remember a winning spell in the last five competitions which had interested more than a score of mages. Even those were mainly the favor seeking students of the current council members. War-mage spells were all but ridiculed, by the current council. Twenty years ago, the spirit sphere entered by Nathan the Barber, of the mercenary band NROK, (named after its members, Nathan, Ryan, Oscar and Kevin) had not even made it past the initial judging. However, he made a fortune selling scrolls of it to every mage who could pay the ten turots he was charging. Meanwhile, the winning spell that year, which sped the yield of toebeans by twenty percent, raised only twenty turots for its creator, Jeneal the Farmer. Because of this bias, war-mage entries were nonexistent in the competitions held since Sivle was a novice.

Sivle had already been involved in three wars, including the Golden Aelf invasion of the Southern Kingdom. Not to mention countless minor battles with grendlaar near the Great Chasm. After the Dalmari invasion, he began writing war scrolls in order to be prepared for the next war. The council mages would argue the years of peace far outweighed the number of war years. During those peaceful years, the nature spells, and other spells not from the war-mage repertoire, added far more to the well-being of the various races than did spells which only damaged and destroyed the land.

Sivle knew if the vreen, or even the Golden Aelf, ever conquered one of the other kingdoms, all the crop growing spells would be worthless there. He learned this when the Golden Aelf defeated the Southern Kingdom. It was the reason he eventually left the temple, deciding to learn other ways of using the spirits. He studied under the greatest spellcasters of each discipline. He learned ways to meld the spirits to do his bidding in ways few had ever even considered. He discovered the rules Toron had taught him long ago were based more on tradition and attitude than on any real limitations of the spirits.

Vanessa interrupted his thoughts, appearing with a pitcher of morning beer and another pitcher of mead. Lolark appeared out of nowhere, surprising Sivle with a slap on his back. Sivle had been struck in combat with less force. Lolark went over to his massive chair, reaching a great arm across the table to spear the ham with his dagger.

"Today is the big day, is it not?" the giant paladin asked.

"It is," Sivle replied. Then added hopefully, "Are you by chance coming to watch?"

"Much as I would like to, I have duties at the Open Joust today." Lolark shook his head. "Why they let these farmers and adventurers compete is unknown to me. They ignore the safety protocols and half the time I think they are actually trying to injure their opponent, rather than unseat him."

"Or her, you oaf." Smiling, a diminutive woman walked up, standing beside Lolark. "Is this a community plate?" she asked, smiling.

Rising as she approached and sat, Sivle gave a small bow. "Of course, my lady."

Braxlo, who had stood as well, looked over to Lolark. "Friend of yours?"

Lolark had been slower to rise. He washed down the remains of the pork before putting one arm around the dark-haired waif of a woman beside him. "May I present Lady Vivian the Beautiful, renowned paladin of the Order of the Stone Bear." He raised an arm to flag down the serving girl. "Bring another order of what you brought Sivle, please." Then smiling grandly at Sivle, "On Sivle, of course."

Sivle rolled his eyes but smiled back at the giant paladin as he sat. When the serving girl arrived with the additional platters, Sivle addressed her. "Young Vanessa, may we present a new friend, Lady Vivian the Beautiful. Evidently a dear friend of Sir Lolark the Luckless."

"Pleased to meet you, my lady." Vanessa bowed as she spoke. "If it isn't rude of me to ask, why do some of your titles seem complimentary, but others, well, less so?"

"Titles must be earned, of course," Lady Vivian said quietly. "Some, like mine, are based on appearance or reputation. Others, like Sir Luckless here, derive from certain incidents which seem to attach themselves to the recipient. They used to call Lolark, the Valiant, until a series of misfortunes ended up with him reduced to a blithering fool. He recovered, but received a new title. Much the way Sir Braxlo became the Brave instead of the Heroic."

Everyone looked at Braxlo. He swallowed, cleared his throat, and nodded. "'Tis the truth. And much better to be brave than heroic in my eyes."

"Why?" Vanessa inquired, eyeing the elder knight with a different mindset.

"Anyone can be heroic. It has to do with being at the right place, or wrong place, at the right time. Some men," then looking at Lady Vivian, "or women, are heroic because they become a wren on a bridge. Their only choice is heroism or death. Often, they get both. But to be called brave means you have put yourself onto the bridge, time and time again. Less emphasis on your heroics, considering your skill and bravery instead." Braxlo put another piece of ham in his mouth, looking back at his plate.

"I see." declared Vanessa. Then she turned to Lady Vivian. "Can I get you something other than mead or morning beer to drink, my lady?"

"Bring her the fruity wine," Lolark suggested. Vivian looked at him, then nodded, sending Vanessa to get the pitcher. "Where is Alliandre?" Lolark asked when she left.

"He and Erich had a drinking contest. Both were staggering when I came down. Evidently, they had been at it for some time." Sivle's scowl told them what he thought of the situation.

The four of them sat eating and talking until Lolark declared it was time to leave. Several empty pitchers and a third set of platters sat on the table. The morning crowd gone, the early lunch crowd began to come in. Sivle looked at the pile of dishes before pulling several turots from his pouch and placing them on the table.

"Perhaps we can help with the bill?" Lady Vivian asked.

"No, my lady. The Party of the Seven has plenty of money to cover these minor expenses."

"Then, thank you for your hospitality." Lady Vivian bowed to Sivle. "Lolark claimed the food was the best in the city, but I didn't believe him. Now I can honestly say I have not had better since coming to Foresight."

"I will pass along the word to Lady Arielle." Sivle bowed in return. "I must go as well. Braxlo, would you check on Alliandre and Erich in a couple of hours to see if they are recovered?"

"Yeah," Braxlo grunted in between mouthfuls of ham. He had gotten his second wind and was finishing up what food remained. Sivle knew the plates would all be empty by the time the serving girl cleaned the table.

Lolark escorted Lady Vivian out of the Aerie. Sivle went to the stables and retrieved Highlander to ride to the fairgrounds. Not that he didn't feel up to the walk, but Highlander needed some exercise while in Foresight. He caught up to the two paladins at the bridge, following a short distance behind them, Highlander's large hooves clopping and clanking on the cobblestones.

Once they got off the cobblestones, the roads were in poorer condition than the day before. The dew and the hundreds of people passing over them turned them into a torn-up mess. While the moisture was gone, it was clear it had been muddy. People began walking in lines, gouging a series of narrow troughs onto the road. The city would bring plow horses and gravel at some point, but for now, the trio picked their steps carefully.

Once they got to the fairgrounds, it was even worse. There was no grass to be seen. The pungent stench of animal dung, sweat, and fair food filled the air. They set the lists up next to the stands, while they would hold the Spell Casting Tournament on the other side of the great barns. Sivle spoke some words, motioning with his hands. A great breeze came in from the south, temporarily cleansing the air and bringing the fresh, crisp scent of the prairie with it. Lolark looked back, nodding his approval as the two paladins split off toward the listing grounds.

Sivle continued on, urging Highlander into a slow gallop past the animal barns. He would go in later to check for oxen. He had the feeling there would soon be an enormous demand for the splendid beasts. He wanted to be sure to get as many as possible before that happened. Right now, however, he wanted to avoid the barns before his artificial respite ended and the stench returned. Once he was south of the barns, the spellcaster grounds were clear.

A score of men in robes, a few in armor even, stood around while the council were all seated in hastily built, though luxurious, stands. Not even the king's pavilion was this extravagant. They had brought oversized padded chairs out, a serving tray with pitchers and cups next to each chair. Incense burned in great thuribles. They hung or set more censors throughout the stands. The scent of highcrisp was strong, Sivle suspecting they were burning an incense made from the dried and crushed seeds of the coveted fruit.

As Sivle approached, two apprentices approached him, taking his name and the scrolls he had brought. Both of them selected one scroll and compared it to the scroll Sivle had sent in with his application to be considered in the competition. It wasn't too late for the council to reject his spell, but he was certain they would not. Not just because it was a novel spell, but because Sivle's reputation was such, they would cause even more suspicion regarding the direction the Mage's Council had taken in recent decades.

Indeed, there was talk of reconstituting the Red Crest Magistry as a counter to the Mage's Council. Only two other mage organizations remained, neither of them gaining any significant patrons. The Stein Virki dwarves had the Stone Mage Fraternity, limiting their magics to earth and stone spirits. Likewise, the Blue Water Mages Guild began with only water and sea spirits. They only opened to all spirits after the fall of the Red Crest Magistry.

Sivle paid his dues to the council, registering with them. His declarations that mages should share their research, along with his insistence on continuing to research battle spells, made him somewhat of a persona non grata in the official mage community. Despite this, he knew he would make a small fortune with the spell he was showing today.

When he got closer, he noticed several priests arguing next to the stands. As he rode by, he could hear the raised voices. One of them, Revered High Priest Jean-Paul the Teacher, called to him. "Lord Sivle, what do you think of High Priest Malcolm's latest submission?"

Sivle rode over and dismounted, tying Highlander to the rearmost support for the stands. He calmly approached. In as calm a voice as he could muster, he told them honestly, "I have not studied her latest submission in detail, only briefly skimming it. She is a learned and meticulous researcher, so I would read her writings with an open mind."

"Given your history with her, I am surprised at your answer," the aged priest challenged him. "If I told you she claims the vreen are actually spirit wardens, like the aelf and dwarves, what would you say then?"

"I have often wondered how the vreen can reproduce so quickly. And there is no doubt of their ability to make use of the spirits in ways no other race seems to. We learned that only too well during the last uprising."

Jean-Paul scoffed. "By that standard, humans must be spirit wardens as well. However, she seems to imply we are merely slaves, made only to improve on the grendlaar."

Sivle thought carefully before he spoke. He had verified at least one item he had read, regarding the Ghhoam, so he was not ready to dismiss all of the statements High Priest Malcolm Mariotteo had made. But he had not discussed the creation history with the high priest, so he just refused to get dragged into the conversation. "I will study her writings and determine some questions for her. I would advise everyone to do the same."

Still, the elder priest persisted. "She claims spirits created the aelf after several other races. How can this be when it is documented Laard the First traveled the world, meeting no other creatures? The aelf protect the Great Tree, surely that proves they were the first to be created. And what evidence has she provided of these Ghhoam? Surely someone else would have encountered them."

Sivle spoke as diplomatically as possible. "I cannot answer those questions, Master Jean-Paul. Perhaps you and the other priests should bring these questions to High Priest Malcolm?"

"You are being evasive. Surely you cannot believe this blasphemy." The high priest was getting angrier with each moment.

"Master Jean-Paul. I agree this goes against everything I have been taught. It is also contrary to my own scholarly work. But you ask me to comment on something which I have not read. I cannot ascertain the soundness of her arguments, or the logic she employed to reach her conclusions." Sivle put his arm around the seething elder priest. "I would counsel calm discussion of each point, one at a time. Perhaps with enough eyes and voices investigating her claims, they can reach the truth. Only through the analysis of evidence can we truly learn anything. I believe you taught me that when I first came to the Great Library to study."

Jean-Paul thought about this carefully. "Perhaps I have let emotion get the better of me. But this is unthinkable. If this is true, it will undermine many of our traditions and teachings. There will be schism." Muttering to himself, the old priest returned to the group of now shouting priests, raising his hands. He spoke too softly for Sivle to hear, but the volume from the group went down noticeably. Several minutes went by, then the priests separated into small groups and went away. Some stalked back to the city, others sat in quiet discussion with themselves, while others prepared to watch the Spellcaster's Competition.

***

Fairwind and Ariandel went to the far end of the dueling grounds. "Let's try the juggling drill Sivle taught us," Fairwind said as she began picking up some blacknut-sized stones and threw them in the air.

Ariandel selected three stones, at first juggling them, then adding air spirits to keep them in motion. When she added a fourth stone, she lost control. Fairwind kept her stones oscillating in the air, but her pattern was wildly inconsistent, forcing her to walk back and forth to keep control. Soon both of their white robes were damp with sweat from the effort. After an hour of practice, Fairwind could remain in one place, while Ariandel kept four stones in the air for over a minute.

Fairwind called a stop to the drill, using the air and aether spirits to chill the wine before pouring each of them a glass. As they sipped, she passed on some tips. "I found if you spin the air a quarter turn while you are bringing the stone up, it stabilizes the stones. Also, if you can form a continuous path for each stone, weaving around the paths of the others, the pattern is easier to hold for long periods. Perhaps we should start with one or two stones and build up."

That proved to be the key to mastering the drill. Over the next two hours, they improved from one stone, to tossing four stones all at once into the air and catching them in the pattern. Both sat next to each other a pace apart and held the stones in pattern, slowly decreasing the size of the ellipses until they were even tighter than Sivle had used. At this point, Fairwind began attempting to separate her stones into four stones each as Sivle had done.

First, she added some of the stone spirit to separate the stones. Once she split the stones, she removed the stone spirit, struggling to hold the stones together. She fought against gravity and the stones bouncing off of each other until she lost control. One of the tiny stones broke off and struck her in the cheek. More stones slowly broke off, going their separate ways. She dropped the stones, looking over to Ariandel.

Ariandel had her stones moving in uniform arcs in front of her and had woven fire around each stone as she had with the dirt clods. She began to add aether when she started losing control of her stones. Fairwind noticed the stones getting closer and closer together. She immediately began weaving a spirit shield against the coming explosion. She cursed, as she should have had them create the shield before practicing the drill. She had thought the drill harmless enough, but this was why mages followed rules in the first place.

She covered herself with the shield and began expanding it to cover Ariandel when the stones touched. The stones exploded in a thunderclap of fire and molten rock, lifting the two female aelf into the air and throwing them back, tumbling toward the inn. Stunned, Fairwind shook her head, trying to reorient herself to stand. She failed in her first attempt, but soon made it to her knees to look for Ariandel. Seeing her three paces in front of her, she crawled over.

Ariandel was laying crumpled in a smoldering pile. The blast had charred her skin other than her left shoulder and head, where Fairwind had covered her with the shield. The remnants of Ariandel's robe were burning where the shield had protected it. The rest burned away. Fairwind grabbed it and pulled it off so it would do no further damage to the unconscious aelf. Checking the charred body, she realized Ariandel was still breathing although the raspiness indicated she likely wouldn't be for long. Pulling a vial from one of the hidden pockets in her robes, she poured the contents into Ariandel's mouth. Then, struggling to rise, she made it to her feet, staggering back to the tavern.

She had made it halfway there when three paladins came through the door, stepping closer to her. One of the female paladins cradled her head in her hands, and she slowly regained her senses. The paladin lifted Fairwind off her feet, carrying her inside the Aerie.

***

Sir Guillermo, paladin of the Order of the Wren, rushed past Fairwind as he went over to the blackened, aelf-shaped body on the ground. Summoning all his strength, he laid hands on her head and chest, sending a complicated weave of aether, sea spirit, and his own fauna spirit through the scorched body. Slowly, as the burned body began healing, the charred flesh fell off, new skin knitting itself underneath. Sweating now, Sir Guillermo pushed harder, forcing more energy from his own life force into the body. Opening his eyes, he saw the naked body lying beneath him, the still-healing skin red and mottled where it had been

2

scorched off in the blast. Another paladin, Lady Hyacinth, saved him from further embarrassment, laying her cloak across the healing aelf. Sliding his hand to her sternum, he finished his healing.

***

Fairwind returned to see Ariandel's eyes flutter and open. Relieved her student still lived, she bent over and hugged her. Ariandel hugged her back and whispered in her ear, "I'm so sorry." Fairwind "tsked" her and then helped her to her feet, keeping the cape wrapped around her. The paladins escorted them inside. She noticed as they walked through the tavern all their friends had left. She waved a summons to Lady Arielle as they walked by. The two paladins helped them to their room. After lying Ariandel down on the bed, Fairwind returned the cloak to the banner commander.

***

Jason entered the Wyvern's Aerie proudly wearing a brand-new uniform, complete with a red sargent sash. His sargent had met him earlier, bringing him to the guard headquarters. There, his captain had brought him into a meeting with the Captain of the Guard, as well as his own sargent and several other captains. They all discussed his performance, which had not been quite exemplary, then requested a demonstration of his skill with the sword. Worried he would have to face the captain again, instead he faced his own sargent.

The duel went well, with Jason defeating his sargent six times out of ten. While not dominating, it certainly impressed the captains. There were concerns raised he had not yet been a squad leader, but one of the watch captains, Captain Del Morgan, needing a sargent, offered Jason the position. His new captain introduced him to his new patrol earlier this morning. The captain observed as he taught his new squad sword and shield right away.

He spent an hour drilling them as Alliandre had drilled him, then met with his new captain. Then it was time to fit him for armor.

"I have a set of cuir bouilli I could use," he told the quartermaster.

"Is that so?" Looking at the young man, the older man challenged him. "Why don't you get it then, and we will see if it can be of use."

When the quartermaster saw it, he immediately called in the captain.

"Where did you get this?" the captain asked.

"I trained with a fighter, and he purchased it for me. He said it was a gift for being such an excellent student," Jason replied, his voice trembling a bit. He didn't understand what he had done wrong, but something clearly irritated Captain Del Morgan.

"And who is this knight, that he would purchase such armor for a guardsman? This breastplate is made from Stein Virki steel." The quartermaster held a vambrace up. "This cuir bouilli is better than the chain shirt you wear."

"He is not a knight," Jason stammered. "His name is Alliandre Del Nileppez. He won the Open Melee Tournament."

This brought silence from the quartermaster. The captain's expression seemed less annoyed. "It will be easy enough to verify." Turning to the quartermaster, "Put this in with my armor. It seems our new sargent has a generous benefactor."

They provided Jason a new chain shirt and coif with a large, round buckler. A sleek, long sword completed his new accoutrements. Everything glistened as he looked in the large steel mirror.

***

Jason was feeling incredibly pleased with his appearance as he entered the Aerie. He immediately looked over to the table where Alliandre usually sat. Not seeing him, he looked around for Vanessa. He tried to catch her eye, but she seemed to be studiously ignoring him. Dejectedly, he walked up to the bar to ask about Alliandre. Seeing the one-armed barkeep, he cautiously sat down and ordered some of the sweet mead. Once the drink was served, he spoke up.

"Excuse me, sir," he quietly began, "has Alliandre left already, or do you know where he is?"

Sir Andras looked at the guard sargent suspiciously. "Naw, laddie. He is out of sorts, up in his room still. If ye be here to arrest him, best ye wait 'til he sobers up."

Jason stared at the barkeep. "Arrest him? No, sir. I thought I would come by and show him I was promoted and thank him again for training me."

"Well then, laddie, why didn't ye say that right off? I didn't recognize ye in yer new uniform. Made ye a full sargent, did they?"

"Yes, sir. I wanted to thank Master Alliandre. Without him, I would have never been promoted, or even thought about making sargent." Jason glanced over as Vanessa passed behind the bar, checking something on her tray.

"Ah, laddie, I hate to take the surprise from Alliandre, but he left ye something in case ye stopped in." Turning to go, Sir Andras seemed a bit excited. "I'll be right back to ye."

Sir Andras returned a half minute later, carrying a bundle of cloth. Laying it on the bar in front of Jason, Sir Andras scooted a nearby customer down a seat. Jason looked at the roll, then untied the cords securing it. Seconds later, he unrolled the bundle to find a sword belt and scabbard, complete with an ivory-handled sword. He drew the sword part way, admiring the pattern of swirling metals on the blade. He was unsure of whether it was good or bad, but it was the finest sword he had ever seen, much less held.

"This can't be for me. Is it?" Jason looked up, his voice curiously hoarse and this throat rough, though he couldn't say why.

"Aye laddie. Lord Sivle finished it yesterday and Alliandre brought it down with instructions to give it to ye if ye stopped in." Raising a shield from underneath the bar, he placed it in front of the young guard. "This too is for you, laddie. It has itself a command word, 'sciath,' to shield ye from arrows as well. I think Lord Sivle added it just to show off to the wee aelf girl. Repeat it so I know ye will remember it."

"Sciath," Jason said softly.

Sir Andras overwhelmed his own emotion with a slap on the bar. "Now then, laddie, just because ye are friends with Alliandre, dinnae think ye are getting out without paying yer bill." The old barkeep turned around muttering to himself as he refilled another customer's drink.

Jason wrapped the sword back up, drinking his mead while he tried again to catch Vanessa's attention. When he did, she came over, genuinely surprised to see Jason. She congratulated him on his promotion, then quickly turned away again when the table of paladins called out. Clearly, she was not impressed, or at least not impressed enough to pause in her duties. Jason had hoped the new promotion might make her reconsider her proposal. Instead, she made it clear she was not interested in him, no matter what rank he might hold.

Jason, who had been so proud when he entered the Aerie, finished his mead before slinking out to drop off the sword and shield to the quartermaster. It was clear Vanessa was out of his reach. Even though Alliandre had been so kind to him, he figured the warrior had much more important things to do than talk to a common guardsman, newly promoted to sargent or not. He carried his gifts proudly, but not even they could replace the emptiness in his heart.

***

Fairwind and Ariandel had not been in their room long when Arielle entered with a jar and tea service for two. She scooped out some gray sludge from the jar and added it to each of the cups. Then she added several spoons of sugar before filling the cup with hot water. Fairwind grimaced as she looked at the jar of ointment. Ariandel and Fairwind forced the acidic tasting liquid down. The sugar seemed to help, but the taste still clung to Ariandel's mouth. However, her mind cleared. Fairwind stood and hugged Arielle.

"Thank you, Your Majesty. We are so grateful to the Aerie and you for the great effort you have taken to ensure we are well taken care of." Fairwind released her hug, turning to her now sitting student. "Remember, in a few hours you are going to be exhausted, so plan on retiring early tonight. In the meantime," turning to Arielle to include her, "no one is to say a word of this to Sivle. He will be upset with us for trying to move further than his training. My not requiring you to put up a spirit shield in the first place will also upset him."

Arielle smiled but nodded. Ariandel looked at her and nodded as well. Arielle waited for a moment before taking the tea service back out the door. Fairwind turned again to Ariandel and reinforced her earlier admonishment. "We should go support Sivle now in the Spellcaster's Competition. Make sure not to say anything about this to him, or he may refuse to train you, or me, any further."

"Surely, he would not blame you for my mistake," Ariandel protested.

"Sivle is profoundly serious about the power of the spirits. If he finds out I allowed you to train without a spirit shield, he will be terribly upset. I have no desire to have a mage of his power upset with me. You should be concerned as well."

Perhaps it was the residual effects of being severely burned, or the euphoria of the healing tea, but Ariandel was defiant. "Again, you act as if Sivle is some legendary mage. He is powerful, yes, but I am sure I could find a hundred mages to train me in the skills he has trained us on. I know I slept with the grendlaar, but I was only trying to imitate what he had shown us before."

Fairwind scolded her again. "Do not think for a moment you understand the knowledge Sivle has of the spirits. And be respectful, if not of him, then at least of me." Softening her tone, she continued, "Just believe me when I say he will be upset with both of us if he finds out what happened today. I wish to have him finish the lesson. If you wish to have him to finish the lesson as well, be respectful."

Considering this carefully, Ariandel relented. "I will, of course, be respectful of Lord Sivle." She rose and bowed to Fairwind. "I promise I will say nothing of my failure today." Fairwind stepped over to hug her once again.

"I am glad you survived. Now, let us go cheer for his success in the contest. I will be surprised if he does not do well. Perhaps we can gain some additional insights seeing what all the mages have come up with." Releasing Ariandel, the two began dressing to go out. Fairwind discarded her white training robes, donning a sturdy linen and satin dress, cornflower blue with gold and red embroidery. Ariandel dug through her pack, selecting a woolen dress of plain brown before adding a bright blue sash and a matching blue shawl. Looking at each other, they both laughed at the difference between them. Then they hugged once again and began their trip to the fairgrounds.

***

As Fairwind and Ariandel were leaving, Alliandre exited his room. Dressed in a red satin coat with black trim over a matching red silk shirt with black ties at the chest, he looked as well-groomed and nobly dressed as Ariandel had seen him. His red tights and black boots completed the ensemble, along with a sword at each hip. Ariandel thought the swords looked out of place. She wondered why he wore them in town when everyone else was forbidden from carrying weapons. Alliandre saw the two aelf and scowled, then bowed his head in their direction. Putting a more pleasant expression on his face, he said, "Good morning, Your Highness." Then nodding to Ariandel, "Cara Ríoga."

"Good morning, Alliandre," Fairwind replied. "Ariandel and I are on our way to see Sivle compete. Would you be so kind as to escort us?" Ariandel gave her a look of disgust, but then returned to a neutral expression, though not before Alliandre had seen her.

"I intend to scout out the Open Jousting Tournament, but I would be happy to escort you if you do not mind me leaving you there. Do you need me to armor up?"

"No, we should not meet with any trouble. It is more for appearance's sake. I gave Braxlo the day off, as I thought we would train all day. But we decided to witness Sivle's triumph today."

"Very well then, Your Highness." Straightening his back, fixing a scowl on his face, he led them down the stairs and out to the fairgrounds. Keeping his hands ready to draw his swords, they were given a wide berth the entire way, even as they walked through the crowded gates. True to his words, he left them at the Spellcaster's Competition and walked back past the animal barn to watch the Open Jousting Tournament.

***

The competition began. As expected, there was only one other battle spell entered. It was from a high priest, who combined fire into a whirlwind of air to create a column of flame which came from the sky and immolated a straw scarecrow brought out for the demonstration. There had not been a prominent war-priest since the Great War. Most of them were killed in the fighting. The few who remained had sworn off their studies to honor the Great Treaty. There were a few who took up the mantle over the years, but they struggled to find followers, and most of the temples died off.

A half hour later, Sivle began his presentation. Ariandel caught Sivle looking up at her and Fairwind. It surprised her, as he seemed inexplicably happy to see them. He waited as the novices set up a scarecrow in an open area. They had set a score of posts in the ground. He addressed the council. "My lords. My demonstration requires multiple targets."

"Nonsense," the head magistrate, Lord Aaron Golden Hair, told him. "We have studied your stamins, and one target shall suffice to demonstrate the effectiveness of your spell. Proceed, or withdraw."

Sivle seemed a bit disgruntled as he cast his spell. A dozen bright lights flew from his fingers to the scarecrow, exploding in a tight fireball, completely incinerating the straw man, as well as the post it was on. The Mage's Council seemed less than impressed; Ariandel could see why. While the number of fire bursts coming from Sivle was impressive, individually they seemed to have little effect. The size of the burst around the scarecrow was much smaller than a standard fire burst. One member of the council called out, "How is this different from a flame blast, other than being quite a bit smaller?"

Fairwind let out a small gasp. Ariandel saw Fairwind was upset.

Still, she smiled, feeling vindicated Sivle was not as great a mage as his friends seemed to believe. Then Sivle looked over. Ariandel tossed her head, still with a satisfied grin on her face. Sivle began gathering spirits again, and after a minute, recast the same spell, only this time he sent the dozen fire bursts at separate posts spanning the demonstration grounds. Setting alight twelve posts, the Mage's Council was in an uproar. After they settled down, they decided Sivle had violated their rules, sending him away. The anger on his face was clear as he bowed first to the council, then to the other contestants before leaving the demonstration grounds.

Sivle walked toward them, scowling at the shocked look of several of the spectators. Several of the other mages had their mouths agape as well. He went to the novices who had collected his scrolls, taking them. Then he turned toward Highlander, no doubt to return to the Wyvern's Aerie.

Ariandel walked toward him while Fairwind froze in place. "What's wrong?" Ariandel asked the statue which had formerly been her teacher.

"Did you see what he just did?" Fairwind asked, still all but motionless.

"Yes. Your 'greatest mage ever' just got kicked out of the contest."

Fairwind looked at her, eyes flashing angrily. "Think about what he just did. He cast the same spell twice. And if I am not mistaken, he could probably cast it again, taking just about as much time as he did the last time."

Ariandel thought about this for a second, then the implications hit her. If Sivle could cast a spell multiple times without re-memorizing it, even a spell as weak as the one she saw, he would be invaluable to an army. If he could do this with more powerful spells... she shuddered to think of what he could do. It was a minute before she realized she was just as frozen in place as Fairwind had been. She looked around. Several other mages were looking at Sivle in awe as well. A small crowd was following him as he strode off.

Fairwind grabbed her arm and pulled her in an unladylike sprint across the uneven ground toward the disgruntled mage. When they reached him, Fairwind stood in front of him with her arm outstretched, her hand in an explicit command for him to halt. He averted his gaze, maneuvering around her, but she would have none of it. "Sivle Si Evila Drol Revo. As a princess of the High Aelf, I command you to stop."

Staring daggers at her, Sivle halted his march. Then he looked over at Ariandel, spitting, "Come to gloat?"

Ariandel looked down in shame. She had scoffed at seeing him disqualified, but now understood he differed greatly from other mages she had encountered. Maybe not with the power of his spells, but with his ability to weave the spirits. She looked up at him and apologized. "My lord, I am sorry for taking any satisfaction in your dismissal. I understand not only was it undeserved, but I have not given you credit for your mastery of the spirits. For that, I am terribly sorry." She actually did feel sorry for the obvious embarrassment he had suffered and continued, "I am truly honored to have had the privilege of training under you, for however short a period. I understand if you refuse to train me further, I have dishonored myself with my behavior toward you after the kindness and patience you have shown."

The crowd had caught up to them, but a look from Fairwind kept them back for a few moments. She grabbed Sivle and said, "Let's fly," as she cast a spell, slowly lifting from the ground. Sivle repeated the spell and together they lifted above the throng of spellcasters about to swarm them. They flew straight toward the Aerie, leaving Ariandel to fend for herself. She ran after them, barely escaping the clutches of the pursuing mages.

Ariandel was never a fast runner. The exquisite boots Fairwind had bought her did not make it easier. The high heels required precise steps lest they drag and trip her. Out of the corner of her eye, she saw Drullock running from the jousting lists, changing course to intercept him. As large as he was, it surprised her how fast he moved. Soon she realized she could not catch him. She shouted several times, but her voice was not loud enough to pierce the distance and the noise of the fair. She cast a minor spell Toron had taught her.

"Drullock, help me. Please," she said in her normal voice.

The freakishly large fighter turned and looked for the source of the message as if she had spoken directly into his ear. He slowed as their eyes met. She knew his first priority would be Sivle, but she hoped he could see Fairwind and he were already inside the walls of the city. On the other hand, she could feel the hands reaching out to catch her dress. Then she realized that if she wanted his help, she should have used his proper name.

She burst into tears of relief when he pivoted, heading directly toward her. She ran to him. She made it within a score of paces away when a hand caught her dress, slowing her momentum. She fought to keep running, but a brawny hand had a hold of her. Short of tearing the dress off, she could only struggle. Then a red blur went by her. She heard the crunch of bones breaking, feeling a rough hand shoving her away from the curiously subdued mob.

"Stop, we only want to ask the blue mage how he did it," one woman in the crowd shouted.

"Go no further. When he wishes to explain himself, he shall. But I swear on the spirits enchanting my sword I will kill the first of you who attempts to pass," Alliandre's voice boomed as Ariandel ran away from the throng of mages, trotting again to the castle. She heard the tell-tale *shring,* as Drullock pulled his sword from its scabbard. She scolded herself again, as she once more used the nickname in her head. When she reached the gate, she stopped and looked back to see Alliandre still holding several stubborn ones back. Most, however, had returned to the spell grounds. She was almost run down as a squad of the City Guard ran out to investigate.

Her thoughts quickly shifted to getting to the Aerie as soon as possible. Winded from the sprint and the scare, she settled into a fast walk through the maze of streets. She had not even made it to the bridges when Alliandre appeared beside her, riding Sivle's destrier. He escorted her the rest of the way to the Aerie. She looked over at the warrior, who seemed intent only on her safety.

"Thank you, Alliandre. For this, and for earlier. I apologize for not calling out for you by your proper name." She lowered her eyes as she continued walking.

"I am only happy I reached you before the crowd had time to assault you further." Alliandre's tone actually sounded sincere to her. She looked up as he continued. "Although truth be told, they just wanted to find out who Sivle was and where he was staying. Once the guard showed up, they disbanded."

Inside the Aerie, she found Fairwind, Erich, Sir Andras, and a man she had never met sitting at the table around Sivle. Pitchers of chilled liquid sat on the table. By the looks of it, Sivle was no longer angry. He was joking and laughing as Erich poured two glasses of the drink. As she reached the table, walking around to Fairwind, the men rose and Sivle reached out and handed her a glass.

Erich raised his glass. "A toast! To being a thorn in the council's side. Here is to the weaselly bastards never figuring out what just happened."

XI

✦

Queen's Protector

35th of Frendalo, Year 1124 AGW

Vanessa rode sidesaddle on Vandion's gorgeous warhorse. He said it was his father's before he died. He mounted it the day they buried his father, riding off to make his fortune. He had not made his fortune yet, but he promised if they finished their surprise at the Aerie, they would impress the Southern Kingdom queen enough to recommend him to one of the schools of magic. With her support, he could become a successful mage and earn money selling potions and other small magic items. Vanessa remembered how much some of the materials cost and thought how much more they would sell for once they were enchanted.

She also thought about how much she was making this Jubilee. With everything paid for, she could keep her tips, and with three more days of Jubilee, she could make as much in tips as they would for the fall crops. Of course, she had spent everything she had made so far on her surprise. Even so, the coming year they would have money enough for a wedding. Perhaps even some extra to buy some piglets to raise and butcher. Vandion seemed to be picking up the farming well. She hoped maybe in a couple of years to be able to leave the Aerie and stay at the farm full time.

They arrived at the tavern early, but found Diana already there, unlocking the massive door where supplies were brought in. Diana was dressed in her sturdy woolen dress; she seemed to own dozens of them. This one was a greenish gray with mint-colored embroidery around the collars and cuffs. Over it was her white apron which went down to her low black boots. Her hair in a bun, the elderly woman looked to be long past working in kitchens. Despite her age, Vanessa knew Diana had more energy than she did. She was always cleaning or tidying up or fetching supplies when she wasn't serving tables.

Vanessa thought of her own plain dress. She had only two dresses which were nice enough to wear to the tavern, one of those having been given to her by Marion. This one was not as nice. It was woven with meadow green-dyed threads mixed with light brown threads. The pattern was not consistent, which gave it the appearance of waving grass in the fields. Vanessa thought the gold piping at the sleeves and the brass buttons made it look very regal. The green threads complemented her eyes and made them look even brighter when the light hit it right.

Vandion wore his best black leather trousers with a violet shirt under his heavy, dark gray, woolen overcoat. A chill filled the air, particularly this early before sunrise, and Vanessa tightened her heavy cloak. As they rode up, Vanessa waved.

"Good morning, Diana," she said as Vandion helped her down from the horse. "I didn't know you got here so early. I thought Sir Andras would be here."

"Oh no, dear." Diana finished opening the door and waved her over. "Her Majesty and Sir Andras do not arrive for over an hour now. They leave the preparations for the day to John, Jean Marie, and me. Jean Marie and John will get here soon, though. I always open up and light the fires and sweep the floors." Diana locked the heavy door behind them after they entered and turned to Vanessa once again. "And who is this dashing young man?"

Smiling broadly, Vanessa grabbed Vandion's hand. "This is my fiancé, Vandion. He is working the farm right now, but he is an aspiring mage and has worked on a gift for Her Majesty." Then, turning to her fiancé,

"Vandion, this is Lady Diana. She is in charge of all of us serving girls and is one of the queen's most trusted friends."

With the introductions over, she led Vandion over to inspect her work. He looked at the stone and cast a small spell from a scroll which made the hidden wire glow brightly for a moment, then disappear again into the stone. Diana frowned, but she said nothing. Then Vanessa took Diana with them downstairs to the cellar pantry, where Vanessa had laid the other wire. Again, inspecting her work, Vandion declared it perfect, and cast another spell from the scroll. The wire glowed as the former had, but this time it seemed to create a sheet of light to the ceiling above it. Then the glow, and the light, disappeared again into the stone. Vanessa bent down and looked at the floor, noticing the wire was still there. Only it seemed to have changed to the same color as the surrounding stone, perfectly camouflaged.

"Oh dear," Diana sighed. "You should have spoken to Sir Andras before doing something like this. Her Majesty does not like surprises, particularly magical ones."

"But wait until you see what it does." Vanessa excitedly pulled Diana back up the stairs to the kitchen. Walking over to where the wires were in the ground, she stood and spoke. "Pantry."

She disappeared, returning seconds later with a large sack of turnips and another of heart roots. "See, no more running up and down the stairs. And we don't need to bring so many sacks up the stairs to get ready for the meals."

"We will have to show Her Majesty and see what she thinks." Diana shook her head doubtfully before turning to Vandion. "But thank you, Master Vandion. I am sure Her Majesty will recognize the potential of this and will be grateful for your efforts."

"Thank you, Lady Diana." Bowing as he held her hand, he added, "I am not yet a master, but I am sure Lady Arielle will soon appreciate the spirit in which it was given. Please do not blame Vanessa. It was my idea to repay everyone from the Southern Kingdom for their treatment of my only love. Now, though, I am afraid I must be going. We had hoped for a chance to meet everyone, but I must get back to the farm.

The days are getting colder and we need to get some crops in so we can sell them in the market." Vandion kissed Vanessa one last time before leaving through the door they had entered.

Vanessa looked at Diana, smiling. Diana smiled back at her, then handed her a broom. "Oh child, I do hope the queen likes your surprise. But that apple is off the tree. As long as you are here, you may as well help clean up. Jean Marie and John will be here shortly. Let's give them a surprise by having the hall cleaned before they get here."

***

Alliandre rose early in order to get in his firstmeal before he left for the Selection of Champions. He also hoped Marion would still be there. He was disappointed in the latter, but not the former. Marion was preparing for the event as well. Diana told him they were at the Golden Palace, with the queen herself doing her hair. According to Diana, she would not be ready for some time. Alliandre thought she looked lovely each time he had seen her and was curious why she would need any enhancement to her appearance now. Diana laughed when he said as much while she set before him a platter loaded with sweet cakes and another with various meats surrounding a bowl of eggs.

Looking closer, he noticed all the meats were cuts of beef, including slices of the tenderloin several inches thick. It was rare anyone would slaughter a cow for meat. They were too valuable hauling wagons and carts and plows for farmers to cut up to eat. Only when they were ill or died naturally did you turn the animal into roasts and steaks, grinding up to mincemeat anything which would have been waste; however, the meat was tough and gamey. Then they rendered down the fat and tallow for cooking, with the bones and horns used for various implements or ornamentation. The hide, of course, would be turned into leather. But normally only wealthy nobles would pay for a healthy animal to be slaughtered just to eat.

Diana returned with a pitcher of morning beer, which she knew Alliandre preferred, along with a pitcher of mead with ice crystals on the side. Alliandre had already loaded his plate up with the eggs and one each of the meat selections. By the time Braxlo, Fairwind, and Ariandel had joined him, he was on his second helping, his morning beer finished. Braxlo's eyes lit up when he saw the platter of meat. Waiting while Fairwind and Ariandel served themselves, he skipped the eggs and went for the eye of rib steaks, taking two of them before grabbing the empty pitcher of beer and cursing Alliandre. Alliandre just smiled, making some unintelligible comment through his mouthful of food.

Diana returned soon enough with more eggs, another pitcher of beer, and a decanter of wine for Fairwind. "Silver wine for you, Your Highness. Lady Arielle has received some and allotted a small cask for you."

Silver wine, from the vineyards north of Silver Lake, was valued throughout all the kingdoms. Whether it was due to fear of the priests and paladins at Silver Lake Keep, or respect for the quality of the vineyards, even the vreen and centaurs avoided the vineyards in their various uprisings. Common Aelf and their priests tended the grapes and made the wine. They sold the limited pressings each year based more on the relationship with the aelf and priests than the price one was willing to pay. Arielle was on extremely good terms with the aelf there, receiving at least one cask every year. Fairwind poured herself a glass of the wine before offering half a glass to Ariandel.

"It is a bit early for wine, is it not?" Ariandel queried her.

"You drink silver wine whenever you have a chance," Fairwind scolded as she passed the half glass of golden liquid to her.

***

Ariandel put the wine to her nose, inhaling slowly and deeply. Fragrant oak and pear met her nostrils, with a bit of peach right at the end. Swirling it in the glass, it held onto the crystal marvelously, showing great legs for such a light wine. The halo in the glass was a shimmering silver ring which seemed to reach up the glass. Tasting a small sip and holding it in her mouth, first sour apple and then adamon exploded in her mouth. As it rolled on her tongue, the sweetness revealed itself, balancing the initial acidity. Finishing with a bit of butter and heart root, it left her palate dry and refreshed. Ariandel had tasted many fine wines in her travels. She could understand why Fairwind was so happy to have this. Even at breakfast, it was refreshing, not even needing fruit juice to cut the tannins of the grapes.

The four ate in relative silence until Sivle and Erich came down. Sivle looked much more cheerful than the previous day. Even Erich looked to be in a celebratory mood, with a charcoal coat over his black silken shirt. Woven into the fabric of the coat looked to be small threads of different shades of purple, which gave it an almost mystical sheen. It was not noticeable unless you were close. With Erich sitting right next to her, Ariandel couldn't help but notice. He still wore his customary black pants, but they were tight fitting today, tucked cleanly into low, soft, black boots. She thought she noticed a silver bracelet, but then realized it was a small throwing knife hidden in his shirt cuff. She looked again to be sure, but it was gone.

Sivle was regal in a golden robe which looked like they might have made it with actual gold threads. A turquoise shirt was danger-ously close to making him look like a palace boy, but the large holy symbol around his neck dispelled that illusion. His bright blue trousers peeking from the bottom of the robe and turquoise boots to match his shirt completed his ensemble. He was busy loading his plate, looking questioningly at Fairwind and the decanter next to her. It appeared to Ariandel that Fairwind pretended not to notice, so he went to the mead.

"Today is the day for you, my friend." Sivle raised his freshly filled glass to Alliandre. "Hopefully, nobody chooses you as their champion before Marion."

Everyone laughed at the jest. It was humiliating to the requestor for a champion to refuse her favor, dishonorable for the knight refusing a favor he had already agreed to receive. Most requestors negotiated with their champions several days before the actual formal selection. As Alliandre was not a knight, it was unlikely some strange noblewoman would request to bestow her favor on him when so many actual knights were in town.

"Marion has already named me her champion. I take part only as a courtesy to Princess Marion. Prince Lucas also requested I put my name on the official list of champions as a formality only." Alliandre continued eating a perfectly reddened piece of the tenderloin with just a sword blade's width of brown sear around it.

Lolark showed up shortly afterward, looking magnificent in fully articulated plate mail, which shimmered and almost hummed with mystical energy. He carried a large shield across his back, over his great sword. A long sword hanging casually at his left hip completed his armament. It looked almost like a short sword on his massive frame.

The serving girl, Vanessa, came over to notify them they needed Diana in the kitchen. She looked unusually cheerful, even smiling playfully when another patron pretended to reach for her shapely behind. Shaking her finger with pursed lips, she smiled before leaving to get the next platter. Fairwind poured another glass from her decanter of Silver Wine, ignoring all inquiries about it. Sivle and Erich were discussing some declaration from the high priest of Foresight.

Alliandre and Lolark fought over the platters, each trying to outdo the other until Sir Andras walked over. "You laddies better be gettin' ready to head over to the lists. The ceremony'll be startin' soon enough."

***

Alliandre rose with the rest of the fighters. They excused themselves before leaving the Aerie. Alliandre was the only one not armored. His pack was already on Aeris, waiting for the order from the king to don his armor and join the ranks of the other nobles. It was tradition for the king to raise to knightly status any commoners who made it to the tournaments through their merit until the tournament was over. If they won, the king would make the status permanent.

The three headed to the fairground directly from the stables, Alliandre leading the way with Aeris. Despite the crowd, people made

298 - DANIEL E MYERS

room for the prickly behemoth he rode. Even in battles, the grendlaar would try to part their lines to allow him to ride through unmolested, their spears ineffective against the coarse spines of "hair" and thick hide. Likewise, many insolent visitors had found themselves with small abrasions after rubbing up against Aeris when they refused to yield. Alliandre was pompous enough to ride to his destination, leaving it to others to get out of his way or suffer the consequences.

Once they arrived, members of the King's Guard took their names. The three friends went over to the list field to wait. Several score of knights gathered there already, a steady stream quickly filling the field. An hour later, a horn signaled the queen was ready to speak. All the knights turned toward the king's stands, which were filled with women. A line of women wound around the list grounds as well. Apparently, several hundred women desired to bestow their favor on the knights doing battle. It did not surprise Alliandre to see many women dressed in gold and green at the end of the line.

The queen herself began speaking, a bard enhancing her voice so all could hear. "Knights and Lords of the realms, let me welcome you to Foresight and thank you all for helping us celebrate the anniversary of the formation of the Central Kingdom. King Henry the Great sends you his highest regards, wishing you good health during the coming days."

A cheer went up among the participants, with a chant of "Long live King Henry the Great!" repeated at least half a score of times before the queen regained control of the crowd.

"As is customary, there are some ladies who would like to present some of you noble knights with a small token of their favor, hoping it will bring you courage and skill in your battles to come." The queen took a sip of wine while whistles and cheers arose from the benches of commoners enjoying the spectacle. "You know I do not enjoy giving long speeches as much as my illustrious husband does, so I will get right to it. When a young lady calls you to receive her favor, come to the stands to receive it. Then you may leave with her to get any encouragement she would like to provide. But the jousts begin at noon, even if the encouragement exhausts you."

Everyone laughed at this, even the usually dour Braxlo. The palaces set up a small tent city on the fairgrounds, for any deciding not to take the long walk to the city. The queen began calling the names of the noblewomen in the stands, who came up and announced the name of the knight they chose to whom to present their favor.

At first, the pace was slow due to the crowding of the knights in the list field. Only once near the end did a knight fail to respond. It was because of the pronunciation of his name, not his reluctance to accept the favor of the young pleasure princess presenting it. As the crowd thinned, the pace quickened. Not surprisingly, Fairwind called Braxlo away. Then Lady Vivian called Lolark. Surely Marion's stature as a princess put her in higher standing than a paladin. Alliandre stood, frustrated as the ladies called knight after knight. At the end, the queen stood with one last lady. Alliandre was happy it was Marion, at least. Many in the crowd had left as most of the knights were gone, the few who remained quieting down when the queen raised her hand.

"It brings me great pleasure to present the princess of the Southern Kingdom, who has broken tradition, selecting a commoner for her champion." The queen paused, giving the crowd time to digest this. The commoners in the crowd began cheering as the nobility began whispering to themselves. "Lady Marion is one of our Jubilee Royal Court and should have gone much sooner. I wanted to bestow my favor on her champion as well, so I would call Alliandre Del Nileppez Drol Hulloc to step forward."

The citizens of Foresight, the visiting tradesmen, vendors, and the farmers attending Jubilee, stood and cheered wildly. Alliandre guessed it was because one of their own was being recognized by the queen. Yelling and cheering, perhaps they hoped to see the bestowal of a noble rank, or a knighting, at least. As soon as Alliandre reached Queen Persephone, they quieted down, not wanting to do anything to ruin their shared success.

In the stands opposite the commoners, Alliandre could see the discomfort among the nobles gathered. Most knew several of the final warriors in the Open Melee entered the Grand Melee. Most understood why Marion might want to give her favor to an unknighted warrior, not want to be seen courting knights from the king. However, the queen was giving her favor as well, which meant there was something going on of which they were unaware. Some feigned outrage, but they watched attentively as Alliandre strode forward, his long stride hastening him across the list to the spot below Queen Persephone and Marion.

Marion stood while the queen pulled a sky blue sash from the chair next to her. In the center was the silver castle representing the Central Kingdom. She lowered it to Alliandre, commanding him, "Wear this sash proudly. During the rest of Jubilee, you shall be the Queen's Protector, given all rights and privileges such a position entails."

Cheers arose from the remaining people in the stands across from the queen. Even the nobles stood, raising a subdued, but sincere, cheer. They expected the queen would give the commoners knightly privileges during the tournaments, but this red-clad warrior merited some more scrutiny. Many would pass silver coins to their "acquaintances" who could investigate the background of the new Queen's Protector. They whispered among themselves as Marion stepped forward to speak. Speaking softly, the bard's power sent her voice clearly across the list for all to hear.

"Alliandre. You have always had my favor, since we were young. You have always brought honor and dignity to it. But today, I want everyone to know you are bound to me, and I to you. So, I present this token of my favor." She tossed a small piece of rolled-up cloth. It unrolled to reveal a pennant with two shields. One had the Wyvern Rampant of the Southern Kingdom on it. The other had Alliandre's Snow Dragon head with the sword through it on the flaming bend sinister. A laurel garland wrapped around the two shields. Rolled inside the pennant was the smaller version made to tuck into Alliandre's armor, which he had worn during the Open Melee Tournament.

Alliandre bowed before walking to the edge of the stands to join Marion and receive his encouragement. He was disappointed when the queen joined him instead. He bowed and simply said, "Thank you, Your Majesty."

"It was nothing. Before Marion distracts you too much, I have to make this clear." The queen's voice turned stern. "You now represent me and the Central Kingdom. This means any dishonor you bring to the field reflects on us."

Alliandre understood now why she gave him the special award. Another warning to keep the young duke-ling alive through Jubilee. He sighed and bowed his head to the outstretched hand of the queen. "I will strive to bring nothing but glory to your house while I wear this."

"I trust you will." The queen withdrew her hand, stepping in to give Alliandre a hug. Whispering in his ear, her voice almost broke. "We all know this is not fair to you. You deserve better. I am truly sorry." Releasing him, she turned and walked back to the stands.

Marion was waiting for him, looking radiant. Alliandre did not think she had ever looked as beautiful. Her long black hair, normally pulled back, was curled, flowing around her shoulders. The locks usually framing her face were joined by a half score more, covering her ears before cascading down the front of her jade blouse. Metal threads in the blouse caused it to shimmer, changing shade in the reflected light. Closed at the neck, it clung to her, appearing to be painted on her skin, rather than draping over it. She dyed her lips a shade of red which matched his armor. They looked wet, like water beading up on a freshly lacquered breastplate.

He had known her since she was born, yet somehow, he was seeing her for the first time. He stood there awkwardly, mesmerized by her beauty, until she stepped forward to give him a hug. "Let's get going. We need to get you armored up if you are going to compete today."

"What? Wait, I don't joust. Besides, with Aeris, it isn't fair to the others. I just came to get your favor and perhaps get some time to spend with you." Alliandre stepped back to look at Marion, knowing it was a mistake as he was once again drowning in her beauty.

"You joust today. You don't have to win, just compete." She moved in next to him, walking toward the impromptu tent city, dragging him along. "But remember, I will be in the stands, so don't lose."

"Yes, Your Highness," was his only reply, as he picked her up and carried her the rest of the way to the tents.

***

Arielle came into the Wyvern's Aerie accompanied by Jean Marie, as was somewhat uncommon. Sir Andras was already in the tavern, which was also uncommon. There were already several tables full of nobles drinking morning beer or tea, depending on their inclination. The smell of meats roasting and bacon frying wafted in from the kitchen. Arielle inhaled deeply, smiling. Looking to her feet, the floors were immaculate, the empty tables scrubbed and polished. Sir Andras was behind the bar, making sure the mugs and glasses were in order, as well as checking on the levels of the beer kegs. He had made a full keg of morning beer since he expected a large crowd for breakfast. He was not disappointed. An empty keg sat over to the side, the new keg looking light as he tilted it to check the level.

Erich was sitting with Fairwind and her lady-in-waiting. It surprised Arielle that Fairwind had a suitor, but she was happy for the aelf princess. Fairwind was quite old to have not had courtiers yet, though far too young to be considered a spinster. It would be another hundred years before that happened. Although eligible to be courted fifty years ago, none had approached the king. Perhaps it was the constant traveling or her abandonment of the court. Perhaps the fact she was an accomplished battle mage discouraged potential suitors. Most likely, though, it was her taking a knight of Dragonsbane as her protector. Many of the aelf had lost close relatives to the humans. Many still distrusted all knights from that order. The knights themselves had, for the most part, long lost any antipathy for the aelf.

Arielle walked to the kitchen to say good morning to everyone when Diana pulled her aside. "Begging your pardon, Your Majesty, but young Vanessa and her fiancé were in early, preparing a surprise for you. I will let her show you, but I thought you should be aware. Evidently her fiancé is a mage in training."

Arielle looked at her longtime mistress of robes and sighed. "Should I be concerned?"

"No, My Queen." Diana replied truthfully. "It appears she tried for something quite useful, but I know how you are about magics in the castle. Or the Aerie, in this case."

Arielle was against magic in the castle. Having studied spell-casting many years ago under a former pleasure princess, she was shocked at how seemingly innocuous spells could remove coin or information from an unsuspecting patron. While she never had occasion to try anything so unscrupulous, she absolutely forbade the use of magics in the private chambers in the castle. Likewise, while there were many magics in the kitchen, they were cast by people she knew and trusted. They were also of limited duration. Though less expensive to make them permanent, she would not allow it.

"Well, when she gets a break, tell her I would be interested in seeing it." Arielle dismissed Diana to get back to work, then began helping fill orders of roasted meats and vegetables.

When Firstmeal ended, Vanessa shyly walked up to the former queen. "Excuse me, Lady Arielle, but Diana said you would like to see my surprise."

"I would indeed, young Vanessa," the queen said brightly. "I understand you worked hard behind my back to set this up."

Vanessa blushed. "Yes, my lady. I had to set the iridium wire on the ground, but my fiancé did all the genuine work this morning. We have been working on this for months. I saved all my tips. We even sold some of our crops to raise the money. But you have been so good to me. I wanted something to show my appreciation."

It was Arielle's turn to blush. To think a tavern worker would give up her tips to pay for some sort of enchantment in gratitude humbled her. She immediately changed her tone. Surely the young girl could not have afforded any enchantment which could threaten the Aerie. "Well, dear, please show it to me. I am excited to see your handiwork." Vanessa led Arielle over to the spot in the kitchen. "Pantry," she said, disappearing immediately.

Arielle stepped where she had been and repeated the command. She found herself in the pantry cellar, beneath the Aerie kitchens and dining hall. A wall of light surrounded her, but slowly dissipated. Surprised at the scope of the enchantment, Arielle gasped. She was particularly skeptical of portals. Her initial reaction was to have it removed. However, she saw the excited face on Vanessa, running up with two bags of heart root.

"And this is how we return." Vanessa motioned for Arielle to leave the space. Stepping into it, she simply said, "Kitchen."

Arielle followed her moments later, noticing no sheet of light surrounding her. She looked over at the kitchen staff all gathered around. She hated the idea of a portal within the Aerie, but saw the convenience it would provide. Thinking quickly, she decided on the most diplomatic answer.

"This is marvelous and will save many old knees from going up and down the stairs." Looking around, she saw Diana and Jean Marie smile at her joke. "But just to be certain, since he is here already, let's ask Lord Sivle to look at it and let us know if it is safe." Turning to Vanessa, she continued, "No offense to your fiancé. Lord Sivle is an accomplished mage. He can ensure this will not fail and leave someone in the aether." Vanessa nodded her approval.

***

Alliandre rode atop Highlander, uncomfortable as he was unused to handling the much smaller warhorse. He rode in Sivle's saddle as well, as his saddle was too large for the destrier. These two things together made him a bit wobbly as he lined up in the list opposite the champion of the Open Joust. As large as Lolark, he rode a horse even larger than Highlander. The two nodded as the marschall dropped the banner. They spurred their horses forward. Halfway down the list, the two lances made impact.

Alliandre was too quick dropping his lance, unused to the slower gait of Highlander. He caught his opponent, aptly named Festivus the

Large, on the bottom of the shield. It deflected off, breaking off the tip on the lower part of the cuirass. However, it gained him no points, counting as a miss. Festivus' lance hit Alliandre's shield square on, and the tip broke off. Both horses seemed to move too slowly for a proper hit. Alliandre planned on changing that.

The second run, Alliandre spurred Highlander to a gallop right away, charging full speed when the two met. This time he had the timing right, his lance shattering as it drove the shield of his opponent back, affecting the larger man's aim slightly. Festivus' lance hit Alliandre's shield on the inside, the tip breaking off cleanly. The two lined up for their last run at each other. Both men raised their lances high in salute.

As he did the previous time, Alliandre spurred Highlander quickly to gain momentum. However, the warhorse stumbled on the list, almost going down. Alliandre recovered, muscling his lance in place just before Festivus' lance tore into his pauldron. Alliandre's lance glanced off the shield, rising into the air as it deflected up. The two men squared off again, saluted each other, then retreated from the list.

The rest of the day went better for Alliandre, shattering many of his lances. He even knocked two men off their horses. Unfortunately, as they tallied up the points at the end of the first round, he was not among the top scorers, so he walked toward the stands to watch the end of the tournament. He got invited to sit next to Prince Lucas, and a few rows behind Marion, while he watched the knights who had made the cut display their skill. He was a bit surprised Festivus the Large had advanced, deciding to cheer him on along with another of the commoners who had made it this far.

He also stood and cheered when Lolark or Braxlo jousted. Lolark had the advantage of size and strength. He had won tournaments in jousting long before he won any with hand weapons. Riding a destrier related to Highlander, he seemed to shatter every lance, only failing once against a large, dark-skinned earl from the Northern Kingdom. Sir Lolark also fought Sir Rodney to a draw, even though he came close to knocking the duke-ling from his horse.

He sat still when Sir Rodney the Magnificent knocked one of the Smithson knights off his horse twice. He cheered vociferously when Baron Clarence Del Gatemouth Drol Brown extended his long arms, catching the duke's son squarely on his encranche. The force knocked him back, moving his lance out of place. Sir Clarence's lance continued, catching in his arrêt. He leaned into it, driving Sir Rodney from his saddle while Sir Rodney's lance glanced harmlessly off his shoulder. The next two runs saw both lances shatter, leaving Sir Rodney with the deficit in points. A dwarf commoner with form-fitting armor nearly knocked Sir Rodney off his horse as well. Each shattered their lances in the first two runs. The commoner shattered his third lance while Sir Rodney's lance glanced off the encranche. Sir Rodney lived up to his name but failed to get named to the top ten for the final round.

The top ten jousters paraded across the list, each champion lowering his lance to his sponsor. Then the final jousting began. The first joust saw Sir Ewan the Terrible opposite Lady Serena. Six shattered lances later, they raised their lances in salute. Most of the other jousts likewise saw evenly matched opponents shattering their lances until Queen Persephone named Earl James Del Jones the jousting champion. Alongside him were Sir Richard the Ravishing, and Sir Lolark the Luckless.

The champions stood in a receiving line in front of the king's stand to be congratulated by the royals and their guests. Marion gave Lolark a hug when she got to him, her arms barely making it around even the waist of the huge paladin. Lord Ferdinand congratulated the giant man as well, before he and Marion moved to Sir Richard.

Alliandre clasped wrists with his friend with a big smile. "It is good to see you on the victory stage, my friend. Why didn't you tell us you entered the joust? We would all have come."

Smiling himself, Lolark teased, "Paladins are humble and unpretentious. I only told my close friends, so everyone else should be here." Still smiling, "I thought jousting was beneath you. How did you get added to the list?"

Alliandre smiled at the hazing, raising a hand to the sash across his chest. "The queen demanded I, as her protector, join the list. I think Marion may have had something to do with it as well."

"I see." Lolark grinned. Marion looks unusually beautiful today. Did you get her favor as well?

"I did." Alliandre reached to the fabric tucked into his armor. "She helped me with my armor even."

"Helped you with your armor?" Lolark laughed. "Is that the only encouragement she gave you?"

His face turning pink, Alliandre retorted angrily. "You would sully the name of the princess by implying she would behave so crudely? I suspect your Lady Vivian encourages you in that manner, but not Marion."

Seeing he had struck a nerve, and not wanting to antagonize Alliandre, or have a repeat of the beating he had taken days earlier, Lolark apologized. "Of course, my old friend. I meant nothing by it, only teasing. You know I hold Lady Marion the Virtuous in the highest regard. So be honest, what encouragement did she provide?"

Alliandre's pink face grew redder. "Do you swear not to tell?" Seeing Lolark's head nodding up and down, he leaned in conspiratorially, glancing around to make sure no one else was nearby. Seeing the area was clear, he spoke in a low voice. "She rented a tent. When we went inside, there were candles around a large tub filled with steaming water, surrounded by drapes. She called out and in came Lord Ferdinand."

"Wait," Lolark stopped him. "Who is Lord Ferdinand?"

"He is Marion's prince in the Jubilee Royal Court. The young man who just congratulated you. Anyway, he took me over to the bath, holding a blanket up to screen me from Marion. I began undressing when two princesses from the Palace of Swans came over. They stripped me and put me in the bath. As they poured the scalding water over me, the scent of lavender and highcrisp overwhelmed me. Then the ladies stripped as well, joining me in the tub where they washed me very thoroughly." Alliandre's eyes and voice rose on the word "very."

Lolark stared at him in disbelief. "While Marion was watching?"

"Yes." Alliandre turned even redder. "It was like they wanted to see how far they could take it while Marion was standing there, only able to see my face. She laughed each time I fought off the overly aggressive cleansing. She laughed a lot. And she encouraged them, teasing me mercilessly. Thankfully, it did not last long. Then the girls dried me off before dressing me in brand new tights and a brand-new arming jacket Marion had purchased. Then Sir Ferdinand lowered the blanket, and he and Marion helped me with my armor."

Lolark let out a deep laugh. "Then you and Marion did not actually get any time alone."

Alliandre shook his head. "No, although I guess while I was carrying her over to the tent, we were basically alone. But Sir Ferdinand acted as her chaperone and nobly carried out his duties. I am glad she became friends with him."

Braxlo approached the two men at this point. "And what stories are you telling to raise such a raucous laugh?"

Lolark smiled but said nothing. Alliandre turned even redder, if that was possible, mumbling something unintelligible.

A familiar face interrupted them, wearing armor lacquered orange and yellow. His helm was the same color as Alliandre's armor, with polished brass reinforcements around the eyes and down the center. "It seems the dog has friends who are quite skilled, at least. Congratulations Sir Lolark on your triumph today. It must be quite satisfying to have defeated so many much younger opponents."

Lolark looked at the newcomer. "Sir Rodney, it disappointed me not to have faced you in the final jousts. You speak so highly of your own skill I was sure I would meet you more than the one time today."

"Well met, Sir Lolark. I must admit it disappointed me as well." Bowing again to the elder paladin, Sir Rodney turned to Alliandre. "I noticed the commoner didn't make it past the first elimination. Do you see the difference between fighting actual knights compared to vreen and grendlaar?" Sir Rodney squared off against Alliandre, pressing his breastplate against the scaled torso of the taller man.

Braxlo interposed himself, forcing Rodney back with a mailed hand

and a gentle but firm shove. "I would warn you, Sir Rodney. Queen Persephone has granted Sir Alliandre her personal favor and named him Queen's Protector. Any slight to him could be misconstrued as a slight to the queen. It would serve you well to remember your courtly manners, lest you force others to come to the queen's defense."

Alliandre smiled to himself. It seems like the queen had made sure they both would have to be on their best behavior toward each other. Letting the inside smile show on his face, he bowed slightly to his gayly armored antagonist. "Your skill with the lance seems to be the equal to your skill with the sword. I am interested to see what happens when we meet tomorrow."

"Your skill with the lance far exceeds your skill with the sword. I am sure what the result will be when we cross swords tomorrow. No excitement for me there." Sir Rodney then bowed again to Lolark before turning around, barking softly as he left.

Braxlo turned to his friend, noticing an unexpected smirk on his face. "I thought you would be angrier, Alliandre."

Alliandre broke into an actual grin. "Do you think my skill with the lance is greater than my skill with the sword?" Smiling fully now, he continued, "I must have impressed him out there today."

Lolark laughed deeply for the second time that day. Then Braxlo slapped his friend on the back hard enough to break the spine of lesser men. Guiding the other two of them over to where the champion stood, Braxlo cajoled them. "Come, let us meet up with the earl. Perhaps we can get invited to his celebration party tonight."

Alliandre laughed. "Why don't we just talk to Her Majesty. I am sure we can get the Aerie to throw Lolark a party like none other."

Lolark shook his head. "I have honored the favor of Lady Vivian, and she intends to honor me in return."

"Besides," Braxlo wrapped his arm around Alliandre, "Lady Arielle does not own part of the Jade Palace and won't be able to provide anywhere near the same entertainment."

Alliandre rolled his eyes but followed his friends to meet the jousting champion.

**

Alliandre and Braxlo left the Aerie for the Jade Palace on foot after bathing and changing into more appropriate attire. Alliandre wore his girdle under his ornate red gambeson with the orange and yellow flames seeming to rise from the black trousers. Braxlo joked that if he was trying to ingratiate himself with Sir Rodney, then perhaps he should have added some jewels as well. Alliandre thought about it. Other than the black trousers, the colors were those of the Wyndgryph. But the matching scale design on the pants and gambeson looked nothing like what the foppish knights would be wearing. He doubted any of them would be carrying the multitude of swords he wore.

They approached the marble columns with green veins running through them, the hallmark of the Jade Palace. Rumors were they mined the marble from the actual Jade Hills, hundreds of hursmarcs to the west, bringing them all the way on wagons. Alliandre thought it unlikely, since the trip would either go east over the mountains or south around them, through land besot by vreen and centaurs. Either way, they would have to first travel through the lands of the Volmen barbarians and the six kingdom warriors. Still, the six columns stood out, as did the marble stairs and great silverwood doors.

Walking through the doors brought them to the foyer with more columns and a marble floor. Alliandre appreciated the construction. Like a keep, the columns would prevent anyone from getting past, but allowed the guards and others behind them to observe or attack from safety. Looking up, he noticed several grates, likely for circulation. They could easily be removed to rain death down upon unlucky patrons or others intending to do harm. Behind the columns and on the ceiling, large panels of silverwood with carvings and jade accents decorated the walls. Banners hung from the walls in the center of the two sides, depicting scenes of women on couches. Alliandre had hung around Erich and Robin enough to recognize the symbols showing the imprimatur of the Thieves Guild on each banner.

Once inside the foyer, two princesses greeted them, promptly taking their sword belts to be stored away. Alliandre balked at first, as he loathed to leave his swords. He relented when he saw Braxlo surrender his sword. Once unarmed, they went into the main hall. Here were more princesses, an army it seemed. Many of the knights engaged in wrestling or other feats intended to impress the onlooking princesses. Alliandre laughed to himself. For half a score of malnots, the princesses would be overjoyed to be taken to a room. Short of that, it was unlikely they would be so impressed. Braxlo gave him a knowing smile, graciously allowing a princess to guide them over to a luxurious couch.

They had not been there an hour when a familiar face came over. Alliandre and Braxlo stood as Prince Valian approached them. As they clasped wrists, Braxlo warmly greeted the prince. "Well met, Prince Valian. I thought you said you could not stay for Jubilee. Surely the allure of the Jade Palace didn't hold you here?"

Prince Valian laughed before responding, "I left Foresight right after my meeting with the king. I was obligated to return, but not for the pleasures of the Jade Palace. The Great Queen has commanded I test the mettle of young Alliandre here. I stopped by the Aerie to find him. They told me he would be here."

Clasping wrists himself with the prince, Alliandre looked a bit puzzled. "Why would the Great Queen wish to test my mettle? Is there some quest she would like to send me on?"

"No, my friend. When I told the Great King of your defeat of the paladins, the Great Queen wished to know if the bloodline of the Del Nileppez family still ran strong. She asked me to challenge you in a friendly duel. She requested a blood duel but does not require it. Don't worry," Prince Valian raised his hands in a peaceful gesture. "The Great Queen has commanded I do no harm to you, although I am worried she has less concern about my health." Smiling broadly, the prince continued, "If you would oblige me, it would be my great honor to cross swords with you. At the time and place of your choosing, of course."

Alliandre considered the prince's request. He could think of no reason the Great King and Queen would even know he existed, much less concern themselves with his swordcraft. But here was the prince, wanting to duel him. And not just a duel, but a blood duel, where he could use his enchanted swords, as well as his enchanted armor. But the prince could use his as well. Alliandre shuddered to think of the ancient weapons and armor the prince would be using. Centuries of enchantments and protections. He thought about it before deciding he had an advantage if the prince would agree to one request.

Reaching his arm out again, he addressed Prince Valian. "If it would please you, Your Highness, I would be happy to duel you. Perhaps we could use this as an opportunity to entertain the knights and ladies here tonight. In this way, I could repay the earl's hospitality, and you would get your duel."

The prince pondered the request for a moment, then clasped wrists with Alliandre. "No armor then?"

"No armor. I suspect it would not matter anyway if tales of your skill are true." Alliandre smiled. "Even if I am able to strike you, trust me, I will not allow myself to become an enemy of the Great King. Or the Great Queen."

"Then if Earl James will allow us our swords, let us prepare."

***

Braxlo cleared an area in the center of the room. Knights, lords, and princesses curiously gathered around. They requested their swords, and after a time, a princess brought their swords and their scabbards to them. Alliandre attached his sword belts and slid the sword breaker scabbards behind his back, while Prince Valian attached his sword belts. Alliandre noticed the two matching swords, each with a Silverwood handle and a bright sapphire in the pommel. Both swords crackled with energy, even within their scabbards.

Braxlo held up his hand, moving to the center of the room. With a voice needing no assistance from a bard, he announced loudly. "Ladies and Lords, may I present to you, Prince Valian of the Great Aelf."

This got the attention of many in the room, several aelf getting down on one knee to recognize Prince Valian. From the back of the room, a voice yelled out, "To the Great King of Kings. May the spirits protect him and his sons."

Every knight in the room responded, "To the Great King. May the spirits protect him and his sons."

After bowing deeply, Prince Valian raised his voice, responding as was tradition. "To the Kings of the Human Realms. May they forever live in brotherhood with the aelf."

"To the kings," everyone repeated, as those with glasses raised them.

Braxlo continued after the din had subsided. "Prince Valian has challenged a descendant of the fabled Del Nileppez line, Alliandre Del Nileppez, to a blood duel."

A hush exploded in the hall. Within seconds of the words "blood duel," every mouth was silent; every eye was on the two men facing each other.

Braxlo continued, "Earl James has been gracious enough to allow them to settle the duel here, for your entertainment." Earl James stepped forward, to wave and to be acknowledged. It was his party, after all.

Braxlo then began the formal introductions. "I am Sir Braxlo the Brave. I will supervise the duel to ensure no outside interference. As this is a blood duel, I will offer no aid or call any halts. The duel ends when one party has been blooded and acknowledges the defeat." The crowd murmured as Braxlo continued, "Prince Valian, as you have issued the challenge, I ask Alliandre to choose the weapons."

"Dueler's choice," Alliandre's clear baritone rang out.

"Combatants, please meet in the center of the hall." Braxlo waited until both Prince Valian and Alliandre were in place, then raised his arm, shouting "Begin" as he dropped it.

Prince Valian circled Alliandre cautiously, before springing forward in a viper strike combined with a moon scythe to test his defenses. A small smirk appeared on Alliandre's face. The prince had watched him duel days before, having had a chance to scout him, so why was he testing his defenses now? With his girdle was on, Alliandre tested the prince. Fading back to draw the prince in, he performed a tiger's claw followed by a leopard pounce followed by a succession of thunder strikes, forcing the prince's swords to defend high. After one of the thunder strikes, he lunged into a viper strike.

The prince's sword should have been out of position, but with almost superhuman reflexes, the prince brought his sword down and deflected the blow. A heartbeat later, he executed an eagle's talon to take advantage of Alliandre's extension. It was half a heartbeat too long. Alliandre was already pulling back when the blow came down. Even so, he barely parried the strike. The two continued to circle each other warily.

Prince Valian impressed him. Several times he had drawn Valian's swords out of place. Each time, Valian still blocked the lightning quick strikes. It was almost as if the prince knew what Alliandre was going to do, even before Alliandre had decided on it himself. Again and again his two swords met the prince's two swords, sending sparks and mystical crackles off the point of contact. The prince began sweating, but Alliandre knew he still had another level inside him. He increased his pace even more.

The four swords were blurs as the two combatants ran around, circling each other, lunging in and out. Bending reed, gale wind, arrow strike. Prince Valian even countered his strength-enhanced windmill slash attacks. If not with ease, at least with certitude. Normally, a parry needed to slow the blade, preventing it from penetrating armor. Here, any parry or block which did not stop the blade entirely, or direct it away from the body, would not prevent the blades from cutting through the clothing the two of them were wearing. But neither had even damaged a thread on the other's coat.

Something about the prince's defenses bothered Alliandre, but he could not figure out what it was. It wasn't so much Prince Valian was sloppy, but the prince's blocks and parries did not flow from the motions of the swords. Several times the prince had abruptly changed the sword direction mid-stroke to make the parry in time. With the speed the swords were moving, many would likely not notice. But Alliandre had studied the sword for the last twenty years, almost to the exclusion of all else. He sped up and tried a few more combinations on the prince, confirming what he had thought.

Alliandre knew what he needed to do. The problem was doing it. He did not want to risk two of his favorite swords, especially when he had two sword breakers which were made for the task at hand. He executed a spinning blade mill, sheathing one of his swords. As expected, Prince Valian leaped to attack. Parrying with a cow tail, Alliandre drew one of the massive sword breakers from his back. Using the hooked end, he caught the prince's right-hand sword, forcing Valian to retreat to free it. This gave Alliandre the break he needed to sheathe his other sword, drawing the second sword breaker.

A small smile came across the prince's face. "You think a larger sword will help you?" He advanced once again on Alliandre.

Alliandre gave Prince Valian a smile of his own. "I have been attacking your defenses, but I think perhaps I have been going after the wrong target." He began swinging the two massive swords in a steel curtain.

No longer attacking the prince, he was only interested in striking Valian's enchanted swords. The smile left Valian's face for a second, but then returned. Lunging forward, he perfectly executed a pierce the waterfall, followed by several seconds of a steel curtain of his own. The four blades became an actual wall of steel, all four moving faster than the eye could follow. A minute later, Prince Valian retreated. Somehow, a slight cut had appeared on his hand. He held it up for all to see.

"I have completed my task. I yield." Bowing to Alliandre, he sheathed his swords and moved over to clasp wrists.

Alliandre looked at his opponent suspiciously. His sword breakers did not have razor-sharp edges. They were used to sunder swords and steel weapons, not injure opponents. To be sure, they would leave a nasty gash if they struck someone, but there was no chance they would leave a nice clean cut like Prince Valian was displaying. Perhaps the prince simply did not want his swords destroyed. Since honor had been upheld, Alliandre stepped over and clasped wrists with Prince Valian.

XII

∞

The Grand Melee

36th of Frendalo, Year 1124 AGW

Sivle was the first down the stairs to the Aerie's dining hall. Fairwind and Ariandel had gone to bed early the previous night. While it was not like the princess to sleep this late, Sivle had detected the scent of his healing balm emanating from their room. He would wait to let them tell him of whatever gave cause for its use. If history was any sign, he would never find out. But they all had their secrets, he supposed.

Braxlo and Alliandre had stayed late at the earl's party, and Lolark was likely still otherwise engaged. Erich had been at some guild meeting the night before, coming in at dawn reeking of death. Likely he would be out until mid-day. It was just as well, as Sivle wanted some time to reflect on his recent discovery. Part of him wanted to go to the Mages Guild straight away and show the frauds their ways of thinking about the spirits was wrong. But humility held him in check. Perhaps he was an anomaly, or the "tricks" he had done could be explained somehow.

Arielle disrupted his reverie with a tray of sweet cakes and sausages. Laying it down, she asked quietly, "Sivle, could you do me a small favor? One of the serving girls, Vanessa, and her fiancé prepared a small enchantment for the Aerie. You know how I feel about enchantments, but she seemed well meaning, so I would ask you inspect it to ensure it poses no danger to my staff."

While her words and tone indicated a request, Arielle had raised Sivle. He would voluntarily stop breathing before he would deny her anything she wished. "It would please me to do so, if it would calm your mind, My Queen."

Arielle walked Sivle to the kitchen and demonstrated the portal. Sivle examined the floor of the kitchen carefully for several minutes before following Arielle to the pantry. Once there, he noticed the shimmering wall, examining the floor where the wall disappeared into. Several minutes later, he stood and said only one word. "Curious."

Arielle brought them back to the kitchen, looking at Vanessa, who had come in, watching apprehensively. "Well, what is your opinion, Sivle?" the former queen asked.

"Well, it is a little curious." Sivle tried to be diplomatic as he explained it, with Vanessa standing right there. "The magic is not extraordinarily strong and will probably not last more than a score of days before it will need to be recharged. The range of the magic in the kitchen is quite short, perhaps a score of paces, no more, and seems permanent. It was nicely done. The receptor in the pantry would seem to have a range of a hursmarc or more. But it will have to be recharged every three weeks or so, depending on how much use it gets. It is not how I would have set this up."

"How so?" Arielle questioned him.

Sivle paused a moment. He could see the tension in Vanessa's face and did not want to be overly critical of her efforts. So, he put the best face on it he could. "It is not pushing or pulling from both sides. Rather than creating a portal to the pantry, the kitchen receptor merely triggers the pantry to open a portal and take you there. The receptor in the pantry triggers a portal to the kitchen. All the magic is originating in the pantry, which makes sense if it is a young mage. It is far easier to link receptors than to create portals. Once she made the originating portal, it would have required her to re-memorize the portal spell to enchant the kitchen or use a scroll. This way she could do it in one trip without scrolls. It also explains why the strength of this enchantment in the kitchen is so much weaker than the receptor in the pantry."

"Is there any danger, then?" Arielle sounded less than totally convinced.

Sivle knew it would be disappointing to Vanessa, but he was obliged to answer truthfully. "A bit. If someone could examine this portal, I suppose they could link another receptor."

"You suppose?" Arielle was accustomed to translating Sivle's nuances.

Sivle sighed. "Someone could link another receptor if they examined the receptor in the pantry." He saw Vanessa's face drop and could see the tears already forming. "But, if it pleases Your Majesty, I can add a glyph to prevent it from opening over two portals in a minute. At any rate, in a few weeks, it will no longer work, requiring someone to recharge the spells. If you wish to let it fade, you can do so then."

Vanessa spoke up helpfully. "I am sure Vandion would recharge the receptacle for free. He is the one who cast it in the first place."

"Receptor," Sivle corrected her. "He would have to be careful not to disrupt my glyphs if he did so."

Vanessa had tear marks on her cheeks, but she smiled up at Sivle. "Lord Sivle, if a great mage such as yourself could show him the glyphs, I am sure Vandion could maintain them. He is just beginning to learn. Perhaps you could train him?"

Sivle looked at her directly in the eye. "If he is just a novice in the spirits, he would not be making portals. If he has outgrown his current teacher, he must go to the guild and find another. That is what the guilds are for. I am sorry, but I do not have time to train novices. Nor could you afford me."

Vanessa retreated a bit but held his gaze. "We cannot afford anyone right now. We spent all the money I have made at Jubilee so far on the supplies for this gift."

Sivle's gaze softened, and he put his hand on the young girl's shoulder. "I cannot train Vandion. However, if he would like to journey to my keep, I will see he is trained at the school there, at least in alchemy, so he can earn a living selling potions."

Sivle then turned to Arielle. "Speaking of potions, I have depleted my ointments. Do you think perhaps John would allow me to use a pot on the stove after the blessings are complete?"

"In repayment for a glyph, I think I can arrange it." Arielle smiled and then hugged Vanessa. "Thank you for your thoughtfulness. But no more surprises, please."

Arielle left to fill orders again, and Sivle moved over to the spot on the floor and said "Pantry" and disappeared. Vanessa was bursting. The emotional roller coaster she had put herself through was excruciating, also totally unnecessary in the end. She had never thought there was any potential danger with the portals. She had never even considered there could be. But now Sivle had declared them safe enough, and even offered to have Vandion trained. She couldn't wait to get home to tell him.

"Better get moving, dear, the mutton will not serve itself." Diana gave her a small push as she shook her head. Vanessa dropped back into the moment, skipping over to a tray of sweet cakes.

***

Alliandre roused Braxlo. The two dressed before going down for firstmeal. Braxlo had withdrawn from the Grand Melee, offering to second for Alliandre instead. Alliandre suspected some ruse, but Braxlo seemed sincere. Fairwind had even agreed to release him for the day. She was planning on spending the day with her prince. As it was the third such meeting, she agreed to allow the prince to provide the chaperone. Alliandre thought about waking Erich as well, but he had no reason to be awake before noon. Likely he was already awake, just feigning sleep to be left alone.

Alliandre grabbed his pack, heading to the stairs with Braxlo, locking the room behind them. Braxlo had put on his mail hauberk over a full-sleeve arming jacket, then donned his plate mail. All this he covered with a magnificent tabard of black silk with the Dragonsbane symbol woven in actual silver and gold thread. He had his swords on as well, which surprised Alliandre if he wasn't planning on fighting. His black armor shone, with the only break from the darkness being the Dragonsbane device on his chest and back.

Sometimes Alliandre resented Braxlo's allegiance to the order. He consciously reminded himself Braxlo was out of the order by the time Alliandre became a squire. Still, he wished his friend could tell him the reason the order had rejected him so long ago. Braxlo had inquired, of course, but only came back with bad news. Evidently the grand commander of the order, a descendent of Drake Nileppez as well, had forbidden Alliandre to be knighted because of some character flaw no one ever spoke about.

Feeling his anger rising, Alliandre focused on other things. It wasn't hard as Marion headed over. She had been watching for them and ran to Alliandre as soon as she saw him coming down the stairs. His heart leaped. Her smile and excitement at seeing him were obvious from across the room. She glowed with beauty in Alliandre's eyes. As soon as they met, she greeted him by leaping into his arms and wrapping her arms around his neck. Burying her head in his shoulder, her scent assaulted him. Jasmine and linen overwhelmed the smells of bread and roasting meats from the kitchen.

"Today you will win the Grand Melee. The king will knight you before dark. Mother has already set up a feast, and even has two cows to butcher." Giving him a quick kiss on the cheek, she pulled away from the embrace, grabbing his hand. "You only have an hour before the blessing, so you need to eat quickly. Sivle left half an hour ago."

Braxlo smiled as Marion led them to their regular table. The other serving girl was setting platters of sweet cakes and eggs while several pitchers of morning beer were already weeping onto the rags she had set them on. The two sat across from each other eating, Braxlo at the sweet cakes, Alliandre at the morning beer. Marion gave Alliandre one last hug, then addressed him one last time. "Alliandre, I will see you after the Grand Melee. I told the entire court you are my champion, so you had better win."

"That is my plan," Alliandre replied, right after quaffing a glass. "I shall call out to you by name after they name me champion."

"I would like that," she said, blushing just a bit. She then grabbed a small satchel, running out the door before Alliandre could pour another glass of beer.

Braxlo looked over at his smiling firstmeal partner and grinned. "If that isn't motivation to win, I am sure I do not know what motivation is. I am glad I chose to be your second, rather than face off against you today."

Alliandre smiled back, shaking his head. "With you at my side instead of draining my energy, it increases the odds of my winning tremendously."

Braxlo smiled at the flattery. He grabbed the pitcher to pour himself a glass before it was empty, getting half a glass. Shaking his head, he filled his glass from one of the other pitchers and set the pitcher next to his plate.

"Don't hog all that, Braxlo," Alliandre admonished him. "I will need my energy today."

Braxlo nodded, keeping the pitcher near him. They finished their firstmeal, and all three pitchers of the morning beer, when Sir Andras approached. The one-armed former knight wiped at the table with a rag while the serving girl came out and cleaned the dishes from the table.

"Best ye be headin' to yer blessin'." The pride in Sir Andras' voice made it crack. "Wouldnae want to curse yer day right at the start." Then the old man pulled out a cloth sack and handed it to Braxlo.

Alliandre rose and clasped wrists with his old teacher, pulling him in for a full embrace. "Thank you, Sir Andras. Even more than King Tristan, you have been like a father to me. When I win today, it will be because of you."

"If that be true, laddie, then bring honor to my name. And that means dinnae kill the popinjay dukeling." Sir Andras' voice didn't crack this time, and Alliandre bowed his head slightly.

"It seems everyone feels they must admonish me to keep Sir Rodney alive. And I shall endeavor to do so. But I do plan on teaching him the difference between a wolf and a hyena." The corner of his mouth twitched up. "He seems to think he is the one, while it is clear to me, he is the other."

"I hate to break up this sad parting," Braxlo interjected himself, "but you will see each other tonight, no need for such a long, heartfelt goodbye."

That got a big smile out of both Alliandre and Sir Andras. After clasping wrists with Sir Andras again, the two fighters grabbed their packs and left the tavern. They gave the horses a rest, breaking into a quick walk to work off the morning meal and warming up Alliandre's legs before the fighting. Alliandre's long legs could have easily out-distanced his shorter friend, weighed down with his armor, but the two kept a steady pace, making it to the fairgrounds and the melee field with minutes to spare.

***

The melee field was surprising. After the jousting the previous day, Alliandre expected the ground before the King's pavilion to be torn up, but workers had plowed and packed the ground, then covered it in small pebbles to give the fighters an even, flat surface to conduct their mock battles. Alliandre suspected some enchantments as well, as the gravel surface seemed too well-packed. Workers put up fencing as well, over two hundred paces long and fifty paces wide. Over eight hundred numbered disks lay on the ground, which meant there must have been some late entries.

"Seems there are more disks than I last heard about," Alliandre said to no one in particular.

Braxlo reassured him. "Each of the dwarven clans sent their champions. They arrived yesterday. Every order has at least a few members entered as well. The king had to restrict it to twenty knights per order to keep it from getting out of hand, although he may have intended it to limit the Wyndgryph knights. But you don't have to fight all of them. Half will be gone before you even get warmed up."

Alliandre nodded as Braxlo continued, "And let the others fight for the top numbers. You must fight smart here. Don't go hunting for anyone, and don't get complacent. If you can beat someone quickly, beat them quickly and take your time looking for the next. This many entries mean there will be a lot of sweet cakes for you to eat. Go slowly and take your breaks."

The trumpets blared, and the combatants gathered in rows in the center of the field, directly in front of the king's pavilion. King Henry stood in front, surrounded by the court. Alliandre, catching sight of Marion in the back, also noticed Sivle and the other priests spreading out to surround the fighters. A page stepped out, the trumpets sounding again, signaling the warriors to line up.

Everyone became quiet as the page called out in a clear tenor voice, "Ladies and gentlemen, and others gathered today, I present to you, King Henry the Great!"

The crowd erupted in cheers and clapping while the men and women gathered on the field began chants of "Long live the king!" King Henry waved and clasped wrists with the royal court, then raised his hands to silence the crowd. Alliandre smiled bemusedly at the king. With great respect, he reflected on how King Henry had an uncanny knack for letting the cheering go on and on, reveling in it and letting it build on itself, until just that moment when people began tiring of clapping and yelling. Then the king would raise his hands and signal for everyone to stop before they did so anyway of their own accord.

Stepping forward to the stage, King Henry turned and greeted the crowd. It was mostly nobles now, friends and comrades in arms of those vying for the honor today. He raised his voice, which needed no bardic enhancements. "Welcome friends! As we near the end of our Jubilee, we reflect on the history of our kingdom. Twelve centuries ago, men and women like you see on the field below you carved out the three kingdoms from the grendlaar and vreen hoards which roamed these plains.

Many of the aelf and dwarven kingdoms were concerned, rightly so for our first couple of centuries. Since the Great Truce, the three kingdoms proved a stalwart ally and trading partner for all the kingdoms in the realm." The crowd cheered at this, even the aelf and dwarves, for what he spoke was true.

"Since the Great Truce, none of the three kingdoms have waged war on any other kingdoms. Since the truce declared with the aelf, we have provided forces for our aelf, dwarf and even centaur allies, despite their own incursions, when called upon. In our twelve hundred years, the Central Kingdom has protected caravans and pilgrims alike as they traveled across our lands and even past the Great Chasm. For twelve hundred years, the land has had a peace like it has never known before. For twelve hundred years, the land has known prosperity like it has never known before. And for over a millennium since it was signed, the three kingdoms have upheld the Great Truce."

He continued, "Even when Golden Aelf attacked our sister kingdom to the south, still we held our armies back. We left the Southern King-dom to defend itself, relying on the pact with the aelf to provide for its defense. We all know their defense proved inadequate, yet we still held our armies back, leaving the murder of its people unavenged. For by the agreement of the pact, only the humans who have been harmed can petition the Great Aelf king for redress of their grievances. We held our armies back, and we will continue to hold back our armies. For while I am king, none of my soldiers will make war on any aelf." Raising the royal scepter above his head, the king shouted out, "To the Great King. May the spirits protect him and his sons."

The crowd erupted again with the response to the toast. It turned into a chant, and once again King Henry let it go on until it was just about to fall from its peak before raising his hands to silence the crowd. "Let us remember the history of our kingdom. Let the brotherhood and friendship we have known with the aelf and dwarven nations guide us in our actions today. We come here as friends, competing for honor and glory. We do not raise our swords in anger or pride. We do not use this as a reason to address past wrongs. We will judge infractions of courtesy and honor as harshly as whether a blow is to be counted. We have enchantments to assist our marschalls with one of those standards, but it will be their judgment for the other."

A page walked up, tapping King Henry on the wrist. Surprised, King Henry looked at him and smiled. "Some here did not come to listen to me speak. I am told we have some priests here who need to get back to their priestly duties, so I will allow them their time. We are pleasantly surprised to welcome his Esteemed Grace, High Priest Aisto Cundondur of the Great Aelf."

An aelf of surprising height stepped out from behind the king. He looked like a mage from the Mage's Council, not a high priest of the Forest Spirits. His gray hair fell to his knees, his green and silver robes bedecked with embroidered trees, birds, and other creatures of the forest. On his head was a brown galero, with one gold tassel and one silver tassel. He walked up to the king and bowed deeply. Then he turned to the warriors standing before him and commanded, "Priests. Raise your hands and bless these men and women, aelf and dwarves, that they may use their might at arms to serve and glorify the spirits."

Thirty priests raised their hands, and a kaleidoscope of colors branched out from the high priest to all the other high priests in attendance. "Pob clod i'r ysbrydion. Gadewch i'r rhyfelwyr hyn wasanaethu'ch pwrpas yn eu brwydrau. Cadwch nhw'n ddiogel rhag niwed. Pob clod i'r ysbrydion." In his head, Alliandre recited the prayer to himself. *All glory to the spirits. Let these warriors serve your purpose in their battles. Keep them safe from harm. All glory to the spirits.*

The colors descended on the rows of fighters, and settled on the ground and dissipated, like mist in the late morning sun. Their job completed, a few of the priests returned to the city, but most went to the chirurgeon tent set up at the far end of the tournament field. The blessing finished, the king stood before the people once again.

Raising his hands over the knights and other nobles, he proclaimed, "The Grand Melee is in one half hour. Lords and Ladies, don your armor."

Over eight hundred men and women stood at the ready, anxiously waiting for the opening horn. Five banners of paladins were acting as marschalls, standing between the lines of warriors. Alliandre had ignored Braxlo's advice and bartered for a number in at least the top ten percent of warriors. Ten golden turots had only got him number seventy-three. He had heard they had auctioned the number one spots at two havnots each. Every number in the top one hundred had earned the bearer at least a turot – those that had been sold, anyway.

Mages had gone around with the scrolls to enchant the armor to turn red with a hit, which also sent a tingle to the wearer. These were old spells, and ones which every mage learned as a novice. The Mages Academy in Foresight had been working for months with all of their more advanced students writing the scrolls. This was also an opportunity for the novices to practice casting from scrolls, and they had gone from fighter to fighter down the line, casting them under the watchful eyes of the paladins.

Alliandre thanked the young female mage, who seemed surprised. Then he looked around. To his left, five paces away, stood the largest dwarf Alliandre had ever seen with arms as thick as Alliandre's thighs and wielding a nasty war axe and shield. Dwarves were fearsome in their shield walls, stout in small groups, and individually in battle they were tough to take down, much less kill. But in duels, the protection of the heaviest armor any race wore was not advised. It slowed them down while providing no benefit because of the enchantments.

Likewise, they favored weapons which lacked the reach of long swords. All this contributed to them faring poorly. Still, the spike on the back of his war axe was going to deal a nasty blow, even with the point rounded as it was. And he was a dwarven champion. Alliandre considered leaving him to the last.

Alliandre nodded at the warrior who came up to his breastplate. He must have been over a stride and a half tall. The dwarf grunted and raised his axe slightly in acknowledgement. "Grunhildor. Pleased to meet you, tall man."

"Alliandre. Pleased to meet you as well, tall dwarf." Alliandre smiled, pleased with his jest.

The dwarf looked over at him, and with no change in tone, replied, "I like you, Alliandre. You made me smile today."

Alliandre was just about to speak again when the horns blared, signaling the start of the Grand Melee. A roar went up from the crowd as the lines of warriors advanced toward each other. All thoughts of the dwarf were out of his mind as he looked the twenty paces across to his opponent. A knight from Redton by the looks of him, the blue bend on the red field, with the sailfin rampant in the middle of the bend. The two warily advanced, circling. Alliandre charged and pressed the knight, who dodged and attempted to sidestep around. Almost as if he expected it, Alliandre executed a lightning strike followed by griffin slash and first took out his opponent's arm, then left a mark in his helm. The vambrace and the helm both turned red, and Alliandre returned to his number.

Braxlo was there to meet him and handed him a water-skin. Turning it down, Alliandre raised the faceplate of his helm.

"Nice work," Braxlo told him as he took back the skin.

"Thanks," Alliandre said quietly. Then he said something surprising to Braxlo. "I sometimes feel bad many of the top fighters go out in the first round. Not like the jousting where you get to continue jousting even if you initially do poorly."

Braxlo thought for a moment. "First off, you hate jousting. Second, a true knight wants to fight someone worthy, not some novice or nobleman who entered for vanity's sake. The knight you defeated will go home disappointed. But if you win, he will brag about having faced you nobly and honorably, knowing he would have had to face you, eventually."

"I know." Alliandre cast his eyes up to look for Marion. "It just seems that to have trained and planned and come here, only to have it ended so soon, must be hard."

Braxlo laughed out loud. "You are the only one I know who trains for duels. No doubt it makes you a better warrior in the field as well, but most of us just do our drills and hope when the time comes to use our skills, we don't fall to some errant vreen spear."

Alliandre smiled as well. What Braxlo said was probably true. But he also knew that one purpose of these tournaments was to ensure the knights were well trained, and accustomed to fighting, so when the time came to do actual battle, panic and doubt would not set in. The two men stood silently, Alliandre unable to find Marion, even though he knew she was behind the king. Braxlo watching the battles, as Alliandre should have been doing, looking for who would be the biggest threat.

A page came by to grab Alliandre's number, the two fighters following him to where the page laid it in at the edge of the field. Once the final duel was over, the fighters would be free to fight the opponent of his or her choosing. Alliandre decided he would clear the field away from the large dwarf, forcing the fighting closer to the stands. He hoped Marion could see him at least, regretting not bidding on a lower number to get closer.

Grunhildor returned to his spot to find someone had moved his number and his pack. He walked over to Alliandre's left to look for them. Finding them, he raised his axe to Alliandre while grabbing a waterskin of his own. They stood there silently for a few more minutes until the remaining fighters had all found their packs. Then both put down their visors and got ready to fight again.

Alliandre had made it to the fourth round, engaging a paladin from Blue Keep when his head rung from a blow to the back of his helm. The minor tingling let him know it was a valid blow. Turning to look, Sir Rodney the Magnificent stood there, visor raised. Alliandre was about to charge when the marschall yelled, "Hold. Foul. Warrior, stand firm."

"Just wanted to let you know I was in the area, dog." Sir Rodney lowered his visor and turned to challenge another knight nearby. The paladin came over, waving for a mage to reset the spell to allow Alliandre to continue. Several minutes later, he resumed his duel with the paladin. Rage boiled over and Alliandre poured a steel rain down until a viper strike could catch the paladin's sword out of place. He looked around for Sir Rodney, but another of his order challenged him instead.

More Wyndgryph knights circled around him, barking and growling. Alliandre ignored the distraction, but he could feel his blood rising. It would not be good for the knights if it boiled over. The knight he was currently fighting was trying to engage him in a novice's drill, but Alliandre swept his swords aside and struck him on the leg hard enough to stagger him. Deprived of his mobility, it was easy for Alliandre to swing behind him and catch him in the kidneys with a straight blow. While the steel cuirass stopped most of the force, the point where the cuirass rested on his lower back had to have left a mark.

No sooner had he finished the blow when he sensed another charging at his back. Spinning quickly, he leaped forward, catching the poor man with a lightning strike straight to the gorget. The knight dropped both swords, reaching for his throat. The flat blade could not penetrate, but the force of him charging and Alliandre's strike combined to crush his windpipe. He fell and paladins surrounded him immediately. "Hold!" a young marschall called out. Several tense moments later, the knight rolled to his knees and stood. He tried a half-hearted bark in Alliandre's direction, but all that came out was a cough.

The three remaining Wyndgryph knights began barking again, two of them charging together. Alliandre faced the one to his right, knowing the one to his left would continue the charge. Sure enough, the man in front stopped and Alliandre ducked the blow aimed for his head, even though he caught it with his sword. The other sword blocked the second blow, and the two exchanged thrusts and strikes before Alliandre backed away to the side, then stepped back up to clear the knight's sword and strike him on the elbow.

His couter red, the knight swung his arm behind his back. Alliandre toyed with him for a bit, forcing the knight to retreat over and over before a thunder strike and a fools thrust combined to turn his helm red. The two remaining Wyndgryph knights looked at each other before one of them charged. Alliandre tried several combinations, but whether the knight had scouted him well, or this knight was just much better, they dueled until the trumpets signaled the end of the round. With much barking, the two knights returned to their numbers.

One advantage of having a second was having someone to provide insights from their observations. Usually it was a squire who knew less than the warrior fighting. Braxlo was no squire. "He seems to have a hitch when he raises his left sword above his shoulder," Braxlo offered helpfully as he handed him a waterskin.

Alliandre nodded. He hadn't noticed, likely because the barking had gotten to him. He cursed his temper. But it calmed him down as he gratefully took the waterskin from the black-clad knight. There were still a couple of hundred knights on the field; it looked to be a long day.

"Did Sir Andras send any morning beer?" he asked.

"No, but here is a pear." Throwing him the fruit, Braxlo chided him. "You need to keep your strength up."

Two rounds went by without a sign of the Wyndgryph knights. Alliandre looked for them, but it seemed some knights from Dragonsbane were interested in him.

A wide knight bearing a shield with the Freehold's device emblazoned on it approached him. "So, you have a grudge against Dragonsbane, do you? I would like you to remove your ugly tabard and burn it."

"Careful, Sir Turl. This is Alliandre Del Nileppez. He trained us when we were all squires together, right before they sent him away." Two of the knights raised their visors. Alliandre recognized the golden-haired man as he continued talking. "When they first raised us to squires, he was training knights as well as us squires. How go your battles, Lord Alliandre?"

"I am not yet a lord, nor a knight, but well met, earl's son. Jamrie, isn't it?" Alliandre cautiously sheathed his sword, raised his own visor, and reached out a hand in greeting. "And this must be your friend, Oscar. Glad to see you both."

"This is Sir Turl, our banner commander. He does not like your chosen device. I think he finds it disrespectful." Sir Oscar smiled while clasping wrists with Alliandre as well.

Sir Turl raised his visor. "Markings like those could be the basis of a blood feud, warrior. Perhaps you should rethink your device."

"The Freehold rejected me. I will wear whatever device I decide on and leave it to one of your order to remove it. So far, I still wear it." Alliandre said it with a smile and reached his arm out to the older knight.

"Then I guess I am honor bound to try," Sir Turl also said with a smile as he clasped wrists with Alliandre, the glint in his eyes showing he would enjoy it.

"As are we," Sir Jamrie and Sir Oscar said as the four men replaced their visors. Sir Jamrie went first. Alliandre's swords proved too fast for the young knight. Sir Oscar was wise enough to stay out of reach, but as he lunged into a viper strike, Alliandre spun and circled around him, catching first his elbow, then his helm with two blows thrown all but simultaneously. The glint was gone from Sir Turl's eyes. The two sparred for several minutes when Sir Turl blocked Alliandre's feint, moving his sword out of position to stop Alliandre's eagle's talon as it rung against his helm.

Bowing his defeat, the knight raised his visor as he stood, smiling. "I suppose you can wear your device a while longer, my lord."

"Still not a lord." Alliandre smiled and looked over the field. He found the fighting had moved toward the stands. There was quite a bit of distance between him and the mass of fighters still going at it. Sheathing his swords, he walked toward the others, looking for the Wyndgryph colors.

***

"It looks like your champion is doing well, Lady Marion." The duke had approached Marion from behind, laying his hands on her shoulders.

There were only a few score warriors left, everyone expecting it would end soon. Alliandre approached the mass of fighters near the stands. Thankfully, other than a knavish blow several rounds ago, Sir Rodney had found other warriors to prey upon. The trumpet blared, sending the men back to their stations. Marion noticed the duchess was heading down the row to her as well. Composing herself, Marion put a pleasant smile on her face and prepared for the small talk.

The duchess came up and bowed to Marion. "I wanted to stop and say thank you once again. Sir Rodney witnessing the defeat of several of his knights has given him more respect for Alliandre. We were pleased to see him refrain from baiting him these last rounds. I suspect there will only be a few more rounds, then we can settle this entire matter put and it behind us."

"I sincerely hope so. I feared Alliandre would kill your son when he struck Alliandre from behind while he was already engaged. It would have been fortuitous if they had expelled Sir Rodney at that point." Marion feigned concern, but after Sir Rodney had delivered his dishonorable and ignoble blow, Marion secretly hoped Alliandre would attack him. Sadly, Alliandre seemed to have his temper in check. She believed they would make it through the tournament with Sir Rodney intact.

The duke turned red in embarrassment. "I will have words with him over that. He disgraced the Wyndgryph and our family. I almost went out and pulled him then and there. Truly, I am ashamed. I plan on apologizing to Alliandre when this is over, however it turns out."

Marion nodded, surprised at the duke's admission. "Perhaps if you were to knight him, Your Grace. It would serve two purposes and remove the source of your son's chief complaint against Alliandre."

"There will be no need, Your Highness." The duke looked directly into Marion's eyes, setting his hand gently on her face. "I consider myself an excellent judge of swordcraft. I do not think there are any here, except perhaps Sir Ereg-Drahcir, who can stand against young Alliandre."

Lord Ferdinand interrupted and Marion introduced the duke and duchess to him. They made some small talk until the trumpets announced the next round. The duke and duchess returned to their seats, while Marion tried to guess who Alliandre would go after next. Her heart sunk as she saw two knights dressed in red, orange and yellow make an arrow flight toward Alliandre.

***

"Only a few scores left. It will be three or four more rounds, then a final round of fighting until it is all over." Braxlo took back the now empty waterskin. Alliandre had been fighting for the better part of four hours, radiating the smell of sweat and grime. Alliandre turned to him. "I think it is time to find Sir Rodney. I don't want him to make the final round." Smiling grimly, Alliandre set his sallet and locked it in place over the bevor.

He didn't have to look hard for Sir Rodney, as he and one of his knights were heading toward him. Grunhildor noticed them too and shouted out to him. "Friends of yours?"

"Not in an aelf's life," Alliandre replied. "Just a distasteful duty I am planning on taking care of now."

The dwarf laughed. "Ha! You want I should soften them up for you, tall man?"

Alliandre thought it over, then declined. "No, Sir Grunhildor. It is better I remove them from the tournament myself."

The dwarf nodded, heading toward the knight who everyone seemed to be avoiding, Sir Ereg-Drahcir. Meanwhile, Alliandre met the two Wyndgryph knights in the center of the field. Sir Rodney set his sword on the ground while Sir Johann Quick Blade, Sword Master for the Order, approached. Sir Rodney spoke loudly, "Time to put down the rabid dog, Sir Johann. No need to be merciful and quick. This dog is out of his mind with madness. Thinks he is worthy of a princess. Woof, woof, woof!"

Alliandre seethed, feeling his blood rising again. But he focused on Sir Johann instead of the barking. The two men circled, feinting and testing each other. For five minutes they probed each other's defenses, observing each other's attacks before the duel began in earnest. Alliandre was pushed back, almost losing his arm when Sir Johann surprised him with an otter dive. He had found a weakness in Alliandre's form. Alliandre, while he could find no weakness in Sir Johann's defenses, recognized the flaw in his own defense and corrected it. The round was over before Alliandre found a chink in the man's attack.

Like all sword masters, Sir Johann had learned every form of attack and defense, as well as the counters to each of them. However, Alliandre noticed he slowed up after a vigorous set of blows. Whether it was fatigue or pacing, Alliandre did not know. But he began a series of thunder strikes, followed by a steel rain, increasing the speed until his swords were just flashes of light. Then, finishing the flurry of blows, he threw a lazy eagle's talon. As expected, Sir Johann swung his sword to block it, but slowed the speed to Alliandre's, then threw a viper strike in the gap.

Alliandre flipped his attack into a frog tongue strike with lightning quickness. The change in speed caught Sir Johann unprepared, unable to pull back his strike in time to block the sword now driving into his visor. Acknowledging the hit, he cursed, then bowed and waved over Sir Rodney. Alliandre half expected Sir Rodney to already be charging, taking advantage of the delay when Alliandre waited to make sure Sir Johann was out. But when he turned, the duke's son was walking back to his station. Seconds later, the trumpet blared, ending the round.

***

Duke Randolf was happy to see his son still in the tournament, but apprehensive about the upcoming round. He knew the showdown between his son and the fearsome Alliandre was going to happen, and he dreaded the outcome. He had lost three other sons to battle and resolved not to lose another. So, he had brought in the finest swordsmen and battle masters to train his son from the time he could walk. There should be no greater swordsman on earth.

But somewhere along the line, his son had become arrogant, and Duke Randolf had ignored it. "Better to be confident than hesitant in battle," he said. But arrogance had stunted Sir Rodney's learning, and as he took his rightful place among the Wyndgryph knights, his arrogance made him surround himself with sycophants. Sir Rodney had not faced a serious duel in half a decade, and now he had to face someone well-known for his tenacity and skill with the sword. A natural swordsman, trained from the time he was a child by the greatest swordsman who had ever lived. Six years Sir Rodney's senior, Alliandre was seemingly unbeatable, as his defeat of Sir Johann showed.

Still, his son walked off the field with all the cockiness Duke Randolf despised. That cockiness would get his son killed one day. But he put away his fears and smiled down at his wife. Her unease had grown the last two days as this day got closer, and while she was no longer waking up screaming, she turned pensive and quiet anytime the subject of swordplay or battles came up. It didn't help they were guests of the king, and were constantly in the presence of Prince Lucas, who spoke often of Alliandre.

His wife clasped his hand tight as the new round began, and he watched his son stride confidently forward to do battle with the "red dog". He hoped his son was not striding confidently to his doom. He looked over at his wife and forced a smile, giving her hand a reassuring squeeze. "Alliandre has given us his oath. He will abide by it. There is nothing to fear, my love."

"I hope you are right," she replied as the two men began their duel.

***

Marion looked on as Alliandre and Sir Rodney approached each other. Finally, he could defend her honor. The two men squared off and began fighting. Alliandre began with a charge which ended up driving Sir Rodney back five full paces before the knight recovered and began circling. Alliandre backed up, forcing Sir Rodney to come to him in the middle of the now constricted field, right in front of the stands. The other fighters began pausing their battles to watch these two.

A hush fell across the field as everyone in the stands noticed no one was fighting but the two circling in the middle of the field. Even the wind seemed to die down so it too could say it witnessed the event. Above, almost as if on cue, a lone buzzard began circling overhead, likely expecting a feast once the duel ended. Marion looked over at the duke and duchess, but they, too, were focused on their son and Alliandre.

Marion could see Sir Rodney was talking by the bobbing of his head, but she could not make out his words. Occasionally he would howl or bark, and slowly she could see Alliandre stiffen. She silently prayed he did not lose his temper and make a mistake, while also hoping he would lose his temper and kill the boorish knight. *No*, she thought to herself. She didn't want Sir Rodney dead. Her family had made an oath, as had Alliandre. She fervently withdrew her unspoken desire of a moment before.

Alliandre began raining blows down upon Sir Rodney. Despite being somewhat overwhelmed, he fended off every attack. Marion didn't know if it was the tension, or if the timekeepers had stopped keeping time, but it seemed like this battle was going far longer than the standard round. She looked over at the trumpeters. They were all sipping wine, not even prepared to blow the note which would stop the fighting. Sir Rodney began raining blows of his own down on Alliandre, but her champion easily deflected or blocked them, even managing a few thrusts to slow the attack.

Then Alliandre stood straight up and began circling Sir Rodney like a drillmaster circling his students. Something was about to happen.

***

Alliandre charged Sir Rodney as soon as they were clear of the other combatants. Sir Rodney parried his initial thrusts and strikes, but Alliandre began a gale wind attack, which forced the knight back. Sir Rodney adjusted to the flurry of blows and began circling. Alliandre stopped his attack, retreating to the center of the field. He was determined to defeat Sir Rodney in front of everyone.

Sir Rodney taunted Alliandre, "So, the dog thinks that by barking louder, we will take him seriously. But you are toothless." Cautiously, Sir Rodney approached, barking and howling to further humiliate his red-armored opponent. "In fact, I give you too much credit by calling you a dog. You are nothing but a toothless boar. Big and scary looking, but in the end, easily put down." Sir Rodney began a flurry of blows of his own. Once again, Alliandre defended them easily, slowing the attacks with some well-placed thrusts of his own.

"Then come put me down, wolf pup. Let us see who is tooth-less." Alliandre charged, throwing a series of thunder strikes, pushing Sir Rodney back again. He knew Rodney's weakness now. Circling, he waited until Rodney closed. He began an eagle's talon with his right sword, which Sir Rodney easily parried with a priest's block, followed immediately by thrashing the grain. Alliandre blocked the thrashing the grain with a crescent moon while simultaneously squaring off and throwing an eagle's talon with his left sword. And over and over, the pattern repeated itself as both fighters began the advanced drill for aelf style two-sword fighting.

"So, we are practicing sword drills?" Sir Rodney sneered inside his helm. "Have you reached the limit of your knowledge of swordcraft?"

"Not at all," Alliandre responded, "I merely thought I would give you a lesson, since you seemed to have trouble when I attack forcefully."

"Noighk Noighk, little piggy. I can do this all day." As if to empha-size his point, Sir Rodney fell into a more relaxed pose and steadily beat out the rhythmic cadence against Alliandre's swords.

"At this pace maybe, but how about if we speed up the drill?" Allian-dre doubled the speed of his attacks. Sir Rodney's stance became much less relaxed as he fought to keep up. Alliandre continued his lesson. "Do you know why we teach this drill, little wolf?"

"Of course. It is to teach the strokes. Everyone knows that." Sir Rodney moved one foot back to better brace himself against the increasing speed of the drill.

"Partially." Alliandre was in full teaching mode now. "These strokes are the basis for all other strokes and parries. Once you have mastered these, then the remaining ones come easier. Like steel rain."

Alliandre switched and began throwing vertical strikes from all areas upon Sir Rodney, albeit much slower, forcing Sir Rodney to defend them. As soon as Sir Rodney began adjusting, Alliandre went back to the drill.

"So, it seems you are a master of drills, toothless pig. I am NOT impressed." Alliandre sped up the drill again. Sir Rodney's breath was coming hard. "We don't use drills in the wars. If you had known that, perhaps you would not have forced Prince Lucas to carry you home, all but dead, fighting vreen of all things." Then Sir Rodney launched a viper strike. A common trick elder knights used on squires when the squires were just learning the drill.

Sir Rodney had sent the attack with his left hand. Alliandre had expected he would use his dominant right hand. Nonetheless, Alliandre used an assassin's block with his right hand to parry the viper strike. Then he stepped up with a punch block to Sir Rodney's right sword, pivoting immediately to come down with an eagle's talon on Sir Rodney's outstretched left forearm. The movements were too fast for Sir Rodney to even react to. Sir Rodney's vambrace creased as his radius broke. For half a second Alliandre's sword was pinched in the cuir bouilli. As he freed his sword and pivoted back to square off against the knight, Alliandre continued his lecture.

"I have fought in enough wars. Do you know why the elder knights perform that trick on the newer knights? I am guessing you don't, else you would not have tried it on me." Alliandre's voice was calm and measured as Sir Rodney tucked his now useless arm behind his back.

"All I hear is a pig grunting," replied Sir Rodney, his voice gruff with pain.

"It is to teach the novices not to grow complacent once they have mastered the drill." Alliandre swatted a combination at Sir Rodney's remaining sword to drive it out of position, then tapped his helm with the flat of the tip. "To train them to always monitor their opponent's swords. Which is why it was so easy to counter. You surely didn't think I was a novice, did you?" Once again, Alliandre drove the single sword Sir Rodney furiously fought with off to the side. Once again, he tapped the unguarded helm. "Now you are bereft of a sword and have as good as lost this duel, wolf pup. How weak you must be to have lost to a toothless old moor-pig."

"Don't think your defeat of me will change anything." Sir Rodney laughed. "Tomorrow I will announce my intent to court the lovely Lady Marion. By the time Adimon comes, I will have bedded her properly. If she pleases me, I may even wed her. But she will no longer be Marion the Virtuous when I am done, pig. Not that she is too virtuous now, from what I have heard."

Alliandre's eyes flashed red. He had steeled himself against the insults the boor would hurl against him. And while he was prepared to humiliate Sir Rodney a little, he had planned to do no real lasting harm. But he was not prepared to stand by while this pig impugned Marion's honor. He bore her favor, and even if he had not, he would normally have demanded a blood duel over the insult. Rage overtook him, bloodlust curling his lips. He would show this pompous grackle what it meant to challenge Alliandre Del Nileppez Drol Hulloc. And he would kill him for disparaging the name of Marion the Virtuous.

Once again, he drove Sir Rodney's sword to the side. This time, instead of tapping his helm or delivering a finishing blow, he stepped in. With a thrust of his sword and a spin of his left arm, he caught Sir Rodney's remaining arm, locking it with his arm and his sword. Then slowly, Alliandre maneuvered his sword in until the flattened point was pressing on Sir Rodney's helm. By positioning and torquing his own arm, Alliandre used the leverage of his sword and Sir Rodney's trapped arm to force Sir Rodney's head forward toward the ground. Sir Rodney stepped forward to avoid falling, but he was twisted and bent over. Alliandre's sword ground against his helm where the visor hinged, wedging the helm from his head.

Alliandre saw his opening. The chain mail coif Sir Rodney wore slid down into the helm of the bent over knight. Only the ties of the gorget protected the back of his neck. A sliver of bare skin revealed itself above the arming jacket. Alliandre slowly cocked his body, twisting to his right, preparing to put all his might into the final blow. He looked up into the stands. He could see Marion standing, hands clasped and mouth moving as if praying, saying the same brief prayer over and over. In front of her stood the duke and duchess, Duke Del Mornay standing like a solid oak while the duchess clung to him like a bird in a storm. As Alliandre's sword paused, the duchess buried her head into the shoulder of Duke Randolf.

***

Marion beamed as Alliandre began toying with the duke's son. His entire demeanor had changed. He looked like the boy who was training the other squires back at Vista. Her mind went back to those days as Alliandre and Sir Rodney began a sword drill. Sir Rodney and Alliandre were trading insults, but Alliandre was completely relaxed. The drill sped up. Sir Rodney struggled to keep up with the speed of Alliandre's swords. Sir Rodney lunged forward. In an instant, Alliandre struck his arm, turning the vambrace red. Evidently, he had hit it solidly, as Sir Rodney gingerly tucked it behind his back.

Then Alliandre stiffened. Even from this distance, Marion could tell his eyes were red, and the duel would not end well. She did not know what Sir Rodney had said, but she clasped her hands together and begged the spirits to carry her voice to Alliandre.

"Don't do it. Don't do it. Don't do it. Please, my love, don't do it."

Then the blow came, and Sir Rodney's helm rolled across the field, a spurt of blood as it separated from the body, Sir Rodney's body tumbling into a limp pile directly where it had once stood.

"He did it. He actually did it," Marion said out loud before she buried her face in her hands and wept.

***

Duke Randolf was rather enjoying his son's defeat. To this point, Alliandre had kept his word and kept his son alive. The blow to his forearm might be a harsh lesson, but even he could see Alliandre was toying with his son at this point. The duel was as good as over. Alliandre swatted his son's sword, then nonchalantly tapped Sir Rodney's helm, humiliating him in front of the entire kingdom. They would spread stories of this duel far and wide, and he hoped it was the lesson his son needed. But then everything changed.

"Rodney, what have you done?" the duke said under his breath as Alliandre tensed up. Pausing in his attacks for several seconds, he moved in and wrapped Sir Rodney's remaining arm. He could have ended it there. Duke Randolf gripped his chair as he watched Alliandre twist and pry his son's helm until he exposed the neck. Then Alliandre coiled. Like a serpent pulling back to build power for his strike, his body twisted and compacted. He looked up at the stands. The duke felt like they almost locked eyes. His wife turned and buried her eyes into his shoulder, but the duke could not look away. Alliandre swung, releasing the energy stored in his body. The sword disappeared, moving too fast for the eye to see until it struck, slowed to visibility by the impact as his son's helm parted cleanly with the rest of his armor, a spray of blood signaling the end of the duel.

"It is done," the duke told his wife. Then he pulled her close and held her as she wept.

***

Sir Rodney seethed. Somehow, this commoner had not only defeated him, but he was humiliating him in front of his men and the king himself. None of his taunts seemed to upset the hotheaded warrior, even though his men had told him he was known for his temper and his lack of restraint. Sir Rodney had hoped to goad him into acting dishonorably, or at least attacking recklessly, so Sir Rodney could find an opening to defeat him. But there was no chance of that now. The brute who thought himself a dragon was actually lecturing Sir Rodney on swordcraft. Even more unforgiveable, he apparently had studied much harder or had better teachers.

He remembered his father's words. "The greatest swordsman who has ever lived taught that boy. From the time he could pick up a stick he has studied. Be careful who you go around insulting. The Southern Kingdom was famous for the quality of its knights. No other kingdom could field knights of such skill and valor."

"He is not a knight, father." Sir Rodney remembered how he almost spat the words back. "And if the Southern Kingdom was so powerful, why is their capital covered in eternal night? Perhaps they are just as full of talk as the mongrel."

But now the mongrel had defeated him, humiliating him in the process. Anger and embarrassment fueled him now. Without thinking, he went straight at the red mongrel's weak spot. "Don't think your defeat of me will change anything." Sir Rodney laughed. "Tomorrow I will announce my intent to court the lovely Lady Marion. By the time Adimon comes, I will have bedded her properly. If she pleases me, I may even wed her. But she will no longer be Marion the Virtuous when I am done, pig. Not that she is too virtuous now, from what I have heard."

Sir Rodney stood with his surely broken arm behind his back, looking at the taller man as he paused. Embarrassment turned to fear as, slowly, the man's eyes flashed as red as his armor. A purple hue seemed to ring them, although Sir Rodney knew that to be impossible. Then his opponent tied up his arm, forcing his head down. He braced himself with his leg. He refused to be driven into the ground like a child. The dog forced his head around at an unnatural angle until the autumn breeze blew a chill on his bare neck. Terror overtook him as he noticed his father and mother looking on, his mother turning her head into his father's shoulder because she could not bear to see her only remaining son killed.

Something snapped in Sir Rodney at that moment. All the days his mother pampered and cared for him growing up. All the years his father spent training him, hiring sword masters from around the world to make sure his mother would not have to endure the grief of a lost son again. He realized all the warnings his father gave him were not to belittle him. Somehow, his father had known how this would end. And here he was, watching as he forced his mother to witness the death of another son – him. In his last moments, shame overcame him from the grief he was causing her now. It was his fault. It was his arrogance and lack of honor. It was his refusal to listen to his betters, or even acknowledge they were his betters.

He felt rather than saw the blow. The release of tension as Alliandre's coiled body straightened. The slight rise as Alliandre's feet drove into the ground. The slight movement back as the red-armored giant turned his hips and shoulders and the fall as he swung his sword arm down. Then he felt nothing.

***

Alliandre didn't know if he had ever swung a sword so purely. His entire body, from his foot planted firmly into the ground and driving the movement, to his hips and legs, releasing at just the right moment. The sword may as well have been part of his body as his shoulders drove his arms and his elbow and wrist snapped at just the right instants to move the sword tip seemingly faster than light itself. Keeping his eyes glued to the duke and duchess, instead of them, he saw Queen Arielle the Beautiful, burying her head into the shoulder of Sir Andras when she heard the news of Nathan's death.

The bloodlust left him. In the last moment, he changed the direction of his blow, striking the back of the helm, knocking it off and sending it rolling across the field. Looking down, he could see where his blow had driven the lower part of the helm through the padding and into the skull of his hapless opponent, tearing a bloody gash in his scalp and knocking him unconscious, but still alive. Sir Rodney lay crumpled in a ball, and as his body fell unconscious to the dirt, Alliandre looked around at the remaining combatants, then back up to the stands.

Silence filled the arena. Marion was weeping. The duchess sobbed as the duke tried to comfort her. Perhaps they didn't realize he had spared the "wolf". Looking down, he noticed the body fell away from the stands, the empty helm lying with its top pointing at the crowd with a splatter of blood trailing its path. Trumpets signaled the end of the round as paladins rushed in to lay on hands and raise the body, head still attached to a standing position. Alliandre found Braxlo, walking over to see if he had refilled the waterskin.

"I thought you were going to send his head along with his helm for a minute," the burly fighter said as Alliandre approached.

"I was," Alliandre simply replied as he reached for the waterskin.

"It was a good choice I think," Braxlo reassured him. Then he handed him the waterskin and warned him. "No morning beer, but I found some mead."

Alliandre tasted it carefully, then drank deeply. Then he drank deeply again. "I'll need something stronger than this to calm down completely," he said before the sweet liquid coated his throat. "Three more rounds, I think."

Braxlo agreed. "Should be, but they ran the last round long. Another round as long, it may only be two. It would be two rounds for sure, but everyone just watched you and Sir Rodney. He was the only one eliminated."

"Don't worry, my friend." Alliandre handed back the waterskin, patting his friend teasingly on the shoulder. "I will get us back to the Aerie as soon as I can."

Alliandre spent the rest of the break deciding who to go after. Grunhildor had lost to Sir Ereg-Drahcir, so he decided he would challenge Sir Ereg-Drahcir. He was the best fighter left. He looked for the knight among the small circle of warriors left. He found him almost directly across. The trumpets sounded and Alliandre walked forward, but a woman with a sword and mace intercepted him, interrupting his plans.

"It would be my honor to fight you, red warrior," she said as she approached. "Dishonor should I avoid you."

"Then I will see your honor upheld," Alliandre replied as he raised his swords.

The woman was quite skilled, her shorter mace used primarily as a shield, thrusting out to block and protect her left side. She had mastered its use, making it clear he would have to work hard to get a blow in on her left side. Unaccustomed as he was with fighting this combination of weapons, it took a few minutes before he found where the mace's limits of defense were. A quick succession of frog tongue strikes removed her sword arm, and it was soon after he rang her helm with a thunder strike.

As he turned to look again for Sir Ereg-Drahcir, the trumpets sounded. *That was a short round,* he thought to himself. Then the trumpets sounded again. Confused, he looked around for one of the marschalls, but they looked as confused as he was when the trumpets blared a third time, only a much higher, longer note. Then Alliandre understood. The city was under attack. His first thought was Marion. He looked over to the stands, relieved to see the people moving from the stands in an orderly manner. Looking toward the city, carriages were already on their way out. The commoners and others in the crowd began stampeding to the protection of the city gates. Trumpets were ringing throughout the city, signaling the attack.

His thoughts of Marion changed when he realized what this meant. The Grand Melee was over. His chance at knighthood was over. It was his last chance, as Marion was nearing the age when the queen would be forced to accept courtiers if she wanted a noble spouse for her daughter and allies for their war. Frustration eating at him, he could feel his anger rising. The orphan curse had struck again. "NOOOOOOOO!" he screamed in frustration and rage. Then Braxlo put his hand on his shoulder, breaking his moment of self-pity.

"I have to find Fairwind," Braxlo told him as he handed Alliandre his pack.

Alliandre turned sharply on his friend before regaining his composure. "Of course. Be safe."

He would take his frustration out on whoever had attacked the city. They ruined his chance for knighthood. They would not be happy they chose this day to attack. He looked for Lolark as he made his way quickly to the chirurgeon's tent to find Sivle, to send his friend

346 - DANIEL E MYERS

for his armor and Aeris. He caught sight of Lolark and waved at him. Lolark waved back but continued talking to several other paladins and the king. Alliandre made it to the tent, poking his head inside.

Sir Rodney sat on a table, head bandaged, but awake and almost alert. His arm was in a sling, but otherwise he seemed fine. Several other knights were in bandages, recovering from their own wounds if the blood and bruises were any sign.

"Sivle, we are being attacked," he called out to his lifelong friend.

"I know, we are gathering up the supplies now." Sivle seemed a bit preoccupied, so Alliandre stated the obvious.

"My friend," he began with his voice raised, pausing until Sivle looked over. "I will need my armor and Aeris. I need you to go get them while I stand with the others until the crowd is inside the gates. Who knows how long we have?"

"Twenty minutes," said a paladin who had just entered. "All able-bodied warriors must stand outside to protect the fair-goers. The food stands included. There are grendlaar to the southeast, coming fast."

"Dear spirits. How many?" a young priest asked. "We need to get the wounded out of here."

"Heal the wounded," Sivle ordered. Grabbing a jar of his ointment, he rubbed it on the arm of a paladin nearby. The paladin raised his arm and flexed it several times.

The first paladin raised his voice. "I said all able-bodied warriors must stand outside to protect the fair-goers. Priests, get the guards to carry back the supplies. Return to the city to prepare to take on the wounded. Anyone who can wield a sword, come with me."

Alliandre turned to follow the paladin, shouting back to Sivle. "Go get my armor. And Aeris."

The End

Glossary

Adamon – A small dense fruit, usually dried and used for rations.

Aedengus Duine Fionn – King of the High Aelf

Aeris – A night steed, mounts of the Dalmari. His mother gave birth to him shortly before the Dalmari were driven from the world. He was discovered and bonded to Alliandre Del Nileppez Drol Hulloc.

Aethorn – An instructor or teacher

Ariandel Spéir álainn – Silver Aelf maiden, magician, alchemist, and arcane scribe from the Silverwood Forests. Cara Ríoga to Fairwind Duine Fionn.

Arielle the Beautiful – Former queen of the Southern Kingdom. Owner of the Wyvern's Aerie in Foresight.

Arming Jacket – Foundation garment to which all plate armor parts are attached.

Arrêt – Hook on the upper left of the chest of armor designed to support the lance.

Ath-leasaiche – Group among aelf nations who believe in deeper relationships with the humans, treating them as equals in all things.

Baineann – Aelf for girl.

Banner – A military unit consisting of twenty knights, paladins or soldiers.

Banphrionsa – Aelf for princess.

Banríon – Aelf for queen.

Barding – Armor designed to be worn by a horse or other animal mount.

Baron Jacque Del Broussard – Baron of the Central Kingdom Barony of Northwatch.

Baroness Julia Del Broussard (Del Franos) – Baroness of the Central Kingdom Barony of Northwatch.

Basalonnel Koobelur – Mora-Ghinearál and leader of the Second Golden Tree of the Golden Aelf army.

Beauregard (no last name) – Mysterious mage who for some reasons bears ill will against Alliandre Del Nileppez.

Bend – A diagonal stripe on a heraldic device.

Bevor – Armor designed to protect the neck and jaw. The sallet (helm) sits on top, covering it. Together, they replace a helm and gorget.

Bhean – Aelf for woman.

Bláthálainn Ard-Tiarna – Queen of the Great Aelf during the Great War. A Forest Spirit priest, she was critical in convincing the king to abide by the treaty resulting from the prophecy.

Blood Duel – Duel where normal dueling protocols are not in place.

Bolos – Weapon designed to incapacitate a person or animal by wrapping them inside it. It includes three weights connected with 1-3 foot cords.

Bradnut – Fruit of the bradnut tree. 1/2 to 3/4 inch across, the meat is not fit for human consumption, but often fed to livestock.

Buckler – A small, round shield.

Caltrop – A four-pointed piece of metal designed to stand with one point in the air. Used to slow or injure hooves or the feet of anything stepping on them.

Caparison – A covering for a horse or other mount used to cover it. Usually bears a heraldic device.

Captain Tennille Del Antoine – Lieutenant Commander of the King's Guard in the Central Kingdom.

Cara Ríoga – Royal Friend. A noble title bequeathed by a member of the Royal Family on (usually) close friends who are not already nobles.

Ceannasaí Mór – Leader of an aelf order of paladins or knights.

Chain Coif – Head covering made from interlocking rings. May be worn under, or instead of a traditional helm.

Chain Mail – Armor made by interlocking rings.

Chain Shirt – A shirt made of interlocking rings.

Chanfron – A piece of plate armor covering a horse's or other mount's head.

Chape – The metal (usually) tip of a scabbard or sheath.

Chegando a idade – An aelf coming of age ritual where the young adult aelf is welcomed as an adult of the community.

Chirurgeon – A surgeon or doctor. Also serves as a dentist or butcher.

Coif – A hood normally providing protection and padding beneath a helm.

Comórtas le Haghaidh Banríona – Ceremony where female aelf from each tribe are presented for the King of Kings to choose his wife.

Corónú – Aelf ceremony where the Great King is coronated.

Couter – A cupped piece of armor protecting the elbow.

Crinet – A piece of plate armor covering a horse's or other mount's neck.

Croupiere – A piece of barding (armor) designed to protect the rump of the horse, while the peytral protected the chest.

Cuir Bouilli – Thick leather boiled in water or beeswax to harden and formed into a lamellar or scale armor.

Cuirass – A piece of armor consisting of breastplate and backplate fastened together.

Cuisse – A piece of armor protecting the thigh and upper leg.

Culet – A piece of plate armor consisting of small, horizontal lames which protect the small of the back and/or the buttocks.

Deasghnáth Pasáiste – Rite of passage from childhood to young adulthood.

Del – Naming convention along with Drol began by the Freehold to identify the noble family of its children. Adopted throughout the human kingdoms. Eventually Del described the father's side, while Drol described the mother's side.

Del Nileppez – Renowned Fire Warrior and son of Jerome Nileppez. Famous for defending the gate of the Freehold of Dragonsbane during the first great assault. Despite the wounds, he remained guarding the gate, withdrawing only after the third wave, when the Black Aelf were pushed back.

Drake Del Nileppez – Fourth leader of the Freehold of Dragonsbane and leader when the prophesy was delivered.

Drake Fíor-oidhre – Human King of the Great Aelf. Given the name of Drake to honor the human alliance.

Drake Pyronius – Renowned Fire Warrior and companion of Del Nileppez. Disappeared during the Great War.

Drol – Naming convention along with Del began by the Freehold to identify the noble family of its children. Adopted throughout the human kingdoms. Eventually Del described the father's side, while Drol described the mother's side.

Drullock – A small rodent indigenous to the western plains. Identified by a green, striped body. It emits a foul smelling spray when mating, or as a defense mechanism.

Dryad – A humanoid female thought to live in trees or other forest growths.

Enchantment Judge – Judge during tournaments whose responsibility it is to ensure no enchantments are used to enhance any of the competitors.

Encranche – A piece of armor worn to cover the upper chest and shoulder during a joust. It is where the lance is aimed.

Faulds – A piece of armor worn below the breastplate to protect the waist and hips. It consists of overlapping horizontal lames of metal, articulated for flexibility, which form an apron-like skirt in front.

Felador Ard-Tiarna – King of the Great Aelf during the Great War. During his reign, the prophesy was delivered.

Ferdinand Del Broussard Drol Franos – Son of Jacque and Julia Del Broussard.

Finial – A decorative ornamentation at the tip of the chape.

Fortress Stone – A stone six feet by four feet by two feet frequently used as a cornerstone when constructing fortified structures.

Frederic the Cold – King of the Northern Kingdom.

Galero – A broad-brimmed hat with tessellated strings which was worn by high priests in the Forest Spirit temples.

Gambeson – A padded defensive jacket, worn as armor separately, or combined with mail or plate armor. Produced with a technique called quilting. They were usually constructed of linen or wool; the stuffing could be scrap cloth or horse hair.

Garderobe – A room or compartment with a toilet. Generally opening to a pit or outside a castle wall.

Ghhoam – Immortal beings with great power over the Forest Spirits. Created much of the world.

Currently look after the Mtumwa.

Great Cataclysm – The time before history where the Great Chasm was formed.

Greave – A piece of armor protecting the shin and lower leg.

Greave Loop – A steel loop in the back of the greave where, along with the peg on the front of the greave, the cuisse is attached.

Gron-gohlotsch – Ghhoam living in the Great Chasm

Guard of Vambrace – An additional layer of armor which goes over cowter.

Guardbrace – Extra plate which covers the front of the shoulder, worn over top of a pauldron.

Halberd – A two-handed pole weapon consisting of an axe blade topped with a spike, mounted on a long shaft. It always has a hook or thorn on the back side of the axe blade for grappling mounted combatants. Usually around six feet long.

Halberdiers – Elite soldiers or knights trained to use the halberd.

Henry the Great – King of the Central Kingdom. Distant cousin to Tristan the Bold and Queen Elizabeth. Symbol is a silver castle on a green field.

High Lord Bramaller – Personal valet and best friend of Prince Perhaladon an Trodaí.

Highcrisp – A small fruit, resembling a pear, but with a crisp flesh and a slightly tart, sweet flavor. common in the northern climates. Valued in cooking and winemaking.

Hostra – A large, flightless ground bird originating in the far west. Can grow up to fifty pounds. Their sharp talons and hooked beak are used for breaking up the ground and digging up roots.

Hursmarc – The distance a team of oxen can pull a wagon in one hour.

Iridium – A silverish metal which has been found to hold spirit energies. For this reason, it is used in the manufacture of weapons and armor and devices intended to be enchanted.

Isipongo Hlubi – Chieftain of the Hlubi clan of grendlaar (Mtumwa). One of the thirty-seven
"Great Chieftains" of the grendlaar (Mtumwa) clans.

Itelizi – Elder grackle (Mabwana wa Mtumwa) living in the Great Chasm.

Ityotyosi – Elder grackle (Mabwana wa Mtumwa) living in the Great Chasm.

Jason Si Gladahar – Member of the City Guard and aspiring knight.

Jerome Nileppez – Founder of the Freehold of Dragonsbane. Also instituted the tradition of naming his children with "Del" to signify their nobility. They did this in honor of his brother, who died protecting the Freehold.

Jeshi – Mtumwa unit consisting of ten kikosi kubwa.

Kikosi –Mtumwa unit consisting of ten umndenii.

Kikosi kubwa – Mtumwa unit consisting of ten Kikosi.

Krom-gohlotsch – One of the Ghhoam living in the Great Chasm

Langets – Long, thin strips of metal (usually either two or four) extending from the head of a staff weapon (such as a halberd) down a certain length of the wooden shaft, secured with nails or screws and designed to prevent splitting or breakage of the wood. Also, in some swords and daggers, an extension of the guard located on both flats of the blade, designed to fit tightly over the mouth of a scabbard and prevent accidental unsheathing.

Leaf Dancer – Horse ridden by Ariandel, and trained by the High Aelf Sharasten.

Leathdhéanach – High Priest of the Forest Spirit Temple in the Great Forest. Highest ranking member of the priesthood.

Locket – Metal "throat" of a scabbard or sheath. Also, a piece of jewelry which opens to reveal a jewel or other precious material inside.

Maighdean Mhara – Water nymphs who are half woman and half dolphin.

Marion the Virtuous – Former princess of the Southern Kingdom. Works in the Wyvern's Aerie in Foresight.

Mariotteo Malcolm – High Priest of the Forest Spirit Temple in Foresight. One of the leading scholars of Forest Spirit lore and history.

Marschall – A general or other high military leader, usually in charge of a specific army or fortress. Also, the ultimate referee during martial competitions.

Mid-hanger – A metal hanger around 1/4 to 1/3 down from the throat of a scabbard where a strap mounts.

Mirandel Amhrán órga – Aelfin Bard and renowned as the greatest bard alive. When young, and only a few hundred years removed from the Human-Aelf wars, she wrote many songs about the exploits of the aelf and became quite renowned. Centuries later, she was an instrumental figure during the Great Grendlaar Wars, when the Copper Aelf army was surrounded and near surrender during the Battle of Mystic Pass. She rallied the soldiers, and they made a heroic charge which shattered the grendlaar morale and caused them to scatter, allowing the aelf army to rejoin the main force.

Mortimer Si Brackenwood – Mage and non-guild thief living in Foresight.

Mousekin – A large insect (beetle) which resembles a mouse due to its oval shell and long nose.

Palladium Council – A group of paladins elected from among the most prominent orders to enforce and amend the Palladium Contract. Terms are for six years. The head of the council rotates every other year. Members of the council currently are:

Lady Lamphrey Knoll Slayer – Current council leader – Order of the Blessed Monk

Sir Lester the Clumsy – Order of the Swooping Crane

Sir Dragk the Mountain – Order of the Stone Hammer

Lady Felanor Silver Hair – Order of the Silverwoods

Sir Volinair the Archer – Order of the Bronze Oak

Sir Allistair the Silent – Order of the Blessed Monk

Sir Jeremy the Prince – Order of the Ice Keep

Sir Thomas Del Aquinas – Order of the Golden Sword

Sir Trelimor the Aristocrat – Order of the Black Woods

Lady Ramona the Cruel – Master of Arms – Order of the Flaming Eagle

Sir Gregory Flame Hand – Almoner – Order of the Silver Ram

Lady Vivian the Beautiful – Order of the Stone Bear

Sir Lolark the Luckless – Order of the Silver Cross

Sir Bradley the Just – Order of the Iron Chain

Lady Sherille the Vain – Order of the Copper Woods

Sir Juan the Jester – Order of the Lion

Lady Nancy Sword Breaker – Order of the Blue Dragon

Party of the Seven – A group of adventurers who have played a key role in numerous wars including the Great Knoll War. They consist of the following members.

- **Her Highness Fairwind Duine Fionn** – High Aelf princess, High War Mage, possessed of an unnatural beauty and is seventh in line for the High Aelf throne. Being the youngest daughter, she is free to pursue her own path for the time being, and joined the Party of the Seven.

- **Sir Braxlo the Brave** – Knight Errant of the Freehold of Dragonsbane. Called "Hero of Formount Pass" due to his actions in the Knoll Wars. His banner was ambushed by knolls while going through the pass, and he held the pass against over two hundred knolls while the remainder of the banner fled to safety. When the knights of the banner returned the next day to recover his body, they found him returning from the pass, having fought the knolls all night, ending with the knolls withdrawing at sunrise.

- **Sir Lolark the Luckless** – Paladin of the Silver Cross. Master and Commander of Silver Cross Castle and the Knights of the Silver Cross. Member of the Palladium Council. Inhumanly tall and strong (many suspect giant bloodlines). As handsome as he is big, rivaling even the High Aelf in beauty.

- **Lord Elric the Black** – High Priest of the Black Woods temple and former member of the Tristheim Thieves Guild. One of the few humans to be allowed in the Black Woods. Found by a Black Aelf cleric, he was raised in the Black Woods and became a cleric before leaving and striking out on his own. Later, he became a high-ranking member of the Tristheim Thieves Guild, but left for unknown reasons. Met Sivle at a temple and began adventuring with Sivle and Alliandre.

- **Lord Sivle Si Evila Drol Revo** – High Cleric and Mage. Raised in the Southern Kingdom along with Alliandre and Marion the Virtuous. His mother, Aesther Con Revo, was captured in a raid by the Golden Aelf, and rescued months later carrying twins. She later delivered Sivle and his sister Seltaeb. Several years later Aesther died of a fever, and because the Revo family in Cairthorn were well respected, her children had been sent to the Southern Kingdom to be raised in the court. That was where Sivle met Alliandre and Marion. Seltaeb returned to Cairthorn after the fall of the Southern Kingdom while Sivle went to the Forest Spirit Temple in Foresight.

- **Lord Robin of the Red Crest** – Mage of the Red Crest Magistry. Began in the Thieves' Guild at Stonebrook as a child. He was also fascinated by the mages, and studied on the side while becoming a guild master. Left the guild and concentrated on magic the last fifteen years. Met with Erich by chance, and the two became friends.

- **Alliandre Del Nileppez Drol Hulloc** – A direct descendent of Drake Nileppez, he was orphaned as an infant and raised in the Southern Kingdom. After the fall of the kingdom, he trained in the Freehold of Dragonsbane for several years, but upon failing to be knighted, he left the order and began adventuring with Sivle Si Evila Drol Revo. He collects swords and strives to be the greatest swordsman alive.

Pauldron – A piece of armor which covers the shoulder (with a dome-shaped piece called a shoulder cop), armpit, and sometimes the back and chest.

Perhaladon an Trodaí – Prince of the Black Woods.

Persephone the Fair – Queen of the Central Kingdom. Half Copper Aelf daughter of the Mayor of Tristheim.

Peytral – A piece of barding (armor) designed to protect the chest of the horse, while the croupiere protected the rear. It sometimes stretched as far back as the saddle.

Plackard – A piece of armor worn over the breastplate, designed to protect the belly.

Plate Mail – Armor made from separate, interlocking plates.

Point (or on point) – The lead element in a formation, generally well ahead of the formation.

Pole-arm – A close combat weapon in which the main fighting part of the weapon is fitted to the end of a long shaft, typically of wood, thereby extending the user's range and striking power.

Prince Lucas the Just – Prince of the Central Kingdom and only son of King Henry and Queen Persephone.

Prionsa Ríoga – Great Aelf Royal Prince. Used to refer to the son of the Great Aelf king. Plural Prionsaí Ríoga

Quale Boars – A breed of pig prized for their meat and gentle disposition.

Queen Elizabeth the Widower – Queen of the Northern Kingdom. Distant cousin of Tristan the
Bold and Henry the Great. Symbol is a white owl on a gold bend on a blue field.

Randolf Del Mornay – Duke of the Western Watch

Reaganel Dílis Mór – High Aelf queen of the Great Aelf.

Rebecca Del Mornay – Duchess of the Western Watch.

Redleaf – Referring to the leaf of a plant grown in mostly swampy land, dried and cured in saltwater, then smoked in pipes. Mildly narcotic.

Ridire Báis –A group of Elite Aelf warriors. Death Knights. Used as a title as well.

Ridire Báis Críonna – Great Aelf paladin, and leader of the Order of the Crown.

Rionach Duine Finn – Queen of the High Aelf.

Rubicon – A threshold that when passed or exceeded permits no return and typically results in irrevocable commitment. A point of no return.

Sabaton – A piece of armor covering the foot.

Sailfin – A large fish common in the seas east of the Venting Mountains. Growing over six feet long, it is prized for its mean and large dorsal fin, up to four feet in height.

Sally Port – A small, secure entryway to a fortification. Generally hidden and protected by a fixed wall and/or stairs which must be circumvented to enter. It generally has two doors which are opened independently.

Scale Mail – Armor made from numerous small, interlocking plates or 'scales'. Often worn over chain mail or under heavier portions of plate mail.

Sclera – The "white" (actually it is opaque) protective layer covering the eye.

Sell Swords – Another name for mercenaries. Usually individuals not associated with a larger organization.

Sharastan – High Aelf breeder and trainer of horses. Considered by all to provide the finest horses.

Sir Andras Anarawd – Former Master of Arms for the Southern Kingdom. Currently runs the Wyvern's Aerie with Arielle the Beautiful. Reputed to be the greatest swordsman who ever lived. Lost his arm to a flesh-eating poison as he covered the escape of the queen and her children, and the other wards of the court escaping the Southern Kingdom when it fell.

Sir Anthony the Rash – Paladin of the Silver Cross.

Sir Francois the Boor – Warrior from the Pine Woods.

Sir Marieau Golden Bow – Silver Aelf archer and member of the Silver Guard.

Sir Nelson Stormbringer – Paladin of the Silver Cross. Seneschal of the order. Was Master of Arms of the order when Lolark the Luckless joined.

Sir Richard of the Waste – Knight of the Black Sword. Currently Commissary General in charge of provisioning the Knights of the Black Sword.

Sir Rodney the Magnificent – Wyndgryph knight and heir to the duchy of the Western Watch.

Sir Roger – Paladin of the Order of the Wren. Currently the Almoner for the Order of the Wren. Son of a baron, he trained with the paladins since he was six.

Sir Rudolpho – Paladin of the Knights of the Golden Keep.

Sir Tulamon Straight Eye – High Aelf archer and commander of an archery school near Candetin.

Sir William the Indomitable – Paladin. Prince of the Southern Kingdom. Currently the almoner for the Knights of the Golden Chalice.

Sourfruit – A small citrus fruit grown mainly in the southeast.

Spirit Bolts – A war-mage spell which sends small 'bolts' of aether spirit out at a high speed. These cause damage to flesh and structures alike, leaving a clean slice like a razor cut.

Spirit Cage – See Spirit Jar. A box created from air and aether spirit designed to contain or trap people or animals.

Spirit Jar – A generic term for any object created from air and aether spirits used to contain something, either to protect/store or to imprison it.

Spirit Sphere – See Spirit Jar. A war-mage spell which creates a sphere which encapsulates an opponent, rendering them helpless.

Stamins – The motions to manipulate the spirits to create spells. Each spirit has different stamins to create different results. Mages memorize their stamins to ensure the spell is cast correctly and can be done quickly.

Stein Virki – Dwarven city in the White Hills, next to the West Silver River. It is the gateway to the west, being the most common route through the White Hills.

T'Whorase – Grackle (Mabwana wa Mtumwa) living in the Great Chasm.

Tabard – A loose-fitting, sleeveless tunic worn by a knight (or nobleman) over his armor and emblazoned with his heraldic device.

Tassets – A piece of plate armor designed to protect the hips and upper legs.

Throat – The opening of a sheath or scabbard, often covered with a locket.

Thuribles – A metal censer (incense holder) suspended from chains, in which incense is burned during worship services.

Toebeans – A large bean named for its large size and shape. Often used for livestock feed.

Togra Chun Páirt – Formal request to court a royal daughter.

Tolon Del Versa – Human mage considered one of the greatest of the current time.

Tomorrouel Boeulieuir – Reit-Ghinearál and leader of the Third Golden Tree of the Golden Aelf army.

Tri-Keep – Three adjoining keeps belonging to Sivle Si Evila Drol Revo, Erich the Black, and Alliandre Del Nileppez Drol Hulloc. The lands belonging to the keeps extend from the northern tip of the Black Woods to the northernmost spur of the Great Chasm, south to the foothills. They have contracted with the Black Aelf to yield the land to the growth of the Black Woods until it reaches their fenced lands.

Tristan the Bold – The "Lost" King. King of the Southern Kingdom before it fell to the Golden Aelf. Distant cousin of Queen Elizabeth and Henry the Great. Symbol is a Wyvern Rampant on a blue field clutching a golden nest.

Tristian Mutton – A dish where lamb or mutton is pounded flat, seasoned on one side, then rolled up and roasted.

Turpin Agates – small (pea-sized) gemstones shaped like a teardrop. Also harder than diamonds and extremely brittle, rare, and expensive. Because of the difficulty in cutting them, usually just polished and set whole.

Umndeni – The smallest unit of Mtumwa military organization. Contains one hundred Mtumwa and is led by a Mabwana wa Mtumwa called an Induna. Plural is umndenii.

Valian Tríúa Rugadh – Prince and Lord Marschall of the Great Aelf, Knight Protector and brother of King Drake Fíor-oidhre.

Vandion – Half-aelf farmer/part time mage. Currently betrothed to Vanessa. Lives with her and works her farm while she works at the Wyvern's Aerie.

Vanessa – Serving girl in the Wyvern's Aerie. Father was a soldier in the Central Kingdom army who was killed during the Knoll Wars.

Victor Del Drago – Minor mage and citizen of the Central Kingdom. Former member of the Foresight city guard. His father is Baron Del Drago of the North Reach, but he is the fifth son, and estranged from his family.

Vreen – Lizard-headed humanoids who roam the savannas in the southern, warmer climates. Tribal in nature, they are warlike and reproduce rapidly. While their lifespan is only forty to fifty years, they reach adulthood in five years.

Wodogo – Name given by the Mtumwa to the Ghhoam.

Wyvern – A flying creature often mistaken for a dragon. Unlike a dragon, its front legs are not connected to its wings, and it has no rear legs, instead a long tail with a spear-like tip.

Great Aelf – Aelf of the Great Forest, home of the World Tree. Identifiable by their purple-tinted eyes and their olive skin.

High Aelf – Aelf of the High Forest which surrounds the Great Forest. Identifiable by their golden hair and above average (even for aelf) beauty.

Golden Aelf – Aelf of the Gold Bark Woods, also called the Golden Woods, in the Sleeping Dragon Mountains. Identifiable by the metallic golden hue to their skin.

Silver Aelf – Aelf of the Silver Bark Woods, also called the Silverwoods. Identifiable by the dragon scale pattern on their ears.

Copper Aelf – Aelf of the Copper Leaf Woods, also called the Copperwoods. Identifiable by their coppery (reddish) skin.

Black Aelf – Aelf of the Black Woods. Identifiable by their scent and their jet-black hair.

Iron Aelf – Aelf of the Venting Mountains. Identifiable by their albino skin, white hair, and stocky build. They are the only race of aelf which live underground.

Common Aelf – Aelf living on any of the plains or pine woods. Identifiable by their light brown skin and lighter hair color. Also, more attractive than other aelf races.

Forest Spirits
All spirits reside in the aether
Aether Spirit
Air Spirit
Earth Spirit
Fauna Spirit
Fire Spirit
Flora Spirit
Stone Spirit
Sea Spirit
Water Spirit
Wood Spirit

Cities
Cairthorn – City just west of the Venting Mountains.

Candeltin – Small freehold city/town in the western plains. Inhabited mainly by humans but surrounded by the centaur tribes. Farms growing grains and a large trading bazaar are the main sources of revenue for the town.

Foresight – Capital city of the Central Kingdom. Wealthiest human city and kingdom. The coins of the kingdom are accepted as currency in all of the remaining great kingdoms except the Golden Aelf kingdom.

Stone Brook – City north of the Iron Mountains.

Tristheim – City in the Northern Kingdom.

Vista – Capital city of the Southern Kingdom (now the Lost Kingdom). Often referred to as the Lost City.

Voldair – City in the Dwarven Kingdom of Khartoum in the Iron Mountains. Inhabited mainly by humans, the weapons trading bazaar is the largest in the land. The Thieves Guild is notorious for smuggling anything and everything. It also has the largest Assassins Guild.

Currency

Havnot – Coin of the realm, Central Kingdom. Equal to one hundred turots, and generally held only by the wealthiest merchants and members of the Royal Household.

Dolcot – Coin of the realm, Central Kingdom. One hundred dolcots equal one malnot.

Malnot –Coin of the realm, Central Kingdom. One hundred malnots equal one turot.

Turot – Coin of the realm, Central Kingdom. One hundred turots equal one havnot.

Months

Adimon – First month – Month of renewal
 Canton – Second Month – Month of preparation
 Frescao – Third Month – Month of Planting
 Senacao – Fourth Month – Month of Growth
 Prescao – Fifth Month – Month of Maturation
 Dolmontous – Sixth Month – Month of Reception
 Frendalo – Seventh Month – Month of Harvest
 Diromontous – Eighth Month – Month of Gifting
 Alkadolo – Ninth Month – Month of Mourning
 Essentolo – Tenth Month – Month of Cleansing

Mtumwa Clans
amaBaca
amaHlubi
amaKwenkwe
amaNgqumbhazi
Amatikulu
Bakuza
Bungane
Cetshwayo
Cunynghame
Dinguswayo
Dinuzulu
Ekukanyeni
Fanawendhiela

Gcaleka – Graelshnar's Clan
Ibabanango
Isandhlwana
iziBawu
iziGqoza
IziHlubi
iziKhambazana
iziQulusi
iziWomhe
Kumalo
kwaBulawayo
kwaDvasa
Langalibalele
Mlandela
Mtonjaneni
Ndongeni
Nomantshali
Senzangakona
Sikali
Sikonyela
Tshingwayo
Ulundi
Umhlatuzi
Xhapho

Lightning Source UK Ltd.
Milton Keynes UK
UKHW010307080223
416649UK00009B/257/J